PUFFIN BOOKS
LORE OF THE LAND

During her growing-up years, Nalini Ramachandran aspired to be an artist, a singer, a dancer, an actress and a journalist. When she finally became a writer and editor, she drew on ideas, listened to the music of language, danced to the tune of imagination, acted on impulsive creativity and dug into research, thus inhabiting several worlds and living the lives of multiple characters at once.

Her interest in storytelling piqued when she was working as a fiction writer with India's only all-comics children's magazine, *Tinkle*. Her short stories have been published in anthologies such as *Gifts of Teaching* and *Scary Tales*. She is the author of *Detective Sahasasimha: The Case of the Disappearing Books* and the graphic novel–biography *A.P.J. Abdul Kalam: One Man, Many Missions*. To know more about Nalini, visit www.authornalini.com.

Abhishek Choudhury is a Bangalore-based illustrator. An avid book lover, comics reader and foodie, he has worked across various fields, including theatre, video gaming and animation. He has also collaborated with several reputable publishing houses. More recently, he has illustrated and published *Inferno*, the first graphic novel in his comic trilogy, The Untold Chronicles.

LORE
OF THE
LAND

Storytelling Traditions
of India

Nalini Ramachandran

Illustrations by
Abhishek Choudhury

PUFFIN BOOKS
An imprint of Penguin Random House

PUFFIN BOOKS

USA | Canada | UK | Ireland | Australia
New Zealand | India | South Africa | China

Puffin Books is part of the Penguin Random House group of companies whose addresses can be found at global.penguinrandomhouse.com

Published by Penguin Random House India Pvt. Ltd
7th Floor, Infinity Tower C, DLF Cyber City,
Gurgaon 122 002, Haryana, India

First published in Puffin Books by Penguin Random House India 2017

Text copyright © Nalini Ramachandran 2017
Illustrations copyright © Abhishek Choudhury 2017

All rights reserved

10 9 8 7 6 5 4 3 2 1

The views and opinions expressed in this book are the author's own and the facts are as reported by her, which have been verified to the extent possible, and the publishers are not in any way liable for the same.

ISBN 9780143429234

Typeset in Minion Pro by Manipal Digital Systems, Manipal
Printed at Replika Press Pvt. Ltd, India

This book is sold subject to the condition that it shall not, by way of trade or otherwise, be lent, resold, hired out, or otherwise circulated without the publisher's prior consent in any form of binding or cover other than that in which it is published and without a similar condition including this condition being imposed on the subsequent purchaser.

www.penguin.co.in

There's rarely a bond as selfless as the one between grandchildren and their grandparents.
I dedicate my book to four special people:

My maternal grandfather, K.B.S. Maniam, who enthralled me with his charming tales and gave me the courage to keep writing;
My maternal grandmother, Andal, who instilled in me a love for words and languages;

My paternal grandmother, Visalakshi, who never tired of animatedly narrating fables and folk tales;
My paternal grandfather, Rajagopalan, who perhaps believed that books are the best legacy to leave behind.

Contents

Author's Note ix
Into the Land of Stories xi

1. The Reluctant Storyteller 1
2. The Devil and the Deep Blue Sea 6
3. Of Time and Tide 12
4. In a New Light 18
5. Show Your Mettle 25
6. As Mean as a Snake 31
7. Nature Finds Its Way 38
8. Rebel with a Cause 46
9. Loving to Death 52
10. Talking in Circles 59
11. A Barrel of Fun 66
12. Word of Mouth 73
13. Warhorse 80
14. Act of Faith 86
15. Flying the Coop 92
16. Learn to Teach 95
17. A Stitch in Time 102
18. Ward Off Evil 109
19. Back and Forth 116
20. A Running Battle 123
21. God's Own Country 130

22.	Eye of the Wind	138
23.	Fortune Favours the Bold	145
24.	Praise to the Skies	151
25.	Jewel in the Crown	157
26.	Into the Wild	163
27.	Rite of Passage	171
28.	You Think You're Smart?	178
29.	In High Cotton	183
30.	Turn Over a New Leaf	191
31.	A Kaleidoscopic View	199
32.	No Child's Play	208
33.	Far and Wide	215
34.	Faith Can Move Mountains	224
35.	Set in Stone	231
36.	Different Strokes, Different Folks	238
37.	What's in a Name?	244
38.	Place in the Sun	252
39.	Bringing Back to Life	260
40.	Earn Your Stripes	267
41.	Lost and Found	276

Thank You! 285
Sources 287

AUTHOR'S NOTE

Writing about ALL the storytelling traditions of India is a near impossible task, given the cultural diversity of the country. It is, however, my intention to take you on a brief but brisk tour of such traditions through this book; hence I have chosen at least one storytelling tradition from every Indian state and union territory. Let me begin by saying that this hasn't been easy, as I have had to select thirty-eight out of more than 300 traditions that I was familiarized with during my research. Deciding why a particular tradition should find mention, to the exclusion of another, has been exceptionally difficult as each one wonderfully exhibits its individuality.

There is a lot more to India, its lore, culture and heritage, and this book seeks to only serve as an introduction to the wonderful realm and breadth of the country's storytelling traditions. While personal interpretations and observations have been woven into chapters, some content is based on information available in the public domain, and sources and acknowledgements are duly provided. Thus the inclusion of the entirety of India's lore is an unattainable goal and I cannot claim to be an authority on the same. So, while every effort has been made to present factually accurate and authentic information, I do not assume and hereby disclaim any liability to any party for any loss, damage, or disruption caused by any errors or omissions, whether such errors or omissions result from negligence, accident or any other cause.

Similarly, much effort has gone into making sure the complementary illustrations that bring the book to life truthfully represent the traditions, albeit with a creative twist. Essentially written for young readers, the chosen traditions and concepts in this book have been simplified. Some of the stories may be lesser-known or versions of popular tales. This does not mean that any one story is right and the other isn't, as you will find out if you read on. It simply means that no two traditional storytellers tell a story the same way. Isn't that enriching?

INTO THE LAND OF STORIES

This is the story of Mohini.

Um, no, it's the story of storytelling.

Actually . . . it's the story of storytelling told through the story of Mohini.

So, tell me, when was the last time *you* told a story?

Maybe last night, when your grandfather was narrating a tale from mythology and you kept interrupting him because you already knew it? Or maybe at school, when you played the role of a historical figure?

But what about the time when you excitedly told your father about what happened in class? Or the time when you recounted a nightmare to your sibling? Or when you chatted with your friends about your trip to a wildlife sanctuary?

What? You're not sure if you can call these 'stories'?

But they are!

Storytelling is a tradition through which lore is passed on from generation to generation—be it from grandparents to grandchildren at home or from village chieftains to curious listeners sitting around a bonfire. And these stories comprise *everything*, from history and mythology to science, from local legends and mysteries to rituals, from fictional accounts and gossip to everyday happenings.

Over centuries, creative storytellers have transformed the lore of the land into diverse storytelling traditions of India. And I am going to introduce you to thirty-eight such interesting practices. But remember, these are not the only ones. Last I counted, I had come across nearly ten times that number—I am sure there are hundreds more that I don't know about—and sadly, quite a few of these are on the verge of extinction. My hope behind writing this book and giving you a glimpse of the rich storytelling heritage of the country is that you and I can create some magic together and help these traditions and their stories live happily ever after.

The best part about this book, if you ask me, is that each tradition is unique and tells a variety of tales—of deities and demons, nature and natives, royals and rebels, wildlife and weapons and whatnot! All this, through the story of Mohini, who fights her own battles with storytelling.

So what are you waiting for? Let's journey to where the stories live!

Chapter 1

THE RELUCTANT STORYTELLER

'Once upon a time . . .' Mohini began nervously, the lump in her throat refusing to be swallowed.

'You've said that at least fifteen times in the past five minutes! What happens after "Once upon a time"?' a man, known for his bitter temper, yelled from the last row.

Her cheeks flaming, Mohini shut her eyes tightly in the hope that the impatient crowd would disappear when she opened them again. But they still sat right there before her, only getting more and more annoyed with her.

She made yet another attempt. 'Once upon a time . . . there was a stone.'

'At last!' the same man said mockingly.

'Shush! Let her get on with it,' an elderly lady sitting right in front shouted, waving her printed yellow fan.

But Mohini had run into a stone wall with her stone story. She had no idea what to say next. So when someone else from the audience shouted, 'Go on! We don't have all day!', she resolved to finish it off the same way she always did.

'Once-upon-a-time-there-was-a-stone-and-a-young-prince-kicked-it-hard-and-the-stone-hit-a-wall-and-was-broken-into-pieces.'

And before the audience could make sense of the world's most hurried fairy tale, she mumbled, 'Story's over. Thank you for your attention.'

The children in the front row moaned and those in the last groaned, even as everyone sitting in between shook their heads disapprovingly.

'That's such a *lame* story,' a woman complained, her cat equally upset.

'Lame? Why, that's not even a story! Tsk tsk ... She has clearly been born into the wrong family,' the latest grumbler said.

Mohini pretended not to have heard any of these comments as she sprinted past them, but every single word had stung her like a smarting wound.

———•❖•———

Mohini's destiny had been decided the moment she was born. Everyone in Mithika, the quaint hill-town where the girl lived, knew what she was going to be when she grew up. A storyteller.

Her grandmother Anokhi had regaled the townspeople with mind-boggling tales of the strange and mysterious. And G-Ma, as Mohini playfully called her, had had another extraordinary skill—whenever people went to her with their problems, she'd give them solutions through stories! 'Oh, stories are everywhere. It's what you do with them that makes all the difference,' she used to say.

Then there was Anokhi's daughter, Mohini's mother, Manohari, who could conjure up magical lands and stories of princesses and goblins in no time. On the other hand, Mohini's father, Yash, believed in true stories and real-life heroes. The two were complete opposites, yet they complemented each other delightfully.

And into this family of gifted storytellers was born our dear Mohini, who couldn't tell a tale to save her life. So, naturally, on her tenth birthday when, in keeping with the family tradition, Mohini was made principal storyteller, she'd thrown a fit.

'I'd rather be principal tissue-folder in a restaurant!' she'd told her mother. (Seriously, she *could* think of many different ways to fold a tissue.)

Manohari had laughed. 'I know you have it in you to be a good storyteller. You just need some time, my dear doe-eyed doll.'

It just so happened that Mohini's great-great-great-grandfather, a master storyteller, had started the practice of Sunday Story Hour in

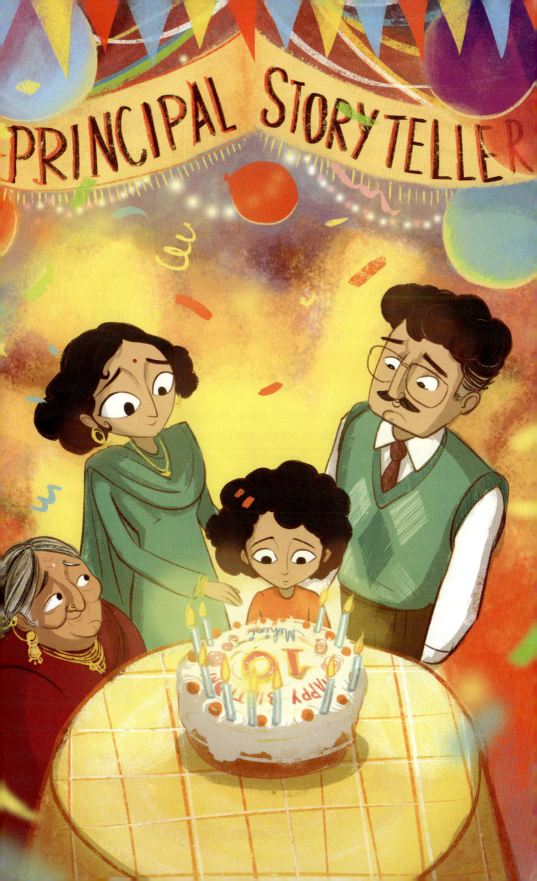

Mithika to keep the tradition of telling tales alive. Ever since, the people of the hill-town had gathered every fortnight to listen to the family weave tales. Anokhi, Manohari, even Yash, had all had their fair share of enthralling Mithika's people during Story Hour.

As principal storyteller now, it was time for Mohini to take centre stage. But the girl showed no interest in the family tradition whatsoever. And after G-Ma passed away, she'd even stopped attending Story Hour. 'Some time' had turned into a *lot* of time. Two years had gone by.

So her mother had finally decided that where a nudge hadn't worked, maybe a push would. She'd literally pushed Mohini onstage during Story Hour that day. And as we know, Mohini had rushed out of the gathering after her disastrous first attempt.

Mohini flopped on to her bed, tears streaming down her face. She couldn't bear the thought of her parents coming back home and looking at her with eyes full of disappointment. *And what about Mithika's people?*

'They won't let go of a single chance to tell me what a loser I am! To them, I will always be the black sheep of my family,' she sobbed.

The way she saw it, there was only one thing she could do . . .

Not waiting for her tears to dry up, she stuffed some clothes into her knapsack. With a pang, she wrote a quick note to her parents and left it on the table.

And then Mohini quietly scurried out of her home. As the afternoon sun almost blinded her, the teary-eyed girl turned to give Mithika one last look.

Screeeech!

'Oh, no! A flat tyre,' Mohini grumbled, stretching herself on her seat. The bus she had boarded had come to an unexpected halt on the outskirts of Mithika. She got down for some fresh air, while the driver changed the tyre.

'Is *that* what I think it is?'

In the distance, she could see the place she'd been curious about for ages. The Eerul Caves. Her townsfolk believed they were haunted. Somebody had once claimed that they'd seen Anokhi there, even as Mohini's grandmother had said that she hadn't left home all day. Certain that the resident ghost of Eerul had played another clever trick, the people of Mithika had decided to stay as far away as possible from the spot.

Despite knowing all this, Mohini felt drawn to the eerie caves. Literally. Only when she had reached the top did she realize that the bus had taken off without her. The situation just got worse from there.

The wind howled. The clouds thundered.

'What? This is no time for rain!' Mohini looked up at the skies, irritated.

And, as though teasing her, a harsh shower erupted, making her run for cover. She was just about to enter one of the caves ahead when she noticed a dirty-looking sign outside:

Trespass at your own risk!

Mohini wondered if she should go in at all, but the heavens roared once again. That was enough for her to decide. She would rather deal with whatever was inside than the rain!

Chapter 2

THE DEVIL AND THE DEEP BLUE SEA

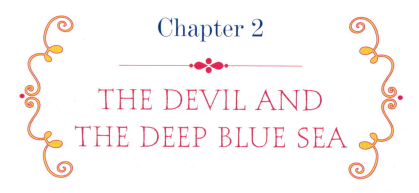

By the warm light of a fireplace, the interiors of the cave glimmered. They were far from spooky. In fact, the place was nothing like a cave! Looking around, Mohini realized it was someone's house, complete with well-furnished rooms and big windows for good ventilation.

'Whoever lives here surely loves books,' Mohini mused, staring at a floor-to-ceiling bookshelf. Yet she didn't understand why anyone, even a reclusive reader, would live so high up in these secluded, supposedly haunted caves.

'Trespasser!' a husky but high-pitched voice cut her thoughts short.

Mohini had expected this. Slowly, she turned around to face the cave-house's owner.

And screamed.

'Shhh! Turn your decibels down!'

The creature in front of her was translucent but colourful, and it seemed to be emitting a strange glow. It had something by way of a face, some ears and horns, limbs—were those hands?—and it ended in a long tail. No feet, though. Ghostlike, it floated in mid-air as it fixed Mohini with an accusing look.

The girl ran out of the cave as fast as she could. But as soon as she stepped out, a bolt of lightning almost struck her foot, making her rush back in. So standing at the entrance, Mohini did the next best thing she could think of: 'Aaaaarghhhh!'

'Would you stop that? My eardrums hurt!' the creature complained.

A sudden wave of courage came over Mohini, and she blurted out, 'Listen, gh-ghost, I-I-I will fight y-you. Don't you dare come near me!'

The 'ghost' burst out laughing.

'M-m-my parents know I'm here . . . They'll be here s-soon, okay!' she fibbed, feeling much less brave after having heard it laugh.

'Really?' The ghost floated towards her.

'Aarrghhh!' Backing away, Mohini held up her knapsack in front of her like a shield.

'Okay, then . . . Nice meeting you too. You can leave now, noisy girl!' The creature turned its back on her abruptly, stuffing its fingers in its ears.

Mohini heaved a huge sigh of relief, but her heart sank when she saw the storm raging outside. She exited the cave once again. It was a pitch-black night, save for the lightning streaks that seemed to be playing hit-and-miss with her. She almost slipped on the wet rocky path and screamed for help, when the ghost's luminous limb shot out of the cave entrance and broke her fall. Pulling her up to safety, it retreated inside.

There was no way Mohini could climb down in such awful weather; and with no light to guide her, the rocks were a sure deathtrap. Trembling, she entered the cave again. The apparition was sitting on a sofa, reading a fat book.

'You're back, huh?' it asked without looking up.

Mohini sat down near the entrance and watched the ghost intently, who seemed least interested in her. And it had saved her life. 'C-can I s-stay here t-tonight?' she asked, mustering up all her courage.

'No,' the creature said curtly. 'Either you leave now or face the consequences.'

'C-c-consequences?'

'Didn't you read the sign outside?

Now Mohini remembered. She bit her lip. 'Um, I'll take the consequences . . .' Her voice fizzled out as she wondered if she would ever see her family again.

'Very well then. Make yourself comfortable, Mohini,' the creature offered.

The girl froze. She hadn't introduced herself. 'How did you—'

'*Please*. It's not rocket science.' The ghost floated into the kitchen. 'You've practically embossed your name on your knapsack, the one you were thrusting at my beautiful face some time back!'

Mohini looked at her bag and recalled having scribbled her name on it with her new marker pen just days ago. Feeling foolish, she quietly edged towards the fireplace.

'If you don't mind my asking,' Mohini hesitated, '. . . *what* are you? I mean, aren't you the gh-ghost of Eerul that everyone fears?'

The creature cackled creepily. Mohini cringed.

'I'm *not* a ghost . . . Ghosts are dead. You can call me a spirit, though. I'm alive, you see,' it said simply.

She didn't really understand the difference, so she went on to her next question: 'Are you . . . a he or a she?'

'Oh, I'm an *it*! A spirit!' the creature chirped.

Mohini observed the spirit for some time. An *it*? This was new to her. Actually, everything about the night was new to her. 'D-do you have a name?'

The creature grinned. 'I have many. But for now, you can call me Katha.'

Mohini stared at the steaming broth that the spirit had just served.

'Eat light and sleep tight. Tomorrow's going to be a day so bright!' Katha gleefully rubbed its hands together and floated away to bed.

The girl wasn't sure if it was wise to have the broth, but it smelled too yummy to be missed. And in no time, she had gulped it all down.

Now that she thought about the day's events, she was certain that she had put herself in danger, not only by agreeing to stay with a spirit, but also by accepting to face the consequences for trespassing into its home. Her mind was filled with dark thoughts: What if the spirit was planning to gobble her up? What if it turned Mohini into a sparrow and kept her caged for life? What if it made her its slave?

Changing into a dry pair of clothes, she curled up near the fire and plotted her getaway, even as her eyelids drooped. *Once this crazy rain stops, I will dart as far away from the spirit as I can!*

When morning arrived, the sun's rays filtered through the entrance and kissed everything golden.

'Good morning, Mohini. Hope you slept well. Now, ready for the consequences?' Katha was floating above her.

But the girl only stared back at Katha, speechless. She had overslept and forgotten all about her great escape! So she started inching towards the cave's mouth ever so slowly, hoping she could make a run for it—

'OWW!' Her head had hit a wall, except . . . wait—there was no wall.

'That's an invisible shield. I've cast a spell on this cave,' Katha said matter-of-factly.

'A spell?'

'Yes, and you just have to do one teensy-weensy thing to break it.'

'Wha-a-at?'

Katha's eyes twinkled. 'Tell me a story.'

It had taken Mohini several minutes and a few repetitions of the request to find her voice back.

'I-I'm sorry, I can do *whatever else* you want me to, but *not this*!'

'Too bad. Tell me a story, and I will let you go. Otherwise, the consequences get . . . *better*, you know,' Katha smiled.

'What do you mean?'

'There's a reason why I put that board outside. I even gave you a chance to leave last night, but *you* decided to stay,' Katha said. 'Now, only a good story can set you free. Until then, you are bound to me.'

'You can't make me stay here forever!' Mohini fumed.

'Okay, go then. But wherever you go, I'll go with you. This is a spell even I cannot undo,' Katha chuckled, especially thrilled at this rhyme.

But Mohini wasn't amused. She tried pummelling the invisible shield, first with her fists and later with her trusty knapsack. Nothing worked. Giving up, she slumped on to the floor and began sobbing.

Completely clueless about what to do with a weeping captive, Katha gingerly offered her some tea, a consoling smile on its face. Having no energy left to fight, Mohini let Katha feed her. The morning tea had such a strange, calming effect on her that she wondered if the spirit had cast another spell.

In between sobs and slurps, she blabbered, 'Look, I come from a family of storytellers in Mithika. But the truth is that I can't tell stories. I just don't have it in me!'

'What a wonderful family you belong to!' Katha exclaimed.

'*Wonderful?* Mine must be the only family in the whole world that has such a silly tradition,' Mohini mumbled.

'That's not true.'

'Why would *anyone* waste their life on stories?'

'*Waste?* Do you know it's stories that help people survive?' the spirit asked.

'Ha! Oxygen is what you need to survive. And food and water!' scoffed Mohini.

'That's right, but stories can give life too.'

The girl went quiet.

'Don't believe me? You can see for yourself. Just come with me.'

Mohini was torn. She didn't want to go anywhere with a creature whose existence she wasn't sure she'd dreamt up or not, but on the other hand . . . 'Fine! But where are we going?'

Katha smiled mysteriously. 'Everywhere.'

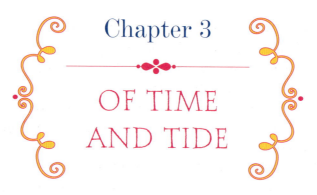

Chapter 3
OF TIME AND TIDE

Katha led Mohini towards the bookshelf, picked a bulky hardback and opened it to a black-and-white illustration of a coastline.

'I know *books* are where you find stories!' Mohini said, keeping a safe distance from the spirit at all times.

Katha sighed. 'Not always . . . Step in.'

Now Mohini was thoroughly confused. 'Um, do you mean I have to *read* this book?'

The spirit only pushed the tome towards her. Thinking that Katha was about to hit her with it, she hurriedly raised her hands to shield herself, shutting her eyes tight.

But there was no impact, only a tap on her shoulder.

Mohini opened her eyes, now completely irritated. She was about to snap at Katha, when her jaw dropped at the scene around her. *She was in the place in the illustration!*

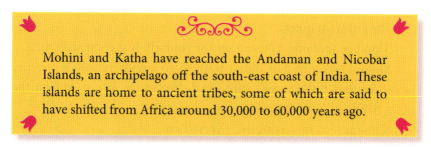

Mohini and Katha have reached the Andaman and Nicobar Islands, an archipelago off the south-east coast of India. These islands are home to ancient tribes, some of which are said to have shifted from Africa around 30,000 to 60,000 years ago.

'*Okayyy*, this dream is getting weirder and weirder!'

Katha's voice dropped to a dramatic whisper. 'There's another name associated with the Andaman Islands. Kaala Paani, literally "black waters".'

'What a strange name! What's the connection?' the girl asked, distracted from the absurdity of the situation.

Katha pointed to the water lapping at her feet. As she watched, the bright-blue water rapidly changed to a dark grey.

Eerie. Lonely. Gloomy. These were the first few words that came to Mohini's mind as she spotted the image of a large structure in the glassy, inky water.

Katha whispered into her ear, startling her, 'One of the most horrible prisons in the history of our country . . . the Cellular Jail in Andaman's capital, Port Blair. *This* is the real Kaala Paani!'

'You said that the islands—'

'Have you no patience?' Katha looked sideways at the girl. 'The British built this jail to house people who rebelled against their rule in India. Today, thankfully, the jail has no prisoners. But it has been preserved as a museum to tell the tale of its unforgettable past, including the story behind the name Kaala Paani.'

Mohini's eyes widened as images of some life-size museum exhibits started appearing on the surface of the water, each showing how prisoners used to be tortured in the jail.

'Whenever the inmates failed to complete their daily tasks—which was actually a lot of work—they were flogged, chained with iron rings and fetters, or even electrocuted. So prisoners knew that landing up in this jail was worse than death.'

Mohini was shocked. 'Didn't anyone try to break free?'

'There was no escape. Even if they got out of jail, how could they survive the dreaded ocean?' As soon as Katha uttered these words, the water turned jet-black.

'Kaala Paani!'[1] Mohini whispered.

'The "water of death",' Katha added. 'Do you like the water?'

Mohini snapped out of her daze, only to realize that the water was blue again. 'No, I—'

---

[1] In Hindi, *kaala* means 'black'. But in Sanskrit, the word *kaal* denotes 'time' or 'death'. Thus, kaala paani also translates as the 'water of death'.

'The native Great Andamanese and Onge tribes too spent a lot of time observing the sea,' the spirit began. 'That is how they'd know when disaster was on its way. But, if you ask me, I'd give full credit to their oral tradition for helping these tribes survive calamity.'

Katha pointed downward, and the girl saw images in the water once more.

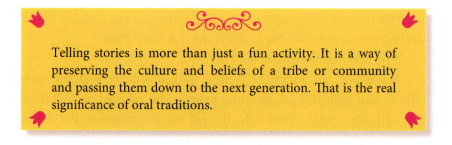

Telling stories is more than just a fun activity. It is a way of preserving the culture and beliefs of a tribe or community and passing them down to the next generation. That is the real significance of oral traditions.

Stream of Stories

'The tribespeople would gather in a clearing after sunset each day. They would dance and sing stories . . . stories of the origin of each tribe, of their gods, such as Pulga, of natural elements and more,' Katha said.

'Who's Pulga?' Mohini asked.

'Shh . . . I'm just telling you!' Katha silenced the curious girl. 'The oral tradition of the Onges had warned them that when the earth shook violently, the sea would recede and then rise like a gigantic wall of water. The only way to escape being washed away was to climb to higher terrain. And *that* is what the tribes did when a tsunami hit the islands in 2004. Stories passed on from generation to generation helped them protect themselves.'

'But what if the landscape was such that the waves didn't reach them?' Mohini asked, trying to be logical.

'Possible.' Katha looked thoughtful. 'Even then, these tribes could have simply run helter-skelter, like many others who were caught in the disaster had done. Instead, they followed the advice of their ancestors and made their way to higher ground.'

'Hmm . . . So, do they have stories about why disasters like tsunamis happen?' Mohini asked.

'Of course they do! The Andamanese believe that their creator-god, Pulga—who lives on Saddle Peak, the highest summit on the islands— punished disobedient people. And Pulga did so by summoning storms and destroying forests,' Katha explained. 'They also believe that long ago, Pulga had caused a great flood, which separated them from the mainland and formed the archipelago.'

'Sooo . . . these islands are the result of a god's wrath?' Mohini asked.

'That's what they say. But there's more.'

The Great Flood

In the beginning, when Pulga created the universe, everything worked according to his will. But with time, humans paid absolutely no heed to his commands. So, to teach them a lesson, Pulga sent a great flood to these islands. All the people, save two men and two women, perished. However, the survivors found it difficult to go about life as usual, for, in punishing them, Pulga had taken away fire too.

Taking pity on the survivors, a kingfisher named Laratut (some believe the bird was the soul of a friend who didn't make it through the great flood) flew to Saddle Peak and stole the fire. But as the bird was flying back, it accidentally dropped a spark on Pulga. Enraged, the god hurled the spark back at the bird, who managed to dodge it. The spark then fell downward and hit the ground right where the four survivors sat shivering in the cold. That is how the tribes were able to use fire once again.

'A prison surrounded by water . . . a god who punished people by sending a flood. One story brought alive through unspeaking things in a museum, another kept alive through oral tradition . . . Stories *can* give life,' the girl said slowly.

'Now you know!' Katha remarked.

Suddenly, Mohini realized that she had unwittingly agreed with Katha's earlier point about storytelling! Her mood turned sour.

'Just because I have heard you out patiently doesn't mean you can drag me along wherever you please. *I am not your puppet!*'

'Of course not. For puppets have a life of their own, you know,' Katha informed Mohini. 'Want to see?'

Not waiting for an answer, the grinning spirit turned Mohini into a puppet, picked her up by the string attached to her head and took off into the air.

Chapter 4
IN A NEW LIGHT

'NEVER do that to me ever again!' Mohini hissed as soon as the spirit had turned her back into her human form.

'How do you expect a feeble, muscleless creature like me to lug your weight around? It's just easier to carry you when you are a puppet,' Katha said casually.

Mohini was about to express some more outrage when she noticed a huge statue of a bull.

'What's THAT?'

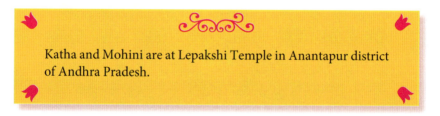

Katha and Mohini are at Lepakshi Temple in Anantapur district of Andhra Pradesh.

'Oh, this is Nandi, Shiva's *vahana*—that is vehicle—and guard. By the way, this place is also known for the legend of Jatayu,' Katha said.

'I thought we were here to learn about some puppets,' the girl said. 'Anyway, who's Jatayu?'

'The vulture from the Ramayana[1] who tried to save Sita from Ravana!' Katha said. 'Don't you know anything?'

---

[1] The Ramayana is an ancient Indian epic that narrates the story of Prince Rama of Ayodhya. Known for its twists and turns and its popular characters—Rama, Sita, Lakshmana, friend and follower Hanuman and the demon king Ravana, among many others—this epic is one of the most revisited tales in the country.

'What's the legend?' Mohini asked, refusing to be needled.

'One story at a time. First, I'm going to tell you about Tholu Bommalata.'

'Tho-loo Bomala-latta?' The girl struggled to pronounce the name.

> In Telugu, the language widely spoken in Andhra Pradesh, *tholu* means 'leather' and *bommalata* means 'dance of the puppets'. So Tholu Bommalata is the 'dance of the leather puppets'.
>
> These puppets are among the largest in the world, with some nearly six feet tall. Characters are created in different sizes as well as attire. For example, there are usually five Hanuman puppets, three of Ravana and two of Rama.
>
> A series of mythological beings, along with the comic husband–wife folk characters Killekyatha and Bangaraku, make up a complete set of 100 puppets. These are preserved in bamboo or tin boxes.

Legendary Shadows

'Tholu Bommalata isn't your regular puppet show. The leather puppets are projected on to a white cloth screen with the help of light from oil lamps,' Katha said.

'Shadow puppets!' exclaimed Mohini.

'Yes, but these are not black or grey like normal shadows. The audience sitting on the other side of the cloth screen sees them as translucent coloured shadows.'[2]

---

[2] The area behind the cloth screen (backstage) is usually covered on both sides and on top with black cloth to keep the light from escaping, instead focusing it on the puppets.

Katha conjured up a white screen and showed her how the puppets danced, and Mohini was riveted. It was as though she was witnessing an actual performance, what with an enthusiastic audience around.

'Ooh, it's like a magical movie!' she exclaimed.

'Sure is. These puppets are made of hide. When the hide is processed, it becomes somewhat see-through. And puppeteers draw the figures on it in a style similar to kalamkari,' Katha said.

'What's that now?'

'Well, kalamkari is a fabric-painting folk tradition of the state,' Katha continued. 'Earlier, the puppeteers would travel from village to village, putting up Tholu Bommalata shows during festivals. It was believed that the show would bring good luck to the village!'

Light, Colours, Action!

'All Tholu Bommalata puppets are created in profile, except Ravana, because all ten of his heads have to be shown,' Katha added.

'Wow! So he's the only one who looks at the audience? The other puppets look at each other?' Mohini queried.

Katha smiled and nodded. 'A typical Tholu Bommalata performance begins with the worship of the elephant-headed god, Ganesha, whose puppet is pinned on to the screen. After this, Goddess Saraswati is evoked, and a comic episode between Killekyatha and Bangaraku is played out. The troupe leader then introduces the story that is enacted by six to eight members. The performance lasts all night, only ending around sunrise with thanksgiving songs. You know, puppeteers memorize the dialogues for the entire play.'

'I'd never remember even if I tried.' Mohini was impressed. 'Are all the troupe members puppeteers?'

'See, each puppet is handled by a single puppeteer. Others lend their voices, making sure that every character sounds distinct. Narrators and voice actors sing too, while musicians play traditional instruments,' the spirit revealed.

'So they are multitalented,' the girl observed.

'Yes, you can say that. Most members do everything—from readying the hide to making the puppets dance, but only a handful of puppeteers can draw the puppet forms perfectly,' Katha said.

'But how do they make the puppets move?' Mohini asked.

'Hmm, let me explain this as simply as I can. The puppets are pressed against the screen and manipulated with bamboo sticks that are attached to their backs. The different parts of the puppets—wrist, elbow, head and so on—are stitched as joints, so that the puppeteers can move each part separately,' the spirit replied.

'What's that sound? Something's happening!' Mohini was intrigued.

'Aha! Get ready for an action sequence! They are building up suspense by stomping on wooden planks,' Katha continued. 'You'll now see them create some special effects.'

'Like what?' Mohini was certain Katha was fibbing.

'Well, how do you think they show a beheading scene?'

'Oh, no, they destroy the puppet!' Mohini knitted her brows.

Katha laughed. 'No, that's not what they do. The head can be separated, see? It's simply removed by the pull of a string.'

'Cooool!' Mohini breathed.

'Hey, have you heard of the word *sutradhaar*?' Katha asked suddenly.

'A sutradhaar is a narrator, of course. I come from a family of storytellers, remember? I know that much!' Mohini rolled her eyes.

Katha suppressed a smile. 'I'd say the word sutradhaar comes from puppetry since it literally means "holder of strings". In light of this, puppeteers think of themselves as creators. After all, *they* breathe life into their puppets and make them portray different emotions, even if they are painted with the same expression,' the spirit explained.

'So *this* is how puppets have a life of their own,' Mohini said.

'And there's more... In the eleventh century, Somadeva, a storyteller from Kashmir, wrote a collection of fables called *Kathasaritsagara*. One of the legends in it was about Shiva's wife Gauri.'

A Creator's Wish

Once, Gauri was enamoured by the dolls that a carpenter had fashioned. So Shiva brought them to life to make her happy. Seeing his creations alive and dancing, the carpenter prayed to Shiva to grant the boon of life to the dolls forever.

> Shiva agreed, and thus puppets came to have a life of their own because they could now tell stories. In honour of this boon, puppet shows are held for nine nights during Mahashivaratri, the festival of Shiva.

'Ohhh . . . But hey, you've totally forgotten about Jatayu,' the girl pointed out.

'I haven't. You do know that Sita was kidnapped by Ravana, right?' Katha asked.

'Yes, but what has Jatayu—'

'Shh . . . *listen*.'

The Broken Wing

Ravana was on his way back to his island-kingdom, Lanka, with Sita, riding his flying chariot. Just then, Jatayu, the vulture friend of Rama's father, Dasharatha, attacked Ravana and tried to rescue Sita.

Unfortunately, the bird was no match for Ravana's power. The demon king cut off Jatayu's wings, sending him crashing to the ground.

It is believed that Lepakshi Temple now stands where the vulture had fallen. The temple even got its name from Rama's words to the injured Jatayu: *'Le, pakshi'* (Rise, bird).

Mohini sat wondering if all this could be true. *Was it just a story?* The performance ended as the sun soared in the clear sky.

'I'm kind of hungry,' Katha said abruptly. 'We should leave.'

'*You* should leave. I'll find my way from here, thanks.' Mohini tried to slink away.

'But the spell—' Katha caught her by the hand.

'Arrgh! I'm tired of you using this stupid spell against me like a weapon!' she groaned.

'Did you say *weapon*? That calls for another story. Want to hear it? Of course you do!'

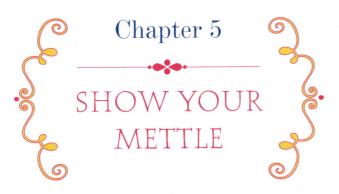

Chapter 5
SHOW YOUR METTLE

Mohini's heart was pounding even as her knees trembled. Promptly, she sat down. It was all she could do to not scream in horror.

'K-Katha?' she called out feebly, but the spirit didn't respond.

Carefully, she peeped down. Scary as the sight of the water gushing below was, the sound and engulfing coolness calmed her nerves. She sat still for a long time before noticing *what* she was sitting on. A long bamboo bridge at a great height above the water, gently swaying in the wind.

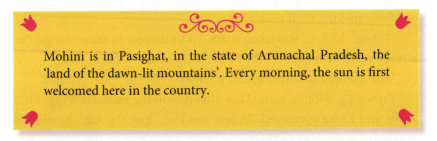

Mohini is in Pasighat, in the state of Arunachal Pradesh, the 'land of the dawn-lit mountains'. Every morning, the sun is first welcomed here in the country.

'Some bridge, huh! I guess we are about a hundred metres above sea level.'

Though startled, Mohini was relieved to hear the spirit's voice. She had never thought that the presence of the very spirit she had feared a day ago would now put her at ease.

'Wh-where did you disappear?' she asked, looking around for its unusual form.

'Tiny food break. But I'm here now,' it said, still invisible.

'Here I am freaking out, and you're thinking of food?' she asked accusingly.

'Now, now . . . Tell me, do you know why this bridge was constructed?'

Mohini sulked in response.

'So that people could easily cross the beautiful river you see below, the Siang,' Katha informed her.

'Crossing this bridge is *easy*?'

'Not everyone's a scaredy-cat like you!' the spirit teased.

Mohini thought it was a good time to change the subject. 'What's the weapon story?'

Blade of the Blacksmith

'The people of the state's Adi[1] tribe are expert bamboo and cane craftsmen. Their bamboo houses, the everyday cane objects they use, as well as this hanging bridge show off their awesome skill,' the spirit said, suddenly making itself visible.

'Whoa!' Mohini was taken aback. 'Why do you do these things? I'm already on the edge of . . .' The bridge swayed and Mohini froze.

'The element of surprise, don't you love it?' The spirit grinned.

Frowning, Mohini turned her attention to the bamboo bridge once again, and Katha continued. 'Where was I? . . . Yes, the Adis. Music and dance are important to their way of life. And one of the unique folk forms of the Adi-Pasi[2] people is Pasi Kongki.'

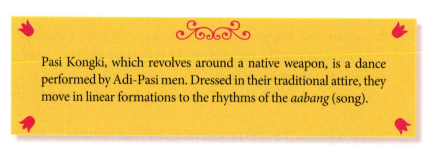

Pasi Kongki, which revolves around a native weapon, is a dance performed by Adi-Pasi men. Dressed in their traditional attire, they move in linear formations to the rhythms of the *aabang* (song).

---

[1] In their native tongue, *adi* means 'hill man', as the tribe lives in hilly regions.
[2] Adi-Pasi is a subtribe of the Adi tribe.

'The aabang sung during a Pasi Kongki performance tells the story of the tribe's legendary journey from their homes in the hills to the markets on the plains below. It highlights the hardship they faced while travelling through the rough terrain on foot as well as on the arduous upward climb on their return,' Katha explained.

'I'm so glad we don't have to cross valleys to reach a market in Mithika! Sounds difficult,' Mohini said. 'But what did they go to the market for?'

'They went to obtain metal to make a weapon called the *dao*, a kind of sword.'

'So Pasi Kongki is about the dao?' Mohini asked.

'Yes. Apart from the journey, Pasi Kongki also includes the men's interaction with the blacksmith, whom they call *pasi mide*. You see, they handed the iron that they'd procured from the market over to him. In a way, the dance also upholds the great skill of the blacksmith, who crafted customized sharp-edged daos for the tribe's men. Each dancer usually holds a dao in his hand when performing this traditional dance.'

'Why don't women participate in this dance?' Mohini inquired.

'That's an important question. The Adis follow the slash-and-burn method of agriculture, which is known as Jhum cultivation.[3] In this practice, the men cut down trees and clear jungles to create farmland. The main farm work is mostly done by the tribes' women in Arunachal Pradesh. In their free time, the Adi-Pasi men practise cane and bamboo craft or make weapons.'

'Oh!'

'And so it was the men who embarked on the risky journey to purchase iron and obtain the daos, making Pasi Kongki an all-male dance. Similarly, Ponung, a music-and-dance form celebrating the harvest season, is performed only by women,'[4] Katha elaborated further on the Adi-Pasis' gender roles and occupations.

---

[3] Even though it has its advantages, Jhum cultivation requires patches of jungle to be cleared and burnt. To protect the state's forest cover, the people of Arunachal Pradesh are now gradually discontinuing this technique.

[4] However, the *miri*, as the lead singer-cum-dancer of Ponung is called, is usually an elderly man.

'If they were ready to climb down and up a hill for it, the dao must be an important weapon,' Mohini mused when the spirit had finished.

'Oh, yes, it's an indispensable part of their daily life!'

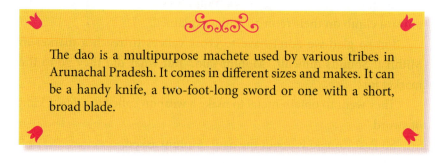

The dao is a multipurpose machete used by various tribes in Arunachal Pradesh. It comes in different sizes and makes. It can be a handy knife, a two-foot-long sword or one with a short, broad blade.

Wonder Weapon

'Craftsmen use the dao to cut, peel and carve bamboo and cane into works of art and domestic items. Even the dao sheath is made like this. Blacksmiths use the dao to create other weapons, such as arrowheads and spears. It has been part of historic wars and the headhunting rituals of some tribes. The Adis also use the dao to give form to religious figurines, clear forests for Jhum cultivation and, most importantly, build hanging bridges,' Katha told Mohini with a wink.

'You don't mean . . .?' She gaped at the spirit wide-eyed, finally turning to give the bridge another good look.

'I do! *This* hanging bridge that you are sitting on right now was also built using the dao.'

'Unbelievable!' the girl exclaimed. 'How did the pasi mide think of creating an amazing weapon like the dao?'

'Ah, so you think the dao is a human creation? Interesting!' Katha smiled.

'It isn't? You said the pasi mide—'

'Well, another tribe in the state has a legend related to this weapon . . .'

Of Men and Monkeys

Thousands of years ago, humans lived with monkeys, one kind among many. One day, the Supreme Being, who watched over all mankind, felt that it was time to give humans a distinct life, separate from that of monkeys. From hunter-gatherers, he decided to transform humans into farmers. And to make this shift, he distributed a dagger to each of them, with which they were supposed to clear forests, build houses and create farmland. This dagger was the dao.

Humans soon realized that only the dao was not enough. They needed another weapon too, and that was fire. But the monkeys, who were the guardians of fire, kept it in a pot out of everyone's reach, atop a tree. Since they couldn't reach the treetop themselves, these humans sought the help of an army of red ants living in the tree. As planned, the ants stung the guardians, who hurled the pot of fire at them. Bad aim led to the flames landing on the ground. And the humans, who had been waiting under the tree, escaped with it.

Now that they had both, the dao and fire, humans came up with the idea of Jhum cultivation, or the slash-and-burn technique. And happy with their innovation and cleverness, the Supreme Being gave humans thorough knowledge of farming.

Mohini had too many thoughts bubbling in her head.

'But in Andaman, they had another tale about humans obtaining fire!'

'*Sigh*. Why should there be only a single story about anything?' Katha asked. 'There is always room for interpretation and imagination. A story can be told in a zillion ways!'

'So stories have multiple lives and meanings, just like the dao!' the girl said.

'And stories can help build bridges too,' Katha added.

Mohini knew this was true. She remembered how G-Ma resolved issues between squabbling parties simply by telling them stories.

'You too can be like the dao . . . flexible. Let go of your stubbornness and show your mettle!'

The girl ignored Katha's advice, randomly remarking, 'Farming is *such* a boon to mankind.'

'True, but it comes with risks. Snakebites, for one!'

Suddenly, the spirit's eyes twinkled with a familiar gleam, as though it had a crazy idea. Without another word, it grabbed Mohini's hand, ready to drag her along the length of the hanging bridge.

'Wait, I'm not—AAAAAAAAAAAAAAAAAAAAAAAH!'

Chapter 6

AS MEAN AS A SNAKE

Mohini's head was reeling by the time she reached the other end of the bridge.

'You're as mean as . . . a *snake*!' rasped Mohini.

'Congratulations! You just used a simile, one of the easiest methods of characterization,' Katha said. 'Congratulations also for overcoming your fear of walking—well, *running* across the hanging bridge!'

But when Mohini turned to look at the bridge again, it had vanished! What lay before her now was the vast stretch of a river.

'This river is a lot calmer than the previous one,' Mohini noted as her heartbeat slowly returned to normal.

'Is it?' Katha grinned. 'What if I told you the two are one and the same river?'

'It can't be!'

'River Siang is also known as the Brahmaputra,' Katha said. 'The river travels through many countries, and through many states within India.'

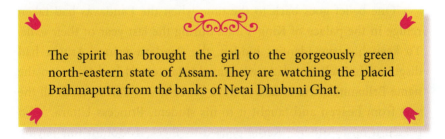

The spirit has brought the girl to the gorgeously green north-eastern state of Assam. They are watching the placid Brahmaputra from the banks of Netai Dhubuni Ghat.

'How about a swim?' Katha asked.

'No, thanks!' Mohini cringed.

'Why not?'

'Because I don't like getting drenched.'

Katha smirked. 'Thanks for the information!'

'Wha . . . Meano!' The girl frowned.

'By the way, snakes are *not* mean,' Katha said in response to her earlier comment. 'Why they attack farmers is another story altogether. But I'm going to tell you about Oja-Pali, especially Sukanani Oja-Pali, which is related to these reptilesssss. Ha!' The spirit slithered snake-like around Mohini.

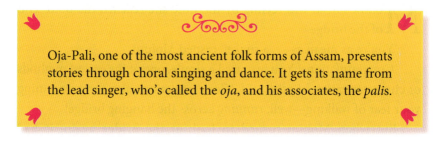

Oja-Pali, one of the most ancient folk forms of Assam, presents stories through choral singing and dance. It gets its name from the lead singer, who's called the *oja*, and his associates, the *pali*s.

Music from Heaven

'Before we get to Sukanani Oja-Pali, let me tell you how the tradition began,' Katha said.

Suddenly yawning wide, Mohini settled down on the banks. 'Oops, sorry! Go on.'

'One belief goes back to the time when the Pandavas had taken refuge in the palace of King Virata during the last year of their exile. To keep his true identity hidden, the Pandava prince Arjuna had disguised himself as a lady who taught dance and had taken on the name Brihannala. He is said to have brought Oja-Pali to earth all the way from heaven and taught it to his student, Princess Uttara,[1] who passed it on to others.' Katha paused to check if Mohini was paying attention before continuing—she was rapt.

---

[1] Princess Uttara was the daughter of King Virata.

'The second theory is that a weaver named Parijati Byasini once had a dream in which she heard strains of lilting music coming from heaven. She was so enchanted by it that she too began singing and dancing. Thus was born Oja-Pali. Parijati is even said to have created the art form's costume based on her dream!'

'So which of these versions is true?' Mohini asked.

'Um, no clue. People believe what suits them,' the spirit replied, shrugging.

Mohini understood, for her father had often told her, 'Histories differ based on who tells them and for whom they are told.' She was snapped out of the memory by the spirit's excited voice.

'. . . a third version too. Oja-Pali is said to be associated with poet and musician Vyasa-kalai and have its roots in the tradition of Kathakata, which uses verse, dance and drama in storytelling. And then others talk of the singing style of brothers Barbyahu and Sarubyahu—who sang mythological and religious tales during the reign of the Koch kingdom in the region—as having been popularized as Oja-Pali,' the spirit said.

'Sooo many stories about *one* tradition!' Mohini was amazed.

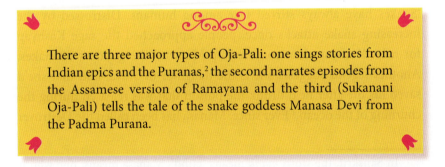

There are three major types of Oja-Pali: one sings stories from Indian epics and the Puranas,[2] the second narrates episodes from the Assamese version of Ramayana and the third (Sukanani Oja-Pali) tells the tale of the snake goddess Manasa Devi from the Padma Purana.

'The oja, who is skilled at singing, dancing and dialogue delivery, leads the narrative while the palis sing after him in chorus. The tale

---

[2] Literally meaning 'ancient' in Sanskrit, the Puranas are texts that include tales from Hindu mythology. Some well-known ones are Brahma Purana, Vishnu Purana, Shiva Purana, Bhagavata Purana and Padma Purana.

progresses through the oja's conversations with the *daina pali*, or his "right-hand" assistant,' Katha explained.

'Hey, that's just like us! Each time you narrate a story, you have conversations with me. So you're the oja, and I'm the daina pali!' Mohini grinned.

'Ha ha! Incidentally, the daina pali is also the one who adds a touch of humour to the narrative. And you're funny too, my right-hand assistant!' Katha said, although Mohini was unsure if this was a compliment or not.

'Mudras—hand gestures or stances—are a key element of the Oja-Pali dance. The oja transitions from one mudra to another smoothly, where each gesture denotes something.' Katha moved its limbs gracefully, forming a colourful blur.

'Nice! It's like dancing mainly with the hands,' Mohini said. 'Okay, so tell me about Sukanani Oja-Pali and Manasa Devi.'

The Mind of Manasa

'Snakes have always stirred fear among humans. Distressed by the increasing snake attacks once, people approached the sage Kashyap for help. Kashyap then conjured up Manasa,[3] the goddess of snakes. Another legend suggests she is the daughter of Shiva, and that she'd saved his life after he'd drunk the poison that was released during the churning of the ocean.[4] Ever since, Manasa has been called the Destroyer

---

[3] In Sanskrit, the word *mana* means 'mind'. Manasa means 'one who is born from the mind'.

[4] The churning of the ocean of milk, also known as *samudra manthan*, is the basis of a popular tale in Hindu mythology. The gods and their rivals, the asuras, together churned the ocean for amrit, or the nectar of immortality. Various items emerged from the ocean before amrit did. One of these was a poison so potent that it could destroy all of them. The gods prayed to Shiva, who readily drank the poison and held it in his throat. This is why Shiva has a blue throat.

of Venom. And there's yet another tale: Chandi, Shiva's wife, was so unhappy with the attention he was showering upon his daughter that she blinded Manasa in one eye,' Katha said, its tone dramatic.

'Ouch! Manasa is a half-blind goddess then,' Mohini noted.

The spirit nodded. 'Shiva couldn't bear to see his daughter suffer because of Chandi's wrath. So he abandoned her under a tree. And from his tears of regret emerged Neta, a mother-like friend for Manasa. Neta became a washerwoman, and it is on these very banks that she lived. Which is why this place is called—'

'Netai Dhubuni Ghat,' Mohini completed, looking around her intently.

'That's right! The "banks of Neta the washerwoman",' Katha continued, smiling. 'An interesting story about Manasa is performed through Sukanani Oja-Pali.'

All for Devotion

Rejected by her father, Manasa was determined to make people worship her, even if by force. But Chand Sadagar, a trader, refused to pay his respects to her with his right hand, because that was the hand he used to worship Shiva. Angry at this irreverence, Manasa caused his business to fail. She even took away the lives of his six sons by getting poisonous snakes to attack them.

Some time later, Chand Sadagar's seventh son, Lakhindar, got married to a girl named Behula. Manasa got to know of this event and sent a venomous serpent to kill Lakhindar on his wedding night. By the time Behula saw the serpent slithering out of their chamber, it was too late. According to custom, when the lifeless Lakhindar was floated down the river on a raft, Behula insisted on accompanying him. Throughout the journey, she prayed to Manasa, and after many months, the raft reached the banks of River Brahmaputra at Netai Dhubuni Ghat. Taking pity on the distraught Behula, Neta took her and her dead husband to Manasa.

To placate the goddess, Behula performed the Deodhani dance for her. Pleased, Manasa promised to not only undo the effects of the poison on Lakhindar, but also to bring Chand Sadagar's other six sons back to life, as well as bestow prosperity on the family. But she had one condition: the trader must worship her.

When Behula recounted the bargain to Chand Sadagar, he gratefully agreed to honour Manasa, albeit with his left hand. This time, Manasa did not mind.

In the end, everyone got what they wanted: Behula got back Lakhindar, and Chand Sadagar, his sons and his business, while Manasa came to be revered as a popular goddess throughout the region.

'Oh, good, it's a happy ending!' Mohini cried. 'What's the Deodhani dance, by the way?'

'It's a unique feature of Sukanani Oja-Pali. Dressed in red, girls perform the dance to please the goddess Manasa just like Behula had done,' Katha answered.

The more she thought about it, Mohini realized she liked the fact that Manasa was neither all-good nor all-bad. Just like people. 'You know, the female characters—Chandi, Manasa, Neta, Behula—are so different. Yet each one was determined in her own way. If they put their minds to it, women can do so much,' she concluded with an oddly wise gleam in her eye.

'Including telling stories in order to save an entire community from starvation,' Katha added mysteriously.

Mohini waited for the spirit to tell her more. But the girl was so sleepy that her eyes shut soon, sending her into a deep slumber.

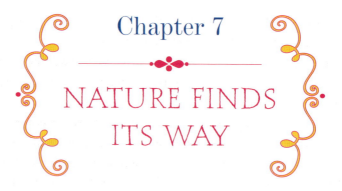

Chapter 7
NATURE FINDS ITS WAY

Mohini couldn't figure out how long she'd slept. What she did know, though, was that she was hungry. And that she was in a different place, resting against the trunk of a gnarled old tree. Looking up, she spotted Katha snoozing on a branch. Immediately the girl thought, *This is my chance to escape!* But she didn't know where to go. *Not Mithika for sure.* As she analysed her situation, an old fear crept into her mind: *What if Katha is actually waiting for the right opportunity to eat me up? What if it is only distracting me with these stories?*

Katha stirred a little. Freaking out all over again, Mohini scooted from there. Only when she was convinced that the spirit was far behind did she slow down. Now sauntering through unfamiliar territory, Mohini saw that the houses on either side were made of mud and that the walls were covered with bright, colourful paintings. An open window showed her that the interiors were painted too.

Mohini and Katha are now in the Mithila district of Bihar, the birthplace of Sita.

'Oh, there you are!' a familiar voice piped up behind her.

Mohini shrieked. She couldn't *believe* the spirit had already found her.

Katha only rolled its eyes. 'What's with you? . . . Here, I got you some delicious litti chokha.[1] You must be starving.'

Even as she inspected the dish, her suspicions about the spirit still strong, her stomach growled in response. Surrendering, she took the plate of food from Katha.

'And now you want me to tell you about these lovely paintings, right?' Katha asked, pointing to the painted walls as Mohini dug in.

'I know you're tired of me, so I'm going to be nice and let you go without a story . . . IF you can tell me what this painting is about,' proposed Katha, pointing to an image on one of the walls.

'Woohoo!' Mohini was thrilled that her freedom was only a see-and-tell description away! However, just a few minutes of staring at the image deflated her excitement.

'Why can't *I* choose an image that *I* want to talk about?' she whined.

'Because between you and me, thanks to the spell, *I* make all the important decisions.' Katha looked smug.

'*Fine!* This is just a painting of a tree with some animals and birds around it. There's no *story* here,' she declared hastily, polishing off her meal.

'Ouch!' Katha yelped. 'You just lost your ticket to freedom, my friend.'

'Oh, why am I not surprised! So what is the story?' Mohini demanded, upset that the spirit had tricked her again, but secretly pleased that she would hear a new story.

'Uh-uh, not so quickly. You need—'

'Background. I know, I know,' Mohini completed, sighing. 'You should have been a history teacher!'

From Mithila to Madhubani

'Mithila was a green region—full of flowers, wildlife and waterbodies. So it came to be called Madhubani, meaning "forest of honey",' Katha said.

---

[1] Litti chokha is a traditional Bihari delicacy. Litti, wholewheat dough balls stuffed with a spicy gram flour mixture, are eaten with chokha, a dip-like gravy made of mashed potato, tomato and brinjal.

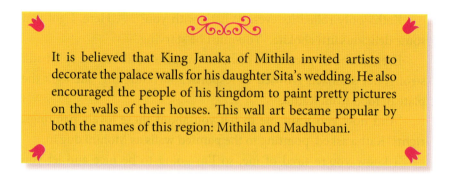

It is believed that King Janaka of Mithila invited artists to decorate the palace walls for his daughter Sita's wedding. He also encouraged the people of his kingdom to paint pretty pictures on the walls of their houses. This wall art became popular by both the names of this region: Mithila and Madhubani.

'You know, this art form used to be practised only by the women of the region. For generations, it was handed down from mothers to their daughters. While painting, the women sang folk melodies about the art and some other tales,' the spirit continued.

'But tell me . . . how did the women save the community from starvation by drawing on the walls of their homes?' Mohini asked, recalling Katha's introduction to these women artists.

'By doing something that *you* have been refusing to do. They shared their talent with the world!' the spirit pointed out. 'Between 1966 and 1968, a severe drought hit the otherwise lush plains of Mithila. Agriculture could no longer be practised and families were starving. So the region's women started producing and selling Madhubani paintings on paper and cloth. This brought in money, with which they could start their lives all over again.'

'Wow!' Mohini was impressed.

Parts of the Art

'In Madhubani, religious art tells the stories of gods and goddesses; social art is about everyday activities, such as farming and village life, as well as women's concerns, such as patriarchy, equal rights and female feticide; and nature art, naturally, gives glimpses of the natural world,' Katha explained.

'Oh, so *this* painting belongs to nature art . . .' Mohini said, staring at the image of the tree on the wall. 'But where is the story in it? You were lying, weren't you?'

'Not at all. Madhubani uses symbols and patterns from nature to convey important messages. So, unlike what you believe, this is *not* "just a painting of a tree with some animals and birds around it". This is the Tree of Life!' Katha answered emphatically.

The Wish-Fulfilling Tree

Kalpavriksha, or the Tree of Life, a wish-fulfilling tree, appeared during the churning of the ocean. Legend has it that when Shiva told Parvati about the tree's powers, she meditated under it and wished for a daughter. Soon, a beautiful girl child emerged from the Kalpavriksha, wrapped in roses. Shiva named her Aranyani, meaning 'goddess of forests'.

In paintings of the Tree of Life, the elements of energy, light, air and the sky are denoted through the sun; parrots, peacocks and elephants represent the earth; fish and lotuses stand for water.

In Madhubani art, certain symbols—the sun, the peacock, the elephant, fish and the Tree of Life itself—are believed to be signs of good fortune. As forests and trees, particularly the entities Aranyani and Kalpavriksha, represent life, Madhubani renditions of the Tree of Life depict their respect for *prakriti* (nature), which is considered the female form in creation.

'Madhubani art, like most folk traditions, shares a special bond with nature, from which it even derives its tools and colours. Women collect seasonal flowers and plants to make specific dyes,' Katha explained. 'The artists then use them to draw directly on the surface freehand.'

'Oh? Don't they draw a rough sketch? And what happens if they make a mistake?' Mohini asked.

'Nuh-uh! There's no place for an eraser in Madhubani. Artists know to turn even their mistakes—big and small—into great works of art.'

> Madhubani has four styles: Bharni, where the drawing is filled in with colours, is practised by Brahmins; Kachni, made up of black and red lines, by the Kayastha community; Godna, which has its roots in tattooing, by the Dusadh people; and Tantric, which involves yantras, by those who have knowledge of tantric art.
>
> Earlier these communities would stick to their individual styles. But now, a single painting may have elements of all four styles.

'Ah. Do all these communities paint the same stories then?' Mohini asked, totally hooked now.

Katha's eyes brightened. 'Not always. For example, Kayasthas tell the story of Chitragupta, the god who maintains records of each human being's behaviour on earth, as the community believes they are his descendants. The Dusadhs, on the other hand, narrate the story of their king, Salhes.'

A Humble King

Centuries ago, there was a time when Shailesh (Salhes in the local dialect), a skilled man from the Dusadh community, ruled over

Mithila. As he protected the then mountainous region from a number of intrusions, Salhes came to be known as the king of the mountains.[2]

Once, a neighbouring king, Kulheshwar, invited Salhes to a game of dice. The one to lose would serve as gatekeeper at the other's palace. And so, when Salhes lost, Kulheshwar dismissed his palace guard, Chuhadmal, and appointed Salhes to do the job. The king of the mountains faced grave insults as Kulheshwar's new guard. Only the four sisters who worked in the palace's garden—Reshma, Kusuma, Dauna and Hiriya—treated Salhes well.

Meanwhile, Chuhadmal, unceremoniously discharged from his duty, swore revenge. He dug a two-mile-long tunnel to the palace, through which he sneaked in and stole the queen's precious *hansuli* (necklace). An enraged Kulheshwar blamed Salhes for this theft, as he was the guard on duty, and imprisoned him.

However, the four sisters suspected that Chuhadmal was the culprit. So they went to his house in his absence to investigate. There, they found his wife wearing the stolen hansuli. The sisters offered to draw decorative Godna art on her body in exchange for the ornament. And Chuhadmal's wife, who had no clue that the hansuli gifted to her by her husband was the queen's, agreed.

Once the tattooing was completed, the four sisters promptly took the necklet to Kulheshwar and narrated the entire episode. As a result, Chuhadmal was punished, while Salhes was restored as Mithila's king.

'Yeah! Girl power!' Mohini shouted happily. 'Godna art helped rescue Salhes *so* many centuries ago . . . and his stories are being told through the same art form till date!'

'Nature and art find their way across time. It's the circle of life,' Katha said.

'But why did Kulheshwar punish Chuhadmal? He only stole from the king because he was unfairly thrown out of his job,' Mohini questioned. 'He's not *exactly* a thief, is he?'

---

[2] In Sanskrit and Hindi, *shail* means 'mountain' and *esh*, 'god' or 'king'.

'Well, that is a never-ending debate . . . Speaking of thieves, there's an interesting one you should know about. But first, let's have a snack,' the spirit proposed, handing out some popcorn.

'But I just ate. I can't stuff myself,' Mohini protested.

'Oh, stop whining. I know you're done. My dear Mohini, take just one!' it said in a sing-song voice.

Raising an eyebrow, Mohini popped one into her mouth.

CRUNCH!

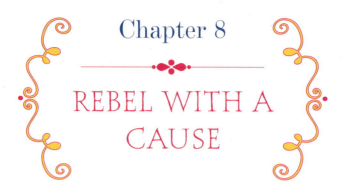

Chapter 8
REBEL WITH A CAUSE

No sooner had she swallowed the popcorn than she began sweating profusely.

'It's getting really hot!' she panted, wiping the sweat from her brow.

'Yeah, what do you expect? Look how close you're to the flames.' Katha pointed.

'Flames?' Mohini turned around with a jerk to face a huge, blazing bonfire.

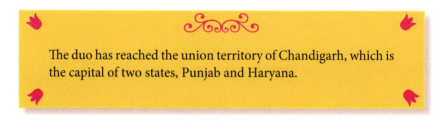

The duo has reached the union territory of Chandigarh, which is the capital of two states, Punjab and Haryana.

'We're here to celebrate the festival of Lohri,' the spirit announced.

'Hey, I know about Lohri! It's a harvest festival, right?' Mohini said.

'How bright you are—like the glowing embers of this bonfire!' Katha teased.

'Do you always have to be sarcastic? Anyway, just tell me about the interesting thief. What's he got to do with Lohri?'

'A lot! This festival, among many other things, is a storytelling tradition—one that keeps alive the legend of Dullah Bhatti,' Katha replied.

> The festival of Lohri is dedicated to the god of fire. At the end of winter, people from the Sikh and Punjabi communities celebrate Lohri to mark the harvest of rabi crops. They offer til (sesame) and rorhi (jaggery), along with popped corn and puffed rice, to a bonfire that they pray to.
>
> When said together, til and rorhi form 'tilrohri' or 'tilohri', from which the festival came to be called Lohri.

'As part of the festival's customs, children go to every house in their neighbourhood, singing folk songs and collecting sweets. These songs narrate the exploits of a legendary hero, Dullah Bhatti. Not just kids, even grown-ups sing his praises while dancing around the bonfire,' Katha began.

'But if Lohri is about fire and agriculture, then why do they sing about this Dullah Bhatti?'

'Be patient, won't you?' Katha said, pointing towards the bonfire.

Mohini blinked a few times before she saw clear figures taking shape in the high-reaching flames.

A Social Bandit

'Back in the day, during Mughal emperor Akbar's reign over Punjab, land tax was forcibly collected from the people. Sandal, a Muslim–Rajput zamindar in the town of Pindi Bhattian,[1] and his son, Farid, opposed this new rule. An irate Akbar ordered the death sentence for father and son, so that no other landlord from the region would ever defy him. Farid's wife, Ladhi, who was expecting a baby at the time of this tragedy, gave birth to a son soon after. She named him Rai Abdullah

---

[1] Pindi Bhattian was in the Punjab region of pre-Partition India.

Khan Bhatti. Now, it so happened that Akbar's son Shaikhu, whom you may know as Jahangir, was born on the same day. Shaikhu being a weak child, the royal astrologers advised Akbar to get a Rajput woman to nurse and take care of the newborn if he were to grow up to be a strong and brave prince. And whom do you think Akbar chose for this role? Ladhi!' Katha narrated.

'How strange! Did she agree?' Mohini asked.

'Yes, Ladhi reared Dullah—as Abdullah came to be called—and Shaikhu with equal care, despite knowing full well that Akbar caused her husband's death. The children grew up together in the palace and were close. When Dullah was a teenager, someone revealed to him that his grandfather and father had been murdered by Emperor Akbar— his best friend's father. Furious, Dullah immediately left the palace and went on to become a rebel, taking to highway robbery,' Katha finished.

'He must have been *really* angry,' Mohini said.

'Oh, yes. But there's another version of this story. It seems Shaikhu had a tiff with Akbar around this time. And it was on Shaikhu's encouragement that Dullah took to highway robbery, only so that he could take from the rich and give to the poor. This made him a popular hero among the masses,' the spirit said.

'Uh-oh! That mustn't have gone down too well with the emperor?'

'Well, it's said that Dullah became so invincible that Akbar changed his capital from Delhi to Lahore for nearly two decades to put an end to the rebel's activities. However, he ordered that Dullah be hanged in the same way as his forefathers had been. Doing this, Akbar assumed, would bring him to his knees. But Dullah accepted death without fear. And ever since, folklore has remembered and celebrated him as the Robin Hood of Punjab!'

> *Dulle di Vaar* (The Epic of Dullah) is also narrated by *dhadi*s, the ballad singers of Punjab. Using the *dhad*, a small drum, and the sarangi to create the background score, the dhadis sing of Dullah's life and battles. Unfortunately, over time, only a few portions of the entire narrative have survived.

'Hmm, but all this *still* doesn't explain how Dullah is connected to Lohri!' Mohini pouted.

'Remember I told you about children going around the neighbourhood and collecting sweets during Lohri?'

Mohini nodded.

'That is said to be a reminder of the way Dullah distributed among the poor what he took from the rich. It recalls his Robin-Hood-ness, his kind-heartedness,' Katha said, pointing to the flames once again.

The Marriage of Mundri

Dullah Bhatti was more than just a rebel and a robber. He also protected the girls of that region, who were often at risk of being kidnapped and enslaved by Mughal officers.

Once, a Mughal officer threatened to abduct Mundri, a beautiful girl who was engaged to be married. The girl's father requested the parents of the groom-to-be to bring forward the wedding date, but they refused, fearing the officer's reaction. Mundri's father then approached the only man who could protect his daughter . . . Dullah Bhatti! A secret ceremony was arranged in the forest. Dullah lit a sacred fire there and performed all the rituals that were traditionally done by a bride's father himself.

As a mark of respect for the hero and his act of bravery, people sing a special song at Lohri even today, dancing around the bonfire to the beats of the dhol:

> *Sundar Mundriye, ho!*
> *Tera kaun vichara, ho!*
> *Dullah Bhatti walla, ho!*

> (O beautiful Mundri!
> Who will think about you?
> Dullah of the Bhatti clan will!)

And so the song goes on, ending with lines that congratulate the couple:

> *Sanoo de de Lohri!*
> *Te teri jeeve jodi!*

> (Give us Lohri!
> Long live, O Couple!)

'Wow, you sing so well, Katha!' Mohini said.

'I know, I'm just too good!' The spirit winked.

Then Mohini fell quiet for a while, mulling over the story.

'Mundri was a complete stranger, yet Dullah acted like her father during her wedding ceremony . . .'

'Ha, and then there are people who betray their own family,' Katha said softly with a smirk.

Mohini looked at the spirit curiously, but Katha remained silent. So she waited, her eyes caught by the arresting orange flames.

Chapter 9

LOVING TO DEATH

Mohini vigorously rubbed her eyes, unsure of what she was looking at. The bonfire seemed to have transformed into a kiln, and clay moulds lay nearby.

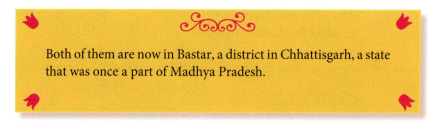

Both of them are now in Bastar, a district in Chhattisgarh, a state that was once a part of Madhya Pradesh.

'Are you going to teach me pottery?' Mohini asked, amused.

'I could teach you a zillion things, if it hadn't been for your mood swings!' Katha chuckled.

Mohini found this comment totally unnecessary. Hadn't she been attentively listening to the spirit all along, despite her displeasure at being spell-bound?

'How much do you love your grandmother?' Katha asked suddenly.

Mohini stared fiercely at the spirit. 'H-how do you know her?'

'You know, you'll do well as a detective,' Katha remarked.

'*Huh?* What?'

'Why are you suspicious of EVERY. LITTLE. THING?' The spirit paused. 'Most kids love their grandparents. It was just a general question!'

The girl wasn't fully convinced, but she replied to Katha's original question nevertheless. 'I love my G-Ma . . . my grandmother . . . TO DEATH!'

'If you love her to death, would you die for her? Would you *kill* for her?' Katha asked, its voice low.

These aren't easy questions to answer, Mohini thought. *Certainly not with a simple 'yes' or 'no'* . . .

'Complicated, isn't it? Think about it. In the meantime, I'm going to introduce you to another complicated thing: Ghadwakam,[1] the fascinating metal craft of the Ghadwa tribe,' the spirit said.

> Ghadwakam, the art of casting or moulding, is a centuries-old, lost-wax technique used to create brass and bronze sculptures.
>
> It gets its name from the Ghadwa tribe, but it has other names too: Bastar art, because it originated in the Bastar region; bell metal craft, as the metal used for moulding is the same with which bells are made; Dhokra in Odisha and West Bengal, where the art form is practised too.

Labour of Love

'The well-known statue *Dancing Girl*, sculpted around 2500 BCE and later unearthed in Mohenjo-Daro, is proof that the lost-wax technique was in use at the time of the Indus Valley Civilization. In the Bastar region itself, this method of metal craft has been practised for more than 200 years,' Katha continued. 'Here, the people came across this idea by observing the native *sataru* insect inside a cave.'

'An *insect* taught them the art form?' Mohini was flabbergasted.

'So they say! This insect had apparently hollowed out its *dengurbhil*, or waxy hive. And some molten metal had found its way inside, settling in the dug-out space. This lesson from nature gave the village folk the

---

1   Also spelt as Gadhwakam or Gadwakam.

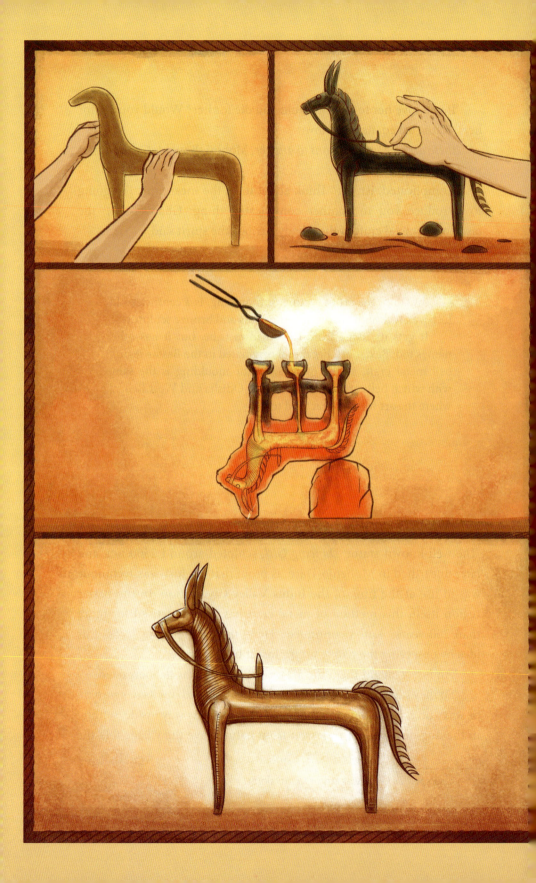

idea for Ghadwakam,' the spirit said. 'But the process is not as easy as the insect may have made it seem!'

> First, black agricultural clay is kneaded with rice husk and cow dung. With this, the sculptor creates a rough mould of the final sculpture. For example, to sculpt a horse figurine, the clay is shaped to form a horse. Holes are made at the bottom of the mould for liquefied metal to be emptied into later. In the next few days, the sculptor applies a number of coats of a muddy mixture on the mould.
>
> Next, with a tool called the *pichki*, noodle-like beeswax strands are squeezed out, which the sculptor carefully places in patterned lines all over the mould. These lines are then smoothened, and decorative designs are created on this surface with some more wax strands. After this, a few coatings of a mixture—of fresh clay from riverbeds, coal and cow dung—are applied on the wax detailing. Lastly, a layer of mud (from ant or termite hills) mixed with husk is applied on the mould.
>
> Once it has dried, the mould is baked in a kiln. The heat causes the wax, which is sandwiched between the innermost and outer layers of mud, to melt.

'Oh, no! The wax melts? That means the sculpture's lost?' Mohini asked, aghast.

'Yep, this is a nervous time for the sculptor. In a way, his wax creation *is* lost. Everything now depends on the next stage—' Katha began.

'*There's more?*' Mohini was baffled.

The spirit nodded. 'The final stage of this complex art form is the pouring of molten bronze or brass. The slightest mistake would mean that the sculptor must start all over again! So the liquefied metal is *slowly* tipped in through the holes that were made in the mould right in the beginning. Once it cools down inside, the metal becomes solid again.'

'Sooo . . . the metal sculpture has formed between the layers of mud, right?' Mohini asked.

'You've got it!' Katha smiled. 'When the sculptor breaks the outer clay mould, the metal sculpture is revealed. The statuette is then polished with care, and voila! The masterpiece is ready!'

Mohini felt a surge of respect for the perseverance of the Ghadwas. 'Is this what you'd meant when you'd asked me about dying, or even killing, for love? As in, the sculptors love their art . . . but . . . but they have to kill it at one point. Kind of. And when the wax melts and the sculpture's gone, doesn't a part of them die too?'

'Looks like the wax in your brain is making way for solid metal!' Katha joked. 'So it is with storytelling. A trial by fire will always help your ideas take shape as solid stories.'

Mohini didn't quite know what to make of that, but she understood this was Katha's way of prodding her into telling it a story. And there was NO way she was going to fall for that one.

Metallic Memorials

'Anyway, do you know why Ghadwakam sculptures are unique?' Katha asked her.

'Because of the complicated process, of course!'

'That too, but mainly because every piece is individually created by hand. There are no ready-made moulds,' the spirit said. 'The Ghadwas use this craft to sculpt many figures, such as the Tree of Life, the mahua tree, objects from their community life and tribal deities like Danteshwari Devi, Mouli Devi and Rao Dev.[2] But almost every household in the region is sure to have the metallic figurines of one particular tribal couple, whose legendary love story supposedly played out in Bastar nearly 600 years ago.'

---

[2] Rao Dev is a folk god of the people of Bastar. Like Ayyanaar, the protector-deity of Tamil Nadu, Rao Dev too is believed to ride a horse and keep a watch over villages in this region.

Jhitku–Mitku: A Love Story

Mitku (some Ghadwas call her Mitki) was the only sister of seven brothers, all of whom loved her dearly. So possessive were they about Mitku that when it was time to get her married to Jhitku, a wandering musician whom she was in love with, the brothers wanted the couple to stay with them even after their wedding. Jhitku agreed, and the couple began leading a happy life.

Around this time, the brothers encountered a peculiar problem. The water from a nearby river frequently flooded their farmland, completely destroying the crops. The brothers built stronger bunds, but the force of the flowing water broke them down each time. One night, they saw a dream in which their tribal goddess said that the sacrifice of a good man would put an end to this problem forever.

Without voicing their intentions, the brothers informed Mitku the next morning that they were taking Jhitku to their farmland. Mitku, however, had a premonition. She waited at the door till evening for everyone to return. One by one, the brothers entered the house and said, 'Jhitku is coming.' But Jhitku never returned. Anxious yet determined, Mitku went looking for him.

When she spotted a lifeless Jhitku near the river, she realized that her brothers had selfishly sacrificed her husband to save their crops. Stricken with grief, Mitku too jumped into the river.

Since then, Jhitku–Mitku have been revered as gods by the people of Bastar. Ghadwas depict the star-crossed couple in ornate attire and headgear. Jhitku is shown as playing a musical instrument, serenading Mitku. Some depictions include two *rakshak*s (protectors) standing guard near the couple. No one can separate them now.

'That's so tragic!' cried Mohini, her eyes moist.

No one said a word for a few moments. Then the girl spoke in a quiet, barely steady voice, 'I don't know if this sounds silly, but Jhitku seems like the wax that vanishes suddenly . . . a-a-and Mitku, the metal that follows after, making their love story immortal. Just like in Ghadwakam.'

Katha took a while to respond. 'Sometimes you amaze me, little one. You express such complex ideas with such simplicity. Just like artists do in Warli.'

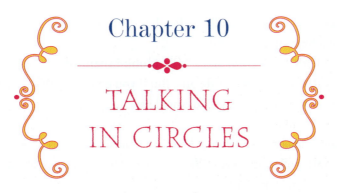

Chapter 10

TALKING IN CIRCLES

'Follow me,' Katha said, entering a house nearby.

Once inside, the spirit drank some water directly from an earthen pot and handed a glassful to the girl. Even as she was gulping down the cool drink, Katha swooshed out.

'Wha—Uff! What are you doing, going here and there?'

An irritated Mohini strode out in search of the spirit and immediately, the pleasant smell of wet earth welcomed her. The kiln had evaporated! She was now surrounded by glossy-green grass that seemed to have been recently bathed in a fresh shower.

'H-how did you do this?'

'Magic!' Katha winked.

'As if I didn't know *that*!'

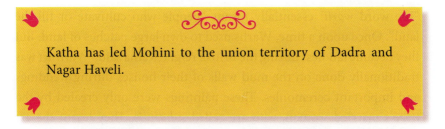

Katha has led Mohini to the union territory of Dadra and Nagar Haveli.

Mohini patiently waited for the spirit to begin telling her about Warli, but . . .

'What? I'm done telling stories! It's *your* turn.'

Not again! Mohini was exasperated. 'AAARGHHH—'

'You know, I'm actually rather happy about this . . . I've always wanted a human helper arou—'

'Well, it's NOT going to be ME,' Mohini snapped.

'We'll see about that, little one. But if you go on like this, refusing to tell stories, you *will* end up like Ahankar.'

'What is that?'

'Later, alligator. First comes Warli, you must know surely,' Katha said.

Mohini rolled her eyes. 'Why do you kick up a fuss when you're going to tell me anyway?'

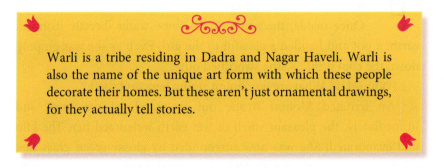

Warli is a tribe residing in Dadra and Nagar Haveli. Warli is also the name of the unique art form with which these people decorate their homes. But these aren't just ornamental drawings, for they actually tell stories.

Stick Silhouettes

'The word *warli*[1] essentially means "people who cultivate or till the land". Once upon a time, Warlis used to own large patches of land. But they became landless during the British reign,' Katha said. 'Warli art was traditionally done on the mud walls of their houses during weddings and important ceremonies. These paintings were only created by the tribe's married women, who are called *suhasini*s. They learnt the art from the elderly women of the tribe, who are believed to have received this knowledge in their dreams.'

'Dreams? *Sigh*. I wish I could dream up stories too,' Mohini mumbled. *Huh? Did I just express an interest in storytelling?*

---

[1] Warli originates from the word *waral*, meaning 'a piece of tilled land'.

'I knew it! So you *do* want to tell tales!' Katha stood with its hands on its slender waist.

'Whatever!' Mohini frowned to cover up her slip. 'So tell me, since it's done on the walls, is Warli like Madhubani?' she went on to ask.

'See for yourself,' Katha said, taking her around the mud house they had just come out of.

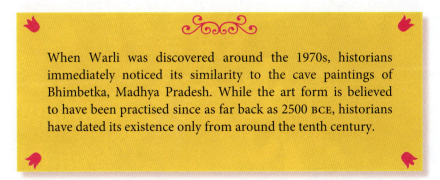

When Warli was discovered around the 1970s, historians immediately noticed its similarity to the cave paintings of Bhimbetka, Madhya Pradesh. While the art form is believed to have been practised since as far back as 2500 BCE, historians have dated its existence only from around the tenth century.

Mohini looked stumped. '*Are you kidding me?* These are just stick figures. Even a child can draw them! How is this art? And how on earth do you tell whole stories through it?'

'Believe it or not, they do this in a rather unique way. You see, the art form was created by the tribe as a pictorial tool of communication and storytelling since they could not read or write back then. The ritualistic Warli figures were kept simple so that every child in the tribe could learn to draw them. But don't let these line drawings fool you—they may *look* easy, but they convey deep messages,' Katha explained.

A Story in Geometry

'Today, Warli is divided into two categories: the ritualistic and the commercial. Ritualistic paintings are the ones drawn by suhasinis. For weddings, they paint the image of Palghat, their goddess of

marriage. This image, known as Dev Chowk, is unveiled at night by the *bhagat*,[2] who plays the drum and prays to the gods to protect the couple from evil spirits,' Katha continued.

'How is commercial Warli different?' Mohini studied the mud wall, where Katha magically made many Warli drawings appear and disappear one after another.

'I'm telling you! Commercial drawings are done on paper, cloth, wooden coasters and whatnot! Of course, sometimes Warli artists are invited to illustrate murals too. Not just women, even the tribe's men are Warli artists now. While modern-day motifs, such as the bicycle,

---

[2] The bhagat is the tribe's spiritual healer, who is also a keeper of Warli mythology.

the computer and cityscapes, have crept into their artworks, they continue to paint stories that they've heard from the tribe's traditional storytellers, as well as daily scenes, such as farming, hunting, cooking . . . even merrymaking!' Katha finished.

'Hey! What's this?' Mohini asked, pointing to the latest illustration on the wall.

'This is a popular Warli theme—the Tarpa dance! It depicts a chain of dancers in a spiralling circle around the *tarpa*[3] player,' the spirit explained.

Warli art is painted with a bamboo stick, using a white pigment made of rice paste, water and gum. The walls on which they draw are made of sticks, mud and cow dung. Artists use only two colours—mud-brown for the background and white for the figures. Usually, the strokes are drawn from bottom to top. All themes and scenes are painted using line work and basic shapes, such as the circle, triangle and square.

---

[3] Tarpa, a musical instrument, is a common motif in Warli narratives.

'Now you will want me to believe that these shapes have meanings?' prompted Mohini.

'Yes, the circle comes from the sun and the moon, which the Warlis revere; the triangle from mountain peaks; the square, they say, symbolizes the waral. Most Warli figures are drawn using two triangles that meet at a point: for example, an inverted triangle on top of an upright one is how the human body is illustrated. This represents balance,' Katha summed up.

'Interesting . . . But you know what I like the most about Warli?' Mohini asked, answering her own question. 'That it expresses emotions even without showing faces for the illustrated figures!'

'Hmm, your brain seems to be working well in my company.' Katha grinned.

'Of course! Hey, you haven't yet told me what Ahankar is,' she reminded the spirit.

'For that we'll have to peek into Warli mythology.'

Kahankar and Ahankar

In the old days, there lived the two Warli tribesmen Kahankar and Ahankar. The former made up and told tales while the latter only listened.

The two friends once wandered into a forest and spent much of their time telling stories. Days passed, but the two unmindfully sat in the same place, engrossed in stories. Food was never on their minds, for stories fed their souls. And so there came a day when the duo passed away, having starved all along. Soon, a group of passers-by, who'd spotted the two unidentified dead friends, took them to their own village and buried them there.

> Some time later, the families of the two friends came looking for them. They reached the same village and were directed to the men's burial spot. But when the families dug up the graves, only their bones were found. This led to a big question: Which one was Kahankar and which Ahankar? The villagers had no clue.
>
> Devising a curious test, the families took the bones to a nearby river, immersed them in the water and waited. Some bones floated up, while the others sank right down. And so the families knew. Kahankar's folks picked up the floating bones as they were his, while Ahankar's collected the ones that had drowned; and all returned home.

'Eh? What kind of story is this? How did floating and sinking bones help them identify their family members?' the girl quizzed.

'They were not just *any* family member. They were Kahankar and Ahankar,' Katha pointed out with a slight smile.

'Um, *so?*'

'Kahankar was the storyteller, the maker of tales. Ahankar,[4] the listener, was the taker of tales. The former shared his knowledge, and so his bones were light and they floated up. The latter took it all in and hoarded information, so his bones became heavy and they sank,' Katha explained.

Day had turned to night even as Katha had lightly narrated this weighty tale. Seeing the spirit float delicately in front of her, the girl felt a sudden heaviness settling in her limbs. Did she really want to be like Ahankar? She sat numb, gooseflesh glistening on her arms in the full moon's light.

---

[4] In Hindi, *ahankar* means 'ego'.

Chapter 11

A BARREL OF FUN

Katha was worried. Mohini hadn't spoken at all since the previous night. Although she had slept well, she'd woken up feeling blue. The story of Kahankar and Ahankar seemed to have unsettled her. To cheer her up, Katha began strutting on tiptoe—rather, *tiptail*—while making odd faces. Mohini was confused for a bit, but then a smile slowly spread across her face.

'Phew!' The spirit wiped off an imaginary drop of sweat from its brow.

The sunny morning suddenly turned into a pleasant dusk, and Mohini found herself in a large clearing, surrounded by thick shrubs and trees. A group of tall men with well-sculpted bodies, wearing traditional attire decorated with peacock feathers and seashells, soon marched into the glade.

'The Siddi, a tribe that came to India from Africa ages ago,' Katha introduced them.

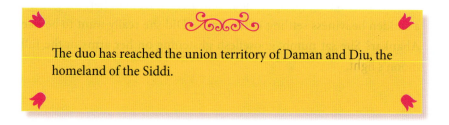

The duo has reached the union territory of Daman and Diu, the homeland of the Siddi.

The men began making the same kinds of faces that Katha had pulled just a few minutes ago.

'Katha, I'm fine. They don't have to do this to get me to laugh,' the girl said.

'Glad to know you're fine. We must eat now, I opine,' Katha said, pulling a plateful of khandvi[1] out of thin air. 'And by the way, these men aren't doing this for you. It's part of their ritualistic dance!'

'Making faces is part of a ritual?' Mohini asked doubtfully as she picked up a squishy yellow piece of khandvi.

'Yup! It's called Siddi Goma.'

'What's Siddi—never mind,' muttered Mohini, still haunted by the Kahankar–Ahankar story.

To a New Home

'The first Siddi people came to Gujarat through Port Bharuch in 628 CE. Some more were led to our country by the Arabs around 712 CE. They were called Zinjis then. From the fourteenth century onward, the number of Siddi immigrants swelled further. They were captured and brought here by Indian noblemen, and later on, by the Portuguese, as slaves,' Katha said.

'Slaves?' Mohini was shocked.

'Unfortunately, yes. The reigning kings of the time hired them as soldiers, but most ended up doing menial jobs. Some Siddis were deployed to guard the coasts because of their physical strength. This is why much of the Siddi population today can be found across the western coastal regions of Gujarat, Daman and Diu, Maharashtra, Goa and Karnataka.'

---

[1] Khandvi are tempered pinwheel rolls made of gram flour and are a local speciality.

Siddi Goma is an energetic dance form. Its name comes from the Swahili word *ngoma*, meaning 'drum, dance, music and rhythm'. Since the Siddis of this region mostly speak Gujarati, Siddi Goma is also called Siddi Dhamal.[2]

---

[2] In Gujarati, *dhamal* means 'drum'.

Dance of Delight

'Siddi Goma or Siddi Dhamal is performed by a group of twelve men—four lead singers and drummers and eight dancers. All of them paint their faces and are dressed alike, in peacock feathers over bright skirts as well as shell belts and headgear,' Katha said.

'Goma begins with one of the performers walking in on tiptoe, holding stances and making faces while letting out animal-like cries and mimicking bird calls. He repeats the name of the tradition, "Goma", a couple of times. The singers then begin crooning and playing the drums as the dancers make their appearance in two groups of four, one from the left and the other from the right. Different kinds of drums, small and big—the one played by the singers is as large as a barrel!—are integral to Goma music,' the spirit continued.

'They look so happy . . .' Mohini observed as the Siddis began performing.

'Oh, yes, it's a happy dance. They sing praises of the tribe's ancestral saints, especially Baba Gor.[3] Actually, it is to spread Baba Gor's message of freedom and joy that Siddis perform Goma. In the olden days, the tribe also performed Goma to express their delight after a successful hunt,' Katha told Mohini.

---

[3] He is also called Bava Gor.

> Baba Gor was an Abyssinian[4] trader, whom Siddis worship as a saint. He is said to have come from Nigeria and settled in the hills of Rajpipla, near Bharuch. There, he began the mining and trade of precious stones, especially agate. This gem is also called Babaghuri after the saint.

The spirit noticed that even though Mohini's mood had improved, she still wasn't asking any questions. Her brow was lined in concentration as she studied the dancers.

So it continued. 'The dancers smoothly move their necks and waists to the drumbeats, gliding from one side to the other. But the fun is in the climax. Watch!'

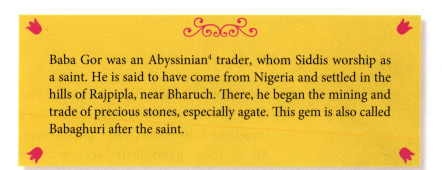

At once, a dancer threw a coconut in the air, jumped up and broke it into two with his head.

'WOW!' Mohini couldn't help but let out a squeal.

'Oh, and guess what? At times, a dancer walks barefoot over burning embers. Siddis believe that the dance leads them to miraculously receive healing powers,' Katha added.

'How I wish the kings and noblemen had respected the Siddis! It is *so* weird that they would make them their slaves instead,' the girl said.

'That's because enslaving the brave and the strong usually makes the oppressor feel more powerful. But true courage cannot remain hidden for long. It makes an appearance, sooner or later . . .'

---

[4] Ethiopia was also known as Abyssinia.

Warrior Extraordinaire

His name was Malik Ambar, and he was a Siddi slave. Brought to India around 1570, he was sold and resold again and again, until he became the serf-cum-confidant of Chengiz Khan, the chief minister of Ahmednagar, also a Siddi. From Khan, Ambar learnt statecraft and warfare. Upon Khan's death, his wife set Ambar free. And through perseverance, Ambar earned a respectable position in the region.

At that time, Emperor Akbar was planning to annex the southern sultanates, including Ahmednagar. The Nizam Shahi Army of the city had already lost to the Mughals and Ahmednagar Fort was besieged. Ambar realized that if he wanted to protect the region from the Mughals, he had to earn the trust of the Nizams. So he had his daughter married to Murtaza Nizam Shah II, who ascended the throne. And Ambar was appointed as the sultanate's regent to manage the affairs of the state on behalf of the king, who was too young to rule.

A guerrilla[5] genius, Ambar helmed an army of 50,000 men, comprising Siddis and Marathas. Together, they pushed back the Mughal forces. His trusted lieutenant in this attack was Maloji Bhosale, Shivaji's[6] grandfather.

Ambar went on to build a splendid city nearby, which later came to be named Aurangabad after Mughal emperor Aurangzeb. Interestingly, after Ambar's death, his guerrilla techniques were largely adopted by the Marathas, led by Shivaji, during their battles against Aurangzeb.

---

[5] Guerrilla warfare consists of a smaller group of warriors adopting clever military methods to fight a large organized army.

[6] Shivaji, the popular king who founded the Maratha Empire, fought Mughal rule in the Deccan Plateau.

'Not just their war techniques, there's another Siddi thing that can influence others pretty quickly,' Mohini piped up. 'Their joy!'

'Rightly said, little one,' Katha shouted back so that she could hear its voice over the drone of the drums. The Siddi performance they had been watching was reaching a crescendo. 'Let's join the Dhamal!'

Katha dragged the girl into the dance. And they did their little jig oblivious to the Siddis, just as the Siddis danced oblivious to everything around.

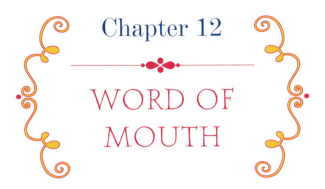

Chapter 12
WORD OF MOUTH

Warlis create paintings to ward off evil spirits. Siddis dance to get supernatural powers and honour the spirits of their ancestral saints. Mohini's mother would have *loved* these tales, but her father would have surely disapproved of them. Anokhi would have only smiled mysteriously. The girl wondered if spirits were for real or just figments of people's imagination . . . Oh, wait, here *she* was, stuck with a weird *spirit* that just wouldn't let her go—'Whoops!'

Some steps had suddenly appeared below her feet and she'd almost lost her balance.

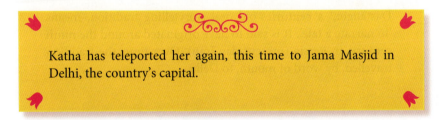

Katha has teleported her again, this time to Jama Masjid in Delhi, the country's capital.

'Why are we here?' Mohini asked, irked at having once again been plucked from one place to another without warning. 'I've been here some four times already. Can I please just go home now?'

'Sure. But there's one condition: You have to tell everyone in Mithika that you were spell-bound to a supercool psychedelic, ingenious spirit. And if they don't buy what you say, then you'll be back with me!' Katha grinned devilishly.

'I might as well stay back then. No one will believe a word of a story about a spirit! Except my mother,' Mohini said sourly.

'Okay, let's get this straight. If you *do* narrate your adventures with me to anyone, then you will have told a story successfully. Now, about belief . . . Isn't it fun when bizarre things happen in tales? Even though they don't seem believable, your mind still imagines them clearly, as though they're actually happening? Tell me, what's your favourite story?' Katha asked.

Mohini didn't really have to think about this. 'The one of Aladdin and the magic lamp.'

'Do you know why?' Katha didn't wait for her to answer. 'Because it has a genie and a flying carpet. It's magical!' The spirit clicked its horns together and a spray of glitter engulfed Mohini. 'A good story is one that makes the unreal seem real and—'

'The real seem unreal!' Mohini completed. 'That's *exactly* what G-Ma used to say.'

'That's exactly what Danstangoi does,' Katha said, looking up at the Jama Masjid's lofty minarets.

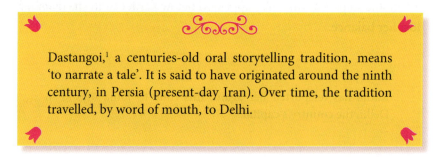

Dastangoi,[1] a centuries-old oral storytelling tradition, means 'to narrate a tale'. It is said to have originated around the ninth century, in Persia (present-day Iran). Over time, the tradition travelled, by word of mouth, to Delhi.

Dead yet Alive

'Around the eighteenth century, when the struggle for Independence was gathering momentum, the Urdu language was much in use in Indian arts and literature.' Katha began giving her the context. 'After the mutiny of 1857, several *dastangos*[2] shifted from Delhi to Lucknow.

---

[1] In Persian, *dastan* means 'tale' and *goi*, 'to tell'.
[2] Storytellers who practise Dastangoi.

Soon, every nobleman's household as well as almost every street in these cities had its very own favourite dastango—'

'EVERY STREET HAD A STORYTELLER?' Mohini was truly taken aback. 'I thought only Mithika had storytellers in abundance!'

'Oh, no-no-no, you're highly mistaken, my friend. In pre-Partition India, there used to be so many storytellers that an entire street was dedicated to them! It was called Qissa Khwani Bazaar, meaning "the market of storytellers",' the spirit told her.

'What a relief I wasn't one of them! Can you imagine if I was? Just one story from me would have had the whole street shutting up shop!' Mohini said with a nervous laugh.

Katha did not want to encourage the girl's underestimation of herself, so it chose to ignore her remark altogether. 'Around the nineteenth century, people started preferring realistic tales.'

'Like my dad!' Mohini interrupted.

'I see.' The spirit smiled and continued. 'Also, suddenly, everyone wanted stories in English! The love for the English novel extinguished the life force of this oral tradition. So when Mir Baqar Ali, the last known traditional dastango, died in 1928, the tradition lost its voice entirely.'

'You mean no one practises this storytelling art form now?' Mohini asked, almost dismayed at the thought.

'Stories change after the interval, my girl! Nearly seven decades after that, a group of researchers and storytellers decided to reinvent Dastangoi. All they had to go on was a tome of tales and an audio clip of Mir Baqar Ali narrating a short story. Just from that, Dastangoi was given a new life, perhaps even a new form.'

'Yay!' Mohini clapped her hands.

Dastangoi requires only three things: a captivating story, a masterful storyteller and a keen audience. The storytellers dress in a plain white *angarkha* (tunic), a churidar and a cap. The stage has a mattress for dastangos to sit on, with bolsters on the sides and candles glowing nearby. In front of the dastangos are bowls of water to drink from during the performance.

'Earlier, Dastangoi used to be a solo act. But these days, a pair of dastangos performs together. A range of topics, like political events and retellings of children's classics, has been added to the tradition's bag of stories. And guess what's back? . . . Urdu!' Katha said happily.

Everlasting Dastans

'Oh, so they not only brought back the art form, but also the language in which it was told?' Mohini was impressed. 'But how does Dastangoi make the unreal real, and the real unreal?'

'Ah, that! Well, dastangos take their audience into the realms of magic, love, adventure and even war. One tale that has caught the fascination of nearly all storytellers is that of Amir Hamza, who was believed to be Prophet Muhammad's uncle. Hamza's adventures are full of twists and turns; djinns and demons; beauties and beasts; *tilism*,[3] talismans and tricksters,'[4] Katha finished.

'Oh, come on! You have to tell me more!'

'Okay, okay! Even Emperor Akbar was enamoured by Hamza, you know. Not only did he tell these tales like a dastango, but he also commissioned the creation of the epic in the Mughal miniature style of painting. *Hamzanama*, as it was called, was made up of 1400 folios depicting various episodes. Each folio, about four-and-a-half feet long and three feet broad, had handwritten text on the back, which storytellers read aloud. But it was *Dastan-e Amir Hamza*, a forty-six-volume tome of Hamza's exploits, published in 1881, that helped researchers and storytellers reinvent Dastangoi,' Katha explained.

'Do I get to hear a Hamza story then?' Mohini was looking at Katha expectantly.

---

[3] Meaning spells.
[4] Tricksters, or *aiyyar*s, are a common and interesting element of Dastangoi tales.

Amir Hamza and the Dragon

Once, when Amir Hamza travelled to a neighbouring land, he heard the anxious cries of a crowd. The region's ruler, who was hosting Hamza, informed him that a dragon had made their life hell. Every now and then, the animal breathed fire, burning down everything in its way for miles around. As though this destruction weren't enough, each time it inhaled, it sucked into its mouth everything from miles around—people, homes, trees, animals!

Upon hearing of the kingdom's woes, Hamza immediately offered to slay the dragon. As he strode to the dragon's lair on his steed, Ashqar Demon-Born, the locals followed him. All along, they wondered how he would single-handedly bring down the huge beast.

When they reached the lair, everyone kept a safe distance, but not Hamza. He rushed the dragon, drawing his sword. Leaping on to its back, he thrust the blade deep into the animal's spine. With a low moan, the dragon turned towards Hamza angrily, clouds of smoke escaping from its mouth and darkening the whole scene.

Was Hamza safe? Had the dragon ended him? People waited with bated breath for the air to clear. And when it did, they saw a dead dragon and a triumphant Hamza.

'Hurrah! He's superhuman!' Mohini giggled. 'Tell me, Katha, what does Hamza mean? I like the sound of the name.'

Katha stared at Mohini, slightly taken aback. 'Who are you, child? Are you an aiyyar playing tricks on me?'

'Very funny! I get it, it was a silly question.' Mohini turned away.

'Not at all! It's a brilliant question,' Katha assured her. 'Okay, it's difficult to explain, but I'll try . . . In many languages, to pronounce certain letters in a word, particularly consonants, the glottis—that part of the throat which comprises the vocal cords—needs to be closed. So the passage of air through the throat is restricted. When you say "Uh-oh!", it results in a momentary silence between "uh" and "oh", right? Such a consonant or letter is called the glottal stop. While the word itself is spelt using these consonants, the sound or pronunciation can't really be written down because there is no letter in the alphabet to denote it. In Arabic, the glottal stop is known as hamza.'

'Uh . . . I *think* I get it—' Mohini's eyes widened in mid-sentence, as though a bright thought had flashed through her brain. 'It makes complete sense!' Her voice was squeaky with excitement. 'Like the glottal stop, the Hamza tales are meant to be *told*, not *written*. They are perfect for oral traditions like Dastangoi!'

Katha hugged Mohini—it really just plunged into her with its barely there body. But the girl was still quite surprised by this sudden, and unique, display of affection. She awkwardly looked up at the now dark sky, only to realize that the moon seemed to be smiling down at them.

'I have one more question . . . Why was Hamza's steed called Ashqar Demon-Born?' Mohini asked as Katha loosened its embrace.

'I'm telling you stories of fire-breathing dragons and you want to know about horses! But hey, your wish is my command, Master Mohini!' Katha bowed low, as if it were Aladdin's wish-granting friend, Genie.

Within the blink of an eye, a horse with a glossy dark-blue coat—the colour of night—trotted towards them.

Neeigghhh!

Chapter 13
WARHORSE

The horse disappeared into the horizon after dropping Mohini and Katha off on the outskirts of a village. The girl was a little disoriented, for the horse had galloped across unseen lands—all of which was a blur—at the speed of light, maybe faster. Yet it seemed as though the whole night was past them as dawn was just breaking.

In the distance, Mohini noticed a group of men, each holding a sword, the sun's rays glinting off the blades. Had Katha brought her to a battlefield? Yikes!

Mohini and the spirit have arrived in Bicholim taluk in the state of Goa.

'Is this truly Goa? Where are the beaches?' Mohini quizzed. Looking side to side and down and up for answers, she found Katha perched on the branch of a cashew tree, busy talking to a yellow-throated bulbul.

'After a brilliant comment comes a silly question. That's *so* Mohini!' it was telling the bulbul. Turning to her, the spirit replied, 'There's more to Goa than beaches, girl—just as there is much more to what you are watching than those glistening swords.'

'Does this have *anything* to do with Ashqar Demon-Born?' Mohini asked.

Katha simply shook its head.

'I knew it! Cheat!'

'Well, Ghode Modni isn't about Hamza's steed, but it's still about horses!'

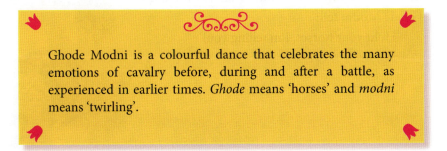

Ghode Modni is a colourful dance that celebrates the many emotions of cavalry before, during and after a battle, as experienced in earlier times. *Ghode* means 'horses' and *modni* means 'twirling'.

The Twirl of Triumph

'Hey, look!' Mohini was excited, now that the men in the distance emerged dressed in vibrant costumes, astride horses. But . . . 'Those horses—they're not real?'

'Nope. Let me tell you about the attire of the dancers. They are dressed like Rajput cavalrymen, but their pagri or turban is in the style of Maratha warriors. Sometimes they even wear floral headgear. What really sets apart their costume is the dummy horse frame that they wear. And when they twirl rhythmically, holding the bridle in one hand and the sword in another, to the music of the dhol, *tasha*—a drum played with sticks—and cymbals, viewers get the impression that both rider and stallion are dancing together,' Katha explained.

'Ohh! They look spectacular!' Mohini gasped as the dancers inched closer.

'You know, a similar dummy horse dance is practised in Rajasthan. That's called Kachchhi Ghodi. And there's one in Tamil Nadu too, called Poikkaal Kudhirai Aattam,'[1] the spirit told her.

'Wow! That means one storytelling tradition is scattered across the country under different names,' Mohini noted. 'But what stories does Ghode Modni tell?'

'Hold your horses, I'm telling you!'

March of the Marathas

'Ghode Modni recreates the many victories of the Ranes[2] over the Portuguese, who had colonized Goa. The dance, which, by the way, is not choreographed, begins at the village border, where the troupe declares mock war. The dancers then ride through the village. The most thrilling part is when they lock swords, effortlessly twirling along with the frames. After they reach the temple of their village deity, they return to the starting point,' Katha said.

'But they aren't singing any story . . .' Mohini said, not taking her eyes off the swirl of colour that the dancers were.

'That's right. No folk songs are sung. But the performers do break into the war cry "*Har Har Mahadev!*"[3] every now and then,

---

[1] In Tamil, *poikkaal* means 'fake legs'; *kudhirai* means 'horse'; *aattam* means 'dance'. So Poikkaal Kudhirai Aattam stands for the 'dance of the horse with fake legs'.

[2] Maratha warriors who had Rajput roots.

[3] There are a few commonly accepted interpretations of this war cry. One of them suggests that since *har* means 'every' in Hindi and Mahadev is another name for Shiva, the call means 'Everyone is Shiva'. Another explanation is that since Shiva is known in Hindu mythology as the destroyer, the cry encourages those going to war to destroy evil.

just as the Maratha warriors used to in battle. Some dancers, who do not wear the horse frame, carry war accessories such as emblem-bearing flags and banners throughout the performance,' the spirit added over the sound of the clanking swords.

'It looks like a parade style of dancing to me . . . you know, since they keep walking and dancing,' Mohini offered.

'Good observation! Some people say this tradition evolved from ghode *mandani*, the parade of horses brought in from Arabia and Persia, observing which the king would evaluate the animals' fitness and strength. But locals believe that the dance symbolizes a funny episode actually! Once, a group of thieves that had entered the village ran away after this dance was performed! Ever since, Ghode Modni is performed to keep away thieves who may be lurking nearby,' Katha narrated with a wink.

Mohini chuckled. 'That's a new one. I didn't know storytelling could even fight crime.'

'Oh, storytelling can do lots of things,' the spirit said. 'Anyway, the most accepted version, though, is the not-so-comical one—Ranes versus the Portuguese.'

Raging Ranes

In 1510, Goa came under Portuguese rule. For centuries after, the Ranes led many rebellions against these colonizers. But three names that have been etched in Goan history are Dipaji Rane, Kushtoba Rane and Dada Rane.

A huge setback for the Portuguese came in 1852, when they faced stiff opposition from Dipaji Rane. In a surprise attack, Dipaji and his army took over Fort Nanus from the Portuguese, driving them out of the Sattari region.

Kushtoba Rane led an uprising in the Sanquelim region in 1869, in which Portuguese police stations were attacked. He is also remembered as a local Robin Hood, for he took from the rich and gave to the poor.

In 1895, Dada Rane looted the government treasury and brought the entire northern region of Goa, including Bicholim, under his control. He also made sure that the Portuguese created a Maratha battalion within their forces.

Ghode Modni, which celebrates the Ranes' rebellion and victories, is popular in Sattari, Sanquelim and Bicholim districts, all of which were the power centres of the Rane reign.

Mohini pondered a while over how different Ghode Modni was from Dastangoi. 'Just when I thought storytelling could be simple, you make me watch this zesty dance.'

'What can I say—variety is the spice of storytelling,' Katha said emphatically.

'But one thing's common. Both traditions tell tales of bravery,' she pointed out.

'Yup. Now that I've told you about a fearless hero and the courageous Marathas, how about the tale of a warrior–monk?'

'*Warrior–monk?* Aren't these two words . . . like opposites?' Mohini asked unsurely.

'You bet!'

Chapter 14
ACT OF FAITH

For the shortest second, a white light flashed all about them. 'Woah!' Mohini's mouth fell open. Everything around her was made of smooth marble.

> Their next stop is a Jain temple in Patan district of Gujarat.

As Mohini admired the marble carvings, Katha began, 'Chalukya kings who ruled over Gujarat took an interest in Jainism. Not only did they have many Jain temples and libraries built, but they also commissioned several manuscripts. In time, Patan became the hub of Jain manuscript painting.'

Mohini nodded, her eyes caught by a sculpture. Katha didn't say anything for the next few minutes as it watched her.

'What? Aren't you going to tell me about the warrior-monk?' she asked, briefly glancing at Katha before craning her neck to see the motifs on the ceiling.

'Nah, I'll wait till you're done looking around. I have *all* the time in the world,' it said sarcastically.

'Weirdo! Why bring me to such a beautiful place if you don't want me to admire it?' Mohini grumbled. 'All right, I am all ears. You were saying something about manuscripts?'

'Jain manuscript painting,' Katha repeated.

A Decorated Doctrine

'Jain manuscript painting is said to have originated a century and a half or so after Mahavira, the last Jain *tirthankara* or spiritual teacher, attained nirvana.[1] But the art became prominent more than a thousand years later, from the fifteenth century onward. At that time, the Svetambara[2] sect's *Kalpa Sutra* or Book of Sacred Precepts was the most popular painted manuscript,' Katha said.

Jain manuscript painting refers to the miniature illustrations in the sacred texts of Jains. *Kalpa Sutra* preserves the life stories and teachings of the tirthankaras,[3] especially Mahavira, through a mixture of miniature paintings and handwritten, calligraphic text.[4]

'Even though the manuscripts are famous for their art, many include only the names of the writers and the patrons. Not of the artists,' Katha pointed out.

'How can none of them bear the artist's name?' Mohini asked.

'Well, some definitely do. For example, one text that had the names of both its writer, Somasinha, and its artist, Daiyaka, was a version of *Kalakacharya Katha* or Kalakacharya's Tale, created around 1416,' the spirit said.

'Hmm . . . Why exactly were these manuscripts created?'

---

1. In Jainism, nirvana refers to freedom from suffering. Some scholars suggest Mahavira attained nirvana in 527 BCE.
2. There are two sects in Jainism: Digambara and Svetambara. Monks of the latter sect are identified by the white robes that they wear.
3. There are twenty-four spiritual teachers in Jainism.
4. The text, usually in Prakrit or Sanskrit, was written using the Devanagari script.

'So that after a Jain manuscript was ready, patrons who commissioned it could gift it to a Jain monk. The monk read aloud from it during Paryushan. The rest of the time, the book was stored in the *bhandara*, the library of a Jain temple. Since the creators, patrons, purpose and content were all related to Jainism, the art form also came to be known as Jaina painting,' the spirit explained.

'Paryushan is a festival, right?'

'Yes, it is!'

> Paryushan is an eight-day-long Jain festival, which focuses on self-purification and forgiveness. Kalakacharya had instructed that *Kalpa Sutra* must be read during this time.
>
> A copy of *Kalpa Sutra* is taken out in a procession to a Jain temple. Monks narrate the story and teachings of Mahavira to listeners while showing corresponding paintings from the manuscript.

'Hey, is Kalakacharya the warrior–monk?' Mohini asked, curiosity now bubbling inside her.

'Right again! I told you you'd make a great detective.' Katha grinned. 'But before we get to the story, don't you want to know how these manuscripts were created?'

Mohini nodded and shrugged her shoulders, as if to say, 'Yeah, obviously!'

Chronicles in Colour

'For the longest time, Jain manuscripts were painted on palm leaves. Around the fourteenth century, when sultanate rule came to Gujarat, paper was introduced. Thousands of palm-leaf manuscripts were copied on to paper by writers and artists. Palm-leaf strips were narrow, and paper offered more space. So the art became elaborate and decorative. A traditional manuscript was made up of folios or loose sheets. And it had a front and back cover made of paper, cloth or wood,' Katha said, magically making some folios appear.

A cool breeze blew, and the folios flew around lazily. 'Gorgeous! Hey, this person has been painted as though he is looking sideways and in front at the same time!' she observed.

'Ah, yes, an important characteristic of Jaina paintings is the "further eye" . . . as in, even if the characters are portrayed in profile, the other—usually hidden—eye is shown.'

'Ohh! So who is this?' the girl asked, pointing to the person in the painting.

'Guess?'

'Kalakacharya!' Mohini exclaimed.

The Monk Who Fought a War

In Dharavasa, a town in Magadha (present-day Bihar), lived the royal couple Vajra Sinha and Sura Sundari with their son, Kalaka Suri, and daughter, Saraswati. Both Kalaka and Saraswati were initiated into the Jain faith. Over time, Kalaka became an acharya (guru) and Saraswati, a *sadhvi* (nun).

Once, when Saraswati was visiting the city of Ujjain, the region's king, Gardabhilla, happened to spot her. He became so besotted with Saraswati that he abducted her. Kalaka, who too was in Ujjain at the time, requested Gardabhilla to release his sister. But the king refused. Determined, the monk crossed River Indus and befriended a Saka[5] chief. He requested him and some other chiefs to attack Ujjain. They

---

[5] Iranian–Eurasian nomads, who were also called Scythians.

Folio reproduced from 'Captive Gardabhilla. Kalpasutra. C.1375, Western India.JPG' user: Ismoon/Wikimedia Commons/Public Domain/2012

agreed and the Saka Army encamped on the outskirts of Ujjain. When the army ran out of supplies one day, Kalaka magically turned some bricks into gold to purchase the goods.

Soon after, they besieged Gardabhilla's palace. Inside, the king sat practising *gardabhi vidya*,[6] through the knowledge of which he could win this battle. But Kalaka knew that the gardabh (she-ass) guarding the palace entrance could kill 108 people with a single bray. So the Saka archers, along with Kalaka himself, shot arrows right into its mouth the moment it was about to let out the fatal bray.

With the she-ass unable to make a sound, Gardabhilla lost all his powers. The Saka forces and Kalaka entered the fort and rescued Saraswati. Kalaka went on to forgive Gardabhilla.

To honour the monk and his contributions to Jainism, his story, 'Kalakacharya Katha', appears in *Kalpa Sutra* along with illustrations depicting each episode.

Mohini looked thoughtful. 'I don't know why, but this story reminds me of the Ramayana. Just as Rama approached Hanuman and the *vaanara sena*—the army of ape–men—to help rescue Sita from Ravana, who had abducted her, Kalaka too sought the Saka chiefs' assistance in rescuing his sister, Saraswati, from Gardabhilla,' she told the spirit.

'That's an interesting parallel you've drawn between the two epics. So, if we think of these as mythology, it means similar stories can be retold through different characters in different traditions,' Katha said. 'But if we consider these as history—'

'It means similar things can happen to different people!' Mohini finished.

'You said it! All right then, it's time for a break,' Katha said abruptly. Before Mohini could ask what it meant, the illusory Jaina folios began to fade away and a deep darkness took over.

---

[6] A powerful magic through which Gardabhilla could make the she-ass bray so loudly that anyone who heard it would die immediately.

Chapter 15

FLYING THE COOP

Mohini awoke with a start. She had had a nightmare that she'd spend the rest of her life as Katha's slave—cleaning its house, cooking its food, dusting its bookshelf . . .

'NO!' she shouted, traumatized by these visuals that had been playing on loop until then. 'I'd rather be a storyteller!' she groggily mumbled. As she looked about her apprehensively, she realized that she was back in Katha's cave-home. 'Oh, no!' The last thing she remembered was the mysterious darkness that had engulfed her.

Why am I back here? Does this mean my nightmare will come true? Or maybe, just maybe, Katha has had a change of heart?

'But spirits don't have hearts, do they? It would be more a case of "change of mind". This one surely has one of its own, playing mind games with me all the time and expecting me not to mind it at all . . . Aaargh! I'll lose my mind if I stick around with this multicoloured thing!' Mohini muttered away nervously.

'Mind if I interrupt?' Katha had flown in without a sound.

Mohini eyed it suspiciously. She still couldn't shake the feeling that the spirit could read her mind.

'You woke up so soon? It's only lunchtime yet,' the spirit said.

'Why did we return?' she asked sternly.

'Well, I can't keep flying around just because I'm a spirit. And wherever you go, for however long, you eventually return home,' Katha replied matter-of-factly.

'Right, I'll be off to *my* home after lunch then.' Mohini hopped off the makeshift bed.

'Ohhh! Let me rephrase what I said: *You* will eventually return home, *after* breaking free from a spell that has bound you to a place or person . . . or spirit.'

And so the girl had no choice but to spend the entire day doing the very thing she had been dreading—helping the spirit with its daily chores!

At night, she dreamed some more; this time about Kahankar and Ahankar. That story had left a deep impact on her. Just as their bones were being lowered to the waters, a cool draught stirred her awake.

She sauntered to the cave entrance and stepped out to enjoy the breeze and admire the stars. Mohini got nostalgic about how she and Anokhi often spent time watching the night sky together. Then, out of the blue, a strange thought was planted in her head.

G-Ma and Katha are alike in so many ways . . . their sparkling eyes, their mysterious grin, their love for stories—even their belief that one day, I will become a storyteller. Mohini missed her parents. *Katha's company is fun, but for how long will I go on these fancy trips with it?* She was so close to Mithika. If only she could . . . Suddenly, her eyes twinkled. This was it!

Katha had been sleeping soundly, unaware that it had forgotten to create the magical shield at the entrance. Mohini couldn't thank the stars enough! Hers and the ones that shone above. Quickly, she tiptoed in, picked up her bag and crept out.

Freedom had made Mohini utterly cheerful. She had walked far away from Katha, towards Mithika. The happy sun began peeping from behind some hills and she sat down to watch the sunrise, but her mind kept wandering back to the storytelling traditions that Katha had told her about. Could she ever tell stories like that?

Her eyes fell on a step-well that seemed to have appeared from nowhere.

'How strange! I've never seen this here before. Wait, am I not near Mithika?' She looked around and found that she was indeed in unknown terrain, as if someone had simply changed the location while she'd continued on her path. 'Huh! How is this possible?'

'By magic, sheer magic,' a familiar voice answered.

'Not you again! Why can't you leave me alone!'

'Oh, there's time for that, and you know it well. A spell is, after all, a spell!' Katha said. 'Come on, Mohini, admit it. You missed me.'

'Please go away! I know you're trying to make me tell you a story, but that is *not* going to happen. EVER.' Mohini said, frustrated.

'Your grandmother . . .' Katha said.

'What about her?'

'Well, did she also try to get you to tell stories?'

'She did. So?'

'She was your first teacher then,' Katha said. 'Did you know there's a storytelling tradition that is completely about the teacher–student relationship?'

Mohini didn't answer, but it was clear from the look on her face that she wanted to know more. And it wasn't like she could get away instead anyway.

'I'll show you,' said Katha as it led her into the step-well that stood before them.

Chapter 16

LEARN TO TEACH

As instructed, the girl sat down on the steps of the brick structure. She turned, first to look at the multiple arches and then the murky water at the bottom of the well. A musty smell hung in the air. The atmosphere gave her the feeling that hardly anyone visited the step-well these days.

'It's eerie in here. It feels as though this lonely step-well wants to say something,' the girl said uneasily.

'A story perhaps?' Katha's eyes gleamed.

> The spirit has taken her to Meham Baoli[1] in Haryana's Rohtak district.

'Why have we come here?' Mohini asked.

'I'll get to that later,' Katha said. 'But first, let me tell you about Saang, one of the ways in which the people of Haryana tell stories.'

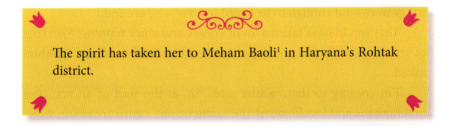

---

[1] In Hindi, *baoli* means 'step-well'.

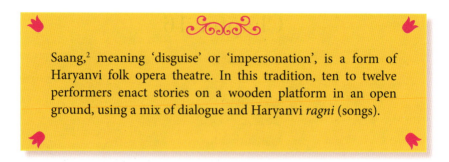

Saang,[2] meaning 'disguise' or 'impersonation', is a form of Haryanvi folk opera theatre. In this tradition, ten to twelve performers enact stories on a wooden platform in an open ground, using a mix of dialogue and Haryanvi *ragni* (songs).

Disguise and Dialogue

'An hour before a Saang performance, artistes sing and play folk melodies to gather the audience. Then they sit in a circle at the centre of the open-air stage, taking turns to stand up and perform their part such that the audience can see them from every side. A single story is narrated over five to six hours,' Katha explained. 'What's also interesting is that traditionally, the artistes didn't use microphones. Yet the dialogues and songs were loud enough to be heard by everyone around.'

'That would have taken a lot of energy and voice training! Speaking of training . . . how is Saang about teachers and students?' Mohini asked.

'I'm coming to that,' Katha said. 'So, at the start of an act, after invoking the goddess Bhavani, the Saang troupe's guru arrives on stage. The artistes thank him and seek his blessings. In Haryana, the guru–*shishya parampara*, or the teacher–student tradition, holds special significance. After all, the battle during which Krishna, the teacher, gave a legendary sermon to his disciple Arjuna was fought on this land—'

'You mean we're near Kurukshetra?' Mohini had heard many stories of the great epic Mahabharata[3] from G-Ma.

---

[2] Also called Swang or Svang.
[3] An ancient Sanskrit epic, it narrates the story of the Pandava and Kaurava princes and the war they fought for power and control over the kingdom of Hastinapur. This war is believed to have been fought in Kurukshetra.

'So you know that that's where the Bhagavad Gita[4] was originally delivered!' Katha was impressed. 'Saang follows this parampara seriously. A novice begins by learning to sing and play musical instruments as well as assisting the chief performer. He then does smaller roles to grow in stature and enact female characters. Finally moving on to play the protagonist, the student—who has by then learnt about every aspect of Saang—forms his own troupe, thus becoming a teacher to a new set of students.'

'That's nice. The guru–shishya parampara will always keep Saang alive!' Mohini said.

'It should. Unfortunately, though, new forms of entertainment are threatening the existence of Saang,' Katha explained.

'Oh, no. Maybe I could learn Saang? And teach it too?' Mohini said thoughtfully. 'But hey, is the student always male? How come he gets to play female roles?'

'There was a time when women were not allowed to participate in such public events. And so men played female roles as well. Although this practice still continues in some places, women too are a part of Saang troupes today,' the spirit replied.

Good Old Tales

'Saang acts are usually in the Bangru language. Performances include mythological tales such as the legends of Raja Harishchandra, Raja Bhoj and Prahlad Bhagat; love stories like the ones of Heer–Ranjha, Nala–Damayanti and Phool Singh–Nautanki; folk tales such as '*Pingla Bharthri*', '*Veer Tyagi ki Katha*' and '*Nanibai ki Mahiro*'. Saang is so ancient that it is said to be the origin of other theatre forms, like khyal, maach, tamasha and nautanki. Which is why tales told across these art forms are often the same,' Katha said.

---

[4] A part of the Mahabharata, it details the conversation that Pandava prince Arjuna had with Krishna—who was his charioteer—on the battlefield, about right and wrong, duty and action, and a number of other complex concepts.

'Hold on, you said "nautanki" twice,' Mohini observed.

'So I did!' Katha smiled. 'Because they are related, yet different. The first Nautanki is a person; the second, a storytelling tradition.'

'How are they related?' she demanded.

'That's a story too!'

A Princess Drama

Bhoop Singh and Phool Singh, although brothers, were as different as chalk and cheese. While Bhoop got married and took on his family's responsibilities, Phool led a carefree life. Once, when Phool returned from a hunt, he ordered his sister-in-law (Bhoop's wife) to bring him water and food. Miffed with his heedless behaviour, she had an argument with him, by the end of which she challenged him to marry Nautanki, the angelic princess of Multan. His ego hurt, Phool left for Multan immediately.

There, with the help of the palace gardener, Phool sent Nautanki a garland he had made. Impressed, when the princess asked to see its maker, Phool appeared in her chambers dressed as a woman. Nautanki offered her friendship to the young girl, but when Phool revealed his true identity, it was love at first sight for the two.

When the king, her father, heard of this intrusion into his daughter's room, he sent Phool to the gallows. Nautanki reached in time, however, and threatened to consume poison. The executioners refused to pay heed, so she turned her sword on them as well as her father! Realizing his daughter's love for Phool, the king set him free. And so Phool got married to the beautiful Nautanki.

'Fascinating! A woman's story wholly enacted by men, where even the hero dresses up as a woman!' Mohini said, remembering that Saang meant 'disguise'.

'Right you are, little one. What's more, Princess Nautanki's Saang became so popular that the audience began referring to the theatre form itself as nautanki. In fact, people colloquially use this word to mean "drama queen". So if I call you a nautanki, you'll know what I mean!' Katha winked.

Mohini made a face before asking, 'But does "nautanki" have any real meaning? Other than being a name?'

'It actually means "one who weighs thirty-six grams". *Nau* means "nine", while *tank* is believed to refer to the ancient silver currency that weighed around four grams each,' Katha revealed.

'What a name to have! But . . . what's the step-well connection?' Mohini persisted.

'Over to another tale for that!'

Jyani Chor to the Rescue

A long time ago lived two friends—Nar Sultan, a prince, and Jyani,[5] a *chor* (thief). Once, when they were on their way to attend a family ceremony in a neighbouring region, they stopped by a river. There, they found a message written on a board floating towards them.

On reading it, Nar Sultan realized that it was a call for help by Princess Mehkade, who was being held captive by Emperor Adli Khan Pathan. When he resolved to rescue her, Jyani reasoned that the prince must attend the family affair instead and leave the rescue mission to him. Nar Sultan agreed.

Jyani, a master of disguise, bravely entered Pathan's territory in the garb of a priest. He then walked into the palace precincts by posing as the son-in-law of a local. Finally, dressed as a woman, he fooled the prison guard and rescued Mehkade, keeping the promise made to his friend Nar Sultan.

---

[5] Pronounced 'Gyani'.

'Um, *step-well*?' Mohini asked animatedly, still not getting how the place and the characters of the tale were related.

'Patience, my dear!' Katha said. 'Legend has it that all the treasures that Jyani looted in his lifetime are still buried somewhere in Meham Baoli. This is why the place is also called Jyani Chor ki Surang!'[6]

'Of all the thieves you've told me about, he seems to be the coolest!' Mohini exclaimed.

'Is that so? Hah! Then you must hear this too . . . Although history does not connect this place to Jyani, *mystery* does! It is said that in those days, every time the officials came to arrest Jyani, he would hide in here. This step-well has been designed like a maze, so the officials always lost their way around and never found him.' Katha floated a few metres above the dark water before slyly adding, 'Nor did they ever come out. Want to look for the hidden gems?'

'Errr . . . the LAST thing I want is to go around a lonely step-well in circles and get stuck, that too with YOU!' Mohini dusted her clothes and bag and got up, ready to leave.

Katha laughed shrilly, its voice echoing off the brick wall. A chill ran down Mohini's spine and she hurried back up the steps.

Safe outside, she looked down once again. Did the baoli truly have valuable riches hidden somewhere? Or what it really protected as treasure was the tradition of Saang, through the tale of Jyani Chor? Some mysteries would never really be unravelled, she guessed.

---

[6] A *surang* is an underground passage or tunnel.

Chapter 17

A STITCH IN TIME

Mohini turned away from the step-well to find mighty mountains all around. Mouth hanging open in awe, she walked towards the edge of the cliff on which she now stood. Dark peaks peeping out of the mist, the fragrance of the surrounding trees, a river snaking down its course way below . . . *Oh, it's all so lovely!*

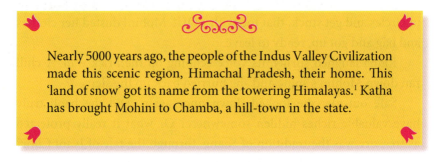

Nearly 5000 years ago, the people of the Indus Valley Civilization made this scenic region, Himachal Pradesh, their home. This 'land of snow' got its name from the towering Himalayas.[1] Katha has brought Mohini to Chamba, a hill-town in the state.

'The Himalayas!' Mohini sighed, staring at the distant mountains unblinkingly.

She bit into the water apple offered to her, fresh and pink. The girl was hungry, the spirit could tell, so it had promptly plucked a few fruits for her.

'I aven't . . . eard'a Chamma . . . befow,' Mohini said between mouthfuls. Slurping up the juice that had trickled all the way down her wrist, she sunk her teeth into another fruit.

---

[1] In Hindi, *him* means 'ice' or 'snow'.

'Well, the story of *Chamba* goes back to the tenth century, when Rajput king Raja Sahilla Varman conquered the territory of Rahnu and made it his new capital. He renamed it Chamba after his beloved daughter, Champa,' Katha said.

Nodding, Mohini pulled out her hanky to wipe her hands dry.

'Hey, pretty handkerchief!' Katha observed.

'Thanks! Ma gifted it to me because I like floral prints,' Mohini said, beaming.

'That reminds me—what can you do with a kerchief?'

'Why, many things! You can wipe your hands with it, sometimes even a leaking nose . . .' Mohini counted on her fingers. 'G-Ma used to tie a knot in it to remember important stuff. And my friend covers his head with it to show respect when entering a place of worship.'

'Is that all?'

Mohini thought hard. 'Oh! I use it to recreate the pretty boat and bird I learnt to make with paper in craft class.'

'Nice. But can you tell stories on a kerchief?' Katha asked, raising its eyebrows.

'*Stories on a kerchief?* I don't think so.'

'Well, if you ask the people of Chamba, their answer will be a loud yes!'

Chamba Rumal preserved stories from the Pahari miniature paintings of the Kangra, Chamba and Guler regions through their embroidered versions on rumals (kerchiefs).

The oldest rumal, but not necessarily the first, dating back to the sixteenth century, was embroidered by Guru Nanak's elder sister, Bebe Nanaki.

Craft on Cloth

'Traditionally, these embroidered kerchiefs were used to cover gifts offered to a deity or a priest, or those exchanged between families of the bride and the groom at a wedding. The rumal itself was an important gift given during marriage,' Katha said.

'So, in a way, people gifted stories to each other,' the girl remarked.

'That's a nice way of putting it.' Katha smiled. 'These needlework miniatures were made only by Chamba's women. What the locals created is known as the folk style, and the embroidery done by royalty is the court style.'

Painting with the Needle

'Pahari miniature artists were specially employed by royalty. After drawing the outlines, the artists suggested colours for the different parts of the drawing. The women then used *pat*—untwisted silk thread—in those colours to embroider the rumal. They only used the complex double satin stitch, because it gave the rumal the distinctive quality of being *do-rukha*, meaning "double-faced",' Katha said.

'Wait, wait, I didn't understand this double-faced bit,' Mohini confessed.

'Glad you asked! So, the stitch was done on the front as well as the back of the cloth simultaneously. This makes the embroidered image on both sides of the rumal look identical, just like mirror images,' Katha explained.

'Okayyy . . . If the image on both sides of a Chamba Rumal look exactly the same, how do we differentiate the front from the back?'

'It's difficult to tell, since no knots were made by the women when beginning or ending the stitches,' the spirit revealed.

'Wow, so they can be viewed and used either way!'

One with Nature

'Chamba Rumals tell stories from the Bhagavata Purana, the Ramayana and the Mahabharata. Many of Chamba's people believe in the god Vishnu, so episodes from the life of Krishna, who is an avatar of Vishnu, are often depicted. For example, Krishna's marriage, Raas Leela and more. The rumal *Godhuli* shows Krishna and other cowherds bringing their cows back home at dusk,' Katha told Mohini.

'Oh, so it's only stories from mythology,' she said.

'That's not true. Royal women replicated the murals that adorned palace walls. Hunting scenes, the game of *chaupar* and the pastimes of royalty also make up the sewn narratives. A majority of the rumals include flowers, trees, animals and birds to depict the close ties that gods and human beings share with nature,' the spirit said.

'Flowers, yay! They must make the rumals look *so* pretty!' Mohini smiled, picking up a stray rhododendron flower.

'My dear girl, flowers are much more than just pretty things!'

Minjar Mela Jalus

A *jalus* or 'procession' is taken out by locals during Minjar Mela, a festival of Chamba, to offer *minjar* (tassels that symbolize maize shoots) to River Ravi for prosperity. One of the many origin tales of this festival goes back to the tenth century.

An elderly woman who'd gone to meet the then king presented him with minjar (maize flowers)[2] as she didn't have any valuable gift for him. Touched by her gesture, the king declared that the humble maize would be commemorated through Minjar Mela from then on.

'If that doesn't convince you, let me tell you about the time when flowers became the cause of—wait for it—a battle in heaven!' the spirit said.

---

[2] Since tassels symbolizing minjar or maize shoots are offered during the festival, they are called by the same name.

Parijata Haran

When the lovely Parijata, a wish-granting tree, emerged during the churning of the ocean, Indra, king of the heavens, took it away and planted it in his garden, Nandan Kanan. Krishna's wife Satyabhama, on her visit to Nandan Kanan, took a fancy to the Parijata flowers. She argued that the tree belonged to everyone and could not be enjoyed by Indra alone.

Krishna agreed with her and uprooted the tree to take it to earth, plant it in his garden and share it with the people of Dwaraka. Indra was furious when this theft came to light. A battle ensued between him and Krishna, in which the latter won.

The rumal that narrates the story of '*Parijata Haran*'[3] scene by scene shows Indra riding Airavat, the white elephant, and Krishna and Satyabhama seated on Garuda, the mythical eagle.

Mohini had never thought flowers could play such an important role in stories. As she traced the outline of the floral prints on her hanky with her finger, a confusing thought occupied her mind.

'You know, Katha, I've been thinking about good and evil . . . based on the tales you've been telling me, actually . . . Characters who I think are heroes go ahead and do—do things that are not *really* right. And then there are characters we could view as, I don't know, anti-heroes . . . but some of *their* actions seem positive . . .'

'Ah, a thought as deep as the ravines around us! I have just the tradition to dive right into,' the spirit said with a knowing look in its eyes.

---

[3] '*Parijata Haran*' literally means 'Abduction of Parijata'.

Chapter 18

WARD OFF EVIL

Just as the girl began suspecting that the spirit might ask her to jump off the cliff, it handed her a wooden mask. 'Wear this!'

Mohini fumed, 'This is a clown's mask, and I am NOT a clown!'

'Oh, don't be a spoilsport. Just wear it!'

'FINE!' Mohini put it on, but seeing the spirit burst into a fit of giggles, she took it off immediately.

She noticed that the weather had turned cold. Biting cold. The mountains were still there, but they looked different now. In fact, every mountain seemed to be of a different ashen shade. Big clouds cast equally big shadows on some of them, even as a few peaks wore snowcaps. Across the barren grey-brown expanses that lay in front of her, strings of colourful little flags fluttered in the wind.

'Prayer flags,' Katha announced.

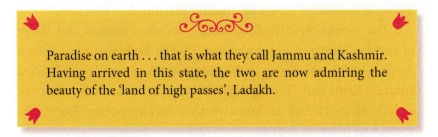

Paradise on earth . . . that is what they call Jammu and Kashmir. Having arrived in this state, the two are now admiring the beauty of the 'land of high passes', Ladakh.

'Where were we? Ah, yes. Good and evil,' Katha began. 'The staples of many a great tale since time immemorial. They make the characters in a story so much more interesting.'

Mohini nodded in agreement.

'When you saw me for the first time, what did you think I was—good or evil?' Katha asked.

'*Definitely evil!*'

'And what do you think of me now?'

'Not . . . evil,' she replied, not wanting to flatter the smart-alecky spirit.

'Exactly! Not being evil does not make me good, just as not being all good does not make you evil,' Katha said. 'It's these two supposedly opposite words that the entrancing Cham dance explores.'

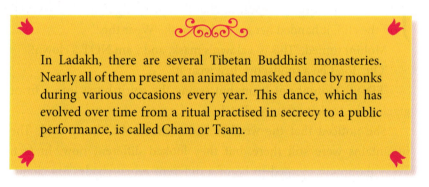

In Ladakh, there are several Tibetan Buddhist monasteries. Nearly all of them present an animated masked dance by monks during various occasions every year. This dance, which has evolved over time from a ritual practised in secrecy to a public performance, is called Cham or Tsam.

Of Dance and Demons

'Dancing monks . . . How fun!' Mohini exclaimed.

'The monks wear multicoloured brocade costumes and dance in circular formations to traditional Tibetan Buddhist music. Cham dance, which is an offering to the gods, is primarily made up of sacred mudras,' Katha said. 'The highlight of the performance is the mask that each monk wears. And you know what's doubly interesting? The monks themselves make these masks!'

'They must be so talented! But is the dance performed for a particular reason?' she asked.

'Yes, for the happiness and benefit of everyone. And yet some people refer to it as the "devil dance" or the "dance of the demons".'

The girl knitted her brows in confusion. 'What do *monks* have to do with *demons*?'

'A story from the life of Padmasambhava might hold the answer . . .'

The scene around Mohini changed in an unbelievable blur of hues. When it finally came into focus, she found herself, along with the spirit, in the vast courtyard of a beautiful *gompa*.[1]

The Vajrakilaya Dance

Padmasambhava, the founder guru of Vajrayana Buddhism,[2] was looked upon as the protector of mortal beings against demons. When Samye Monastery, the first monastery in Tibet, was being built in the eighth century, demons began creating obstacles and did not let the construction proceed. It was then that Tibetan king Trisong Detsen invited Padmasambhava to ward off the evil spirits.

The guru arrived at the site and performed the powerful Vajrakilaya dance, which comprises making various mudras and praying to deities. An important element of his dance was the *kilaya*[3] that he held in his hands. Through this ritual, he chased the spirits into a skull fixed atop a pyramid made of dough, thus ridding the place of demonic trouble.

This dance is considered to be the origin of Cham.

---

[1] A Tibetan Buddhist monastery.
[2] In Sanskrit, *vajra* means 'thunderbolt' and *yana* signifies 'journey'. In essence, Vajrayana Buddhism encourages people to focus on their real self, which, like the thunderbolt, cannot be destroyed.
[3] The kilaya or the *phurba* is the ritualistic dagger used by the guru in his dance. It is said to possess supernatural powers and can thwart evil.

Behind the Masks

'Oh! So Cham is performed by the monks to get rid of evil,' Mohini said.

'Actually, it's much more than that. The use of masks adds layers of meaning to the dance. What we see is not what may be, and what it may be, we may never see!' Katha rhymed.

'I don't understand a thing when you talk like this,' Mohini complained.

'Okay, okay, let me rewind and simplify. So, days before the performance, while meditating, the monks visualize the protective deity they wish to invoke during their Cham routine. They choose one of the eight guardian deities of Tibetan Buddhism called *dharmapalas*.[4] This is when they also begin making the mask to portray that particular deity, which they wear for the main performance. Have you got it so far?'

Mohini gave it a thumbs up.

Katha continued. 'The monks wear long-sleeved robes to hide weapons, such as the phurba, the vajra, the spear and some chains. With these, they threaten and destroy evil, which is symbolized by an effigy made of dough. And—'

---

[4] Dharmapalas are 'protectors of the law'. Dharma means 'law' and *pala*, 'protector'.

'Wait, wait! If these masks are depicting protectors, why is Cham called the "devil dance"?' Mohini asked.

'Hmm, you're asking some tricky ones!' Katha scratched its bald head. Then it clicked its horns together, flailed its limbs and mumbled some incomprehensible chants . . . and, lo and behold, Mohini was playing audience to a Cham performance!

As the monks appeared one behind another, wearing magnificent masks and briskly moving to the mesmerizing sounds of the drums, trumpets and cymbals, Katha explained, 'See, evil is not just the devil or demons. It could mean anything that harms us. Even our own vices . . . anger, ego, hatred, all of that. So when the monks wear the protector masks and dance, the vices or demons inside them are cleansed. Only compassion prevails. Does that make sense?'

'Compassion? Then . . . w-why do the masks look so . . . so fierce?' Mohini asked, watching the dancers with rapt attention.

'Because when evil sees something as ferocious as itself, it feels afraid. And think about it, why should the face of good always be soft and kind?' the spirit asked.

Mohini wasn't sure she understood these difficult ideas fully, but she figured what Katha meant was that good and evil coexist. And that it is up to the good in a person to push the evil out.

'The masks, they don't have holes near the eyes!' Hers had been caught by a mask that drifted towards her in mid-air, and she wondered how the monks danced perfectly without even seeing where they were going.

'Well, it's said that they see through their mind's eye,[5] the eyes of the wrathful protectors they embody.'

As Mohini mulled over this revelation, Katha added to her curiosity: 'You don't think such a complex tradition would tell only one tale, do you?'

The Monk in the Black Hat

In ancient Tibet ruled King Ralpacan, a follower of Buddhism. But his evil brother, Langdarma, murdered him and took over the throne. He then began destroying Buddhism.

---

[5] The masks are designed and worn in such a way that the monks can, to an extent, see through the opening made for the mouth.

Pelgyi Dorje, a disciple of Padmasambhava, decided to put an end to Langdarma's atrocities against Buddhism and the monks. First, he smeared soot all over his white horse. Then he wore a black hat and a reversible black coat with long sleeves—in which he hid a bow and arrow.

On reaching Langdarma's palace, he began performing the Cham. Intrigued, the king came out to watch the dance. Finding an opportune moment, Pelgyi let loose the arrow, killing Langdarma instantly, and fled on his horse.

Stopping by a river, he wore his coat the other way around, now sporting its white side. He washed the soot off his horse as well, returning it to its original coat. So when the king's soldiers searched for a man dressed in black and his black horse, they found neither.

'Ah. That explains the long sleeves,' Mohini remarked.

'Yup. It is said that the Black Hat Dance, which is a part of Cham, commemorates Pelgyi Dorje's victory over Langdarma,' Katha told her.

'So many stories are hidden in one tale, just as a mask would hide so many . . . umm . . .' Mohini struggled to find the right word.

'Personas!' Katha completed.

The girl scanned the gompa with some more interest. Its whitewashed walls, red pillars and arches, and yellow-framed windows sharply contrasted with the muted hills visible beyond, even at dusk. Her attention was drawn back to the courtyard as she saw the dancing figures of the monks fade away. 'It's amazing how Cham dance is choreographed to use up all this space.'

'And yet there are dances that are performed in a space as small as a stuffy box,' the spirit gave away.

'No way!'

'Yes way! This way!' Katha pointed to a little wooden box lying on the ground.

Chapter 19

BACK AND FORTH

'Are you insane? How will I fit—' Mohini was protesting, but Katha simply pushed her into the box, which was no bigger than a pencil holder.

Next thing she knew, she felt as though she was falling down a deep, bottomless pit. After an indefinite amount of time, she landed with a thud near a shady tree. The spirit had already reached before her and lay stretched out on a sturdy branch that arched just a few inches above the ground, away from the glare of the harsh sun. Inexplicably, it was afternoon again.

> The two are now in Jharkhand. The name of the state literally means 'bushland'. And it is home to one of the largest adivasi communities of the country, the Santhals.[1]

'Let me guess . . . You're going to tell me about a Santhali tradition that is connected to . . . the forest!' Mohini said confidently, looking at the woods around.

Katha nodded. 'Santhals live in harmony with the forest. And they are particular about passing on their culture to the next generation . . . their language, music, dance, art, woodcarving, all of it!'

---

[1] The Santhal population is spread across the eastern regions of India, not just Jharkhand.

'Woodcarving?' she asked, settling down on the curving branch.

'Yes, they make a number of household items, musical instruments and even puppets with wood,' Katha said. 'Tell me, is there a form of puppetry that is neither glove nor string puppetry? Neither shadow nor rod puppetry?'

Mohini thought for a few seconds about this seemingly random question. *Tholu Bommalata is shadow puppetry. Rajasthan's Kathputli uses strings.* Her father had brought back a pair of these puppets from a trip to the state. Rod and glove puppetry too she had heard of. 'No,' she finally replied.

'Oh, but there is—Chadar Badar!'

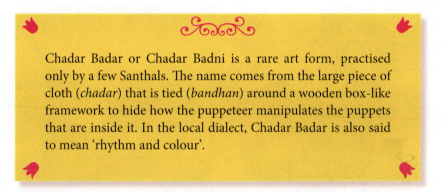

Chadar Badar or Chadar Badni is a rare art form, practised only by a few Santhals. The name comes from the large piece of cloth (*chadar*) that is tied (*bandhan*) around a wooden box-like framework to hide how the puppeteer manipulates the puppets that are inside it. In the local dialect, Chadar Badar is also said to mean 'rhythm and colour'.

Rural Engineering

'Do the puppeteers carve the wooden puppets themselves?' Mohini remembered that the Tholu Bommalata puppeteers made their own puppets.

'Yes, the puppeteer is first and foremost a carpenter and woodcarver. He constructs a six-foot-high wooden structure, the central element of which is a hollow bamboo pole. At the top of this pole is a cage-like frame within which is a circular rotating stage,' Katha elaborated.

'A rotating stage!' Mohini was thrilled.

'And on this interesting stage are two groups of puppets, each about seven to nine inches tall. On one side are the male drummer puppets, playing the traditional drums *tamak* and *tumdak*, and on the other are the dancing girl puppets. Their show resembles the actual back-and-forth dance of Santhali women,' the spirit said.

'You mean, these wooden puppets move?'

'Only the arms of the male musicians are movable, while the arms as well as the heads of the dancing puppets can be moved,' Katha answered.

'But how do the puppeteers make them move inside such a small space?' the girl asked.

'Slightly technical stuff, but I'll try to explain,' the spirit said. 'So, each hand of the puppet and every puppet itself is attached to strings that are connected to sticks. These are, in turn, controlled by the main string that passes through the hollow bamboo pole. When the main string is pulled,[2] it causes the circular stage to move like a see-saw. This makes the male puppets beat the drums and the female puppets dance. At the same time, the stage rotates too. Simple!'

'If you say so! Most puppeteers I know of carry the puppets to the stage. Here, the Santhals carry the stage along with the puppets! That's so cool!' Mohini chirped.

'If only more youngsters would think of this as a "cool" art form. Hardly any practitioners of Chadar Badar, which is considered one of the earliest forms of puppetry, are left. Not many from the younger generation are learning the tradition now.' Katha sighed sadly.

'If more people get to watch it, I'm sure some would be interested in learning the art form. But is it tough to learn? And what are the stories told?' the girl asked.

---

[2] Sometimes, the main string sticks out from the pole at the bottom. The puppeteer then controls the whole show by tugging at the string with his foot.

Double Performance

'See, the puppeteer travels from place to place, carrying the wooden framework over his shoulder.[3] His troupe includes musicians who play various Santhali instruments as well as dance. In a way, they do both the things that the male and female puppets do! At the end of each performance, they receive money and foodgrains from viewers, which they divide equally,' Katha said.

'Hold on . . . Do *all* Chadar Badar puppeteers make the same musician and dancer puppets?' Mohini wondered aloud.

'Very much so. The stage *always* depicts a traditional Santhali folk dance scene,' Katha replied.

'But why dedicate a whole different puppetry form just to imitate this dance?'

'Ah, there's a saying . . . All Santhali women dance and every Santhali man plays the drums. This is how they forget their worries. Puppeteers recreate the dance scene within the square-foot-wide wooden framework of Chadar Badar to spread joy. And you have to see it to believe it—the audience usually begins dancing along with the puppets!' Katha explained gleefully as Mohini watched some kids and grown-ups walk up the forest path and huddle around a Chadar Badar puppeteer who had arrived nearby.

'If the puppets are the same, then they must be all telling the same story too, right?' Mohini guessed.

'Surprise! The answer is no. The narratives vary, but what remains constant is the dance of the puppets. Chadar Badar puppeteers tell stories about kings who had usurped their land, the Santhals' fight against the British rule and imaginary characters who repent after committing mistakes—all sorts of things, really.'

---

[3] Some puppeteers perform alone, while others are accompanied by musicians, thus forming a troupe.

'Oh?' The girl hadn't expected a set of identical wooden puppets to offer so much scope for storytelling.

Katha went on. 'For a long time, Chadar Badar has been telling tales of Santhal life . . . their customs and social taboos, of their love and togetherness, and their music and dance. The puppetry form is also used to spread social messages related to urbanization, deforestation—'

'Deforestation? But if Santhals don't cut down trees, how will woodcarving or even Chadar Badar exist? They are wooden puppets, after all.'

Katha smiled. 'That's right, but Santhals take only what they need from the forests. They know forests must live and grow if they and their art are to survive.'

'Hmm . . . You said they have stories about music and dance?' Mohini was itching for one of Katha's tales by now.

'Well, there is a Santhali folk tale, but I can't remember if it's a story sung by Chadar Badar puppeteers,' Katha said honestly. 'Still want to hear it?'

'Yes, please!' came the prompt reply.

A Mysterious Dance

Like most tribal communities, Santhals too were oppressed by cunning moneylenders.

Once, a moneylender kept pestering a Santhal man to repay his loan. Tired and afraid of facing him, the man hid in the forest. When the lender came looking for him, the Santhal man's wife casually said that her husband was busy doing the 'backward and forward dance' in the forest. Intrigued, the moneylender agreed to waive the loan if the man taught him this dance.

Seeing a chance to be rid of the moneylender once and for all, the Santhal man made the lender promise so in the presence of witnesses and then took him to the forest. As it was cold, the man lit a fire and the two sat near the flames for a while. When the flames leapt higher, they moved away from the fire. When the embers died down, they moved closer. This went on for a long time.

The lender lost his patience and asked when the backward and forward dance lessons would begin. The Santhal man stared blankly and explained that they had been doing the dance for quite some time now. Going back and forth, away from the fire and towards it, again and again—this was indeed the dance! This is what he had been doing while in hiding in the forest.

Furious at having been tricked, the lender complained to the witnesses, but they said that the dance, whatever and however it was, had in fact been taught by the man. And so the promise had to be kept. The moneylender walked away disappointed, and the Santhal man, joyous.

Mohini laughed aloud. 'That's funny! A dance that doesn't exist solved his money problems!'

'Had *yaksha*s been a part of this tale, they would have celebrated this victory in song and dance too, just like the Santhals,' Katha added, standing up on its tail and stretching its phantom limbs.

'Yakshas? Are you talking about the nature spirits from Hindu mythology and Jain and Buddhist tales?' Mohini asked.

'You seem to know quite a bit about them.' Katha was impressed.

'G-Ma told me about them,' she said.

'Did she tell you about their storytelling tradition too?'

Gauging from Mohini's lack of a reaction, the spirit understood her answer and clicked its magical horns together.

Clink, clink!

Chapter 20

A RUNNING BATTLE

The very next moment, Mohini found herself standing amidst small, vibrantly coloured wooden dolls. But these dolls looked different from the Chadar Badar puppets. 'Where ar—OH!' Just as she was getting used to her new surroundings, there was a green flash.

'WHAT. JUST. HAPPENED? The dolls have grown!'

'These aren't dolls! They are people wearing doll suits, actually,' Katha said, floating beside her. 'The smaller dolls you saw at first are the famous Channapatna toys, whi—'

'Channapatna? Dad told me about them when he came back from a visit there last year,' Mohini said, still trying to make sense of what she was looking at. 'That means we are in—'

> Karnataka—the state known for Mysuru Palace, the ruins of Hampi, the forest of Agumbe and the fictional world of Malgudi.[1]

As they walked past a row of gigantic doll suits that were nearly twelve feet tall, Katha continued. 'Oh, and *these* large doll-suits belong

---

[1] Malgudi is a fictional town, created by the well-known author R.K. Narayan and appearing in many of his works, such as *Swami and Friends* and *Malgudi Days*. The latter was made into a television series, in which Agumbe's surroundings acted as the setting for Malgudi.

to a dance tradition called Gaarudi Gombe. Both Channapatna[2] and Gaarudi Gombe[3] are storytelling forms.'

'Which of these is related to yakshas?' she asked.

'Neither! Let's just keep walking, shall we?'

'Uff! Why would you conjure them up if you're not even going to tell me about them?' Mohini huffed and puffed as she struggled to keep pace with the gliding spirit.

'Just. Annoy you, I must! Want to eat something first?' Katha grinned, seeing that Mohini was indeed peeved. And so they sat down by the roadside and enjoyed some delicious neer dosa.[4]

It was dark by the time Katha and Mohini arrived at their destination. A crowd had gathered around a rectangular stage decorated with festoons. Two oil lamps flickered onstage importantly.

'So beautiful! I love lamps,' Mohini said as she sat down among the audience.

'Then Diwali must be your favourite festival?' Katha guessed.

'Yes, it is! But what's happening here?' The girl looked around, unable to contain her excitement.

'Why, Yakshagana, of course.'

'Yakshagana? Finally the yakshas make an appearance!'

Katha nodded. 'Yakshas served Kubera, the god of wealth. Legend has it that Kubera was driven out of his own kingdom in Lanka by his half-brother Ravana. But some people believe that yakshas belonged to an ancient tribe that migrated from Lanka to Karnataka and Andhra Pradesh.'

'Does that mean yakshas are not mythical beings?'

'In the world of stories, there's a thin line between myth and reality, you know,' Katha said with a wink.

'HOW is it that you say the things G-Ma used to say?' Mohini looked at Katha suspiciously.

---

[2] Famous lacquerware toys made by the craftsmen of Channapatna, a town in Karnataka.

[3] Gaarudi Gombe, meaning 'magical dolls' in Kannada, is performed by dancers while wearing massive doll frames that are usually made of bamboo.

[4] A Karnataka speciality, it is a light, lacy dosa made of rice batter.

Katha smiled. 'Those who believe in stories speak the same language.'

'Hmm . . . So, what is this Yakshagana?'

'Its origins lie in an interesting belief. It seems—and this is another tale altogether—when the wealth of Kubera was returned by the asura king Bali Chakravarthi, the yakshas spent the whole night in celebratory song and dance. They had their own style of music and rhythm, known as Yakshagana, the "song of the yakshas".'

'Did yakshas teach their songs to human beings then?' Mohini asked, wondering how people came to perform it.

'Maybe they did. Maybe they didn't. But the dance, the way it's performed today, has its roots in the Bhakti movement,'[5] said the spirit.

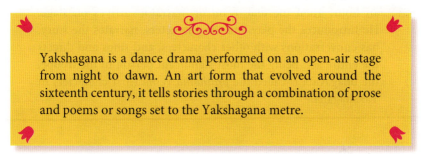

Yakshagana is a dance drama performed on an open-air stage from night to dawn. An art form that evolved around the sixteenth century, it tells stories through a combination of prose and poems or songs set to the Yakshagana metre.

Drama in the Fields

'The tales are narrated, sung and enacted by a group of fifteen to twenty actors. Dance is an integral part of the performance. The use of facial expressions and hand gestures is limited, though,' Katha said. 'Earlier, Yakshagana actors were only men; farmers performed in open fields after the harvest season. Thankfully, women too practise this art form now. You know, by the twentieth century, Yakshagana was taught in schools in villages to help children know and remember mythological stories.'

---

[5] A spiritual movement that helped common people understand that devotion could be expressed without practising complex rituals or following superstitious beliefs.

'Uh-oh, imagine if my school taught storytelling as a subject . . . I would have flunked it with flying colours!' Mohini laughed at her own joke.

'Nope. You just wouldn't be stuck with me then. You would've been able to tell me a tale and break the spell on your very first attempt!' Katha retorted.

'Whatever,' the girl mumbled.

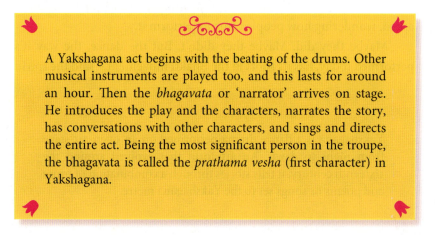

A Yakshagana act begins with the beating of the drums. Other musical instruments are played too, and this lasts for around an hour. Then the *bhagavata* or 'narrator' arrives on stage. He introduces the play and the characters, narrates the story, has conversations with other characters, and sings and directs the entire act. Being the most significant person in the troupe, the bhagavata is called the *prathama vesha* (first character) in Yakshagana.

'As the story unfolds, various characters walk in and out of the stage. Known as *veshadhari*s, their *vesha* or "costume" is in keeping with the character they portray,' the spirit said.

'The costumes and make-up look quite similar to me. How do you know who is playing which character?' Mohini asked, studying the actors who stood backstage.

'Look carefully. Heroic characters wear pinkish-yellow make-up, while red-and-black make-up denotes antagonists or demonic characters. The *mundasu*, or headgear, is also designed differently for heroes, kings, queens and demons,' Katha pointed out.

'Oh, yeah! The mundasu looks splendid!' the girl said.

'The elaborate headgear and their wooden ornaments are wrapped in silver and golden foil and decorated with mirror-work, so that they dazzle under the lights,' the spirit said.

'That's clever.'

Colourful Battles

'The Yakshagana narrative is full of zing and drama. Heroic episodes and battle sequences from the Puranas and the epics often make up the climax of an act. These scenes include quick, energetic dance movements, and much jumping and spinning in mid-air—there, look!' Katha yelled out.

'Now, *that* must be difficult, especially with their bulky attire,' Mohini said without taking her eyes off the character who was practising one such jump.

'You're right. Despite their heavy costumes, the characters maintain perfect rhythmic timing during their spins and land on their feet without losing their ba-a-a-a-LANCE!' Katha had tried to imitate a Yakshagana spin, but failing miserably, it made the girl laugh.

Turning to look at the stage again, Mohini saw that the musicians had begun playing the drums.

'The performance is starting. This one's from the Ramayana,' Katha said. 'The story of Mahiravana.'

Mahiravana

Ravana's brother Kumbhakarna had died at the hands of the Ayodhya princes Rama and Lakshmana and the vaanara sena. Determined to win the war against the princes, the Lanka king called another one of his brothers, Mahiravana,[6] a master sorcerer and the king of the netherworld, to his aid.

---

[6] Some accounts suggest that Mahiravana was Ravana's son.

> Mahiravana abducted Rama and Lakshmana, and took them to his world. There, he planned to sacrifice the two brothers to the goddess Kali. But the loyal Hanuman found his way into Mahiravana's kingdom through an underground passage. At the altar of sacrifice, before the sorcerer could offer the princes to the goddess, Hanuman killed Mahiravana and rescued Rama and Lakshmana.
>
> Once again, the mighty Ravana was left distraught, and lonelier than before.

Spirit and girl had both sat up all night and watched the performance. Dawn had to be breaking any moment now.

'What an act!' cried Mohini, rubbing her eyes vigorously, as a performer retreated backstage, taking the oil lamps with him.

'Wasn't it? Oh, I almost forgot, Yakshagana shares a deep connection with lamps,' Katha told her before stifling a yawn. 'It is performed from November to May each year, and the season's first act is traditionally staged on Diwali, which is also called Yaksha Ratri.'

'You mean, Diwali celebrations are related to yakshas?'

'Oh, yes. Yakshas, known as "the luminous ones", used gem-studded lamps called *ratna pradeep* during night-time. And so in their honour, Diwali or Yaksha Ratri is celebrated by lighting numerous lamps and lanterns.'

'I had no idea,' Mohini said, even as her mind raced to another thought. 'Mythology is so fascinating!'

'You can always be sure to have an unusual story peep out of its mysterious casket,' Katha added.

'Exactly. There are so many goddesses, gods, animals . . .'

'Well, they say there are thirty-three crore gods in Hindu mythology,' the spirit informed Mohini.

Her eyes grew wide in amazement.

'Whoa! When you get curious, your eyes grow as big and bright as the sun,' Katha said, pointing to the yellow sky. It was a new day.

Chapter 21

GOD'S OWN COUNTRY

Mohini had been staring at the rising sun in such a trance that she didn't realize the scene around her had changed—again. Big pink lotuses bloomed in the lake that had appeared near her. And there were coconut trees all around it, dancing to the tune of a light breeze. Not far from her, a bright-blue kingfisher shot into the water like an arrow and was back on its perch in what seemed like a nanosecond, happy with its find—a tiny gleaming fish.

> Katha and Mohini have reached Kerala,[1] the 'land of coconut trees'.

'What does Kerala have to do with Hindu mythology's thirty-three crore gods?' Mohini asked as she collected some cool water from the lake in her cupped palm and drank from it.

'Kerala is known as God's own country! I thought you'd know that.' Katha shook its head, pretending to be deeply disappointed.

Suddenly, something stirred in the water, before a thick scaly tail thrashed into view, drenching Katha.

---

[1] Kerala was named so because of the sheer number of *kera* or 'coconut trees' found there. Another theory suggests that this region was called Cherala after the Chera king who ruled here.

'It's a crocodile! I LOVE CROCODILES!' shrieked Mohini, who'd stepped back just in time.

'Shh! Now, that is the LAST thing I'd expected to hear. Well, watch *quietly*, you brave girl,' Katha muttered as it gave itself a good jiggle for quick drying.

The reptile had turned and was making its way towards the opposite bank, from behind whose dense foliage, a majestic elephant lumbered out.

'Oh, no-no-no . . . We must save the elephant!' Mohini whispered in alarm.

'If Kerala mural artists were around, they would have found much inspiration in this scene,' Katha remarked.

Mohini was disgusted. 'You're so heartless! That poor elephant is in danger and you—'

'You judge too quickly.' Katha scratched its bald head. 'Had *you* been a Kerala mural artist, you would have known that a god is around the corner. For now, let us pause this scene here.' The two creatures seemed to freeze.

Mohini was relieved that what she was watching wasn't real but with Katha around, she could never tell.

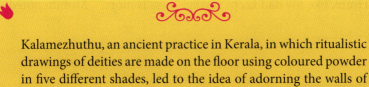

Kalamezhuthu, an ancient practice in Kerala, in which ritualistic drawings of deities are made on the floor using coloured powder in five different shades, led to the idea of adorning the walls of temples, churches and palaces with paintings too. This new art form became known as Kerala mural[2] painting. It flourished as a kind of temple art between the fourteenth and sixteenth centuries.

---

[2] The word 'mural' comes from the Latin word for 'wall', *murus*.

Eco-friendly Art

'Kerala murals are also called Panchavarna[3] paintings because they use only five colours—yellow, red, green, white and black.'

'Eh? They paint gods and skies and water without any blue?' Mohini asked.

'Yep. But new-age artists have started including blue too.'

'Even then . . . are just five colours enough to paint images of deities? I mean, more colours would make them look splendid, even supernatural!' she insisted.

'Aha, you mean gods must look like me?' the psychedelic spirit winked.

Mohini rolled her eyes.

'So I've observed something interesting about the traditions of this state . . . Most art forms in Kerala use a combination of the five colours that I just mentioned. Theyyam[4] uses a lot of red and black. In Kathakali,[5] the attire is chiefly white and red, while the make-up uses green, yellow and black. And if gods can look regal in just five colours, why use more?' Katha explained.

'Hmm, like my dad keeps saying, "Less is more!"' Mohini noted.

---

[3] In Sanskrit, *pancha* means 'five' and *varna*, 'colour'.
[4] An energetic ritualistic dance of Kerala that incorporates mime. The dancer, whose face and torso are entirely painted, wears an elaborate costume. Red is the predominant colour in both the make-up and the attire, apart from black, which is used especially for the eye make-up.
[5] Kathakali, or 'story play' (in Malayalam, *katha* means 'story' and *kali*, 'play') is an ancient dance drama of Kerala. With faces painted in a distinctive style and colourful, ornate attire, the performers enact stories from Hindu mythology. The dancers undergo special training to master the movement of their eyes and facial muscles as mime and pronounced eye expressions are unique aspects of Kathakali.

> The artist applies a mixture of crushed limestone, sand, jaggery, water and neem juice on the temple walls for a smooth finish and to keep insects away. After it dries, the initial sketch is done in yellow and a darker outline in red. The image is then filled in with colours. The wall is left unpainted wherever white[6] must appear. Finally, a black outline is drawn to complete the mural.

The Painting on the Wall

'How do artists know how to draw the gods? As in, how do they know if Ganesha was cute and plump? Or if Saraswati had waist-length hair?' Mohini queried.

'Artists follow traditional texts when they create these paintings. There are also the Dhyana Shlokas,[7] which describe the physical characteristics of the deities, their facial expressions, the number of arms and eyes, the weapons wielded and all that,' Katha said. 'So the artists can easily paint the images of Saraswati, Nataraja, the reclining Vishnu, Vettakkorumakan—'

'Wait, who's that?' Mohini hadn't missed the last, unfamiliar, name.

---

[6] These days, since the paintings are created for commercial purposes on surfaces other than walls, white paint is used.

[7] Dhyana Shlokas are a series of couplets, each of which is about a particular deity. The couplets help devotees and artists visualize the gods clearly.

The Power of a Weapon

During the battle of Kurukshetra, as told in the epic Mahabharata, Arjuna required the *pashupatastra*, the most powerful weapon that can be wielded by a mortal. Shiva assumed the avatar of a hunter, Kirata, and delivered the weapon to him. He and his consort Parvati (who took the form of a huntress) then wandered through forests for a while. During this time, they had a son, whom they named Vettakkorumakan, meaning 'son born during a hunt'.[8] As the boy grew up, he became more and more mischievous, freely shooting arrows and troubling everyone around.

When complaints reached Vishnu, he too disguised himself as a hunter and met Vettakkorumakan. At this meeting, the boy took a fancy to Vishnu's *churika*, a gold sword-cum-dagger. Vishnu agreed to give it to him, if he promised to use weapons only to protect and not cause harm. Vettakkorumakan agreed, and went on to become the protector of forests.

Kerala murals depict him with both weapons—the bow and arrow as well as the churika.

'Shiva and Parvati seem to be really fond of forests,' Mohini noted, remembering the story of Aranyani. 'But, hey, what about the crocodile and elephant?'

'Oh, that story's not hard to get hold of. You'll find it depicted in the largest Kerala mural in the state, at Krishnapuram Palace,' Katha replied, pointing to the animals in front of them, who were advancing towards each other once again.

Mohini held her breath.

---

8   Another interpretation suggests that the name means 'a son for hunting'.

Gajendra Moksham

King Indradyumna, a devotee of Vishnu, was so lost in the thoughts of his god once that he failed to notice the great sage Agastya. Furious, the sage cursed him to be reborn as an elephant. The frightened king apologized but Agastya did not revoke the curse; however, he granted that even as an elephant, the king would worship Vishnu.

Indradyumna was eventually reborn as Gajendra, 'the king of elephants'. Every day, he went to a lake, from which he picked up a lotus to offer to Vishnu. On one such visit, as Gajendra stood in knee-deep waters, someone watched him intently.

It was Huhu, a *gandharva*.[9] Huhu had been so engrossed in singing and dancing with a celestial maiden once that he'd fallen into this lake by accident. Sage Devala, who had been meditating nearby, was so angered by the disturbance that he had immediately transformed Huhu into a crocodile, saying that his return to heaven as a gandharva depended on an elephant.

And so, that day, as Gajendra was about to step out of the lake after picking a lotus, Huhu the crocodile grasped his leg with his strong jaws. Gajendra fought back with all his might, but to no avail. None of the other elephants could help either. Some say the two creatures stayed locked in tussle like this for years and years!

At last, the bleeding Gajendra called out to Vishnu for help. The god immediately came riding on Garuda's back and released his weapon, the Sudarshan Chakra, which beheaded the crocodile. The dead crocodile, as was foretold, changed back into Huhu. Bowing to Vishnu, the gandharva made his way up to heaven. Gajendra, on the other hand, got *moksham*, or salvation.

---

[9] In Hindu mythology, gandharvas are celestial musicians, and are often paired with apsaras, the celestial nymphs who sing and dance like a dream.

> The panel at Krishnapuram Palace shows a compassionate Vishnu atop a fuming Garuda near the crocodile, who is firmly holding Gajendra with his deadly jaws. And Gajendra, despite the excruciating pain, continues to carry the lotus in his trunk. The legend of Gajendra Moksham, of which there are several retellings, is so popular that many Kerala mural artists have painted their versions of it.

'Wow, what an intense story!' Mohini gasped as the lake returned to its original stillness, the astonishing battle that had just played out barely leaving ripples. 'But it's not fair that both Indradyumna and Huhu were punished for being absorbed in what they loved doing the most . . . You know what I liked about both stories, though? That the weapons didn't cause destruction. They transformed—'

She paused, realizing that the crocodile and elephant hadn't disappeared; they were still standing in the lake. Slowly, the reptile swam closer to the pachyderm, but this time, it did not attack. *Did Katha use magic to save this elephant?* She looked sideways at the spirit.

'What? Oh, I forgot to mention. *That* crocodile is vegetarian!' yelled Katha, before diving into the lake for a swim.

'Suuuure. Crocodiles are vegetarian, and fish can fly!' Mohini said sarcastically.

'Didn't I already tell you that you judge too quickly? Crocodiles aren't always the bad guys, you know. And that one really *is* vegetarian.' The spirit said with a straight face.

Mohini watched the crocodile and somehow felt that the spirit was speaking the truth. The predator almost looked friendly as it floated calmly in the blue-green water.

'And for your information, some fish *can* fly!' Saying so, Katha grabbed her legs and pulled her in.

SPLASH!

Chapter 22

EYE OF THE WIND

Mohini *hated* getting wet. Thankfully, the underwater journey—though aquamarine and beautifully vivid—ended soon and they climbed ashore. Sprawled on a bed of warm white sand, she coughed up salty water.

'Yuck! It's up my nose . . . *ugh* . . . it—where are we?'

> Katha and Mohini have swum to Kiltan, one of the ten inhabited islands of the smallest union territory of the country, Lakshadweep. This archipelago is called so as it is believed to be made up of one lakh *dweep* (islands).

'I've studied all this in school, but I've never understood how they ever counted these islands!' Mohini said, looking down the busy beach. Fishermen were casting their colourful nets, people were chatting away happily, kids were playing with the waves.

'The sea is an important part of life here,' Katha said. 'The locals sing songs, dance and swap tales on the seashore. And one of the ways in which they tell stories is Kattuvili.'

Wind in the Sails

'As you may have guessed, the primary occupation of the inhabitants of Lakshadweep is fishing. Fishermen travel to the mainland, especially Kerala, to get basic supplies. People here are really good at building boats. And they make them from locally available materials, like wood and coir from coconut trees as well as oil from fish and crab. Earlier, they used to make these trips only in a special kind of boat that they call *odam*,' Katha began.

'Why is it special?' Mohini asked.

'Oh, because the odams are no ordinary sailing vessels. They can travel far out to sea, making deep-sea fishing possible, and have the capacity to ferry up to 400 tons of cargo.'

'Whoa!'

'Wait till you hear this . . . On the archipelago's capital, Kavaratti Island, the locals used to build a remarkable boat entirely out of twisted coir. Fish oil was applied all over the coir to make the boat waterproof. And the incredible part is, the locals didn't use even a single piece of wood or iron in their construction!'

'They had some skill!' Mohini was astounded.

'Anyway, back to the odams. In those days, fishermen loaded the odams with coir and copra, which they sold in the mainland, and returned with their purchases of rice, sugar and other goods. These sea journeys, undertaken by the men, were long and made the waiting women anxious, who would then sing Kattuvili.'

> Kattuvili[1] is a tradition practised by the women of Lakshadweep's Kiltan Island. Its name translates as 'a call (or request) to the wind'. Through their song, the women appeal to the wind to be steady, to create the gentle push required by the boat's sails and make sure their men return home safely.

---

[1] In Malayalam, the language widely spoken on these islands, *kat* means 'wind' and *vili*, 'call'.

'The lyrics also highlight how much their men mean to them, and the agony the women feel if the wind doesn't accept their pleas,' Katha said.

'Fascinating! They believe that nature will listen to humans,' Mohini said.

'Yes. Earlier, when they assembled on the shore at night to perform Kattuvili, the bonfire they lit acted as a guiding light to the approaching odams. This tradition is on the decline, though,' the spirit admitted.

'Why? Don't they believe in talking to the wind any more?' Mohini was confused.

'Nature's whims still exist, but something else has changed . . . For the longest time, odams were the only mode of sea transport. But their construction declined when mechanized and chartered vessels made an appearance on the horizon. With the sails absent, the need to invoke the winds waned. And this has resulted in the near extinction of Kattuvili,' Katha explained gloomily.

'Oh, no!'

On seeing Mohini's face fall, Katha roused its own spirits and suggested they go on a cruise. With a click of its horns, a boat was conjured up onshore.

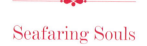

Seafaring Souls

'Lakshadweep has many more sea-based traditions. The fishermen of Amini Island would sing songs during sea journeys. In rhythm with the rowing of the boat, the men would croon about their love and life, the changing face of the islands and their legendary characters,' Katha said.

> The archipelago is also known for Bhandiya Jehun, a dance with colourful metal pots, which expresses the joy a young woman feels when her beloved returns from a long voyage.
>
> The women sing about how their men have brought back presents, such as perfumes, jewellery and fine clothes, from faraway lands. The dance is traditionally performed near a pond, where the women gather to fill water. Tapping on the metal pots that they carry adds energy and tempo to their graceful twirls.

'On Kavaratti, locals teach children about the many species found in the waters, such as the lionfish, sailfish, octopus, tuna and the *parava meen*, through folk songs,' the spirit explained as their boat sailed on effortlessly.

'What are parava meen?'

Before the spirit could reply, a few glistening bluish-silver fish leapt out of the water around their boat. Squinting, Mohini saw that they had—it couldn't be!—translucent *wings*.

'Told you so!' Katha laughed. 'Parava meen[2] is what they call these mirrorwing flying fish.'

Their tail fins wriggled through the surface of the water, and now they were flying above it! They were fast, lightning fast. And in just a few seconds, they'd disappeared undersea again.

'Some islanders even have songs dedicated to these flying fish, pleading with them to bite the bait, which these fish manage to dodge expertly,' Katha informed a stunned Mohini.

'I thought f-flying f-f-fish existed only in the im-imagination . . . a-and in s-s-stories,' she stammered, still finding the sight unreal. And just when she thought this couldn't get any better, they saw a dolphin breach. Mohini squealed with delight and clapped her hands.

'Looks like it's story time!' Katha announced.

---

[2] In Malayalam, 'parava' means 'bird' and 'meen', 'fish'.

The Unlikely Guide

In the seventh century, lived a saint named Ubaidullah. While on a visit to Mecca, he dreamt that Prophet Muhammad wanted him to head to Jeddah and from there, sail off to distant lands and spread the message of Islam. The saint followed his dream. But the ship he boarded from Jeddah was wrecked by a storm.

Ubaidullah survived and held on to a floating wooden plank. Miraculously, a wayfinder appeared in the form of a dolphin and led the saint to the shore of Amini Island, where he began propagating Islam.

There, he fell in love with a local woman, Hameedat Beebi, and the two got married. But not all was well. The lives of the saint and his wife were threatened by a few people who opposed his work. Just as they were about to be attacked one day, Ubaidullah invoked the Almighty to protect them. And so the attackers suddenly turned blind. By the time they got their vision back, the saint and his wife had disappeared! The duo had managed to escape to Andrott Island. Ubaidullah preached Islam there as well and across some neighbouring islands over time. But Andrott became his final resting place.

This story has been passed down from generation to generation through oral tradition. Thus, the locals in most of these islands revere the dolphin and refrain from hunting or eating the animal. They have noticed that dolphins, terns and tuna often travel together. So when fishermen want to locate tuna shoals, the dolphin acts as their unlikely guide.

'While some sea-based folk forms of Lakshadweep are still alive, those such as the cyclone song, tide songs and the street song have gone with the wind. Kattuvili is at the edge of similar danger,' Katha continued.

For Mohini, who had often lamented not knowing what stories to tell, Lakshadweep was a big lesson. 'Sometimes, just the way we live becomes a memorable story. And sometimes, storytelling becomes a way of life!'

'You're right. The way we live is a story indeed,' Katha assured her, making the boat speed up.

Chapter 23

FORTUNE FAVOURS THE BOLD

Mohini was horribly seasick. Katha had made the boat fly over the water every now and then, keeping pace with the feisty parava meen. But the girl couldn't endure it. Finally taking pity on her, Katha lightly touched her hand and the two rose into the air, leaving behind the sea and the fish and the smell of salt. Spirit and girl were now floating through dusk-pink clouds, fluffy like cotton candy.

'WOW,' she breathed, her hand going through a passing cloud.

As they descended slowly, Mohini noticed a temple atop a hill ahead. 'What's that?'

'I'll tell you. First, you need some rest,' the spirit said, deep concern on its face.

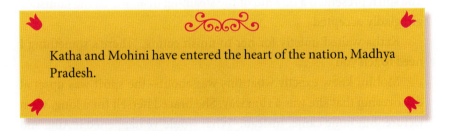

Katha and Mohini have entered the heart of the nation, Madhya Pradesh.

'Ughh . . .' Mohini moaned. 'I do feel terrible!'

'Do you want some water?'

'NO! No more water! I'm still . . . *ugghh* . . .' Mohini flopped down on the grassy patch they'd landed on.

'Aren't you hungry?'

'Nope, I don't want *anything* right now.' The girl shook her head.

'Umm . . . Do you want to reach out to your parents?' Katha asked, now feeling truly guilty.

'Oh, no! They'll get worried. As it is, after I ran away from home—'

'YOU RAN AWAY FROM HOME?' Katha was shocked. *'But why?'*

'Because I was expected to tell stories to the people of my town. As always, I tried but couldn't. I was tired of failing. And listening to comments about how bad I was in comparison to the GREAT storytellers in my family . . . Ohh . . . Don't make me talk, please!' Clutching her gurgling stomach, she closed her eyes.

When she awoke, it was around midnight. She had slept for a long while and was feeling much better. Her eyes slowly adjusting to the darkness, she found the luminous spirit staring into the pitch-black distance. It looked rather troubled, she thought. 'Katha?' she called out.

'You're awake so soon?' The spirit floated towards her hastily.

'Yeah, I'm fine now. Don't worry!' she said.

'Well, that's a good thing . . . Wait, what's that rumbling? It's your tummy! You must eat now . . . please? How about some bhutte ka kees?'[1] The spirit presented a bowlful of the steaming dish, which the famished girl gladly accepted.

Katha waited quietly for her to finish eating. 'There's something I need to tell you . . .'

Mohini knew exactly what this was about—the spirit was upset at discovering that she was a runaway. She braced herself for a long, stern lecture. But none came. Instead, 'What would've happened if Alha and Udal had also run away every time they faced a challenging situation? Would people still remember them?' it asked her, looking away.

Mohini knew by now that even the smallest reference Katha made was eventually related to how tales are told. 'Another storytelling tradition?'

'Yes, the ballad of Alha and Udal.'

---

[1] A speciality of Madhya Pradesh, the dish is made of grated corn.

Ballad of Battles

'In the twelfth century, the Chandela king Paramardi Deva, who was also known as Parmal, ruled over a place called Mahoba[2] in the Bundelkhand region. His army's generals were two brothers, Alha and Udal. News of these two men's bravery spread like wildfire throughout the region, so much so that Jagnayak, Parmal's court poet, wrote a collection of poems on the duo's military feats, in a metre that came to be called the Alha metre,' Katha recounted.

'That's pretty cool, having a metre named after yourself. But what kind of feats are the brothers known for?' Mohini asked.

> This *veer kavya* or 'epic poem' written by Jagnayak is known as Alha Khand. It is recited and sung till date by bards of the Alhait community, who are called *alhet*s. As the epic has been passed down through oral tradition over the years, people sing the ballad today in several dialects.

'The epic poem narrates the story of King Parmal, his generals Alha and Udal, and the fifty-two battles they fought and won. So fearless were the two brothers that even Prithviraj Chauhan, the great Rajput king of Delhi, who wanted to annex the Chandela kingdom at that time, was defeated by them many times over,' Katha said.

'I don't remember reading about this in my history textbook. We did have a chapter on Prithviraj Chauhan, though . . .' Mohini recalled.

---

[2] After the country was divided into various states, the Bundelkhand region came to span parts of both Madhya Pradesh and Uttar Pradesh. Today, Mahoba lies in the Bundelkhand area of Uttar Pradesh.

'Well, we can never tell what actually happened. There are so many sides to a story. And, as you now know, so many versions of the same story,' Katha said, shrugging.

Warrior Act

'The ballad praises the courage and sense of honour of the warrior brothers. Often, the alhet enacts the roles of multiple characters as they appear in the epic. A troupe of musicians plays the dholak and the nagara, adding rhythm to the alhet's energetic narration of the tale,' the spirit explained as it magically transformed Mohini into a mini version of an alhet, complete with a twirly moustache.

Used to Katha's stunts by now, Mohini was barely alarmed and immediately started twisting its ends.

> The alhet dresses up like a warrior, mostly sports a curling moustache and even carries a sword with him, which he unsheathes at key moments in the recitation. He looks every bit the heroic figure that the ballad had set out to create. So evocative is his rendition of the verses that it instils patriotic fervour in the listeners.

'The epic ballad is usually sung during monsoon. At times, the audience sits through the bard's performance despite the rain.' The moment Katha spoke these words, a sudden shower began.

'Oh, no! Just when I was getting over my water woes!' Mohini frowned as her magical alhet costume melted away.

'The rain really likes you,' Katha teased, dragging her into a nearby shed for cover.

Wiping off the raindrops from her hair and face, Mohini asked, 'So what happened to Alha and Udal? Did they become kings and marry princesses?'

'*Sigh!* More interesting things happen to characters in stories, you know. I wish kids would devour more than the staple fairy-tales-and-bedtime-stories diet!' Katha complained.

Living Legends

Alha and Udal were devotees of the goddess Sharda, also called Maihar Devi. Every morning, they would be the first to get a glimpse of the goddess and offer her their prayers.

It is said that in one of the battles against Prithviraj Chauhan, Udal lost his life. Angered by the murder of his brother, Alha sought revenge from Chauhan and was about to kill him. But Maihar Devi appeared in front of him and asked him to spare Chauhan's life. To show his respect for the goddess, Alha severed his own head as offering. Moved by this sacrifice, Maihar Devi revived the brothers and granted them a boon, that of immortality!

Even today, nearly 900–1000 years since this episode, the two brothers are believed to be the first devotees to visit the temple early each morning.

'They say, "Fortune favours the bold". You ran away from your difficulties, Mohini, but Alha and Udal faced them head-on each and every time. Isn't life about how you want to be remembered?' Katha asked her.

Mohini was silent for a few moments, her head bowed as she pretended to inspect something on her shoe. *Katha is right*, she thought. Perhaps she should have spoken to her family and told them that she should follow another dream? Or she could try harder and learn the nuances of storytelling? Her complete lack of interest in the subject *was* changing, thanks to a crazy spirit's silly spell.

'I feel . . . more than the boon, it's Alha and Udal's heroism that has kept them alive for centuries, through stories,' she said, not answering Katha's question directly.

Mohini contemplated if *she* could be a hero like them. What did she want people to remember her for? The sound of bells tolling in the hilltop temple cut short her chain of thoughts. 'There's still time for sunrise. Why would anyone visit a temple this early?'

Katha grinned mysteriously. '*That* is the Maihar Devi temple. You know who her first visitors are, don't you?'

Chapter 24

PRAISE TO THE SKIES

From the solemn temple bells, Mohini's attention was abruptly diverted to a melodious voice. Her surroundings transformed quickly, as though a stage was undergoing a scene-change for a new act. A few bushes scooted left even as some trees jumped to her right. But time seemed to have stood still, for the night sky stayed put.

> Mohini and Katha are now in the homeland of the celebrated Chhatrapati Shivaji Maharaj: a 'great nation' in itself, Maharashtra!

The girl felt as though she was being pulled in the direction of that voice, although her thoughts were still with Alha and Udal. *Are they really still alive? Do they look as young as they used to? Do they present themselves to the people who sing their ballads?*

'Hey, what was the story you told the people of your town that provoked such a strong reaction?' the spirit asked gently.

Ordinarily, Mohini would have flatly refused to answer. But for some reason, she found herself repeating the story to Katha.

'So . . . once upon a time, there was a stone, and a young prince kicked it hard, and the stone hit a wall and was broken into pieces.'

Katha rolled its eyes dramatically. 'Alas! If only this were a story at all, you would have broken my spell.'

'That's why I keep telling you that I CANNOT become a storyteller!' Mohini said sternly, walking ahead of the spirit.

'Well, your "stone" needs a little devotion and some character. Once you do that, you could even make a god spring from that thing,' Katha suggested.

'And how do I do that?' She whipped around to face the spirit.

'Kirtan will show you how,' the spirit said, pointing to something behind the trees ahead.

Mohini now spotted the source of the sweet-sounding voice: a simple-looking man in a kurta, dhoti and turban, holding the stringed tanpura in his hand and completely lost in his song.

'Is his name Kirtan?' she asked, confused, to which Katha chortled in response.

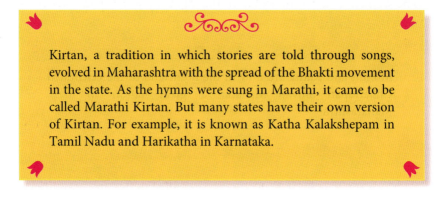

Kirtan, a tradition in which stories are told through songs, evolved in Maharashtra with the spread of the Bhakti movement in the state. As the hymns were sung in Marathi, it came to be called Marathi Kirtan. But many states have their own version of Kirtan. For example, it is known as Katha Kalakshepam in Tamil Nadu and Harikatha in Karnataka.

Singing Saints

'He's a *kirtankar*.[1] Doesn't he remind you of somebody?' Katha asked, jerking its head in the direction of the dhoti-clad singer, who was now singing towards the stars.

Mohini thought hard as she observed the man. 'Hmm . . . He looks like a saint, doesn't he?'

---

[1] A Kirtan singer.

'Good!' Katha was impressed. 'Before you ask, yes, I'll tell you what a saint has to do with Kirtan . . . Ever heard of the sage Narada?'

'Of course!'

'Well, according to mythology, the praises sung by Narada, of Vishnu, can be considered to be the earliest Kirtan. Since Narada is usually perceived as a wandering saint, singing and playing a stringed musical instrument, that's what kirtankars do too. They dress up like Narada and go from village to village, spreading the message of devotion,' the spirit explained.

'So are all kirtankars saints?' Mohini asked.

'Not exactly and not always. Kirtankars are very much like me,' Katha said haughtily, and Mohini made a face. 'It's true! Kirtankars are multitalented and well read. They not only tell stories and sing beautifully, but also act and dance whenever the performance requires them to do so. And oh, they answer the difficult philosophical questions that their audience asks. I do all of these things, you know it!' The spirit shrugged.

'Give it up for Katha!' Mohini began applauding suddenly. 'A rare kirtankar who sings its own praises!'

The spirit laughed heartily. 'You're trying to keep pace with my sarcasm, eh?'

The girl faked a smile and went on to her next question. 'I've still not understood . . . Do common people sing Kirtan?'

'Yes, but some saints played a vital role in propagating Kirtan among the masses, especially in Maharashtra, through the Bhakti movement. Ramdas, Dnyaneshwar, Namdev and many others. A new spiritual tradition known as Varkari[2] emerged at that time, in which songs dedicated to Vitthal, an avatar of Vishnu, were sung. These simple, soothing hymns called *abhanga*s are still sung by the people of this sect, although they were popularized centuries ago by Varkari saints like Eknath and Tukaram.'

---

[2] Followers of the Varkari belief system make up the Varkari community. Several believers make an annual trip to Vitthal Temple in Pandharpur, singing devotional songs throughout their journey.

'Tukaram . . . Isn't he the saint whom Shivaji respected a lot? I remember reading about him in class,' Mohini said.

'Absolutely! Shivaji was enamoured by the saint's teachings, but Tukaram advised him to return to his kingly duties.'

'A king who was fascinated by a kirtankar!' Mohini exclaimed.

'Yes, but don't you want to know about the king who was infuriated every time his son sang Kirtan, or, for that matter, even took the name of a god?'

Katha had made Mohini amply curious.

The Devoted Son

Hiranyaksha, brother of the asura king Hiranyakashipu, was killed by Varaha, the boar-like incarnation of Vishnu. As an act of revenge, Hiranyakashipu resolved to become stronger than Vishnu himself. Through devoted penance, Hiranyakashipu got Brahma to grant him a unique boon: that he will be killed neither during day nor at night, neither by man nor beast nor by god, neither on earth nor in the sky, neither by any animate object nor by an inanimate one.

Out of fear, the gods attacked the asura king's palace in his absence. Finding this move unfair, Narada protected Hiranyakashipu's wife, who happened to be pregnant at that time. Narada's Kirtans influenced the child while he was inside his mother's womb. And so Prahlada, as the boy came to be named, grew up to be a staunch devotee of Narayana (another name given to Vishnu).

Much as Hiranyakashipu tried, he could not get Prahlada to proclaim him as the most powerful being in the universe. So the asura king plotted to do the unthinkable: kill his own son. He had the boy thrown off a cliff; he made elephants trample the child; he even threw him into a bonfire. But every time, Prahlada called upon Narayana for help and was saved.

> Then came a day when the father lost all patience with his son. He mocked the boy, saying that if his Narayana was omnipresent, then he must be residing in a random pillar as well. The devoted Prahlada answered with a confident yes. Enraged, Hiranyakashipu kicked the pillar hard to prove to the boy that no god would spring from it. But to his shock, when the pillar split, the ferocious Narasimha, the half-man, half-lion avatar of Vishnu, emerged with a deafening roar!
>
> Lifting Hiranyakashipu off the ground, Narasimha placed him on his thigh and attacked him with his claws, instantly killing the king. For a long time thereafter, the god's anger could not be tamed. Finally, Narada requested Prahlada to sing. Hearing Prahlada's expressive Kirtan, Narasimha calmed down.

'Hiranyakashipu was killed at twilight by Narasimha, who was neither man, beast nor god; on his thigh, which was between the earth and the sky; with claws, which are neither animate nor inanimate,' Katha concluded. 'Incidentally, it is believed that Prahlada later listed nine ways to perform bhakti, with Kirtan being one such form of devotion.'

'What a clever tale!' Mohini realized that her stone story *did* lack character and commitment in comparison to this pillar one.

After mulling over a thought for a few minutes, she said, 'Alha and Udal earned immortality despite death. Hiranyakashipu died in spite of getting a boon that defied death. In both cases, devotion won. But Katha, must devotion always be such a serious matter? Can't it be . . . lighter and . . . um . . . playful? Like friendship, or love?' Her face wore a look of deep curiosity.

'Walk around this tree thrice, little one. You'll get your answer,' Katha said. 'Go on, do as I say!'

Chapter 25
JEWEL IN THE CROWN

And so Mohini went around the tree thrice. The first round was awkward; the second was kind of fun; the third, dizzy. She held on to the trunk to stop her head from spinning. When she steadied herself, she saw that the full moon's radiant beams had spotlit the whole place.

'Wow!' she smiled at Katha. 'It seems like a never-ending night. What did you do?'

'Some nights last for years!' Katha grinned back.

She wanted to know what the spirit meant but she was distracted by a group of dazzling figures walking towards the tree in a single line.

'Are these celestial beings? Are we in *paradise*?'

'No such luck yet!' Katha broke her reverie.

> The spirit and the girl are back in the country's North-east. This time, in a place that has a strong connection with dance: the 'land of jewels', Manipur.

Mohini couldn't take her eyes off the approaching party. 'So elegant . . . and divine!'

The group's attire played a shining role in lending them this appearance, no doubt, but it was also the poise with which they carried themselves. Then there was the magic of the full moon too.

'You are about to witness a joyous dance between a god, his love and his lovers. A blissful display of devotion, a flowing play of emotion—' Katha began, when Mohini interrupted with a shout.

'Raas Leela!'
'The *Manipuri* Raas Leela,' Katha clarified.

Raas Leela is the dance of Krishna, his consort Radha and the *gopi*s (female cowherds). As many Manipuri people believe in Vishnu, stories of his avatar Krishna and Radha have become part of the state's folk traditions, including dance. While Manipuri dance comprises different types, such as Pung Cholom, Nupa Cholom and Thang Ta, it is often represented visually through Raas Leela.

A Moonlight Tryst

'Raas Leela narrates the tale of how Radha and the gopis were drawn into the forest one full moon night by the melodious notes of Krishna's flute. Through the night, they danced around him. Krishna not only created illusory clones of himself to dance with each gopi, even as he danced with Radha, but he also magically caused that single night to last for . . . guess how long? 4.32 billion years!' Katha revealed.

'Ah, so that's what you meant . . . What a dance it must have been!' Mohini smiled.

'Well, it was a dance of rasas, or emotions . . . Among all the emotions, the dance focuses most on love and its many moods—shyness, playfulness, beauty, desire, devotion, envy, contentment and more,' the spirit explained. 'Traditionally, Manipuri Raas Leela is staged on full moon nights in Radha–Krishna temples. The performance, which lasts up to eight to ten hours, is a combination of Lasya, the gentle feminine style, and Tandava, the energetic masculine style. But the cool part is that both styles are performed only by women.'

'But Krishna . . .?' the girl began.

'Krishna too is played by a young girl!'

Celestial Connections

'Raas Leela has its roots in Vrindavan, in Uttar Pradesh, the home of Krishna. But the Manipuri version was born due to a dream that the region's eighteenth-century king Bhagyachandra saw. In the dream, Krishna appeared to the king with details of this dance and its costumes, asking him to build a temple and conduct the dance there. And so Bhagyachandra had Shree Govindajee Temple built in Imphal. This is where the very first Manipuri Raas Leela was performed on a full moon night, in November 1779,' Katha said.

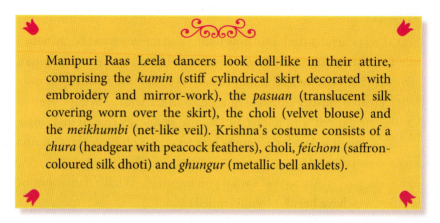

Manipuri Raas Leela dancers look doll-like in their attire, comprising the *kumin* (stiff cylindrical skirt decorated with embroidery and mirror-work), the *pasuan* (translucent silk covering worn over the skirt), the choli (velvet blouse) and the *meikhumbi* (net-like veil). Krishna's costume consists of a *chura* (headgear with peacock feathers), choli, *feichom* (saffron-coloured silk dhoti) and *ghungur* (metallic bell anklets).

Mohini noticed how the dancers were so involved in the performance that they seemed to be observing only their own hand movements and nothing else.

'Dance plays an important role in the everyday lives of the state's people. For every occasion—be it birth, a toddler's ear-piercing ceremony, marriage, even death—Sankirtan[1] is performed,' the spirit said.

'They seem to be as lost in their art as the gandharva Huhu had been,' she remarked.

'Good observation,' Katha said, and then did a double take. 'What a thing to have said!'

The perplexed girl waited for an explanation to follow the spirit's reaction.

'You know, the people of Manipur believe their ancestors were gandharvas. It seems some ancient texts even refer to this region as Gandharva Desa, the "land of gandharvas".'

'Wow, interesting!' The dancers' attire shimmered even more as if to grab Mohini's attention once again.

---

[1] A ritualistic tradition of Manipur, in which performers dance while singing and playing the drums and cymbals.

'Hey, did you know that Manipuri Raas Leela is also known as the jewel dance?' Katha asked.

'Oh? Is it because it's an important dance of the "land of jewels"? Or because the dancers sparkle like jewels, thanks to their lovely costumes?' Mohini guessed.

'Yes, but there's more . . .'

Dance of the Divine

Legend has it that when Krishna was performing Raas Leela in Vrindavan, he requested Shiva to stand guard and not allow anyone a glimpse of the dance. However, Shiva himself saw the dance and was so fascinated that he longed to perform Raas Leela with Parvati.

For this, Shiva chose a hill in a far-off region, where he and Parvati then danced to music created by heavenly beings, most likely the gandharvas. Adding glamour to this event was Ananta-Sesha, the thousand-headed snake who wore a jewelled crown on each of its heads.

As Shiva and Parvati danced—the god in the Tandava style, and the goddess, with elegant Lasya movements—the gems, or *manis*, on Ananta-Sesha's many crowns illuminated the land. When the snake swayed to Raas Leela along with the divine couple, some precious stones fell to the ground. And so the region came to be known as Manipur.

'It must have been such a dazzling sight! How I wish I could've been there!' Mohini gushed. 'You were right . . . Manipuri Raas Leela is indeed about the joy of devotion.'

'Yup, it's intense yet playful,' Katha added.

'It's nice to know that Shiva–Parvati helped bring Krishna–Radha's favourite dance to Manipur,' Mohini noted.

'Well, mythology is full of tales of camaraderie between the gods and the coexistence of their traditions,' Katha said thoughtfully.

'Hmm . . . I was also thinking, dreams are a common theme in stories. So are imaginary beasts, like the dragon or Narasimha or Ananta-Sesha,' Mohini offered.

'Excuse me! What do you mean by *imaginary*? You don't believe such creatures exist?' Katha looked peeved.

Mohini burst out laughing. 'Look, flying fish are one thing. But you want me to buy that there are beings like Narasimha? Half-animal, half-man?'

Katha's eyes twinkled. 'Speaking of the unseen and the unknown, I have an idea to break this spell and set you free.'

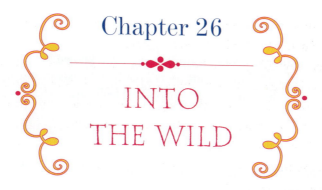

Chapter 26

INTO THE WILD

Though Mohini still couldn't see herself as a storyteller, she did like getting to know about these traditions. Yet her curiosity got the better of her—she simply couldn't pass up on a shot at freedom.

'What idea?' she asked, watching the first rays of the sun lighten the sky.

'Don't be so suspicious! I promise it's simpler than the previous tasks I'd set for you. From here on, the moment you ask me a question, the spell will be broken.' Katha grinned, knowing Mohini's inquisitive mind only too well.

'Unfair! This means that if I want to know more about something and ask about it, the spell gets broken. You can't just leave things midway!' Mohini stomped her feet.

'Says who? *My* spell. *My* rules. I can do whatever I want,' Katha said matter-of-factly. 'All *you* can do is question me. Your time starts now.'

Mohini was undecided. She wanted to be free, but . . . 'Fine!'

'*Fine . . . fine . . . ine . . .*' Mohini's words echoed freakishly as a thick jungle rapidly grew around them. Towering, sturdy trees snaked skyward. Sunlight barely filtered through the canopy of leaves above. A damp, woody smell now hung in the air. And all of a sudden, the girl found herself standing alone, for Katha had become invisible again.

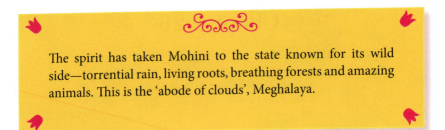

The spirit has taken Mohini to the state known for its wild side—torrential rain, living roots, breathing forests and amazing animals. This is the 'abode of clouds', Meghalaya.

'I know you're here,' Mohini spoke to the invisible spirit in whispers.

It was so still that she could hear her heart thumping loud and clear. But another, altogether different, sound bothered her the next minute—that of a growling beast. Leaves rustled behind her but she refused to look, till something breathed down the back of her neck and murmured calmly, 'Yes, I'm here.'

'Thank heavens, Katha! I almost—' She turned abruptly.

Mohini's heart now jumped straight into her mouth, for she stood staring at what had just spoken to her—an unusually large Bengal tiger!

Mohini thought she was going to cry. Actually, she thought she was going to die. Why had Katha changed its form to *this*? Was this the spirit's idea of a prank?

'Jungles are the guardians of stories. Unbelievable stories, when told over and over again, become legends,' the tiger said in a low growl. 'Jungles are the keepers of secrets too. Secrets that are better left buried deep in its uncanny recesses. Digging them out is never a good idea.'

'K-k-k . . .' Mohini's voice didn't leave her throat, even though she was sure the spirit was doing this deliberately to get her to ask it a question.

'Perhaps if I told you about how the jungles of Meghalaya are no less than any other storytelling tradition you have known, it might ease your fear . . .' the tiger said, fixing its glassy gaze on Mohini.

> Meghalaya follows a unique system, by which local communities take on the responsibility of protecting some jungles. The state has more than a hundred such public forests that are designated as 'sacred groves'.[1]

Revered and Restricted

'These groves have a number of rules. The very first one is that no jungle rules should be broken when people visit its sacred space. What belongs to the jungle, remains in the jungle. No one is allowed to take even a single petal outside.' The tiger looked pointedly at Mohini's hand, which held a pretty flower.

'I-I-I . . . d-didn't pluck it, I swear!' Her hands trembled. 'I p-p-picked it up from h-h-here,' she stammered, placing the flower back on the forest floor, where she had found it.

The tiger only nodded and continued. 'Needless to say, deforestation is forbidden.'

'P-people will hardly enter the f-forest then,' she mumbled timidly.

'Not true. Do you see those monoliths? They've been erected by the locals in memory of their loved ones—it is also how they pay their respects to their ancestors. Some visitors also come here to perform rituals to appease the jungle protector, U Ryngkew U Basa, who makes sure both locals and outsiders follow the rules. Anyone who disobeys the laws of the jungle pays for it—if not through illness, then with their life,' the tiger finished menacingly.

---

[1] This system not only protects the environment but also helps the communities preserve the ancient medicinal herbs that grow in these groves.

> For ages, the Khasi people of Meghalaya have believed that U Ryngkew U Basa was sent to their land by God to protect their forests from the vices of man.
>
> According to legend, U Ryngkew U Basa is believed to appear either as a snake or a tiger.[2] Justice is delivered to wrongdoers by the snake. But if miscreants apologize and return to the forest what they have taken from it, the snake forgives them. On the other hand, innocent people entering the jungle or seeking shelter in it are protected by this guardian in the form of a tiger.

Shifting Shape

Mohini was utterly confused. Who *was* this talking tiger? But she dared not ask, lest the spell be broken.

'The state's people share an inexplicable bond with the tiger. Some clans believe that each time folks walk through a forest, a tiger escorts and protects them. And then there are others who believe that the tiger chooses human beings to become one of its kind, granting them the ability to transform into a *weretiger*,' the majestic animal told Mohini, who stood rooted to the spot.

Not taking its eyes off the shivering girl, the tiger strode towards a sprawling tree and sat on its haunches on a smooth rock before continuing. 'Some say that men, especially witch doctors, can turn themselves into a tiger by licking a mysterious stone. Others believe that people enter the tiger's realm in their sleep. Their *rngiew*, which

---

[2] The protector, a supernatural being, can appear in any form—human as well as animal—but that of the snake and the tiger are believed to be more common.

is one's essence or spirit, crosses over to the other side in their dream, where an unusually large tiger, U Ryngkew U Basa, waits for them. The protector then asks them to shed their human form and wear the garb of a tiger—hide, fur, claws, fangs and whiskers. Through this ritual, man acquires the powers of a tiger.'

Daring to glance at the tiger's striped face from the corner of her eye, Mohini gave a half-smile. So *this* was Katha's plan, the girl thought. *By telling me these tall tales, it wants me to believe in fantastical beasts!*

The tiger chuffed to regain Mohini's attention. 'These men and women, having successfully transformed into weretigers, then follow their protector. Every following weretiger has to walk exactly over the paw prints of the previous one, all the time wiping away the mark behind it as it moves forward. The tiger at the rear makes sure all paw prints are completely erased.' It paused, noticing the girl clear her throat.

'Footprints are erased . . .' Mohini was careful to leave the thought hanging, making her question sound like a statement.

'The secret of shape-shifting must never be shared,' the mighty tiger said. 'It is a power given to mankind to help protect the sacred forests. Any human—weretiger, to be precise—found misusing the power will be punished by the protectors!'[3]

'There must be a reason for the existence of these stories . . . I mean, legends . . .' Her voice was barely audible.

The beast stooped low, its muzzle so close to the girl's head that her teeth chattered, and said, 'Maybe it all goes back to a creation tale.'

---

[3] In Meghalaya, different tribes, even individual clans, have their own set of beliefs as far as the lore of the weretiger is concerned. One of these legends suggests that men and women who metamorphose into tigers are actually spies of their respective clans. Once disguised, they easily gather secrets and report them back home. Since it would be easy for anyone to trace a weretiger by following the paw prints—and no alert spy would be careless enough to leave behind such evidence—they have to be completely wiped away.

The Tree and the Tiger

In the beginning, when God created humans, Dieng-iei, a 'gigantic tree', acted as the connection between them. Over time, the tree grew so enormous that the sunlight didn't even touch the earth. A deep fear of darkness gripped the people and they found it difficult to go about their everyday work.

So, armed with axes, they marched to the tree and began hacking it down. Knowing that this job would take several days, they left the tree partly cut and retired home in the evening. But the next day they found the tree intact, as though they hadn't inflicted a single blow on it. Once again, they began cutting it down, only to discover later that their work had been in vain. This went on for many days. The tree continued to heal its cuts and stood strong.

Seeing their despair, Phreit, a little wren, revealed that after they left, a tiger would come by and lick Dieng-iei's cuts. And immediately, the tree would revive. Phreit suggested that the people leave their axes tied to the tree at dusk.

That night, when the tiger came and licked the tree, it cut its tongue on the blades around the trunk. Hurt, the tiger went away. And then the people successfully felled Dieng-iei.

Furious, God severed all ties with mankind. The destruction of the tree caused natural disasters and led to misunderstandings between animals and humans. Frightened and ashamed, the people apologized to God and promised never to pick up the axe to harm forests.

Hoping the humans had learnt their lesson, God entrusted the protection of the sacred forests to them. But, to ensure that they never disobeyed him again, he sent a protector to live among them in the sacred groves—U Ryngkew U Basa.

'It's a clear message to human beings to save trees, protect animals and let the forests live,' the girl observed.

The tiger grunted in agreement.

Mohini was itching to ask the spirit something about the weretiger legend. If only Katha hadn't tied her tongue so wickedly! But before she could figure out a way to turn her question into a statement, the tiger bounded far away from her. 'Hey, Katha! Wait for me!'

'I'm here, little one.' The spirit stretched lazily and yawned wide, before emerging from behind the rock on which the tiger had sat. 'No idea how I dozed off. The jungle's too cosy.'

'Y-y-you're h-here!' the girl stuttered. 'I thought you were the—'

'Tiger?' Katha completed, scratching its bald head. 'Nah. Anyway, we should go.' The spirit led her towards a hidden passage at the base of the huge tree.

Before entering the hollow, Mohini turned to look for the tiger in the distance, who too had stopped to catch one last glimpse of her. It held her gaze for just a second, then disappeared into the thick, dark jungle with a roar that ripped through the trees.

Chapter 27

RITE OF PASSAGE

As Mohini followed Katha down the musty tunnel in a daze, she couldn't decide if the tiger in the sacred grove had been real.

Scrambling out of the tunnel's exit, Katha directed her attention to a house unlike any she had seen before. Propped up on bamboo stilts, the house had a thatched roof and a bamboo porch. Through an open bamboo door, she could see that even the flooring was made of bamboo. Bamboo objects occupied the room: chairs, baskets, containers, a water jug, musical instruments and more.

> The magical tunnel has led Mohini and Katha to Mizoram,[1] the 'land of the hill people'.

'You still look lost. Something bothering you?' Katha asked with a straight face.

It was right. Mohini hadn't been able to gather her thoughts yet. Luckily, though, she remembered accepting Katha's challenge of no questions. 'Bamboo seems to have been used for almost everything in that house,' she said.

---

[1] *Mi* stands for 'people'; *zo* means 'hill'; and *ram* is, 'land'.

'You're making me curious.' Katha raised an eyebrow in wonder. Why wouldn't the girl ask a question? After all, didn't she want to be free?

When Mohini didn't react, the spirit replied, 'Yes, the people of Mizoram use bamboo for one of their most popular folk rituals too. It's called Cheraw dance.'

Step It Up

'Cheraw dance, which has existed since the first century, has been a part of Mizo culture ever since the state's people resided in the Yunnan province of China. So, around the thirteenth century, when they shifted from there to present-day Mizoram, the ancient art travelled with them. Versions of this dance exist in Myanmar, Thailand, the Philippines and Indonesia,' Katha said.

> In Cheraw dance, also called bamboo dance, dancers step in and out of a grid of long bamboo poles. Two groups of four men sit in parallel rows opposite each other, with a bamboo pole resting horizontally in front of either group. Over these base poles, each pair of men facing one another holds two bamboo poles, beating them together and apart. In all, eight poles are clapped over the two base poles, creating the rhythm and tempo for the dance. Sometimes, men sit on four sides, so that four base poles form an outer square. Six to eight women carefully step over the crossed poles without letting them close around their ankles.

'Um, this sounds *super* confusing,' Mohini said.

'But not to the dancers, look! They smoothly cross over from one side to the other, not once missing a single step, nor bumping into one

another, nor looking down at the shifting poles,' Katha commented as eight women and eight men, carrying bamboo poles, appeared. And as the cool evening breeze picked up, they started gracefully hopping across a grid in front of the bamboo house.

'They really don't look down! Wow!' Mohini was amazed by their skill.

'The dancers, inspired by nature, often mimic the movement of trees and birds,' the spirit said.

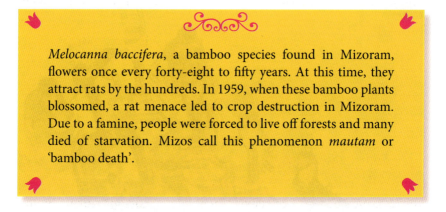

Melocanna baccifera, a bamboo species found in Mizoram, flowers once every forty-eight to fifty years. At this time, they attract rats by the hundreds. In 1959, when these bamboo plants blossomed, a rat menace led to crop destruction in Mizoram. Due to a famine, people were forced to live off forests and many died of starvation. Mizos call this phenomenon *mautam* or 'bamboo death'.

For the Afterlife

'Mizos conduct rituals to appease spirits and pray for a good afterlife for those who leave the mortal world. Cheraw, for the longest time, was a dance performed to ensure the safe passage of the departed to Pialral.[2] Which is why, it's important to perform Cheraw with precision and utmost concentration. A mistake could mean that the person they are practising this ritual for may not reach Pialral,' Katha explained. 'Any questions?'

Mohini shook her head from side to side.

---

[2] According to Mizo mythology, Pialral is the paradise awaiting one after death.

'Okay, then let me tell you about the soul's journey to Pialral.' At this, a blackboard appeared and hovered in front of the girl. The spirit traced a diagram on it with a piece of chalk and began, 'See, the souls wander to Lake Rih Dil first, before heading to the mountain called Hringlang Tlang, from where they catch a final glimpse of the people they lived with. The souls then drink from the spring Lungloh Tui—'

'This reminds me of something,' Mohini interrupted. 'G-Ma had told me a few stories, where, you know . . . souls long to return to their families . . .'

'Aha! That's where the Lungloh Tui helps. It's a spring that erases their memories, so they don't remember their past lives any more. The souls then pluck the flower Hawilo Pâr and wear it in their hair. This flower weeds out their desire to return, helping them move on. The souls are now ready for a new life in either Mitthi Khua or Pialral. All souls travel to Mitthi Khua, the "land of the dead". But only a chosen few can pass on and enter Pialral,' the spirit revealed before adding, 'But even though the dance's origin lies in this complex belief, these days, Cheraw is performed during happy ceremonies too.'

'Phew! Complicated stuff,' Mohini mumbled.

'Let me confuse you a little more. Mizos say, "Rih Dil is the largest lake in Mizoram, but is situated in Myanmar,"' Katha said. 'Ask me why!'

But Mohini only stared at it blankly.

'Fine, I'll tell you anyway! That's because the lake is situated between Mizoram and Myanmar, but international boundaries suggest it belongs to the other country,' the spirit explained.

'It's a *real* lake . . . Interesting!'

'Yup. Even more interesting is the story of this lake.'

A Lake with a Heart

Rihi and her younger sister lived with their father and stepmother. The woman didn't like the girls much. So she convinced her husband to get rid of them. First, the father took his younger daughter to the forest and killed her. When Rihi went looking for her and found her lying lifeless in the forest, she was devastated.

Lasi, a noble spirit, who saw Rihi grieving, took her to an enchanted tree. Rihi used the tree's magic and brought her sister back to life. Alive once again, the younger sister felt thirsty suddenly. Not finding water around, Rihi used the tree's powers once more to turn herself into a lake and satiate her sister's thirst.

Over time, Rihi changed form and wandered the land as a white *mithun* (bison). She finally settled in her present-day location and turned into a lake again.

A symbol of sacrifice and life itself, crossing Lake Rih Dil is considered the most important passage for all souls. While *dil* means 'lake' in the Mizo language, it means 'heart' in Hindi. And strangely, Rih Dil happens to be a heart-shaped lake!

Though moved by Rihi's selfless love, the girl contemplated why so many stories she had heard or read since childhood portrayed stepmothers in a bad light. 'It's quite unfair that all stepmothers are made to appear wicked. I'm sure they're not all evil.'

'Of course they're not. Well, it depends on what the storyteller wants to believe or wants people to believe. Or it could just be a mode of characterization . . . Stereotypes!' Katha shrugged.

'If I ever tell a story about a stepmother, I'll make her nice and kind,' the girl said with an air of certainty. 'Oh, it just occurred to me that

Meghalaya's legend is about a tree that was killed by humans, while Mizoram's folklore remembers a tree that gave life to a human.'

'It's good to see you make these connections. Because storytelling *is* about unlikely connections,' Katha said. 'Now, would you believe it if I told you that somewhere, cotton is related to headhunting?'

Mohini's eyes gleamed with curiosity even as she reined back the question at the tip of her tongue.

Chapter 28

YOU THINK YOU'RE SMART?

Katha almost launched into the next storytelling tradition, but it suddenly remembered a supremely important thing. 'Hey, your time's up. Had you asked me a question by now—*This one was so easy!*—you could've been a free bird. But . . .' Katha shook its head in disappointment.

'Woohoo! I won!' Mohini jumped with joy.

'Okay . . . Looks like you're still reeling from the shock of seeing the tiger.' Katha peered at her. 'For your information, you've *lost*.'

'Nope, I wanted to show you that I could get you to tell me stuff without me having to ask questions. I WON!' Mohini squealed.

'Ah, you're playing games with me.'

'I'm beating you at your own game, Katha! You think you're smart, huh? Well, I'm smarter.' Mohini winked. 'Now that the task is over, you *have* to answer my questions,' she added quickly, for she suspected the spirit might slyly change the rules of its spell.

'I'm a spirit of my word. Ask and you shall seek . . . Let me guess, you want to know about the tiger of Meghalaya.'

'*Sometimes* you're smart.' Mohini laughed. 'So, that tiger wasn't you? As in, you weren't the tiger?'

'Nope.'

'Then who was it?'

'A tiger, but of course!'

'Uff! Was it a tiger or . . . a weretiger?'

'I thought you didn't believe in such *imaginary* beasts?' Katha teased the girl, who scowled in response. 'I have no idea, really. I didn't see its claws or paw prints,' the spirit said honestly. 'A tiger is four-clawed; a weretiger, which is actually human, has five claws. Five fingers and five toes, so five claws—get it? That's how locals differentiate between the two. That's also why the beasts cautiously erase their pug marks.'

Mohini thought about this and announced, 'This tiger was big, very big. It *had* to be U Ryngkew U Basa, the jungle protector!'

'If you insist . . .' Katha said, happy that the girl had begun believing in stories without hesitation or mistrust. 'Here's a treat.' The spirit held out a bowl of broth made of steamed bamboo shoots and vegetables. 'From a recipe quite old, some comfort food for a night so cold!'

'Yummm!' Mohini said with a loud slurp. 'Never thought bamboo would taste *so* good.'

Watching her enjoy her meal, the spirit asked at last, 'Let's have some honesty here, little one. Why didn't you free yourself?'

'I guess I *have* started liking the company of my ethereal friend,' Mohini confessed. From the fantastical realm that Dastangoi had taken her through to the uncanny yet convincing world of Meghalaya's jungle lore, she was somewhat getting an idea of the power of storytelling.

'Is that so?' Katha moaned with much melodrama. 'This calls for a special rhyme, lo:

Dear me! A lovable spirit and an obstinate girl.
Together in a spell caught,
That too, forever!
My head's in a whirl
At this frightful thought,
And how my bones shiver!

Mohini chuckled. 'You don't have bones! Anyway, I've been thinking about something—we're like Vikramaditya and Betaal. We share a love–hate equation, just like they did.'

'What's a Vikramaditya? And who's Betaal?'

Mohini didn't believe Katha. 'You've told me SO many stories and about SO many storytelling traditions. How can *you* not know them?'

'Well, a smart spirit needn't be a know-it-all,' Katha tried to cover up.

'In that case, allow me, O Smart Spirit, to add to your storehouse of knowledge,' Mohini proclaimed playfully. She cleared her throat, took a deep breath and began, 'Vikramaditya was an able king, loved and respected by the people of his kingdom. Once, a sage requested the brave king to bring him a particular corpse for some important rituals. A shrewd spirit called Betaal that dwelled within that corpse had been causing obstacles for the sage. Vikramaditya agreed to help.'

'You think I'm like Betaal, a *shrewd spirit*? Ouch!' Katha touched its heart, pretending to be hurt.

'Wait, wait, there's more . . . The moment Vikramaditya pulled down the corpse, which hung upside down from the branches of a tamarind tree, and heaved it on to his shoulder, the corpse spoke. It was Betaal! To make their journey interesting, for Betaal knew where Vikramaditya was taking him, the spirit told him a story followed by a riddle at the end. If the king solved the riddle, the spirit would soar away. But if he kept mum despite knowing the answer, the king would lose his life. At the end of the first story, Vikramaditya answered the puzzle and Betaal flew back to the tree. The poor king brought the spirit down again . . . and so it happened again and again and again, twenty-three times—'

'Oh, then that's twenty-three stories that Betaal told the king,' Katha interrupted her.

'No, twenty-four stories. After the last story, the king failed to answer the riddle. So the spirit let him carry the corpse to the sage. Including the Vikramaditya–Betaal outline story, they are twenty-five tales in total. That's why the text, written by Somadeva—the one you mentioned when you told me about Tholu Bommalata in Andhra Pradesh, remember?—is called Betaal Pachisi, "Twenty-Five Tales of Betaal",' the girl said emphatically.

'Impressive! I've still not understood how Betaal would get away at the end of a tale, though.'

'Um, okay, let me give you an example.' Mohini thought for a bit, as if recalling something. 'Ah, yes!'

Knowledge and Wisdom

When Vikramaditya was making yet another attempt to carry the corpse to the sage, Betaal began telling him a tale about the sons of a Brahmin.

There was once a Brahmin who had four sons, not one of whom was intelligent. In the hope that knowledge would change them, he sent them to a learned guru. The guru taught them all he knew, including the art of recreating life. The four sons were now ready to return home.

On their way, as they passed through a dense forest, they chanced upon some bones. The brothers decided to test their skills. Their father would be proud to hear about it later, they thought. So the eldest brother assembled all the bones to give the dead being its true form. The second brother used his magic to add flesh to the bone structure. With his powers, the third recreated skin and hair to make the being look exactly like it used to. In front of the four brothers now stood a lifeless lion. The youngest brother then chanted some mystical mantras to breathe life into the animal. No sooner had the lion returned to life, than it pounced upon the four young men, killing them instantly.

Betaal ended the tale there and asked Vikramaditya which of the four brothers was the most foolish. The king didn't want to speak, but not answering meant death. So he told Betaal that the brothers had knowledge, but that they didn't have the wisdom to understand when *not* to use it. While all four were equally stupid, the youngest was the most unwise, because no sensible human would make a dead lion come alive.

Thrilled that Vikramaditya had once again given the right answer, Betaal flew back to the tamarind tree and hung upside down, its wicked cackle filling the eerie night.

'Now have you understood how we are like Vikramaditya and Betaal? You've been telling me about storytelling traditions and have bound me by your spell. Betaal too told tales, entangling Vikramaditya in the web of his riddles!' Mohini's voice was quivering with excitement.

'That's true. But for all your smartness, you've missed one crucial point,' Katha answered. 'After the twenty-fourth tale, their association breaks.'

'Yeah, that's because Vikramaditya was unable to answer—'

'Like Betaal, I too have finished telling you about twenty-four storytelling traditions,' Katha said slowly.

Mohini did a quick mental count. 'You're right. That's so cool! Give me a high five!'

As Katha's palm touched Mohini's, the spirit began fading. 'It's time for us to part too, little one. You did wonderfully!'

The girl had seen Katha turn invisible way too many times. 'Nice try, Katha, but in our case, your spell can't be broken, until I—!'

Chapter 29

IN HIGH COTTON

Mohini froze.

'I TOLD KATHA A STORY! A proper one, without goof-ups or hurried endings.'

The spirit had led her into telling a tale, after all. Her family would've been so happy had they been there. She beamed, thinking about how she had broken the difficult spell. Then she grew sad. Had Katha truly disappeared?

More questions cluttered Mohini's curly-haired head: *Where am I? How will I get home? Are there more storytelling traditions? What about headhunting? How could Katha go away leaving the trail incomplete?* Instead of feeling invincible in freedom, she felt even more helpless.

Rowrr! Rowrr! Rowrrr!

The girl wondered if a jungle dog had sniffed her presence and whipped around to check what beast had found her.

'Up here! Rowrr!' the voice said.

She craned her neck to look up a nearby tree, the morning sun flickering through the leaves and in her eyes. On a high branch sat an enormous black-and-white bird, with beady eyes and a large yellow beak, looking straight at her.

'Lost? Need directions? Some motivation? Rowrr!' The bird flew down to a lower branch.

'Katha, is that you?' Had the spirit come back, having changed form to mislead her?

'Rowwrrr! *Puh-leeze* don't call me funny names! I am the great Indian hornbill.[1] You can call me Tenem, but make sure to remember the "great" part,' the bird introduced himself.

'Oh, hi.' She had met a talking tiger, so a curious talking hornbill was no big surprise.

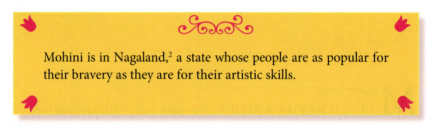

Mohini is in Nagaland,[2] a state whose people are as popular for their bravery as they are for their artistic skills.

Glad to at least know where she was, Mohini was about to ask the amusing bird to help her get back home. But a lilting song distracted her. 'What's that, Great Tenem?'

'I like the sound of *that*. Follow me . . . rowrr!' Tenem croaked, spreading his large wings, and Mohini had to jog to keep up.

The hornbill led her to a clearing, where a few women sat around, simultaneously singing and working.

'Nagaland is home to sixteen tribes of Tibeto-Burmese origin—wonderful, all of them! So, let's see . . . there's the Angami, Ao, Chang, Lotha . . . the Konyak, Rengma, Sumi—they're also called Sema, by the way—and . . . Wait, you don't need to know about all sixteen, do you? Anyway, *these* are Sumi Nagas, a warrrrrior tribe!' Tenem pointed to the women. 'Hear that? They're singing a song called "Ayekuzule".'

'The name sounds so sweet, just like their song. Is the Naga language easy to learn?'

---

[1] The hornbill is admired and revered by most tribes of Nagaland, for it holds a significant place in their culture and folklore. The state even hosts Hornbill Festival, an event during which each tribe presents its multilayered traditions, especially through music and dance.

[2] The name Nagaland is said to have evolved from the Assamese word *nahnga*, meaning 'warriors'.

'Uh, NOPE. 'Cause, well, there's no one language of the Nagas,' the hornbill told her. 'Some sixty—that's right!—dialects are spoken here. Most tribes don't understand another's language.'

Inching closer, Mohini saw that the women were working with cotton, the fibre lying in puffy white heaps in cane baskets. *Is this connected to what Katha had left untold?* the girl pondered.

So she asked Tenem, 'Does "Ayekuzule" have anything to do with cotton?'

'Rowrr! It has everything to do with cotton!'

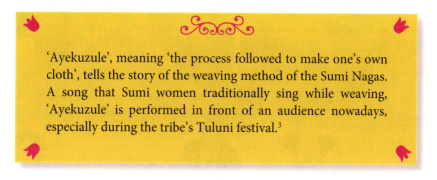

'Ayekuzule', meaning 'the process followed to make one's own cloth', tells the story of the weaving method of the Sumi Nagas. A song that Sumi women traditionally sing while weaving, 'Ayekuzule' is performed in front of an audience nowadays, especially during the tribe's Tuluni festival.[3]

Weaving a Song

'Listen up. So, during a performance, the women demonstrate each aspect of the weaving process . . . rowrr! First, they clear land for farming and sow the cotton seeds, of course. When it grows into an abundant plant—say, about this big—they pick the oh-so fluffy cotton bolls. Girl, do you know how cotton is deseeded? No? By flattening it on a slab of stone! Then it's rolled on to a wooden spindle and spun into thread. After that, the threads are dyed in such beeeeautiful natural colours . . . the loveliest shades, really, before finally being woven

---

[3] This event marks the end of seed-sowing. Weaving begins after the first rice of the season has been consumed.

into cloth. Whoops, almost forgot the finishing touches—cool symbolic patterns are stitched on it, making the cloth ready to be worn!' The bird finished with a dramatic swoop around Mohini, who'd giggled through his crazy narration.

'All of this is done by hand?' She was in awe of the women's skill and strength.

'Yeppity yep. Through "Ayekuzule", the tribe's elderly women—such sweethearts, I tell you!—pass on the knowledge of weaving to young girls. Know why weaving is such an important tradition here? Chiefly 'cause it's related to the Naga custom of headhunting. Rowrr!'

As soon as Tenem had uttered the last word, Mohini knew that Katha, even in its absence, was closing the loop it had begun.

'Headhunting?' she asked to make sure she'd heard right.

'That's what I said! Aren't you paying attention? Headhunting was a ritual practised by some Naga tribes, especially the Konyak. Remember them? When an enemy from another tribe was killed, his head was preserved as a trophy. Awesome tattoos on the face or chest of the victorious warrior also indicated his headhunting achievements . . . rowrr!' Tenem said.

'For some reason, headhunting—collecting heads as trophies—reminds me of the goddess Kali,' Mohini said. 'But is headhunting practised even today?'

'Nah. As with everything, new, less extreme beliefs have replaced these old customs. Now warriors wear miniature pendants that are designed like heads instead. Clever, right? The most common signs of a warrior's feats are still found as motifs on the traditional shawl worn by them, though. These are also handwoven by the tribes' women . . . What a talented bunch!' The bird snapped his beak shut a few times, as if in applause.

'Tenem, I mean, Great Tenem . . . this traditional shawl,' Mohini paused to word her question carefully, 'could it be considered a storytelling tradition?'

The hornbill tilted his head thoughtfully. 'Rowrr! Yes, of course! The textiles of the Naga people differ from person to person, based on their gender, achievements and the tribe or clan they belong to. Some tribes believe that if an undeserving person wears a warrior shawl, he may face illness, or worse . . . death,' Tenem rasped. 'But yes, the motifs do tell stories.'

'Ohh? What signs are found on a warrior's shawl?' Mohini asked, her curiosity undeterred.

'So many, but they are different for every tribe. The Ao, Rengma and Lotha people paint the motifs instead of weaving them—extra information, if you care. Oh, I must tell you about *tsungkotepsu*, the warrior shawl of the Ao tribe. It shows an elephant and tiger, signifying courage; a bison, for wealth; a human head, depicting success in headhunting; and the dao and spear, weapons wielded with pride. Mighty birds, such as the rooster, peacock and yours truly, are also found on the shawl,' Tenem decoded the designs.

'Their attire mostly has only three colours . . . black, red and white.' Mohini turned her attention back to the weavers.

'Oh, you have a good eye! Red stands for blood and war, black for the dark aspects of life and white for peace,' the bird explained. 'In case you're interested, the Ao tribe has a legend related to the hornbill . . . Wanna hear? Rowrr!'

Hanging by a Thread

In Chungliyimti, the first Ao village, lived Longkongla. She was an expert weaver, who had magical powers. One day, as she worked at her loom, she saw a hornbill fly past. When she wished aloud that she wanted to possess one of its feathers, a pretty plume landed near her. Over the next few days, the hornbill feather turned into a cocoon, from which emerged a baby boy. Thrilled, Longkongla brought him up as her own son. She named him Ozukumer, meaning 'one who evolved from a bird'.

Years passed and Ozukumer grew into a handsome lad. With the help of her weaving skills and supernatural powers, Longkongla became rich and owned much land and cattle. Jealous of her wealth, the villagers took away her most precious belonging—slyly, they drowned Ozukumer in a river. A distraught Longkongla believed that her son's death was an accident. But when the boy's friend told her that the villagers were behind this horrific act, she attacked a few of them.

When their angry relatives sought revenge, Longkongla spread a layer of millet around her and sat weaving in the centre. The attackers slipped on the millet, and Longkongla killed some of them with her weaving stick. Things had got out of hand. So she prayed to the god Anengtsungba, who pulled her up, heavenward, by a thread, with the warning that she must not look down till she had reached the god's abode. But the cries of her cattle, who wished to go with her, forced her to glance back at them one last time.

The moment she did that, the thread snapped, and she fell to her death on the *kabusung* tree. Till date, the tree oozes a reddish sap, which the Ao people believe to be Longkongla's blood.

A sub-clan of the Ao called Ozukumer traces its lineage to Longkongla's miracle child.

'It's such a dark tale,' Mohini told Tenem in a quiet voice. 'Longkongla must have dedicated her entire life to weaving, but the thread betrayed her when she needed it the most.'

'You're a bright child. Rowrr!' Tenem said, pulling a Naga shawl out of thin air. 'I must go back to feed my kids, but it was super-duper nice to meet you! Keep this shawl, it will take you to your next destination. Rowrr . . . Goodbye . . . Rrrowrrr!'

Wrapping the shawl around herself, Mohini raised her hand in farewell as the hornbill soared away, his yellow beak stark against the grey sky.

Uncertainty clouded her mind. What would her next destination be? Would it be her home? As if on cue, the shawl suddenly clung to her shoulders and transformed into huge black-and-red wings. The next moment, the girl found herself gliding through the sky, her heart in her mouth.

Chapter 30
TURN OVER A NEW LEAF

The wind seemed to have gone out of Mohini's wings. Dropping at an alarming speed, she saw a large, calm waterbody below.

'No, no, no, please! Not in the water!' she prayed aloud.

Just as her toes skimmed the surface, the Naga shawl steered her towards the shore, much to her relief. The girl sat down on the hot, dry sand, catching her breath and taking stock of her surroundings.

In the distance, the afternoon sun glistened over a striking sand sculpture—that of an animated black face with big, round eyes and a bright-red smile. As she tried to figure out what or who the sculpture depicted, the shawl spontaneously burst into colourful dust and evaporated. But it left behind a small piece of something that Mohini couldn't identify.

Why did the shawl bring me here instead of taking me to Mithika? Maybe Katha's here? I must find it, she deliberated. Then staring at the little sand-coloured object that had appeared in place of the shawl, she grumbled, 'But what do I do with *this*? As it is, I have much to figure out on my own. And now here's another riddle!'

'Did you say riddle? I LOVE riddles. I can help you solve it!' a shrill voice squeaked.

Mohini turned around and spotted a small olive-green turtle, about twice as big as her palm. 'Er, hello, I'm Mohini. And you are . . . ?'

'Oh, I'm Ridley,' the turtle introduced herself.

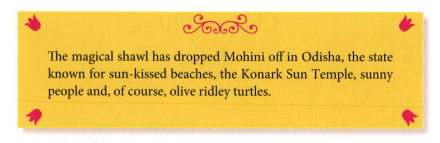

The magical shawl has dropped Mohini off in Odisha, the state known for sun-kissed beaches, the Konark Sun Temple, sunny people and, of course, olive ridley turtles.

'Thanks, but I'm not exactly sure why I'm here. See, I'm looking for my friend Katha,' Mohini found herself saying.

'Ah. What's that?' the turtle asked, staring at Mohini's palm.

'No idea.' She shrugged and waved it about.

'Hey, I know what this is! Maybe it's a clue. Which means, your friend is in Raghurajpur,'[1] Ridley said with certainty.

'How do you know that?' The girl looked flummoxed.

'Simple! This is a piece of dried palm leaf. And people in Raghurajpur make beautiful art such as Tala Pattachitra. I just put two and two together. Let's go now,' Ridley urged.

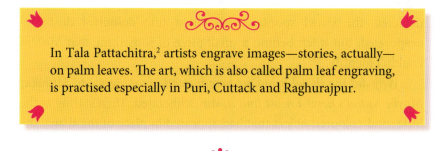

In Tala Pattachitra,[2] artists engrave images—stories, actually—on palm leaves. The art, which is also called palm leaf engraving, is practised especially in Puri, Cuttack and Raghurajpur.

Panels on Palm

'Ask me how Tala Pattachitra is made!' The turtle gently nudged the girl with her head.

---

[1] In this heritage village, almost every house belongs to an artist. Thriving with traditions such as Pattachitra, woodcraft, Gotipua dance and more, Raghurajpur is an art lover's delight.

[2] The name, meaning 'illustrations on palm leaves', has its roots in the Bengali words *tala* (palm), *patta* (leaf) and *chitra* (illustration).

'Tell me, how?'

'Dried palm leaves are cut into rectangular strips, usually about one inch in breadth. Two or more of these strips are glued and then stitched together. The artist then uses a *lekhani*, an iron stylus, to etch images on them,' Ridley eagerly told Mohini as they neared the heritage village.

'For a tiny creature, you know an awful lot,' Mohini said, carefully picking the turtle up and holding her in her hand.

'Oh, I pester my mother with a lot of questions,' the turtle answered sheepishly. Mohini was pleased to know that someone else shared her brand of curiosity.

'You know, Katha told me about Jain manuscript paintings, in which images and text used to be painted on palm leaves. And here, Tala Pattachitra uses engraving,' she recalled, trying to see if she could spot Katha along the way.

'Well, Tala Pattachitra emerged from manuscript writing!'

Thousands of years ago, humans used to communicate by painting or inscribing on stones and cave walls. Then came a time, much before paper was created, when people began using palm leaves for communication.

Kings had their chronicles written on them. Temple priests used them to preserve religious manuscripts. Works in Odia literature were painted on tala too. These were called *chitra pothi*s. With Pattachitra (paintings on cloth canvas) becoming popular around the eighteenth century, artists began painting Pattachitra images on the palm leaf. In time, the idea of engraving evolved.

Layers of a Tale

The two had reached the village of Raghurajpur and were now watching a Tala Pattachitra artist seated on the porch of his home, engrossed in his work. Mohini looked in every possible direction, even inside the house, up at the roof and behind some trees, but Katha was nowhere to be found.

'Do they dip the lekhani in ink and then etch?' Mohini asked, observing the black outlines on some tala artworks that lay nearby.

'I used to think the same till my mum showed me how! No, black ink is rubbed on to the image. The ink settles in the etched lines, making them look darker. The excess smudges are then wiped clean,' Ridley explained. 'For coloured images, pigments made from vegetables and flowers are rubbed on to the engravings.'

'Ah! What's that flap he's making?' Mohini asked, watching the artist slice a semicircle on the palm strip.

'Artists glue together the palm strips, remember? Sometimes they etch on the top layer, make a semicircular slit around it, open it and engrave another image on the layer below. So you see an image on top, open this flap-like slit and another image is revealed underneath it!' the turtle replied.

'Do artists only draw mythological tales?' she asked, noticing that one layer of the flaps showed the *dashavatar*.[3]

'Mostly, yes. Tala Pattachitra tells tales of Jagannath, Krishna, Ganesha and many others. It also depicts nature and wildlife.' With her head, the turtle lifted a flap of the Pattachitra in the making, exposing the engraved image of a butterfly.

Mohini had heard of these gods and themes from Katha, except . . . 'Jagannath?'

---

[3] According to mythology, every time the earth has been taken over by dark forces, Vishnu, who is said to be the preserver of the universe, has appeared in a new avatar to fight them and maintain the balance of good and evil. The ten incarnations of the blue god are referred to as the dashavatar.

'Don't you read? The English word "juggernaut" has its roots in Odisha,' Ridley said with pride.

The Perfect God

In the dense forests of Utkala, in ancient Odisha, lived Visvavasu, the chief of the Savara tribe and a devotee of Nila Madhav. This god's shrine was kept secret from outsiders. But around this time, King Indradyumna saw a dream that Vishnu in his best form resided in Utkala as Nila Madhav. So he immediately sent his aide, Vidyapati, to Utkala to find this form of his favourite god.

To win the trust of Visvavasu, Vidyapati married the chief's daughter. One day, upon being coerced by his daughter, Visvavasu reluctantly led Vidyapati to Nila Madhav's shrine. He kept his son-in-law blindfolded to keep the route a secret. But Vidyapati dropped mustard seeds throughout their journey across the hilly tract. In a few days, when the mustard shoots were visible, he led Indradyumna to the shrine. To their shock, Nila Madhav's image had disappeared.

Divine intervention then guided a sorrowful Indradyumna to Puri Beach, where he found a floating log of wood. Back home began a search for an able sculptor to create the most perfect image of Vishnu from that log. Vishwakarma, the divine architect, appeared in the guise of an old carpenter[4] and agreed to carve out the god's form. But he made the king promise that until the image was ready, the door of his room would not be opened.

When the elderly carpenter didn't come out for many days, Indradyumna's compassionate queen got worried. So the door was opened. But by doing this, the king had broken his promise. And they

---

[4] Another version suggests that the elderly carpenter was Vishnu himself.

found that the carpenter had vanished, leaving behind incomplete images of Vishnu as Jagannath (lord of the universe), Balabhadra (Krishna's brother Balarama) and Subhadra (their sister). These unfinished images have been installed at the Shree Jagannath Temple in Puri.

Once, when the idols were bathed with 108 pitchers of water as per custom, Jagannath and his siblings caught a fever, and they could not make an appearance at the temple. Knowing that lakhs of devotees would be waiting, artists were invited to create Pattachitra images of the three gods. The devotees then gladly worshipped the Pattachitra depictions.

This tradition is followed annually till date. After the idols' holy bath, the paintings, each of which is five-and-a-half feet long and four feet broad, take the place of the gods in the temple for a fortnight. Having recovered completely, when the gods return, they are taken out on a grand procession on chariots, known as Rath Yatra. The word 'juggernaut', derived from the presiding deity's name and which has come to mean 'a huge vehicle' as well as 'a powerful being', was used to describe the enormous chariots of these divine beings of Odisha.

Mohini remembered Indradyumna from the Gajendra Moksham story. But pondering about this tale, she said, 'Art and storytelling are actually *worshipped* here.'

'Yes, and it's amazing how even the half-done image of Jagannath is vibrantly depicted in so many of Odisha's art forms. You saw the sand sculpture on the shore, didn't you?' Ridley asked.

'Oh! That was Jagannath!' Mohini exclaimed, recalling the arresting yet odd-looking figure. She glanced around once more, in the hope that Katha would show up now, but when it didn't, she hung her head in disappointment.

'You'll find your friend soon. Come, now, I'll cheer you up with a riddle!' the turtle said. 'If it hits your eyes, you aren't able to see. And yet you need it to see. What is it?'

'Um . . . Light!' said Mohini, placing Ridley down on a stool.

'Wrong! It's sand,' Ridley said, flapping her arms and, in her excitement, accidentally knocking over a pot of black ink.

'Oh, no! What have you done?' Mohini cried, staring aghast at the spilt ink on her hand—and on the strip of palm leaf she'd been clutching. Frantically, she tried to wipe it clean. And, like magic, a message appeared on its surface:

Look for the sign in the design,
But, first, eat a croissant with jam.
If you still truly wish to find me—then fine!
You must know who I am!

Katha

Just then, a strong gust blew from the east, sending some sand into Mohini's eye. As the girl blinked rapidly, she heard Ridley say, 'Told you I'd solve your riddle for you!'

Chapter 31
A KALEIDOSCOPIC VIEW

When the swirling wind died down, Mohini scanned all around for her turtle friend, dusting her clothes and rubbing her eyes. 'Ridley? We solved the riddle only to face another,' she called out. 'What do you think Katha means? This—wait, where am I?'

Ridley was nowhere to be found; nor was Raghurajpur for that matter. Instead, an imposing red-and-white church with gothic arches stood tall in front of her, the world wearing the colours of a rosy dawn. 'Uh, okay? I barely shut my eyes!' she muttered, confused by the passage of time.

> Mohini has reached a cathedral in the union territory of Puducherry.[1] Earlier known as Pondicherry, the place is also fondly called Pondy by residents as well as travellers.

On her guard, she entered the church with soft footsteps so as to not disrupt the proceedings inside. But not finding a soul there, she relaxed and settled down quietly on one of the benches at the back. As she stared fixedly at the altar, for some reason, her mind returned to Ridley's last riddle. 'How can sand make people see?'

---

[1] The name comes from the Tamil *puducheri*, which means 'a new settlement'.

Before she could arrive at an answer, a splendid patch of colour to her right caught her eye. 'What a gorgeous stained-glass window!' she exclaimed, even as a thought flashed through her brain. '*Of course* sand can make you see! It's used to make glass . . . and some people need glasses to see. Oh, that clever turtle!'

Mohini got up and walked around the cathedral, slowly studying the intricate interiors and striking glass paintings. The more she looked, the more awed she was. 'They tell stories!' she whispered.

'So they do,' came a hoarse response from down the aisle. A frail old man leaning on a walking stick stood at the door, a knowing smile playing on his lips.

He ambled in and knelt down at the altar to pay his respects. At his side, Mohini silently prayed that he would tell her more about the place. And almost instantly, her wish was granted, for the man introduced himself as Mr Verrière and, looking around him, began, 'Long ago, my girl, I used to work in a stained-glass factory.'

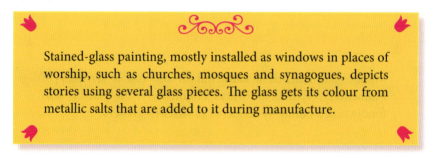

Stained-glass painting, mostly installed as windows in places of worship, such as churches, mosques and synagogues, depicts stories using several glass pieces. The glass gets its colour from metallic salts that are added to it during manufacture.

Fragile Frames

'Making these wonderful windows is difficult indeed. The image is hand-drawn on a large sheet of paper, divided into various parts and colour-coded. Glass pieces of corresponding colours are cut to match the shape of each part and then placed on the drawing,' the old man said, sitting back in a pew.

'That sounds just like a jigsaw. But don't the glass pieces fall off?' Mohini asked.

'No, no—not so easily, my girl! The outlines of the pieces are soldered together with narrow strips of an alloy of lead and tin. And an iron structure holds the painting in the window frame,' he explained. 'Now, tell me . . . did you know that in the Middle Ages, such paintings were called the "poor man's Bible"?'

'Poor man's Bible?' she repeated, unsure if she had heard correctly.

'That's right. Illiterate followers understood Christianity and its teachings mainly through the painted stories of Jesus Christ, the apostles and saints that adorned church windows and ceilings,' Mr Verrière said.

'That's so useful!' Mohini now understood what her G-Ma had meant when she would say, 'Oh, stories are everywhere. It's what you do with them that makes all the difference.' Indeed, some stories teach, some entertain, some make you laugh, some make you think . . .

The sun's rays cast a multihued reflection of a floral stained-glass motif on to the stone floor, making Mohini smile.

'Why, doesn't this colourful reflection remind you of Kolam?' the old man asked her.

'Is that a storytelling tradition too?' Mohini was as inquisitive as ever.

'Oh, yes! Would you like to see for yourself?'

'I would!'

And so they rode on Mr Verrière's cycle, jingling through the quaint streets, and arrived in that part of Puducherry mostly inhabited by Tamilians.[2]

'There!' He pointed his cane towards a street lined with houses, each with pretty drawings just outside their entrance.

---

2   Puducherry is largely divided into two sectors: the French Quarter, where French culture and architecture can be found; and the Tamil Quarter, where Tamil culture is prevalent.

'But . . . that's Rangoli, isn't it? That's what Dad calls it.' Mohini looked confused.

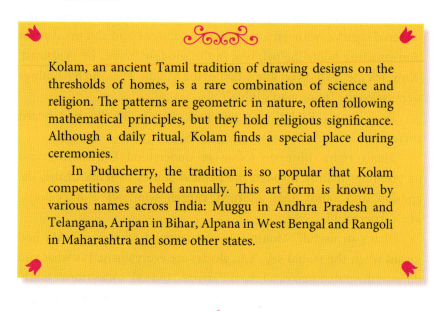

Kolam, an ancient Tamil tradition of drawing designs on the thresholds of homes, is a rare combination of science and religion. The patterns are geometric in nature, often following mathematical principles, but they hold religious significance. Although a daily ritual, Kolam finds a special place during ceremonies.

In Puducherry, the tradition is so popular that Kolam competitions are held annually. This art form is known by various names across India: Muggu in Andhra Pradesh and Telangana, Aripan in Bihar, Alpana in West Bengal and Rangoli in Maharashtra and some other states.

Sacred Lines

'Every morning, before sunrise, women clean the threshold of their house, often using water and cow dung. On the wet mud, they draw Kolam with rice powder. The tradition supposedly gets its name from the Kolam rice[3] that is powdered and used for drawing the designs.'

'Why rice? I thought people used coloured powder,' Mohini wondered aloud as she noticed that some designs were all-white and some, multicoloured.

'Ah, you got me there! Well, these days, people embellish the designs with synthetic coloured powder, but the traditional Kolam of Tamil Nadu is created using rice powder, to feed our winged and crawling friends.'

---

[3] A specific variety of rice consumed by South Indians.

'You mean birds and insects?'

The old man nodded, suddenly patting his stomach. 'Mmm, all this talk of rice and feeding is making me hungry. How about some breakfast?' he said, bringing out two jam-filled croissants from a bag that hung from the handlebar of his cycle.

'Croissant!' Mohini exclaimed, remembering that Katha's note mentioned it. In that case, perhaps the spirit meant that she should look for the sign in the Kolam designs? So she narrowed her eyes and examined the patterns, but there was no sign of Katha yet.

Gobbling his share in no time, Mr Verrière continued. 'Coming back to Kolam then . . . So, another reason for creating it is to keep evil away from homes. You see, it chiefly follows the dots-and-lines principle—a grid of dots[4] is plotted on the floor and loopy or straight lines go around these dots. For evil spirits to not find any opening into the Kolam, and therefore the house, these sacred patterns enclose all the dots. None can be left out!'

Mohini observed a complicated Kolam near her. The old man was right. 'This is fascinating stuff!'

'Sure is. The best part is that several designs can be drawn from the same grid of dots. It's about creativity too!' he said with a toothless grin.

'Oh, I get it!' Mohini's eyes widened. 'It's like . . . the dots are stories and the lines are storytelling traditions. The same tales can be expressed in so many creative ways!'

'That's a brilliant thought, my girl, just brilliant!' he lauded her with a pat on the back.

Drawing Devotion

The white Kolam on the mud-brown earth reminded Mohini of Warli art. 'Is each Kolam a symbol?' she asked.

---

[4] Women draw intricate and difficult patterns, with the number of dots in a grid even going into lakhs.

'Well, Kolam by itself is a sign of auspiciousness. People believe its loopy lines symbolize the cycle of birth and death. Also, each pattern represents a particular deity, or occasion, or season, or day of the week! Most designs are actually prayers in pictorial form. Maybe because it all began with a prayer.' The old man shrugged, growing thoughtful.

The Life-Giver's Request

Long ago, a king who had lost his son prayed to Brahma to revive the boy. Moved by his devotion, Brahma agreed. To correctly recognize the boy he had to give new life to, Brahma asked the king to draw an image of his son on the earth. Once the king drew his son's portrait, the god returned the boy alive and well.

'That is how the earliest Kolam came to be drawn,' Mr Verrière finished.

Mohini recalled what Katha had once told her—'Stories can give life.' At the time, she had not believed it in the slightest. Now she added her own observation to that claim. *Not just stories, even storytelling traditions such as Kolam seem to give life!* But she wasn't so sure of something. 'You said that Kolam usually depicts prayers, but how can a prayer be a story?' she asked.

'Why not? Prayers give you a glimpse into the life of the person who's saying them as well as the gods they are offered to, don't they? See, the Kubera Kolam, drawn to ask for wealth, tells you that the person is in need of money and that Kubera, the lord of riches, can grant the request.'

'Hmm . . . Understood!' Mohini nodded slowly.

'What did I want to tell you next? Oh, yes. Kolam is practised in honour of four goddesses: Bhudevi, the earth goddess, who bears our burden with grace and patience; Tulasi Devi, who protects the household from evil; and the two sisters Sridevi and Moodevi,' Mr Verrière said.

Mohini looked puzzled at the last two names. 'I've never heard of these two deities.'

A Tale of Two Sisters

Moodevi, also known as Jyeshtha,[5] is the goddess of misery, laziness, sleep and poverty. Her younger sister, Sridevi, better known as Lakshmi, is the goddess of riches and prosperity.

Once, the sisters quarrelled about who between the two was more beautiful. When things got out of hand, they approached Brahma, Vishnu and Shiva. As judges, the three gods requested the sisters to walk in front of them a couple of times, so that they could settle the case. The goddesses complied.

Finally, the holy trinity decided that when the sisters walked towards them, Sridevi looked more attractive. But when they walked away from them, Moodevi looked more beautiful. The sisters were happy with this verdict.

---

5   In Hindi, *jyeshtha* means 'elder or eldest one'.

'Huh? What does this story mean?' Mohini asked.

Mr Verrière laughed at her innocence. 'See, it's not really about their looks. Both are gorgeous. Since Sridevi is the goddess of good fortune, she looks pretty when she comes towards you or your home. Moodevi, the goddess of misfortune, looks nicer when she is going away. The three gods just played safe and smart!'

'Ohhh!' Mohini chuckled too, now understanding the tale. 'So the Kolam welcomes Sridevi into homes, but . . . but also acts as a prayer to Moodevi to keep gloom away?'[6]

'You've got it!'

Thinking of both the traditions she had learnt about in Puducherry, Mohini remarked, 'Stained-glass paintings are made once, but they live on for centuries. And then there's Kolam, which one has to create every day.'

'You've got some impressive reasoning skills, my girl,' the sweet old man said, handing her a gift. 'Since it all began with glass—here, remember me by the dance of coloured glass chips!'

'A kaleidoscope!' Mohini was thrilled.

'Pass it on to someone who makes you smile, won't you?' He flashed his toothless grin again and went his way, his cycle tinkling once more.

Saying goodbye, Mohini started studying each Kolam down the street, one after another, more intently. She couldn't decide which one looked prettier, for they were all breathtakingly intricate. But she had another agenda presently. Under her breath, she muttered, 'Where is that sign? *What* is the sign? What if I cannot find it? Will I be stuck in Puducherry forever? Sigh!'

But after several failed attempts at identifying any sign at all, a tired Mohini plonked herself down on the steps of a charming house.

---

6   According to Hindu mythology, when Moodevi and Sridevi emerged during the churning of the ocean, they asked Vishnu where they must stay. Vishnu decided that Sridevi would stay in places that are clean, while her elder sister would reside in unclean surroundings. Hence, Tamil women religiously clean the threshold of their homes and draw a Kolam there.

Absent-mindedly, she began turning the kaleidoscope with one eye shut and the other admiring the beautiful patterns made of the broken pieces of glass. The designs seemed to change from floral stained-glass motifs to geometric Kolam in a brilliant blur of shades. And suddenly, she saw a sign in the design—just as the message on the palm leaf had told her she would! The psychedelic fragments had formed an all too familiar face.

'Katha!'

Chapter 32

NO CHILD'S PLAY

Mohini was out of breath and feeling rather squashed down. Although the journey through the kaleidoscope had lasted merely a second, the suddenness of being sucked in through the eyehole sure had shaken her up.

'Ugh! What is with this teleportation business! Can't I just get to places by bus or something? When I find that crazy spirit, I w-w-w-will—!' Having landed on soft mud, the girl skidded, desperately flailing her arms to find her balance.

'Hey, missy, careful there! You're going to trample me!' said a tinny voice.

Mohini peered at the ground till she found the little thing that had spoken to her. 'You're made of clay!' she exclaimed, as if that were the most bizarre thing she'd seen so far.

'That's mean—I have feelings too, you know? So what if I'm a terracotta acrobat?' the toy spat, poised precariously on a tall clay stand.

'Wow!' Mohini said, bending to get a closer look at the figurine, for she noticed that although he spoke, his face, especially the lips, didn't move.

Attired in splendid green, gold and red and wearing a turban that was a wee bit too large for his head, the acrobat toy too looked her up and down, albeit a little robotically. 'So, you must be the toymaker's new helper?'

'Uh, no . . . not really,' said Mohini, distracted by the colourful array of clay playthings all around the open courtyard, which seemed to be the toymaker's workshop. A potter's wheel lay at a distance; some toys and urns stood basking in the noonday sun; yet another set of dolls waited near a brick wall for a final coat of paint.

Hearing the acrobat click his tongue impatiently, Mohini tore her eyes away from the scene and explained that she was on the trail of her friend, a spirit called Katha.

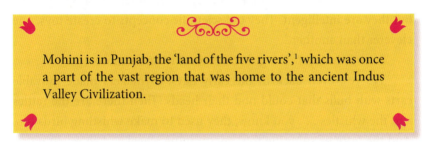

Mohini is in Punjab, the 'land of the five rivers',[1] which was once a part of the vast region that was home to the ancient Indus Valley Civilization.

'What are you called, by the way?' she asked the clay toy.

'I told you, jeez . . . I am an acrobat!' the boy repeated.

'Shush, silly billy! That's not what she wants to know,' chided another toy, a woman dressed in a salwar kameez, with a dupatta covering her head. She sat near the acrobat, working on the charkha. 'He is Shararati—I gave him that name because he's so mischievous,' she said, answering Mohini's question. 'And—'

'She's Soni, a complete know-it-all!' piped Shararati.

'Don't mind him. We are the folk toys of Punjab,' Soni told the girl proudly.

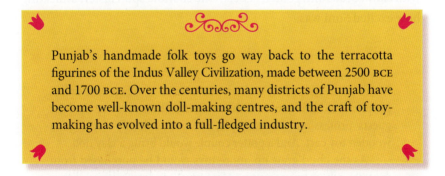

Punjab's handmade folk toys go way back to the terracotta figurines of the Indus Valley Civilization, made between 2500 BCE and 1700 BCE. Over the centuries, many districts of Punjab have become well-known doll-making centres, and the craft of toy-making has evolved into a full-fledged industry.

---

[1] In Punjabi, *panj* means 'five' and *aab*, 'river'.

Moulding Mud

'Whoa! The craft is more than 4000 years old?' Mohini was stunned.

'Yes-yes,' Soni said. 'You know, toymakers might be simple people, but they are intelligent. They use scientific concepts to create toys, one cleverer than another.'

'Science in toys?' The girl was curious to know more.

'Yes-yes, even back in the early days, toymakers made movable carts with bulls that could nod their heads. Then there are the rattles and the whistles . . . you know, they used to make whistling birds too. And the *lattu* or spinning top, my spinning wheel and so much more. Now, don't all these items function using science?' the woman asked.

'I'd never thought of it like that,' said Mohini, realizing how the science of movement, sound, weight and more was a major factor in making toys. 'Hey, Shararati is only made of clay, but you've been decorated with cloth,' Mohini said, suddenly noticing the difference.

'Do NOT compare me with her!' the acrobat rocked to and fro agitatedly.

'Don't listen to him. He's just jealous,' the clay woman retorted. 'Toymakers use clay, wood, cloth, cotton, hay, even paper to make playthings. Some are painted. Others, like me, are fancier dolls adorned with cloth, beads and golden tassels.' The charkha spun faster, indicating how excited Soni was.

Many years ago, when a child was born in a village in Punjab, people would bring toys for the newborn. These toys matched the guests' professions. For example, a carpenter family would gift a wooden toy cart. And a potter couple would bring a clay doll.

As the child grew up, more toys would be purchased from the fairs, which were thronged by toy sellers. But today, children prefer factory-produced plastic playthings over handmade toys.

Mohini understood that the way kids played sure had changed over time. 'So there's a story to every toy,' Mohini said.

'Yes-yes. I tell the tale of the love that Punjab's women have for spinning. They talk and laugh as they sit with the charkha, which is like a friend to them,' the woman explained.

'How I wish I could spin yarn like you do,' Mohini said, spontaneously using a pun. *Oh, why didn't these smart lines come to me in Katha's presence?*

Figures of Faith

'I don't know about this storytelling business, but I do know that folk toys play an important role in festivals and customs,' Shararati offered.

'Oh?'

'Yes-yes. Just before Diwali, Khiloniyanwala Bazaar[2] and Mishri Bazaar[3] in Amritsar are laden with new playthings and treats. There are models of Krishna that show how the waters of River Yamuna rose to touch his feet, pretty Ganesha and Lakshmi idols and, of course, edible sugar toys,' Soni added.

'You mean there are playthings that can be *eaten?*' Mohini wasn't sure she'd understood correctly.

'Yes-yes, Diwali celebrations here are incomplete without *khand khidone*,' the woman said. 'They come in sooo many shapes—elephants, rabbits, fish, even houses.'

'*I* wouldn't want to be eaten. No way!' Shararati complained.

'Just ignore him,' Soni replied.

'I really like Diwali,' Mohini said, bemused by the duo's interaction right from the start.

'Yes-yes, us too. Diwali plays an important role in Sikh history. This was the day when Guru Hargobind,[4] who had been held captive in Gwalior

---

[2] The toys market.
[3] The sweets market.
[4] The sixth guru of Sikhism, who came to be known as Bandi Chhor, or 'liberator'.

Fort, returned home. So Sikhs celebrate Diwali day as Bandi Chhor Divas, literally meaning "the release of the detainees",' the woman revealed.

Mohini found it fascinating that people residing in the same country celebrated the same festival for different reasons.[5] Walking through the rows of clay items now, she remarked, 'Toymakers and potters must be so proud to see their pretty urns and dolls when they're ready.'

'Oh, yes! Our toymaker beams every time he sees *me*,' Shararati said in a bid to irritate Soni, who chose to ignore him as always.

Mohini smiled. She was just about to study the carvings on a terracotta lattu when it slipped from the shelf—but thankfully landed on a cushion below. 'Phew! That was close!'

'We're pretty for sure, but you've just reminded me about a funny folk tale that speaks of our fragility,' said Soni.

Mohini sat down on the floor to listen, perching the acrobat on her knee so he could do the same.

A Good Sale

A potter and a farmer once hired a camel together to carry their respective goods to the market on time. On one side of the camel, the farmer firmly attached his bundle of fresh vegetables. On the other, the potter loaded his clay wares.

Throughout the journey, the greedy camel kept turning towards the vegetables, even managing to eat some of them. The farmer had to constantly scold the animal and guard his goods. The potter had a good laugh at this and mocked him, saying that the farmer may have nothing

---

[5] Diwali is more widely celebrated to mark the return of Rama, Sita and Lakshmana from their exile of fourteen years.

> to sell by the time they reached the bazaar. And that between the two of them, the potter would surely make a better sale.
> When they reached the bazaar, the mahout directed the animal to sit so that the goods could be unloaded. But, with some of the vegetables having been eaten, the weight on both sides was unequal. The camel lost its balance and tripped, crushing all the pottery under its body. And so, while the farmer still had some vegetables to sell, the potter was left with nothing.

'Ah, interesting!' said Mohini, placing Shararati where he had been. Just then, a booming baritone sounded from behind her.

'All these greedy camels give us good camels a bad name!' The source, she saw, was a clay camel with golden harnesses and a patterned rug on his back.

'Yes-yes,' Soni said, laughing. 'Where will you go looking for your friend now?' She turned to Mohini.

Before the girl could answer, the camel on the floor grunted in surprise, suddenly realizing he could move his neck. And then, his feet! 'I can swish my tail, move my jaws and bat my eyelids too!' he exclaimed.

The other clay toys gasped in unison. And then, with faint plops, the camel grew larger and larger, eventually resembling the real animal—hair, hide, everything. 'Hey, look at me!' he whooped.

'I think it's your friend's magic,' Shararati noted confidently. 'Perhaps Pushkar, our camel buddy, might be able to take you to the spirit? Go on, hop on his back!'

'Yes-yes, do listen to him. This time, he's right!' Soni conceded gladly.

And so, Mohini clambered on to the camel's hump and bid adieu to her little clay friends.

'Where to?' she asked her ride.

'Wherever my feet take me!'

Chapter 33
FAR AND WIDE

Mohini had dozed off on Pushkar's back, unable to keep her eyes open through the night. The camel was still galloping at full speed when the ground beneath changed to loamy sand, the fine grains spraying to the side with every stomp. The air became sultry; the morning sun, harsher. Vast dunes lay in ranges as far as the eye could see.

'This feels fantabulous!' the camel shouted, grinning toothily at his new form. 'Thank you, Mohini!'

'You should thank Katha, actually. I bet this is the spirit's magic,' she said groggily, patting the camel's neck. 'Any idea where we are?'

'Let's ask around,' the camel suggested, spotting a desert couple walking towards them.

The man, dressed in a red tunic, pyjamas and turban, was carrying a large carpet-like roll over one shoulder. The woman, wearing a colourful blouse, ghaghra and a dupatta that covered her head, held a musical instrument in one hand and a cloth bundle in the other. The two stopped when they saw Mohini, and the man shouted, 'Who goes there?'

The girl told them that she was looking for a friend, not mentioning that the friend was a spirit. Pushkar too thought it wise to keep mum in front of the strangers. Something told them that not all humans would understand spell-weaving spirits and yapping animals.

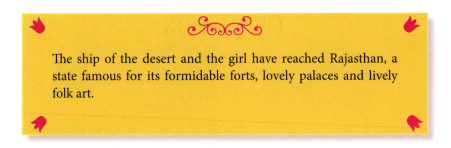

The ship of the desert and the girl have reached Rajasthan, a state famous for its formidable forts, lovely palaces and lively folk art.

'I'm Kanhaiya Lal and this is my wife, Roop Devi. We are heading to a village nearby to read the Phad. Come with us. Someone there should be able to help you,' the man said.

With the girl and the woman riding on his back and the man walking alongside, the camel trotted through the new terrain.

'Uh, what is a Phad?' Mohini broke the silence after a while.

'*This* sacred scroll,' Kanhaiya Lal said, pointing to the large roll. 'We are from the Nayak priest community. People call me *bhopa* or *bhopo*, and my wife, *bhopi*. We're wandering storytellers,' he explained.

Mohini's interest surged at the last word and she let her face show her keen curiosity. Also, after her parents, this was the first time she had come across a storyteller couple!

The journey was long, and the bhopa couple was only too happy to talk about their work.

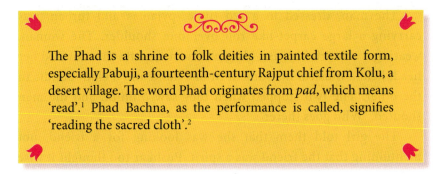

The Phad is a shrine to folk deities in painted textile form, especially Pabuji, a fourteenth-century Rajput chief from Kolu, a desert village. The word Phad originates from *pad*, which means 'read'.[1] Phad Bachna, as the performance is called, signifies 'reading the sacred cloth'.[2]

---

[1] It is also said to mean 'folds'.
[2] The performance or reading is in Rajasthani dialects.

Reading a Cloth

'Pabuji is revered by Rabari camel herders. So we travel from village to village, carrying Pabuji's temple, which is the Phad, to these worshippers. We then sing and narrate episodes from his life to the tune of a stringed musical instrument called the *ravanhatta*,[3] the man began.

'Won't it be easier to build a temple and tell tales there, instead of travelling with a cloth shrine?' Mohini asked.

'But we are nomads! Does it make sense to build a stationary shrine if we are always on the move? Also, not everyone here worships Pabuji. So we'd rather take Pabuji to his believers,' Roop Devi explained.

'That's right. The Phad is kept rolled during daytime and is unfurled only at night to be erected at a spot, which has to be swept clean and made sacred by touching a piece of gold to the ground. When we unroll the Phad, you will see that the story is not painted in sequence. The duty to narrate the tale rests with us for we know how,' the bhopa said.

'But why isn't it painted in order?' Mohini asked.

'Well, you see, while painting, the artists usually divide the Phad into four major episodes from Pabuji's life. But the supposed random order of the panels allows us to move along the length of the cloth during the performance. So when the bhopa sings about each episode, pointing with the ravanhatta bow, I cast light on the corresponding panels in the painting,' the bhopi answered.[4]

'Oh! How long is it?' the girl asked, indicating the scroll, which she saw had several coils.

'A Phad can be around twenty feet long and five feet broad,' Kanhaiya Lal said, smiling and fully expecting to see the surprise in the girl's eyes. 'Narrating the entire tale usually takes more than five days, so we stick to the important events from Pabuji's life.'

---

[3] The ravanhatta is believed to have been created by Ravana.
[4] There are portions of the act in which the bhopi sings while the bhopa plays the musical instrument.

'Whoa! How do you even paint such a large narrative scroll?' the girl asked.

'We don't. We commission artists called *chiteras*[5] to do so,' the bhopi replied.

A Painted Shrine

'Ganesha, the elephant-headed god of storytelling, writing and all things creative, is usually painted in the first panel,' Kanhaiya Lal continued. 'The protagonist, Pabuji, occupies the largest panel in the scroll. Most of the figures are drawn in profile, be it Pabuji, Dhadal, Kelam, even Ravana—'

'Ravana in Pabuji's Phad?' Mohini was confused. The name had made Pushkar curious too, but he continued to trot quietly.

'Oh, you'll know when we narrate it tonight,' Roop Devi assured her.

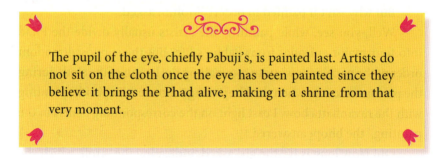

The pupil of the eye, chiefly Pabuji's, is painted last. Artists do not sit on the cloth once the eye has been painted since they believe it brings the Phad alive, making it a shrine from that very moment.

'Only twelve or so Phad artists remain in the world today,' the bhopa said, directing the camel towards a village that was visible from Mohini's perch.

'Why so few?' she asked with concern.

---

5   Phad chiteras are usually from the Joshi community. They were originally *jyotishi*s or 'astrologers', who drew horoscopes.

'Quite a few reasons actually. But if you ask me, it could be because the artists never really taught the art to their daughters—although, traditionally, the first brushstroke of a Phad is painted by a young girl of the family,' he told her.

'They have now started teaching not just their own girls, but outsiders as well. It's a good thing. It's the only way to preserve this tenth-century storytelling tradition and its stories,' the bhopi said.

'Hold on . . . If Pabuji belonged to the fourteenth century, then how can the art form be older?' the attentive Mohini asked.

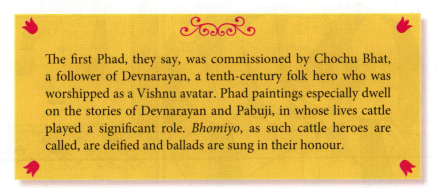

The first Phad, they say, was commissioned by Chochu Bhat, a follower of Devnarayan, a tenth-century folk hero who was worshipped as a Vishnu avatar. Phad paintings especially dwell on the stories of Devnarayan and Pabuji, in whose lives cattle played a significant role. *Bhomiyo*, as such cattle heroes are called, are deified and ballads are sung in their honour.

'Cattle hero?' Mohini—who only knew hero and superhero—didn't quite understand what this term meant.

The bhopa nodded seriously in response. 'But you know, not all bhomiyos are bestowed with this honour and affection. Pabuji, for example, dedicated his life to the protection of cattle. That's why he is so popular and widely worshipped through Phad.'

By the time they reached their destination, the sun was dipping below the horizon. The couple immediately got busy with setting up the shrine in an open space. The villagers trickled in slowly but surely. Soon, there was hardly any space to fit any more people, yet more came. And when the Phad was finally unfurled and a conch sounded, everyone watched with utmost reverence. The girl and the animal couldn't take their eyes off the huge painted tapestry that was teeming with bright figures and action-packed scenes.

'Gorgeous!' they exclaimed together, before Mohini shushed Pushkar, reminding the animal that no one should hear him talk.

As Kanhaiya Lal began playing the ravanhatta and narrating from the Phad and Roop Devi lit up the matching panel, the magic of the story gripped the audience. The famished girl watched eagerly, while relishing the bajra roti and ker sangri[6] that the bhopi had given her earlier.

From Lanka to Rajasthan

Pabuji was born to Dhadal Rathore and a celestial nymph named Kesar Pari. Due to certain circumstances—and that's another story altogether!—Kesar Pari left Pabuji in Dhadal's care, promising to return to her son in the form of a mare years later.

Pabuji grew up to be a strong man. As he went off to fight battles, he was accompanied by his four associates: Rajputs Chando, Dhebo and Salji, and Harmal, a Rabari. On one such expedition, he saw a beautiful mare called Kesar Kalami with the goddess of Kolu, Deval. He promised to protect Deval's cattle in exchange for the mare, for she was indeed his mother, Kesar Pari. The goddess agreed.

Around this time, Pabuji had agreed to give his dear niece, Kelam, a unique wedding gift—she-camels from Lanka. So he first sent Harmal to Lanka, to survey the region and find out about the red-brown camels there. Armed with information that Harmal gave him, Pabuji and his forces rode into Lanka, where battle ensued for the ownership of the she-camels. On the field, Pabuji killed the demon king of Lanka, Ravana, with a spear. That is how he brought the very first camels to Rajasthan. Being a just hero, he gifted half the herd to Kelam and the other half to Harmal.

---

[6] A Rajasthani speciality made from the berries of the native ker tree and the slender beans (sangri) that grow on the khejri tree.

> The epic of Pabuji does not end here and continues to recount his various adventures and the many 'cattle battles' that he fought, which made him the hero he is today. In fact, the Rabari community, to which Harmal belonged, are camel herders to this day. They believe that Pabuji protects their cattle and so are the primary audience of Phad Bachna.

It was nearly dawn when the arresting performance ended, leaving Mohini with the additional revelation that Pabuji had let his arch-enemy, Jindrav Khichi, take his life. As the crowd scattered in twos and threes, Mohini and the camel followed the bhopa couple to the house they were being hosted in. The two chatted about the show in excited whispers, till Mohini finally asked, 'Why did Pabuji let Khichi kill him?'

'I bet you'll get confused if I tell you,' the bhopa said.

'No, I won't!' she insisted.

'All right, then. Some say Pabuji is an incarnation of Lakshmana, Rama's younger brother. One version of the Ramayana suggests that Lakshmana had killed Ravana, not Rama. So it was destined that in their next life, Ravana would kill Lakshmana. Khichi is believed to be Ravana reborn,' Kanhaiya Lal explained as simply as he could, spreading out a mat on the porch of the host's house.

Mohini's head spun. 'B-but Pabuji already killed Ravana to secure the she-camels!'

'Actually, he had attacked a place called Lankesariyo, which was believed to be somewhere near River Sindh. The king who ruled over this region was so evil that he was compared to Ravana. This parallel, over time, led to people referring to the place as Lanka and its king as Ravana,'[7] Roop Devi said, adjusting her pillow and getting ready to wind down.

---

[7] Phad paintings depict this ruler with ten heads, clearly emphasizing his likeness to Ravana. Often, Hanuman's meeting with Sita in Lanka is also illustrated in this section.

'So confusing!' Mohini complained.

'Tell me about it! I thought I was a clay toy made in Punjab. Now, according to this story, my ancestors came to Rajasthan from Ravana's Lanka—oh, sorry, from Lankesariyo, whose ruler was like Ravana!' Pushkar hissed softly, sitting down on his haunches under a banyan tree that shaded the porch.

'Oh, and why did he bring only she-camels?' Mohini turned to ask the bhopa couple, but they were so tired that they had already gone to sleep. Standing under a dim lantern, she recalled what G-Ma used to tell her. 'You can't have all the answers when *you* please!'

Sulking nevertheless, Mohini walked away and plonked herself down on the mud floor, resting her head against Pushkar's flank. Before the sun could peep out and announce the morning, both of them had dozed off.

Chapter 34

FAITH CAN MOVE MOUNTAINS

'Pushkar, why is your hide so hard and cold? Icy cold! Brrrr . . .' Mohini shivered as she rubbed the sleep from her eyes. But neither the camel nor the bhopa couple was around. The girl was not even in Rajasthan! 'Oh, not again!' she wailed.

Tall, pointed, snow-painted peaks rose all around her to touch the azure sky. Mohini found herself on the slope of one of these steep mountains, somehow, and thankfully, in trekking gear. 'Okayyy . . . is no one else around?'

Just as she began to feel a ball of panic rising in her throat, she noticed a strange-looking creature watching her from the intimidating mountaintop. Something about its calm manner made the girl slowly trek towards it. Although it was a strenuous climb, she seemed to be moving up rather effortlessly and quickly. When she reached the summit, she came face-to-face with the peculiar creature, who had waited patiently under the morning sun for her arrival.

It had a large, roundish head with pointy ears and globular yellow-and-black eyes. Its body was covered in snow-white fur—Mohini had never seen a purer white. It had a curly, vibrant mane that was turquoise in colour, just like the hair on its tail and near its paws. Despite its fangs and bright-pink tongue, Mohini was unafraid, though she didn't know why.

'Welcome, friend! I am Seng-ge,[1] a snow lion,' the creature said, baring its canines in a positively cheery smile. 'You may have never seen my kind before, have you?'

---

[1] In the Tibetan language, *seng-ge* means 'lion'.

Now, Mohini knew the Asiatic lion, African lion, liger, tigon, even the snow leopard. But what was a snow lion? 'H-hello,' she mumbled.

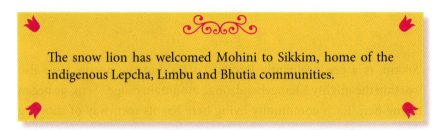

The snow lion has welcomed Mohini to Sikkim, home of the indigenous Lepcha, Limbu and Bhutia communities.

'Sikkim? Now don't tell me this is—'
'The Khangchendzonga,[2] the third-highest mountain in the world!' the snow lion announced.

'WOW, I scaled *this* mountain? Ma and Dad will never believe it . . . Why, even *I* don't believe it!' she chirped. 'Okay, wait, *why* am I here?'

The snow lion raised its paw solemnly. 'Katha wanted me to tell you my story.'

'You know Katha?' *That means I'm on the right track!*

'Oh, yes, we're old friends.'

'Where is it? Is it here?'

'No, you must find it.'

'Yeah, I already know *that*. Do you know who Katha is? Can you tell me?' Mohini asked, hoping the riddle Katha had posed for her would be answered.

But the snow lion said, 'I do . . . And *eventually*, so will you.'

'Hmm . . .' Mohini figured she had to wait to know the answer. So she decided to focus on the present. 'Dad has told me a bit about Sikkim, yet he never mentioned a snow lion.'

---

[2] The locals believe that their deity, Dzo-nga, resides here. The name of the mountain is more commonly spelt as 'Kanchenjunga'.

'Maybe because it's a matter of faith,' the creature said.
'Huh?'

Strong as a Lion

'Sikkim is a predominantly Buddhist state, but the people here also worship the mighty Khangchendzonga mountain range,' Seng-ge began telling her. 'Each community living here has its own way of showing their respect for these mountains. The Bhutia community, for example, performs an entertaining masked dance called the Khangchendzonga dance or Singhi Chham.'

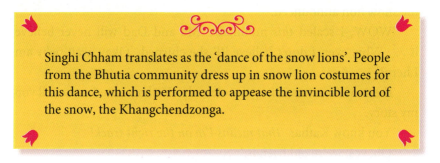

Singhi Chham translates as the 'dance of the snow lions'. People from the Bhutia community dress up in snow lion costumes for this dance, which is performed to appease the invincible lord of the snow, the Khangchendzonga.

'But why worship a mountain?' Mohini queried.
'One important reason is that the people hope the mountain range will spare them a thought before sending down a rumbling avalanche. You know, a single avalanche can sweep everything out of its way and leave behind a blanket of destruction and death!' Seng-ge said with a shudder.

Mohini peered down the deep gorges around, realizing how much power the mountains must have over life in the ranges. Perching gingerly on a rock, she decided not to move much, lest she dislodge a tiny pebble and cause a snowball effect.

> In the eighth century, Guru Padmasambhava visited Sikkim. To preserve the positivity of the place, he meditated in the four corners of the region. He hid Tibetan Buddhist wisdom here, for he knew that worthy followers would find them one day.
>
> Like he had foreseen, monks Lhatsun Chenpo, Karthok Rikzin Chenpo and Ngadak Sempa Chenpo acquired these teachings when they reached Sikkim in the seventeenth century. Together they chose Phuntsog Namgyal to be this Buddhist territory's monarch and had several monasteries built throughout the region. Today, there are around 200 Buddhist gompas that uphold the faith and continue to teach Padmasambhava's ways.
>
> As a mark of honour, a grand 135-foot-tall statue of Padmasambhava watches over Sikkim from Samdruptse Hill. It has been designed to look like two snow lions are supporting the structure.

Demanding yet Dainty

Suddenly, a man in colourful brocade clothes jumped out from behind Seng-ge. And further down the mountain track, she saw two more snow lions. Only, they looked different.

The man in the satin-and-silk attire announced the start of the performance and began moving slowly, waving the scarf in his hand and hopping in a circular motion on one leg. Mohini and Seng-ge watched together, the snow lion explaining the dance to the girl in whispers.

'Singhi Chham begins with the entry of a herdsman,' Seng-ge rasped. 'He controls and directs the dance of the two, sometimes four, snow lions.'

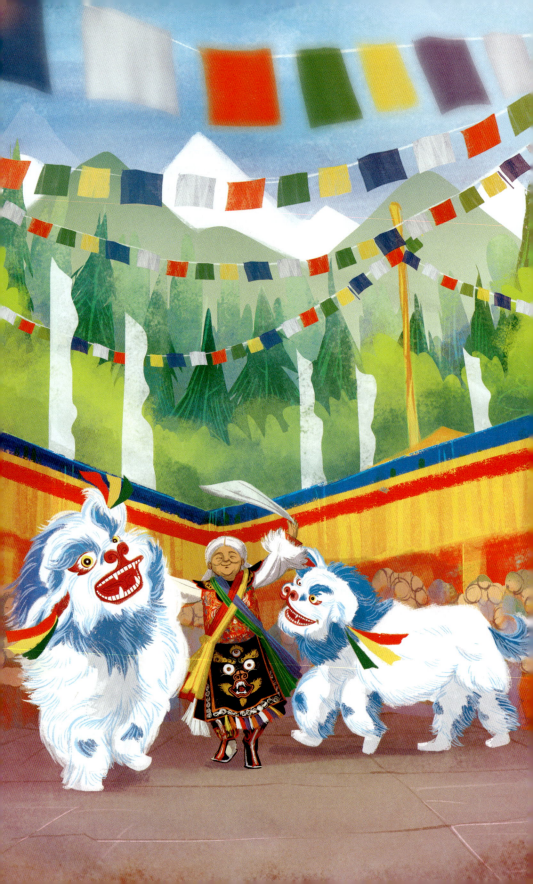

'Now I get why they don't look like you! Those are just *people* in snow lion costumes. You're the *real* deal, aren't you?' Mohini said, her eyes travelling from Seng-ge to the dancing snow lions and back again.

'Am I?' Seng-ge smiled mysteriously as the costumed snow lions tapped their feet, jumped up and down, twirled around and rolled over on their backs.

'Pretty acrobatic! Wait . . .' The girl leaned forward with narrowed eyes. 'Hey, it can't be one person in that costume walking on all fours . . . those snow lions look much bigger!'

'Wise, very wise!' The snow lion beamed at Mohini. 'There are two people inside each snow lion costume. One dancer's legs become the animal's forelegs and those of the other dancer, who stays bent throughout the performance, become its hind legs. Imagine how difficult it must be to hold these postures and mimic a lion's body language . . . twitching the head, scratching the ears, batting the eyelids!'

'They're adorable!' Mohini clapped her hands. 'But Seng-ge, what do Buddhism and Padmasambhava have to do with Khangchendzonga and snow lions?'

The Lion, the Faith and the Mountain

For a long time, the lion has been celebrated as the king of all wildlife. A king is not just a symbol of power, but is also responsible for the protection of his people. Borrowing from this thought, Buddhism represents Shakyamuni Buddha[3] as Shakya Seng-ge or Shakya Simha, meaning 'lion of the Shakya people'. And so the Buddha is often portrayed as seated on a throne held up by eight lions.

---

[3] Gautama Buddha was actually a prince of the Shakya clan, but he became a muni, or 'sage'. Thus, he also came to be known as Shakyamuni, meaning 'sage of the Shakya clan'.

> The snow lion, a mythical animal, is a Tibetan Buddhist icon, along with the dragon, tiger and garuda. Known as the 'four dignities', each of them stands for a set of Buddhist qualities. The snow lion rules over mountains and is a symbol of happiness, goodness and boldness.
>
> But just like the turquoise-maned white snow lions, the snow-topped mountains with their hints of blue have been watching over the people of the land and preserving their happiness. It is said that this is because Guru Padmasambhava commanded the Khangchendzonga mountain range to protect the people of Sikkim. Fierce and playful at the same time, the five peaks of the range together resemble the legendary animal. While the people look up to the mountain as their presiding deity, they have made the snow lion the state's cultural mascot.
>
> Singhi Chham is an ode to this mystical connection between the faith and the mountain.

'Mind-boggling how all the dots are connected in this art form!' Mohini exclaimed, impressed. 'But Seng-ge, I can see you . . . even touch you,' she said, gently patting the snow lion's thick mane. 'Then why do you call yourself mythical?'

'The snow lion is a story as strong as faith,' Seng-ge said, its tranquil smile crinkling its eyes.

'You're a story?' asked Mohini, for she wasn't sure of how to interpret faith.

Seng-ge nodded. 'I am only as real as you think me to be.'

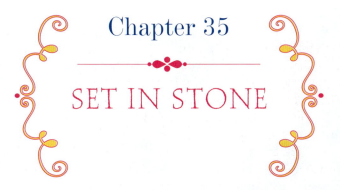

Chapter 35

SET IN STONE

'The fastest way to reach the base of the mountain is to slide down this trail. Don't worry, I'll be watching over you,' Seng-ge had said in parting before leaping away.

Had the snow lion not come across as a serious and kindly sort of creature, the girl would have thought this was a joke. So, putting all her faith in the Khangchendzonga, and Seng-ge, Mohini poised herself at the edge and gave herself the slightest push.

Sky and clouds and mountains became one as she slid down swiftly and smoothly, the biting wind lashing at her face. When she slowed down, she saw the whiteness of snow had given way to a stony grey. And she finally came to a stop at a spot that looked hard and uncomfortable but felt cushioned when she landed on it. Something else was different too—she was in her regular clothes again, which had flecks of ice that were now melting fast.

'Oh!' she gasped when she looked up at the vibrant structure in front of her. 'What a splendidly colourful tower!' The temple entrance was the picture of hustle and bustle—eager kids dragged their parents in by the hand and groups of elderly women ambled in, even as priests hurried past everyone.

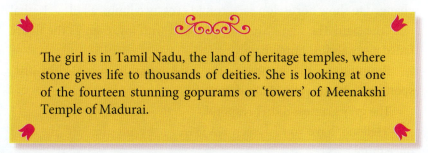

The girl is in Tamil Nadu, the land of heritage temples, where stone gives life to thousands of deities. She is looking at one of the fourteen stunning gopurams or 'towers' of Meenakshi Temple of Madurai.

A few metres from the gopuram stood an elephant, her body covered with chalk drawings. As Mohini studied the designs, the pattern changed to show horns, lop ears, round eyes, two limbs, a tail . . . Katha!

'The sign! The sign!' Mohini whooped with joy, even as the figure faded away almost immediately.

Running to the elephant, she said breathlessly, 'Hello-I-just-spotted-Katha-in-your-chalk-drawings!'

The grey giantess didn't respond.

'Hellooo, have you . . . seen KATHA . . . by any chance?' she tried once more.

Nothing. The elephant continued to relish the bananas at her feet.

Uh-oh, what if this creature isn't a talking one, wondered Mohini, now too used to the absurd to remember the 'normal'.

Finally, Malligai, the temple elephant, turned to face her. 'Sorry, I don't like talking while savouring my favourite food. So what were you asking? Oh, yeah, I don't know who this Katha is, but I, Malligai, can tell you about the tales hidden in the land's temples, starting from here,' she trumpeted, happily swinging her tail. 'This is a nine-storeyed *rajagopuram* or "grand tower", of which there are three more in the complex. This one depicts 1011 tales from the Puranas, while the tower at the southern end of the temple has 1511 characters.'

'No wonder the designs are so intricate!' Hooked, and convinced that Katha would have wanted her to listen to what Malligai had to say, Mohini decided there was no harm in staying here a while.

'Usually temples are built in a specific location, but Madurai is a city that was built around this temple. Isn't that amazing?' the elephant continued, leading her through the entrance.

As they walked around the sprawling temple complex, from one mandapam (hall) to another, Mohini once again understood the potential her stone story had had—the one that had made her leave home. She stood in one spot and was mesmerized by the magnificence of what had been created out of mere stone. Malligai, in the meantime, was gladly indulging a child who had offered a banana in exchange for blessings.

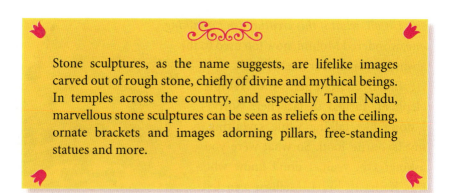

Stone sculptures, as the name suggests, are lifelike images carved out of rough stone, chiefly of divine and mythical beings. In temples across the country, and especially Tamil Nadu, marvellous stone sculptures can be seen as reliefs on the ceiling, ornate brackets and images adorning pillars, free-standing statues and more.

Houses of the Divine

'So, what do you think of my temple?' the elephant asked when she saw the little girl's jaw drop while gazing at some of the carvings.

'It's splendid! All the sculptures are almost in the same colour—grey-brown—and yet each one looks so different,' Mohini noted upon seeing that the figures inside the temple were in stark contrast to the explosion of colours along the height of the tower.

'That's right. More than a thousand years ago, the temples were built using only soapstone, sandstone or granite,' the elephant answered. 'You know, in the olden days, temples also served as a status symbol for the reigning king. And so dynasties commissioned temples to be built.'

'Oh! So, in a way, telling stories in stone made kings feel powerful,' Mohini remarked.

'You could say that. The grander the sculptures, the bigger the reputation of the temple and the royals who had them built. In Tamil Nadu, the Pallava, Chola and Pandya dynasties left their own stamp on architecture and sculpture,' Malligai explained.

> The making of the temples and sculptures took decades, even an entire lifetime. From architects and supervisors to masons, sculptors and artists, everyone resided at the temple site once a king or patron commissioned it.

A passing priest offered a bunch of bananas to Malligai, knowing her weakness only too well. Sharing a few with Mohini this time, she gulped down the remaining.

'You know, ancient scriptures explained how the temples should be built and the statues and memorial stones should be sculpted,' the elephant told her.

'Memorial stones?'

Malligai pointed her leathery trunk to a blank wall in the complex. 'Watch!' the pachyderm instructed as images appeared on it.

Remembering Heroes

'Centuries ago, when livestock and cattle were the lifeline of rural Tamil folk—which they still are—battles used to be fought over these animals. People from neighbouring regions conducted cattle raids in particular villages, and those who died defending their land and livestock were upheld as heroes,' the elephant explained.

'Cattle heroes! I get it now!' Mohini said, remembering Pabuji's Phad.

'That's right. These heroes were honoured by the villagers by erecting *nadukal* or *veerakkal*, "hero stones" that told the story of the brave martyrs.'

'And these were constructed according to what the ancient texts said?' Mohini clarified.

'Exactly. I've heard that villagers chose a suitable rock, prayed to the spirits that may be residing in it to leave it immediately and then ferried it to the village. There the rock was immersed in water for a set number of days. After that, it was brought out for sculpting,' Malligai said.

'Was the hero's story carved as pictures or text?' the curious girl asked.

'Well, both. The stone usually bore an image of the heroes, along with an inscription narrating the story of their life. Sometimes even animals and birds were featured on these hero stones,' the elephant trumpeted, expressing her delight.

'Eh? Did *they* protect the cattle too?'

'They would assist the hero in battle, yes . . . or they were like this rooster,' Malligai said, indicating the fowl's image on the wall, 'which represented its village during traditional rooster fights.'

Mohini was amused as well as amazed at the contents of the memorial stones.

'Once the stone was ready, it was erected at an appropriate site. People then lit lamps, and offered *naivedyam*[1] and prayers,' the elephant continued. 'Another interesting aspect of stone sculpting in Tamil Nadu is the creation of the images of village deities, such as Ayyanaar.'

'Who?'

Guardian of the Night

The myth of the folk god Ayyanaar is deeply mysterious. Some say that he was a tribal chief. Some think of him to be the same as Ayyappan, the god who was born to Shiva and Vishnu, when the latter had taken on the form of a beautiful damsel, Mohini. Others believe his worship is rooted in pre-Vedic pagan practices.

---

[1] Sacred food offering made to a deity; in this case, a memorial stone.

> Ayyanaar, a fierce and brave god, is said to protect villages and its inhabitants from invaders, demonic spirits, as well as natural calamities. Along with his entourage of twenty-one gods, armed with weapons, Ayyanaar rides on his white horse through the lanes at night to keep vigil. By summoning rain, he also ensures the villages have plenty of water and a good harvest. Locals believe he resolves household problems and fulfils wishes too.
>
> Being a village deity, Ayyanaar's statues are normally found near a tank or pond or at the boundary of a hamlet. Offerings to this powerful protector and his accomplices are usually in the form of terracotta horses, which the Velar potters[2] craft with much devotion, to help him in his night-time travails.

Mohini sat deep in thought about how people worshipped protectors as folk deities and also prayed to nature and gods to win their favour. Her eyes brightened at a memory. 'You know, my grandma used to say, "A hero can be idolized, and God is a superhero anyway." Maybe this is what she meant.'

Malligai affectionately touched Mohini's head with her trunk. 'I have to go now, young Mohini. The devotees are waiting to say hello to me—with a basketful of ripe bananas, of course! Come back and visit me whenever you like!'

As the girl waved enthusiastically at the animal's lazily retreating figure, a sheet of paper flew into her raised hand.

Is it another clue from Katha? she wondered. 'Nah, this is just a painting of some women playing polo!' *Sigh! How can I forget what Katha had said when I struggled to decipher the Madhubani Tree of Life? Could this really be 'just a painting' now?*

Even as she stood under the dusking sky, giving the picture another good look, the world seemed to whirl around the girl and her feet were on new soil once again.

---

[2] Members of the Velar community also act as priests in Ayyanaar's shrines.

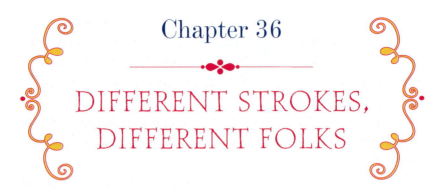

Chapter 36

DIFFERENT STROKES, DIFFERENT FOLKS

'What a relief!' came a shaky voice.

Mohini spun around to see a stately old lady tottering towards her with a hand on her hip. Watching her approach, Mohini thought she was the picture of opulence—an expensive-looking printed sari draped traditionally, gold-rimmed glasses perched on her nose, a dozen diamond-studded bangles around each wrist, *kundan jhumka*s dangling from her ears and a large rose sitting pretty in her neat bun.

'I was trying to straighten this painting, when a strong breeze knocked it straight out of my hands! But I'm glad you caught it before it could fly into the swimming pool. Thank you, stranger,' she said, gently removing the painting from Mohini's grip.

'You're welcome. This is . . .' Mohini trailed off, studying her new surroundings.

'You must be here to see the art exhibition, of course. I'm Gulrukh, the curator.' The old lady smiled, pointing to a gallery behind her.

'Erm . . . no, I'm actually . . . uh, looking for my friend,' Mohini confessed hesitantly.

'That's all right too. Come on, wait inside. Hyderabad is just sweltering at this time of the year—even in the evenings. Oof!'

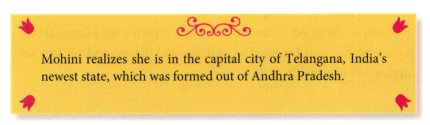

Mohini realizes she is in the capital city of Telangana, India's newest state, which was formed out of Andhra Pradesh.

'Maybe I should find Katha instead of whiling away time inside this gallery!' Mohini mumbled to herself when the lady had walked away. But as she turned to go, she had an afterthought: *No, wait. There must be a reason I was brought here, right? What if Katha has hidden a message or the sign in those paintings?*

So the girl decided to check, starting with one on her right. 'Come on, show me your goofy face now,' she muttered while studying the figures carefully.

Gulrukh had been watching the girl curiously after having installed the rescued painting firmly back in its place. Walking over, she tapped Mohini on her shoulder, asking, 'What are you doing?'

'I-I—am just l-looking for something in the p-painting,' she blurted out.

'Well, you'll need this.'

Mohini stared at the object in her palm. 'A magnifying glass . . . Huh?'

'These are miniature paintings. You need a magnifying glass if you want to see the details,' the curator explained with a grin.

Mohini now looked at the same painting through the glass. 'Whoa! I can see almost every brushstroke!'

'Now, that's the magic of miniatures,' Gulrukh told her.

Miniature comes from *minium*, the Latin word for red lead, which was commonly used for works of art in medieval India and elsewhere. With the introduction of paper, artists began creating detailed illustrations on sheets. Often these were painted with a single-hair brush. So the royals had to hold the painting in their hand and view the fine strokes under a magnifying glass. The colour red and the relatively small size of the paintings together gave them the name 'miniatures'.

In India, four major miniature painting styles have developed: Mughal, Deccani, Pahari and Rajasthani.[1] The one that flourished in the Deccan Plateau (which comprises present-day Telangana), under the patronage of Deccan sultanates, is called Deccani painting.

---

[1] Apart from these, manuscript painting styles also come under miniature paintings.

Royal Landscape

'Deccani painting evolved here in the sixteenth century and it slowly became popular in Bijapur, Golconda, Ahmednagar and subsequently Hyderabad. Between the late sixteenth and the early seventeenth centuries, Mughal miniatures were being encouraged in northern India by Emperor Akbar,' Gulrukh explained.

Mohini remembered that Akbar had commissioned the retelling of *Hamzanama* in the Mughal miniature style. 'So if Deccani is just one kind of miniature painting, how is it different from the rest?' she asked, walking down the gallery and looking at the paintings on display.

'I'll show you. See, Deccani painting was influenced by a number of other styles. Turkish artists who came to the Deccan are believed to have introduced calligraphy into it. They also added pretty landscapes with lilac-hued hills. Then the Iranians brought with them the use of gold in the paintings. From Mughal miniatures, Deccani painting is said to have borrowed the idea of creating portraits and depicting historical events. And since it all happened in India, you will find mythological scenes and gods and goddesses too.' Gulrukh's bangles clinked softly as she pointed towards examples of each characteristic across the hall.

'So it's made up of many parts, and yet it has its own identity. All the—Oh!'

Suddenly, in the middle of that bustling exhibition in a land she had never travelled to, Mohini was faced with the most obvious solution . . . *Could it really be that simple? She too could learn from the storytellers in her family and the ones she had met, but still be a unique storyteller herself!*

Subjects of Opulence

'Ha ha, you seem awfully happy,' the old lady said, watching Mohini hug herself and grin from ear to ear.

'Wha . . . Oh, right. I'm sorry, please go on!' Mohini said, trying to return to the present moment. 'I was just about to say that all these paintings look so rich.' She noticed that many of the displayed art works showed the royals having a good time.

'Oh, yes, they are! You know, some of these colours were produced from precious gems! Deccani painting is about all things exquisite—royalty and deities, music and the arts, nature and architecture, mythology and mysticism,' Gulrukh listed.

'Mysticism?'

'Despite their love for glitz and glamour, the Deccan sultanates also commissioned portraits of ascetics,' she said, pointing to a painting that depicted a sadhu.

But something else had caught Mohini's attention. 'What's this?' It was a most startling painting, showing a woman talking to and feeding snakes!

'A Ragamala painting,' the lady answered. 'The Deccan sultans were fond of music. And Ragamala paintings visually depict Indian classical music ragas. Usually, there's a nayaka, "hero", and a nayika, "heroine". The setting shows the season or time when the raga must be sung,' the curator explained.

'What an idea, drawing an image of music!' Mohini laughed.

'You've got it. The woman in this painting, Asavari ragini, symbolizes the raga by the same name, which is part of snake charmers' melodies.'

'Fascinating! What about this one?' Mohini asked, pointing to the very painting that had flown into her hand at Meenakshi Temple.

'Ah, yes. So, Deccani painting is famous for depicting the freedom and authority that women had in those times,' the curator continued. 'Look around, there are paintings of women riding horses, talking freely to their confidantes, going on hunts with men and playing indoor games and outdoor sports. This painting,' Gulrukh's eyes twinkled as she paused, 'gives us a glimpse of the life of Chand Bibi.'

The Lone Queen

Chand Bibi or Chand Sultana was the courageous and beautiful queen of Ali Adil Shah I of Bijapur (in present-day Karnataka). She knew multiple languages, was an arts and sports lover, a competent leader and a war strategist. After the demise of her husband, she became regent of both Bijapur and Ahmednagar (in present-day Maharashtra).

When Akbar and his son Daniyal attacked Ahmednagar, she ably led her army and defeated the Mughal emperor's forces. Unfortunately, rumours spread that the queen was a traitor, on account of her decision to negotiate with the Mughals later on. And her angry troops themselves killed Chand Bibi.

> A famous Deccani painting shows Chand Bibi playing *chaugan bazi*, or polo, along with other princesses. The bold yet delicate work is a reminder of the power and position the warrior woman once enjoyed.

The story had made the girl sad. 'Hmm . . . All these leaders and protectors—I mean, kings, queens and even gods—must have had such a tough time deciding what's right and what's not. Because so many people look up to them!'

'True, and sometimes people bring down the ruler out of love for their land, as in Chand Bibi's case. And sometimes, the ruler must destroy the land for the sake of the people,' the curator added.

Before Mohini could ask her what she meant, Gulrukh excused herself to welcome some guests who had just arrived. As her figure blended into the crowd of people, Mohini turned to observe the painting of the ascetic that the curator had spoken about earlier. Her mind wandered to where her feet might next. *Where should I go?*

Just then, the girl thought she saw the ascetic's eyes swivel in their sockets.

'I must be tired,' she mumbled, without bothering to look closely. But Katha's face now peeped from behind the ascetic's, clear as day. 'There it is!'

And with a barely audible squelch, the painting pulled her in.

Chapter 37
WHAT'S IN A NAME?

Mohini landed on her behind with a thud. 'Oww!' The scenery was nothing like she'd seen in the painting. The terrain was rocky, yet grassy in large patches. 'Okay, looks like I've time-travelled again,' she said, noticing the golden-red sunrise.

'Kathaaaa!' she called out as loudly as she could, when an irate voice hissed, 'You must *look* before you shout.'

The moment she saw who it was, Mohini stammered an apology, 'I-I-I am r-really s-s-sorry. I didn't see you . . . P-please don't c-curse me!'

The sadhu, who was doing a headstand, opened his eyes. 'Why would I curse you?'

All the stories that Katha had told her ran through Mohini's petrified brain. 'B-because I disturbed your penance . . . but unknowingly,' she clarified.

The sadhu only smiled, picked up his staff while doing a double somersault and landed in the cross-legged sitting position. His dark eyes that had a glint of madness, the wild locks tumbling from his head, his stubble, the ash smeared on his forehead in three lines, his armband of brown beads, the snake tattoo above it and the deep vertical cut between his eyebrows together made the girl very uncomfortable.

She apologized again and was about to leave, when she heard a low whisper. 'Mohini—the charmer, the enchantress . . . or should I say, the *charmed*, the *enchanted*?'

'Huh? H-How do you know my name?' the girl asked, sure that this time her knapsack had not given it away.

"You are a seeker. A seeker of tales,' he said, ignoring her question.

A chill ran down the girl's spine.

'Names tell stories,' the sadhu said. 'Just like the name of this place does.'

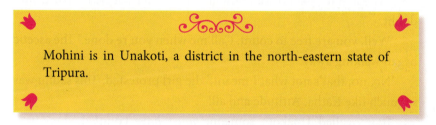

Mohini is in Unakoti, a district in the north-eastern state of Tripura.

'So, um, what story does Tripura tell?' Mohini asked despite her suspicions.

'It tells not one, but many stories. Just like Unakoti.' The elderly ascetic pointed towards a cemented arch in the distance with his staff. Mohini walked through it and was astounded by the sight that met her eyes. Wherever she turned, she saw rock-cut carvings.

'You have an old connection with stories in stone, don't you?' The ascetic smiled cryptically.

Mohini was too stunned to reply.

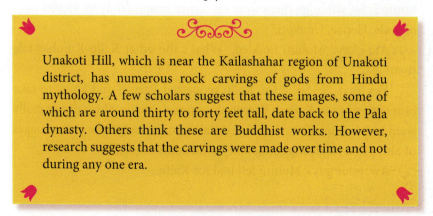

Unakoti Hill, which is near the Kailashahar region of Unakoti district, has numerous rock carvings of gods from Hindu mythology. A few scholars suggest that these images, some of which are around thirty to forty feet tall, date back to the Pala dynasty. Others think these are Buddhist works. However, research suggests that the carvings were made over time and not during any one era.

Let Sleeping Gods Lie

'What does Unakoti mean?' Mohini asked.

'Unakoti translates to "one less than a crore". Apparently there are 99,99,999 rock carvings in this region.'

'Whoa! But *how* do we know it's true?' Her surprise turned into doubt.

'Well, you are free to count. Call me when you're done.' The ascetic began walking away.

'No, no, that's not what I meant,' the girl protested. This sadhu was so much like Katha. Attitude and all!

'If it's called Unakoti, someone *must have* counted, don't you think?' he asked.

Mohini recalled that Katha had told her about there being thirty-three crore gods in the Hindu pantheon. She guessed some things were best left at face value.

'Of the various origin tales, two are related to a local potter and sculptor, Kallu Kumhar,[1] who was an ardent worshipper of Parvati,' the ascetic was saying. 'The first story is that Kallu saw a dream in which he was instructed to engrave images of one crore gods. Kallu slogged and followed the dream's diktat, but right at the end, he carved an image of himself. So, although there were one crore images, only 99,99,999 were of gods. Hence, Unakoti.'

'Ah, okay.' Mohini nodded. 'What's the other Kallu Kumhar tale then?'

'Yes, that . . . So, once, Kallu requested Parvati and Shiva to take him with them to Kailash Parvat, the couple's abode. Shiva didn't really want to take him along, but said if Kallu would sculpt one crore images of Shiva in a single night, then he could come along.'

'Aw, poor guy!' Mohini felt bad for Kallu.

---

[1] In Hindi, *kumhar* means 'potter'.

The sadhu continued. 'The devoted Kallu took up the challenge nevertheless and worked through the night. At dawn, his sculptures fell short of just one piece. So, even though Shiva refused to take him along, that is how the place got its name.'

'You can talk to the gods, but you can't live with them,' Mohini observed.

The ascetic laughed. 'But there's a more popular story of how Unakoti came to be.'

The One Who Was Awake

Once, Shiva and a convoy of 99,99,999 gods (one crore in total) were travelling to Kashi. Passing through a deep forest on Raghunandan Parvat,[2] they decided to rest there that night and resume their journey at the crack of dawn. Shiva warned the group that they must wake up before the first rays of the sun touched the region. Everyone agreed and fell into a deep slumber.

Tired as they were with all the walking, the gods did not wake up as early as planned. Only Shiva was up and about. Annoyed, he cursed them to turn to stone and stay in the forest forever. And so, Unakoti became home to the images of 'one less than a crore' gods and goddesses.

'Uh-oh! All the gods look like their eyes are closed . . . as though they are asleep,' she said, looking around at the rock-cut reliefs. 'What if this story is true?'

---

[2] The region of Unakoti was earlier called Raghunandan Parvat.

'Ah, so you are a believer of stories now. Good, good. But could *this* legend possibly be true?' The ascetic pretended to think while scratching his beard. 'Tell me, who do you think that large image in the centre belongs to?'

Mohini struggled to answer at first, but then she found a clue. The huge face set in stone had a vertical almond-shaped groove etched in the middle of its forehead, indicating the third eye. 'Shiva?!' she sounded both confused and disappointed.

'There are many faces of Shiva here. This is not the only one,' he told her.

'But if Shiva is here, then he didn't leave. If he didn't leave, why were the others turned to stone? If he didn't curse them, because he himself is here, then could the Kallu Kumhar tale be true? But which one . . .' she trailed off.

'You seek too much!' the ascetic observed. 'Stories are not answers to mysteries. Stories build on mysteries. And some mysteries are not meant to be resolved.'

Power of Three

'Is the naming of Tripura a mystery too?' Mohini asked, realizing that places themselves were storytelling traditions as well.

'Oh, it is. And like I told you, there are multiple stories. One says that the state is named after the presiding deity, Tripura Sundari, an avatar of Parvati. A second theory, based on the place's proximity to the Bay of Bengal, suggests that Tripura means "near water".³ But mythology tells of yet another Tripura . . .'

The sadhu was quiet for a long time and Mohini sat pondering over the variety of tales about Tripura's naming. Suddenly, she saw that he was levitating! She stared in utmost silence and awe, even as the agile ascetic, his eyes shut, began narrating a story.

A Killer Smile

The three asura brothers Tarakaksha, Vidyunmali and Viryavana,⁴ all followers of Shiva, prayed to Brahma for immortality; but Brahma refused, reminding them that nothing in the universe was permanent. So they asked for another boon—kingdoms that could only be destroyed by a single weapon, that too, only when the three would be aligned one below another. This wish, Brahma granted.

They hired Mayasura, a master architect and a staunch Shiva devotee, to build the kingdoms. Mayasura created the lands in three tiers: the lowest on earth, constructed entirely out of iron; the central empire in mid-air, built with silver; the topmost in heaven, made of gold. These 'three cities' were called Tripura. Moreover, Mayasura's genius made the three kingdoms move at all times, aligning them only for a single second once in every thousand years. The asura brothers, together called Tripurasura from then on, ruled over a kingdom each.

---

3 In a Tripuri dialect, *tui* means 'water' and *pra*, 'near'. Tuipra eventually became Tripura.
4 Some versions refer to the youngest brother as Kamalaksha.

Seeing that the powerful asuras lived in impregnable cities, the gods felt threatened. They approached Shiva with their concerns. But not seeing the asuras misbehave, he discarded their fears as unfounded. Then they went to Brahma, who reiterated what Shiva had said. They then ran to Vishnu, who understood their plight and suggested that if Shiva was made to believe the asuras were leading a deceitful life, he might listen to them. So, after purposely creating disharmony in Tripura, the gods approached Shiva again. This time, Shiva saw the shameful state Tripura was in and decided to end to it all.

Exceptional war equipment was created to help Shiva wipe out Tripura: Prithvi (the earth) became his chariot; Surya (the sun) and Chandra (the moon), the chariot's wheels; Meru (the mountain) transformed into a bow; Vasuki (the serpent) turned into the bowstring; Vishnu became an arrow; Agni (the fire) was the arrowhead; and Vayu (the wind) was at the tail feathers. But the gods made a big mistake. They thought that Shiva could annihilate Tripura only because of *their* contribution. However, Shiva, who was waiting for the three kingdoms to align, read the gods' minds and only smiled at their naivety.

In an instant, without Shiva having called on the other gods, the three kingdoms began burning. Shocked, the gods asked Shiva for forgiveness and requested him not to render their involvement completely meaningless. Relenting, Shiva then sat on the divine chariot and shot the holy arrow through the three flaming kingdoms.

Mohini now understood that this is perhaps what Gulrukh's parting comment had meant.

'Then Shiva wept for those who had lost their lives. Wherever his tears fell, shoots of a new kind of berry grew. This berry is called rudraksha.[5] Followers of the god, especially ascetics, wear these sacred beads even today,' the sadhu said, even as Mohini stole a glance at his rudraksha armband.

---

[5] Rudraksha means one that is born out of the *aksha* or 'tears' of Rudra or Shiva.

'After the flames of the burning kingdoms died down, Shiva picked up some ash with his fingers and smeared it on his forehead, forming three distinct lines—apparently, these denote the three kingdoms.'

'He's strange,' Mohini said, quietly observing the three-lined ash marking on the sadhu's forehead again. 'First, he smiled. Then, he cried. If he—' She stopped herself, recollecting that all mysteries cannot be explained. And Shiva seemed most enigmatic.

'I was thinking, what if the place is called Tripura because Hindu mythology's holy trinity was involved? As in, Brahma helped create it, Vishnu oversaw how it developed and Shiva destroyed it?' she asked.

At this, the ascetic abruptly got up and walked away. Without turning, he told her, 'Your journey will end where it all began . . . For now, find Sanjhi.'

Mohini hurried after him. 'What's *your* name?' she asked, but he didn't stop to answer.

Just when she had lost all hope of knowing the inscrutable sadhu, his voice quaked from behind the faces set in stone, 'They call me Mahadev!'

Chapter 38

PLACE IN THE SUN

There was a shallow pool of water at the base of some of the Unakoti carvings, cool and crystal clear. Drawing invisible figures on its surface with her finger, Mohini pondered if the sadhu had indeed been Mahadev.[1] Then lying on her stomach and looking at her own reflection, she sighed a troubled sigh. 'I thought I was in search of Katha. Then I figured out I have to *know* who Katha is. And now I have to look for Sanjhi. But *where* do I find her? I don't even know what she looks like!'

Suddenly, at the rocky bottom of the pool, Katha's face—the sign she was looking for—appeared among the ripples, before slowly changing into a colourful painting. Mohini felt inexplicably drawn towards it. And, without sparing a second thought, the girl who disliked getting wet dived headfirst into the pond and grabbed at the painting.

The very next moment, she was spat out by the water and placed all dry on an unfamiliar land, in front of a boy, a few years younger than her, who sat playing marbles by himself. Deciding not to beat around the bush, Mohini said to him cheerfully, 'Hi, my name is Mohini and I'm new to this place. Do you know anyone called Sanjhi? Can you tell me where she lives?'

'Everyone in Vrindavan knows Sanjhi!' the little boy said between giggles. 'Sanjhi is not a girl—it's a way of telling stories.'

'I should've known!' Mohini muttered to herself, deflating. *Where else would Katha hide the sign!*

---

[1] Mahadev, meaning 'great god', is another name for the ascetic god, Shiva.

The girl has reached Uttar Pradesh, a state known for its beauty and poetry, be it through the Mughal heritage wonder, Taj Mahal; the spellbinding Ganga *aarti* at Assi Ghat; or Vrindavan, the land of the divine couple Radha–Krishna.

'Can you take me to someone who can tell me about Sanjhi?' she asked, embarrassed.

'Why, I can tell you myself!' the boy offered, puffing out his chest. 'I'm Gopal and I belong to a family of Sanjhi craftsmen. I've started learning from my father already. When I'm ready to practise it properly, I'll be the seventh generation of my family to do so. Father says that I'll be the BEST!' he rattled on as, clasping Mohini's hand, he led her through the winding lanes to his house.

Deep inside, Mohini wished she too possessed the kind of self-confidence and passion for her family tradition that this boy did. After all, her family had also upheld the skill of storytelling for generations now. Would it die out because of her?

Sanjhi paper art has its roots in the story of Radha and Krishna. While waiting for Krishna at their usual meeting place every evening, Radha would draw Sanjhi designs with flowers and coloured stones. Today, Sanjhi patterns are cut out on handmade paper such that they look like intricately crafted stencils.[2]

---

[2] Sanjhi cut-outs are also made from copper and plastic sheets.

A Spiritual Stencil

'I'm slightly confused. Is Sanjhi the design made using flowers and stones or is it the name given to the paper stencils?' Mohini asked.

'See, the traditional images created with flowers and stones are called Sanjhi. Today, paper stencils are used to make these Rangoli-like designs with coloured powder—on the floor, on the surface of water, even underwater! And they are also Sanjhi. Understood?' the boy explained animatedly.

'Got it. But—'

'Wait here!' The boy ran off to a nearby food stall and brought back an oil-stained paper bag full of snacks. 'Kachoris, bedmi puris[3] and tasty pedhas[4] for us to eat at home later,' he said, his eyes twinkling. 'So, what were you saying?'

'I wanted to know what Sanjhi means,' she said, by now sure that every name had a story behind it.

'My friend's uncle says that Sanjhi comes from the Hindi word *sajaavat*, meaning "decoration". But Father says that the craft is named after the word *sanjh*, which means "evening" or "dusk" . . . the time of day when Radha drew the designs out of her love for Krishna,' Gopal said.

'But Mother has told me another tale. It seems, according to Braj[5] mythology, Sandhya[6] was born out of Brahma's mind as the goddess of dusk. So people worship her in the evening by creating designs with flowers and coloured powder,' he finished.

Mohini was amazed to know that there was a story to even explain why this tradition was practised only during a particular time of the day.

---

[3] Puffed pastry stuffed with a spicy dal mixture. Both kachori and bedmi puri are specialities of Uttar Pradesh.
[4] A popular sweetmeat.
[5] The region around Mathura and Vrindavan is called Braj.
[6] It is believed that Sandhya was also called Sanjhya, and the name was eventually shortened to Sanjhi.

In Braj, a traditional Sanjhi is made with flowers and colours on the floor or in water (inside a shallow basin or on a plate). It evolved into a temple art around the seventeenth century. Only a few temples continue the tradition now, where the design is prepared through the day but revealed only at dusk, after the aarti has been performed.

A Cut above the Rest

Entering the boy's house through a low, arched doorway, Mohini couldn't take her eyes off the beautiful paper stencils that she saw in a corner of the room.

'You know, we make these cut-outs directly on paper—without sketching with a pencil first,' the boy began, seeing the wonder in the visitor's eyes. 'A single wrong cut can spoil the beauty of the whole design. So it takes years of practice.'

'Oh, wow!'

'Father says, "A good Sanjhi craftsman knows how to make the scissors obey him." Believe me, mine do!' The boy grinned wide.

Mohini was completely charmed by Gopal. 'Ha ha, I'm sure! Do you use regular scissors for the cut-outs, by the way?'

'Oh, no. There are special scissors for Sanjhi, which are kept wrapped in a piece of cloth, out of respect,' the boy answered, slowly bringing the tool out to show Mohini.

> The arms of Sanjhi scissors are long and the tips of the blades are curved. This helps craftsmen cut tiny, difficult patterns. The paper is moved around as they cut, so that they can work smoothly in all directions without stopping. To make many identical stencils, they clip two sheets of paper together and cut through them at once.

'Does Sanjhi only tell the story of Radha and Krishna?' Mohini asked, remembering that Kolam wasn't dedicated to any particular deity.

'Well, mostly, because it all began with them. So even the Sanjhi motifs are based on Radha–Krishna stories. You'll find the kadamba tree, below which Krishna used to play the flute . . . and, um, on whose branches he hid the gopis' clothes!' The boy's face turned a delicate shade of pink. 'Anyway, the Tree of Life is another popular theme, because it brings good luck. Oh, snakes are often seen in Sanjhi too . . . like Kaliya, on whose head Krishna danced after subduing him because the snake had poisoned River Yamuna, and Ananta-Sesha, the one Vishnu reclines on.'

Mohini smiled at the mention of this snake, recalling the Raas Leela story that Katha had told her in Manipur.

'Also, since Braj is the land of the Yadavas—cattle herders—cows are *everywhere* in Sanjhi. You know, they are my favourite motif!' From an oak chest, the boy pulled out a transparent plastic envelope, which contained a pretty cut-out of cows that he had created, and shyly held it out to Mohini.

'This is perfect, Gopal!' she exclaimed, carefully running her finger over the design without removing the Sanjhi from the cover.

'Not really . . . there's a mistake. See?' He pointed out a teeny-weeny tear like it was the biggest flaw. 'But Father says I *will* master it some day.'

'Of course, I believe in you!' Mohini said with an encouraging smile.

'Thanks! And then my fingers will create magic, just like Krishna's little finger did.'

A Tussle of Might

As a child, Krishna once saw the people of his village, Gokul, in Braj, ignore their daily chores because they were busy readying things for a ritual to appease the god Indra. He explained to them that what mattered most is that they religiously do their duties of farming, cattle-rearing and managing their homes. Work was worship. So the people returned to their jobs without performing the ceremony.

A livid Indra caused incessant rain and a flood in Gokul. The houses were not strong enough to protect the people from the god's fury. In the heart of Gokul stood Govardhan, a sturdy hill. Krishna lifted Govardhan and rested it on his little finger, inviting the people and the cattle to take shelter beneath it. As they stepped under its shade one by one, the village folk were astonished to see Krishna, who was just a child, lift an entire hill on a fingertip!

For seven days and nights, Indra unleashed his anger through the downpour, during which Krishna patiently held up Govardhan over his people and livestock. At last, Indra accepted defeat. The rain stopped and the sun appeared from behind the clouds. Only then did Krishna ask everyone to go back home, putting the hill back in its place.

Mohini had heard this tale from her G-Ma long ago, but she had not thought much about it back then. 'Look, here's a submerged Sanjhi depicting the same story!' Gopal called out, very slowly turning a water-filled basin in her direction.

The girl was fascinated to see that though the image at the bottom of the basin seemed to move when the water was stirred, the Sanjhi was not disturbed. *Hey, haven't I seen this image somewhere?* she wondered. *Of course! The painting in the pool in Unakoti!* She suppressed a giggle at what was surely Katha's magic at play again.

'There's another method as well,' the boy was saying, 'where the image is formed on the surface of the water instead of underwater.'[7]

'How cool! Sanjhi is just one tradition, but it has so many interesting forms. And you truly are a talented boy,' Mohini said, ruffling his hair.

'Hey, we forgot all about the snacks! Let's eat,' the boy announced.

And so the two ate their fill of fried goodness and chatted some more. Before leaving, Mohini brought out the kaleidoscope that Mr Verrière had given her in Puducherry and presented it to Gopal. 'For the boy with magical fingers.'

He clutched it excitedly and beamed with gratitude.

As sanjh painted the sky a pinkish orange and the clouds formed lilac-grey designs on nature's canvas, a flurry of leaves twirled Mohini around and she was on her own once again.

---

[7] Jal Sanjhi, i.e., Sanjhi created with coloured powder on the surface of water or underwater is practised by very few artists today.

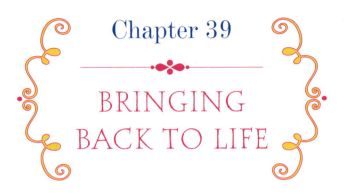

Chapter 39
BRINGING BACK TO LIFE

Mohini sat down to rest under a tree, tired of wandering in a directionless manner. She resolved that she had to end this quest soon. Her heart ached for her parents and she deeply missed her home—even her lost spirit friend.

'So, who is Katha?' She went back to the puzzling question, speaking aloud the answers before shooting them down. 'Is it the spirit of a historian? A teacher, perhaps? Nope, that's not it. Oh, since it keeps changing colours, it must be the spirit of an artist! . . . Nah! Can't be. It has horns . . . A mythical stag's spirit then?'

All of a sudden, a curling tail rolled down from above and a monkey landed on all fours right next to her. Mohini screamed in fright, backing away. The grinning monkey teased her, jumping closer at first, then picked up her unattended knapsack and clambered up to a high branch.

'Thief! Hey, give me back my bag!' Mohini yelled, following the animal up the tree.

The monkey now stood on the very end of the branch, cruelly brandishing her beloved backpack. Mohini leaned forward, not wanting to go nearer, and stretched out her arm. 'GIVE IT BACK!'

And with that, unable to bear the weight, the feeble branch snapped and she fell straight to the ground. 'OW! Ow-ow-ow . . . Just you wait!' Magically, of course, it wasn't a dangerous fall, and she got away with a few bruises.

The monkey only stood coolly beside her, plonked the knapsack down and said, 'Hope you enjoyed the chase!'

'What on—Ouch!' Wincing in pain, she got to her feet and saw that she was no longer in Uttar Pradesh. And it was broad daylight, like the sun had no intention of setting on that long day.

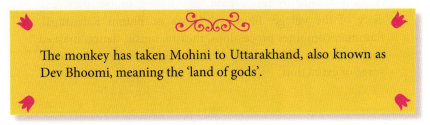

The monkey has taken Mohini to Uttarakhand, also known as Dev Bhoomi, meaning the 'land of gods'.

'Uh-oh! Can't you fall without hurting yourself?' the monkey quizzed as Mohini examined her bruised knee. Without waiting for an answer, the animal bounded away and returned with some leaves. Crushing them in her palms, the primate asked the girl to apply the sticky paste on her bruise.

'No way! That looks gross,' she said.

'I'm your ancestor. Trust me, I know better,' the monkey said, her tone turning grave.

Reluctantly, she complied and a coolness soon spread across her wound, removing a lot of the pain.

'Now, if you could hurry up and follow me—I'm Chanchal, by the way. And we must reach before the festival begins.'

'What festival?' Mohini asked, trying to stand up straight.

'Ramman, of course!'

The monkey hurried on and Mohini limped after her.

Together, We Celebrate

After a short trek, the two reached the open courtyard of the temple of Bhumi Kshetrapal in Saloor Dungra, a village in the state's Garhwal region. Mohini noticed that some sort of a performance was about to begin. More than keen to observe, she found a vantage seat on a slope away from the crowd and sat back.

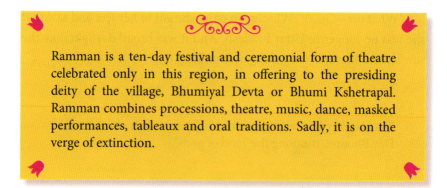

Ramman is a ten-day festival and ceremonial form of theatre celebrated only in this region, in offering to the presiding deity of the village, Bhumiyal Devta or Bhumi Kshetrapal. Ramman combines processions, theatre, music, dance, masked performances, tableaux and oral traditions. Sadly, it is on the verge of extinction.

'Ramman is unique for many reasons. The villagers here organize, fund and participate in this event together. Each community plays a different part in the event. For example, *jagars*[1] are sung by a Rajput community known as Bhalla or Bhalda, while men from the Das community play the drums, and so on,' Chanchal began, perched on Mohini's shoulder.

'That's like one big family!' she said.

'You can say that,' the monkey answered. 'Since the most prominent of these is the enactment of the Ramayana, the tradition was named Ramman after the epic. Apparently, the act comprises eighteen performers portraying eighteen characters while wearing eighteen masks, dancing to eighteen taals and showcasing tales from eighteen Puranas. Scenes from the Ramayana change as per these eighteen taals, which are said to be made up of a total of 324 beats and steps![2] And, before you ask me, no, I've never counted.'

Mohini laughed, for that would have naturally been her next question. 'How do they even calculate while dancing and acting?' Mohini asked.

---

[1] These are ballads, usually sung to invoke gods and ancestral spirits, and include narratives from the Ramayana and the Mahabharata.

[2] Each taal is made up of a set number of beats. Since it is a dance-based performance, the narrative progresses according to rhythm. For example, Rama and Lakshmana's childhood and youth are enacted in the first seven taals, Rama's wedding with Sita and the exile are performed during the eighth taal, and so the sequence changes and goes on till the eighteenth taal, in which their victory over Ravana and the subsequent return to Ayodhya are played out.

'Oh, they have someone keeping track. He ensures that all characters perform perfectly and on beat,' Chanchal said.

Her interest was further roused by the entry of a man wearing a large wooden mask. 'Whoa! That mask looks *heavy*!'

> *Pattar*s, the wooden masks worn in this ritualistic theatre, are created by craftsmen of the Lohar community. The masks usually measure about twelve inches in length and eleven inches in breadth. The ones denoting gods are called *dhyo* pattar, while those of imaginary characters are *khyalari* pattar.
>
> The most auspicious mask, Narasingha[3] pattar, takes about six months to make. Weighing nearly twenty-five kilograms, this mask is worn by a member of the Bhandari community over his head, such that it faces skyward.

Gods in Character

Just as she was trying to digest the information about the masks, she noticed a pole with multicoloured cloth and a mop of black threads fixed at the top resting under a canopy right outside the temple. 'Hey, what's that?'

'Who do you think? That's their god, Bhumiyal Devta! He is kept in the temple only during Ramman; otherwise, the god lives in the house of a villager throughout the year. He promises a good harvest and protects them from hunger,' the monkey said.

Mohini was surprised by this very different depiction of a god. She was too used to seeing gods with faces and bodies, somewhat like

---

[3] In Garhwal, Narasimha is called Narasingha.

humans. And almost all the storytelling traditions she had learnt about had depicted them so. Her attention returned to the performance since the Ramayana act she had been watching changed suddenly. Even day had dramatically transitioned to night. 'Hey, what did I miss here?'

'Nothing. You can't possibly sit here for all ten days. So, I'm jumping ahead in time to show you snapshots,' Chanchal explained, leaping up to grab hold of a nearby tree's branch.

The girl could now see a performer in costume, resembling a tiger, attacking another who seemed to be dressed somewhat like a shepherd.

'Like I told you, the Ramayana is the main act. But the epic's episodes are interspersed with other masked dances,' the primate said, swinging.

> Mwar-Mwarin Nritya shows the dangers faced by the region's buffalo-herding community—wild animals attack them in the jungles when they travel from the plains to the hills to sell milk. Baniya-Baniyain Nritya is about the problems that a merchant couple goes through when they are robbed. Maal Nritya shows the legendary battle between Garhwalis and Gurkhas. Episodes from the Mahabharata and Krishna Leela are part of Ramman too.
>
> No dialogues are spoken throughout Ramman—neither in these performances, nor during the enactment of Ramayana. Tales are expressed only through ballads and dance.

'Ramman ends with Bhumiyal Devta being carried in a procession to another villager's house, where the god will stay until the next

Ramman,' Chanchal finished as a local danced away, carrying the bamboo pole symbolizing the god.[4]

Mohini pondered about how the shrine was brought to the people with the Phad, whereas in Ramman, the god is taken home by the villagers. And then as she met Chanchal's gaze, another thought struck her. 'You know—since we are talking of the Ramayana—when I look at you, I realize . . . Hanuman and the army of ape–men are so important in this whole epic,' she remarked.

The monkey sighed. 'But the people of Dronagiri village in this region are angry with Hanuman. Neither do they have his idol anywhere, nor do they worship him.'

'Huh? Why?' Mohini was shocked.

A Mistake for Life

During the war with Ravana, when Lakshmana was grievously injured, a few medicinal plants were required to treat him. So Hanuman flew to Garhwal, where Dronagiri Hill is situated, to fetch the four herbs: *vishalya karani* (remover of arrows), *sandhana karani* (restorer of the skin), *suvarna karani* (balancer of skin colour) and, most importantly, *sanjeevani* (life-giver that glows in the dark).

But the people of Garhwal refused Hanuman entry into the region, to protect their environment from damage. Hanuman then disguised himself as a sage and pleaded with an elderly woman to show him the way to the hill. Moved by his devotion towards Rama and Lakshmana, the woman guided him to the well-hidden Dronagiri.

---

[4] This gives the impression that the god himself is twirling to the rhythm of the drums.

However, unable to identify the four plants from the several that grew on the hill and not wanting to waste time, Hanuman broke off that half of the hill on which the herbs grew and carried it back. The physician treating Lakshmana found the herbs and healed the prince.

Although sanjeevani gave Lakshmana a new lease of life, Hanuman earned the disfavour of the Garhwali people for tampering with their ecosystem. And because it was a woman who had led Hanuman to Dronagiri, women are not allowed to participate in a ritual during which the hill is worshipped as Dev Parvat.

During a jagar, when the spirit of the hill god is believed to talk to the worshippers through a person, his right hand lies limp throughout, an indication of the lasting damage that Hanuman caused to the hill's right side.

'How can they be angry with a god in this "land of gods"?' Mohini asked, truly perplexed.

'Nature is sacred,' the monkey said, a shadow of remorse flitting across her face. 'Let us not forget that they worship Dev Parvat as well.'

Mohini recalled, 'Though Krishna lifted Govardhan, he put it back in the same place. Could Hanuman have done the same?' Even as she asked the question, she knew there would be no clear answers. What was done was done anyway.

It was nearly dawn. Chanchal let go of the twisting branch and landed right in Mohini's lap, alarming the girl about her injured knee. But she felt no pain! 'Hey, my bruise has healed completely. How . . .?'

The monkey only exchanged a meaningful smile with her in answer, and all she could say was, 'I wish sanjeevani could revive the dying Ramman too.'

Chapter 40

EARN YOUR STRIPES

'Fasten your seat belt,' Chanchal advised her.

'Um, there is no seat belt,' Mohini shot back. 'Are you sure this is a good idea?'

'Trust me, I know better.'

For some unexplainable reason, the monkey believed that Mohini would reach her next destination, whatever it may be, by riding the same branch—what was left of it anyway—that had brought them from Uttar Pradesh to Uttarakhand. So they had walked back to the tree, its dewy leaves glistening under the morning sun. And Mohini presently resembled a witch sitting astride a broomstick.

'Ready?'

'What? No way—NOOOOO!'

The branch shot off like a rocket into the sky. Gripping the splintery branch with both hands, the girl shut her eyes tightly for fear that she might slide off the other end. After what felt like a long while of the harsh wind slapping her face, the branch began descending at lightning speed. Mohini's fingers began slipping . . . the branch started wobbling dangerously—CRASH!

Hurt once again, she sat holding her aching ankle for a while. Then she took in her new surroundings. Wherever she turned, she saw simple mud-walled houses with tiled roofs—but these were no ordinary houses, for they had gorgeous paintings covering the outer walls. *They remind me of Madhubani, but they aren't the same—are they?*

Mohini staggered towards one. A few children, some younger than her and few as old as her, were painting on its walls. As she got closer, she saw that one of them was applying a white coat over old paintings. On the porch sat a middle-aged man, poring over panels of colourful drawings that lay strewn over a cane mat. Many longer, vertical paintings hung behind him from a string, like curtains.

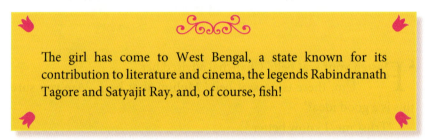

The girl has come to West Bengal, a state known for its contribution to literature and cinema, the legends Rabindranath Tagore and Satyajit Ray, and, of course, fish!

She slowly picked up a painting at her feet, which showed myriad lively fish. It seemed to her that the vividly painted fish were depicting a story. So she examined it carefully, hoping to spot Katha's face hidden in the brushstrokes, like she had in other places.

'Hello? Are you here to do a school project on Pattachitra too?' the man assumed. 'Quite a few students stopped by last week—isn't that so, kids?' The children eyed the girl curiously and nodded.

But Mohini hadn't noticed, for another thought occupied her mind. 'Pattachitra? But this doesn't look like the ones I saw in Odisha.'

'Ah, yes. The name is the same, but the art isn't,' the man revealed.

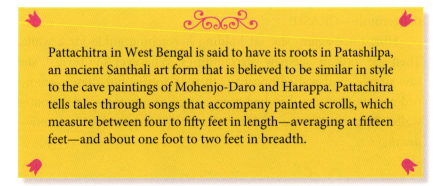

Pattachitra in West Bengal is said to have its roots in Patashilpa, an ancient Santhali art form that is believed to be similar in style to the cave paintings of Mohenjo-Daro and Harappa. Pattachitra tells tales through songs that accompany painted scrolls, which measure between four to fifty feet in length—averaging at fifteen feet—and about one foot to two feet in breadth.

The Ancestor of Television

'We Pattachitra storytellers are called *patua*s,'[1] the man began. 'Since the thirteenth century, or even before that, patuas have been travelling from one place to another, performing stories from the scrolls. Not all patuas could paint earlier, but because these illustrations have become the face of our tradition, now every patua paints too. We've even added the word "chitrakar", meaning "illustrator", to our first names. So people call me Barun Chitrakar, and my wife, Nagma Chitrakar.'

'Interesting! These scrolls look like comics—actually, like scenes from a television show or a movie,' Mohini pointed out.

'Why wouldn't they? Pattachitra is the ancestor of television!' Barun Chitrakar said.

'Oh? What do you mean?'

'In earlier times, when a patua and his troupe[2] arrived in a village or town, people gathered around and listened to them respectfully. They even hosted the whole troupe in their houses for a few days. From zamindars and forest guards to British officials, everyone was a fan of Pattachitra,' he said with a nostalgic twinkle in his eyes. 'We do go around in troupes even now, but it's not the same. People's interest in Pattachitra is wavering.'

'Because of television!' the girl exclaimed, seeing the connection clearly. She had never thought that television, which she and her friends couldn't imagine life without, could have affected a storytelling tradition.

---

1   Patuas are also called *patidar*s, *paitkar*s and *chitrakar*s.
2   A troupe traditionally had ten or more members, including both male and female storytellers. Often, they belonged to one family.

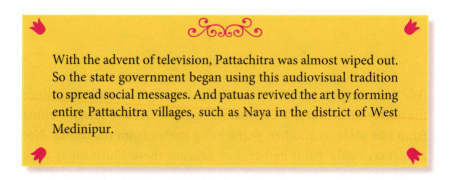

With the advent of television, Pattachitra was almost wiped out. So the state government began using this audiovisual tradition to spread social messages. And patuas revived the art by forming entire Pattachitra villages, such as Naya in the district of West Medinipur.

'So why does a painting style of West Bengal have the same name as that of one in Odisha?' Mohini asked, still confused.

'That's because both paintings use *pat*, or cloth canvas. See, paintings are done on paper and then stuck on cloth.' He showed Mohini the cloth glued to the back of a painting. 'But beyond that, both art forms are very different. In our Pattachitra, there are three types of pat: *chouko* or *choukosh* pat is square and has a single image; *arelatai* pat is a horizontal scroll held by two bamboo sticks at either end; *jodano* pat is a vertical scroll that is created by sewing several sheets of illustrations one below another. These stories are then sung,' the patua explained, handing her an example of each type of pat.

'Ah, okay. Do patuas draw first and then come up with a song or—' Mohini asked.

'Um . . . yes, but some of us choose a theme first, then compose the song. Based on that, the illustrations are created,' he said. 'During a performance, we unfurl the scrolls and narrate the tale panel by panel. This narration is done through *pater gaan* or "patua's song".'

'Understood. And each person in the troupe plays a different character from the story, right?'

'Right! But if a single patua performs the entire tale, voice modulation becomes very important,' the patua replied.

Patuas really did seem like all-rounders to Mohini.

The Making of a Storyteller

'Those children . . . What are they painting on the walls?' Mohini asked, pointing at them.

'Pattachitra is a patua's identity! Without the art, we are nothing. So we train our children from a young age by making them paint on the walls. They whitewash the walls, their canvas, and then start again with new images,' Barun Chitrakar said proudly.

'Oh, so the white paint is like an eraser. How clever!'

The patua nodded. 'Every weekend, the family's children are taught various aspects of storytelling—how to think up a story or theme; how to write songs, compose music and sing it; how to find and mix colours; and how to paint and preserve Pattachitra.'

Mohini was starting to see similarities between her family and that of the patuas. Suddenly, the fortnightly Story Hour made a whole lot of sense. 'What kind of stories do patuas tell through Pattachitra?' she asked, looking at the variety of illustrations around her.

'Oh, so many! Pattachitra has no boundaries when it comes to storytelling. Mythological tales such as those of Savitri–Satyavan, Manasa Devi, dashavatar, Yayati, Shalivahana and Kamala Kamini. There are origin tales of the Santhal community. Contemporary stories such as India's freedom struggle and the French Revolution. Social themes like deforestation, global warming, natural disasters. Lastly, there's *pashu* katha or "animal tales",' Barun Chitrakar trailed off.

'Animal tales?' Mohini grew more curious. G-Ma used to tell her fables while oiling and combing her curly hair. It had been ages since she last heard one.

After a sweetly worded request, the patua took the painting of the many fish from Mohini's hands and, introducing it as one of the most popular Pattachitra stories, struck up a Bangla song in his high-pitched voice.

A Dramatic Wedding

A fish couple was getting married and all species had been invited, except the big fish, for they feared it would prey upon the wedding party.

A small fish said that it would play the drums; two others offered to lift the palanquin in which the fish couple was seated; yet another offered to sing and dance. But just as the mood got merrier, the big fish arrived without invitation, having found out that it was excluded from the guest list. As punishment, it threatened to eat all the fish present there. There was complete chaos, and the atmosphere turned frightening as the big fish opened its mouth wide and was about to swallow a few guests.

The smaller fish chose situational wisdom: they apologized to the big fish and invited it to the party. Having calmed down, the big fish too joined in the celebrations and the wedding took place with no further interruptions.

A riot of colours, this story is usually depicted on a choukosh pat. Titled *Maachher Biye* in Bangla and *Machhli ki Shaadi* in Hindi, it literally means Wedding of the Fish.

'How cute is that!' Mohini grinned. 'But it's tragic too.'

'And relevant. West Bengal is close to the Bay of Bengal. Thus, fish is an important theme and so is water,' the patua said, opening up a long jodano pat.

The Water Monster

It was a normal day in 2004. People were going about their work as usual. Little did they know that their lives would turn topsy-turvy in a few seconds.

The next moment, a gigantic wave—a tsunami—swallowed up their world. Those who fled to higher ground escaped. But not all were lucky. Houses were washed away; so were trees and animals. The wave dragged back hordes of people along with it.

> A 110-year-old man lamented that he had never seen such a thing in his lifetime. Everyone prayed to Goddess Ganga, who was seated atop her vahana, the *hangur* (Ganges shark), to stop this water monster.
>
> Rescue operations went on for days. Journalists reported the destruction, and people elsewhere watched the news on television in horror. It worried everyone that the after-effects of this tsunami would be difficult to bear.
>
> The painted scroll depicts the tsunami as a water monster with bloodshot eyes and fangs, preying upon innocent and helpless living beings.[3] The narration also seems to indicate how the television was able to report the calamity live. Patuas, on the other hand, could tell this tale through Pattachitra only much later.

Mohini thought about how the pat honestly depicted the role that its rival, the television, played in today's world. Then her mind wandered to a connecting thread. 'Both stories are about the strong and the weak,' she said, at which Barun Chitrakar only smiled.

As they sat in silence, staring at the setting sun, Mohini realized that Pattachitra had shown her the other side of the same tsunami tale, which she had heard on Andaman and Nicobar Islands! There, the story had saved lives. Here, patuas told the tale as tribute to the dead, and it helped them earn their livelihood. 'Katha was right all along . . . Stories indeed give life,' Mohini said aloud, struck by the perfect circle she had traced. Wait—what was it that Mahadev had told her? *'Your journey will end where it all began!'*

It dawned on her like a divine revelation. 'It all began on Andaman and Nicobar Islands with the tsunami tale. That means my journey ends here!'

---

[3] The entire episode and the characters mentioned, including the elderly man and the news reporter, are illustrated on a jodano pat. While the tsunami pat stays true to the central theme, each patua's storyline, song and characters vary and so does the style in which the tale is painted.

As soon as she uttered these words, the patua and his scrolls were washed away, as though they had been wiped out with an eraser. Total darkness surrounded her, like she was nowhere at all. The girl looked from side to side, her arms stretched out for an answer. Then, like a guiding star, Katha's smiling face appeared in front of her before flickering away.

The sign!

'But where *are* you, Katha?'

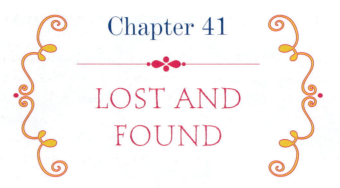

Chapter 41

LOST AND FOUND

Someone, somewhere switched on the lights, placing Mohini in the world again. She blinked, shaken at having possibly solved the big riddle. Or had she? There was only one way to find out.

Squinting in the blinding sunlight, she struggled to see which new locale she had been sent to, and it took her a few minutes to register that she was, after all, standing in front of a very familiar-looking door. When she finally figured it out, she clapped her hands and a delighted squeal escaped her. Not waiting another second, she flung the door open and announced, 'I'm home!'

After a teary welcome, Manohari and Yash chided their girl and then cried some more. With the help of Mohini's friends and Mithika's folk, the couple had frantically searched for their dear daughter, but to no avail. The girl apologized profusely, knowing full well the unnecessary trauma she had caused them.

Mohini then narrated the sequence of events that had led to her sudden disappearance. She held back nothing—her shame at having failed and the fear of facing her parents, her encounter in Eerul Caves, how her suspicion about and irritation towards the spirit turned into admiration. Never interrupting, her parents keenly listened to her extraordinary adventures.

'She's telling tall tales like you,' Yash told Manohari after Mohini had fallen asleep, utterly exhausted and relieved to be in her own bed after many nights.

'But a lot of what she said was based on facts, you know,' Manohari replied.

'Hmm, which is what is confusing me. Even if I want to believe she visited all those places, I'm sure this whole spirit business is nothing more than an imaginary tale.' Yash tucked Mohini in lovingly, before leaving mother and daughter alone.

Deep inside, Manohari knew that what Yash considered fiction was not really make-believe. In the quiet night, she stroked her sleeping daughter's curls and thought of that last visit her mother, Mohini's G-Ma, had made to the Eerul Caves before she'd passed away without warning or fuss. She'd had to lie about it to Mithika's people, of course, because the family's association with the spirit was a prized bond and a well-guarded secret—even Yash wasn't in the know. Manohari had never questioned her mother about the purpose of that visit. How could she? Anokhi had been enigmatic beyond reason and wise beyond belief. But hearing Mohini animatedly go on about her colourful exploits, she understood now that the trip had been made by the doting grandmother to request Katha's help in letting her darling granddaughter find her true calling.

'Your real test is tomorrow, my doe-eyed doll,' Manohari whispered in the ear of the now dreaming Mohini.

The girl woke up in the morning to muffled sounds of her parents arguing softly.

'I won't let you force her. She ran away once—isn't that enough?' her father was saying.

'For *us* to be sure, for *her* to be sure, she *has* to do this today,' her mother reasoned.

'What do I have to do?' Mohini had tiptoed into the kitchen and startled the two.

'Nothing, we're just . . . uh—' Her father struggled to find a cover-up, but her mother was in no such mood.

'Today's the first Sunday of the month. You must preside over Story Hour!'

Mohini immediately felt queasy and her knees buckled ever so slightly. But her mother's hopeful eyes said it all.

'All right, Ma.' She gulped her fears and smiled nervously. 'If I fail again, it just means I have much more to learn.'

As his daughter turned on her heels and confidently walked away, Yash said to Manohari in a low voice, 'She's growing up.'

A little later, he saw Mohini packing her knapsack. Alarm bells ringing in his head, he rushed to her. 'Mohini? What're you up to there?'

'Don't worry, Dad! I'm not running away,' Mohini answered with a laugh.

'Look, you don't have to if you don't feel like it,' he said, kneeling down beside her.

'I know. But Katha has taught me well . . . I'm ready.'

'Once upon a time . . .' Mohini began meekly, but went quiet for over a minute, the longest one she had ever endured.

'Well, well, well, nothing's changed. She still has no story!' a grumpy listener complained.

Her palms were sweaty and her mind, restless. *Which story should I tell? The Vikram–Betaal ones? Nah, G-Ma has already narrated those. One of the stories that Katha told me? But that would surely be cheating and it wouldn't make me a unique storyteller. I have to be imaginative.*

Hoping for a plot to come to her, she closed her eyes. And the spirit's face flitted across her mind for a split second! 'Katha?' she whispered expectantly, but there was no reply.

'Great, now she's talking to herself! Look, can we just go?' a screechy old woman asked.

But the kind lady with the printed yellow fan encouraged Mohini still, 'Go on, you can do it!'

Stealing a look at her parents' supportive faces in the last row, she finally swallowed the lump in her throat, breathed deeply—and simply began again. 'Once upon a time, there was a stone.'

'Excuse me, didn't the stone break into several pieces last time?' The impatient man from the previous Story Hour chuckled.

Ignoring him, Mohini continued. 'The stone lay in an isolated cave. One stormy night, a brave young girl called Maya strayed into this gloomy cave and began playing there with a few coloured stones. That's how she found this one. At first glance, it looked perfectly ordinary. But she soon realized that it was a magical object.'

At this point, Mohini paused and promptly picked up a smooth stone lying among many others. With the edge of her hairclip, she engraved the sun and moon symbols on it, along with the words, 'Use my magic thoughtfully'.

Passing the stone around to make the audience curious, she resumed her tale. 'Maya decided to test its magic. What she didn't know, though, was that the stone had a mind of its own and was a bit of a prankster!' Murmurs of interest rose from the crowd.

'Maya commanded the stone to take her to a beautiful land where everyone wore fine clothes and lived with fantastical beasts. The smart stone obeyed, and Maya found herself in . . .' Mohini paused to think, 'Fabrica! A place where *everything* was made of fine cloth—homes, trees, even people!'

A few people in the audience laughed. They liked this complication in the tale. 'Clever stone!' someone said.

Mohini now brought out two ragdolls from her knapsack. Using them as puppets, she made the dolls talk as though they were the cloth people of Fabrica. 'Two of the cloth people saw how Maya had magically appeared out of nowhere. Convinced that she was no ordinary girl, they rushed to her. "Oh, save us, brave warrior!" one said as the other added, "Yes, save us from the absent-minded dragon! Each time he sings and sighs and yodels and yawns, he breathes blazing fire. He forgets that Fabrica is completely made of cloth!" It was now up to Maya to stop the dragon from troubling the folk of Fabrica.'

The girl paused. 'What should Maya do? Battle and kill the beast?' she asked the listeners on purpose—she needed to buy a few seconds to make up the next part of the tale anyway.

'Hey, not fair! The dragon was just absent-minded. Why kill the poor guy?' cried the lady with the pet cat, who too seemed agitated.

'I agree! Why so violent?' Mohini's classmate, who was sitting next to Manohari and Yash, added.

Without answering their questions, Mohini brought out a paper mask of a dragon's terrible face and slipped it on. She stomped among the audience menacingly, stopping to glare at a few younger children in the audience now and then. Among shrieks and giggles, she croaked, 'The dragon was absent-minded, sure! But he *did* cause destruction! The cloth people *were* afraid of him! And Maya *had* to save them!'

Mohini whipped off the mask dramatically. 'But Maya was fearless. And she wasn't made of cloth! As she faced the mighty dragon, the beast was about to open his yawning mouth and emit a scorching flame. Even as Fabrica's people cowered far behind, Maya boldly commanded the magic stone, "Give me the strongest weapon to stop this fire-breathing dragon's mischief!" The stone obeyed, of course, but . . .' Mohini smiled naughtily to tease the audience.

'It had a mind of its own!' a schoolboy and his father completed in unison, a twinkle in their eyes.

'Exactly! And so the stone did give her the strongest tool to control fire with—it started a downpour! It rained so hard that when the dragon breathed, only black smoke hissed out of his mouth. The cloth people danced with joy. "Hurrah!" they cheered. "Maya has saved the day!" . . . Uh, oh! Not so fast! They suddenly started wailing for they had another problem now.' Mohini looked straight at her worst heckler. 'Do *you* know what it is?' she asked him.

'*Me?*' Every head turned to look at him. 'Um . . . I-I don't know. Maybe the dragon wasn't forgetful any more?'

The children in the front row moaned and those in the last groaned, even as everyone sitting in between shook their heads disapprovingly.

'They were *cloth people*, you dummy! They'd be soaked to their bony threads if it rained all the time!' the lady with the fan said with a wave. The audience erupted into laughter at the brilliant twist and mocked the impatient old man, from whom not a peep was heard thereafter.

Mohini spoke louder to get the listeners' attention again. 'That's right. So . . . perpetual rain was a *bad* idea indeed! Finally, Maya understood the stone's mind and *thoughtfully* commanded, "O Magic Stone, make it rain only on the dragon and only when he's about to breathe fire and destroy Fabrica—but cause the poor beast no harm." The stone obeyed her word for word, and this time, a perfect solution was reached. From then on, the cloth people of Fabrica lived without fear. And the oblivious dragon didn't understand why or how it rained only over his head every time he sighed and sang and yodelled and yawned. But he didn't mind it. You know why, don't you?' she looked eagerly at the crowd.

'Because the dragon was absent-minded,' they chorused and laughed.

'That's right. And so Maya and the smart stone made their way to their next adventure—but that's for another Story Hour.'

Mohini finished to resounding applause, and each listener competed with the other to hoot and clap the loudest. She stood numb with disbelief and joy. She'd done it! 'Mithika has found its next storyteller!' People swamped her with such warm words of congratulation, and Mohini believed it now—she *was* a storyteller. She even heard someone say, 'Anokhi would've been so proud.'

A thrilled Manohari waded through the crowd and hugged her. 'My dear principal tissue-folder is using her craft for storytelling now,' she said, admiring the dragon mask.

'Ma, you remember!' Mohini giggled.

'Good job, my girl! But how about a *real* story next time, eh?' Yash said with a thump on her back. 'Anyway, I'm glad you've found your lost storytelling spirit.'

'Thanks . . . Wait—what did you say?' Mohini asked. All the bustle of the successful Story Hour instantly died down in her head.

'Er . . . That you've found your—'

'HOW could I have been *so* stupid! It had been so clear right from the beginning!' The girl held her head in her hands, angry with herself. 'Ma, Dad, I have to go somewhere,' she told her parents and rushed off.

'But you just came back!' Yash called after her.

However, Manohari, who knew exactly what Mohini had just realized, didn't stop her. 'Go! But don't let anyone see you there,' she said softly.

As the afternoon sun flared overhead, Mohini made it just on time to catch the bus. Thrusting some coins into the conductor's hand, she said confidently, 'Eerul Caves.'

'You thought you could leave me out there and happily read your books here, is it?' Mohini stormed into the cave.

'Yikes!' Katha pretended to leap out of the couch in fright and drop the book in its hand.

'Oh, *please*. I know who you are!' the girl told the spirit.

Katha cleared its throat, drew a deep breath and began:

Yeah, an annoying spirit with oodles of pride,
Who, without your permission, took you on a ride.
Only to suddenly leave your side,
But not without hiding a sign to guide!

Its translucent face displayed a gamut of expressions during the length of the rhyme.

'Nope!' Mohini beamed. 'You are Katha, the storytelling spirit. You're the one who inspires storytellers to tell a good tale and keeps their traditions alive. Isn't it?'

'Bingo!'

'But why did you let me escape all those times?' she queried.

'To see if you came back to me on your own. You didn't at first. So I followed you. But when you kept following my trail even after you'd broken the spell, I knew I'd done my job well . . . Speaking of the spell, you do know that if you want to go back home, you must tell me a story, don't you?' The spirit winked.

'Oh, just you wait! I have not one, but *many* stories to tell you!' And so the girl told the spirit about all the storytellers she had met on the last leg of her journey. Evening turned to night, night to dawn, dawn to noon, but Mohini did not run out of tales to tell.

'Oh, my, you're becoming like Kahankar,' the spirit said, stifling a yawn.

'Shush! I don't mind that one bit,' the girl answered happily.

Katha was exhausted listening to her, but the gushing Mohini simply could not stop telling stories.

THANK YOU!

Authoring this book has been nothing short of living a story, with its many twists and turns. And like it happens in a tale, a number of characters have played important roles in its creation. I extend my heartfelt thanks to:

Every traditional and unconventional storyteller of India, for carrying on the legacy of telling tales;

Every museum, cultural institution and the many individuals and government agencies involved in the preservation of the country's storytelling heritage;

My family and friends—especially Anand P., Poornima Subramanian, Savio Mascarenhas and Swati Ali—for their constant guidance, help and belief in my work;

The wonderful teams at Puffin Books (Penguin Random House India)—editorial, design, typesetting, the printing press, marketing, sales, legal, accounts and other staff—for persevering to get this book published.

A special 'thank you!' to my persistent and gifted editor, Nimmy Chacko; the supportive and approachable editor, Sohini Mitra; the patient and artistic designer, Devangana Dash; the talented and innovative illustrator, Abhishek Choudhury; and the perceptive and eagle-eyed copy editor, Kankana Basu.

Most importantly, a warm smile and much gratitude to each child, teen and grown-up who read *Lore of the Land: Storytelling Traditions of India*. I hope you enjoyed this journey as much as I did.

SOURCES

Andaman and Nicobar Islands

Andaman and Nicobar Tourism. 'Cellular Jail: From a Mute Witness to a National Memorial.' Accessed 4 October 2017. http://www.andamans.gov.in/html/cellular.html.

'Andaman Cellular Jail Light house show.' Filmed 2013. YouTube video, 33:48. Posted by 'Desi Traveller', 6 January 2015. https://www.youtube.com/watch?v=S7t4C0MT4Kw.

Budjeryn, Mariana. 'And Then Came the Tsunami: Disaster Brings Attention and New Challenges to Asia's Indigenous Peoples.' *Cultural Survival Quarterly Magazine* 29-1 (March 2005): https://www.culturalsurvival.org/publications/cultural-survival-quarterly/and-then-came-tsunami-disaster-brings-attention-and-new.

Custance, Arthur C. *The Flood: Local or Global?* The Doorway Papers Series. Reprint of the 1975–80 Zondervan editions, Arthur C. Custance Centre for Science and Christianity. Accessed 4 October 2017. http://custance.org/Library/Volume9/index.html#Abstract.

Kapse, Ram. 'Hundred Years of the Andamans Cellular Jail.' *The Hindu*. 21 December 2005. http://www.thehindu.com/2005/12/21/stories/2005122107881100.htm.

National Geographic News. 'Did Island Tribes Use Ancient Lore to Evade Tsunami?' 24 January 2005. http://news.nationalgeographic.com/news/2005/01/0125_050125_tsunami_island.html.

Pettersson, Anders. 'Historical and Theoretical Perspectives of Literature.' In *Comparative Literature: Sharing Knowledges for Preserving Cultural Diversity (Volume 1)*, edited by Lisa Block de Behar, Paola Mildonian, Jean-Michel Djian, Djelal Kadir, Alfons Knauth, Dolores Romero Lopez and Marcio Seligmann Silva. Oxford: EOLSS Publishers/UNESCO, 2009.

Temple, R.C. *Andaman and Nicobar Islands*. Imperial Gazetteer of India Provincial Series. New Delhi: Asian Educational Services, 1994.

Vaidik, Aparna. *Imperial Andamans: Colonial Encounter and Island History*. Cambridge Imperial and Post-Colonial Studies Series. Hampshire: Palgrave Macmillan, 2010.

Andhra Pradesh

Aakhyan: A Celebration of Masks, Puppets and Picture Showmen Traditions of India. New Delhi: Indira Gandhi National Centre for the Arts with Sangeet Natak Akademi, 2010. Exhibition brochure. Accessed 4 October 2017. http://ignca.nic.in/PDF_data/aakhyan_brochure.pdf.

Brandon, James R., ed. *The Cambridge Guide to Asian Theatre*. Cambridge: Cambridge University Press, 1993.
Centre for Cultural Resources and Training. 'Puppet Forms.' Accessed 4 October 2017. http://ccrtindia.gov.in/puppetforms.php.
Chandaraju, Aruna. 'The Hanging Pillar and Other Wonders of Lepakshi.' *The Hindu*. 27 January 2012. http://www.thehindu.com/features/metroplus/travel/The-hanging-pillar-and-other-wonders-of-Lepakshi/article13383179.ece.
Gaatha. 'Leather Puppets of Andhra Pradesh.' Accessed 4 October 2017. http://gaatha.com/leather-puppets-of-andhra-pradesh/.
Ghosh, Sampa and Utpal Kumar Banerjee. *Indian Puppets*. New Delhi: Abhinav Publications, 2005.
Kuiper, Kathleen, ed. 'Indian Performing Arts.' In *The Culture of India*. Understanding India Series. New York: Britannica Educational Publishing in association with Rosen Educational Services, 2011.
Rao, S. Chithambara (2003 National Award–winning member of Chaya Nataka Brundam, Leather Puppet Manufacturers and Specialists in Leather Puppet Shows) in discussion with the author, Paramparik Karigar Exhibition and Sale 2017.
Ranjan, Aditi and M. P. Ranjan, eds. 'Andhra Pradesh: Leather Puppets.' In *Handmade in India*. Crafts of India Series. New Delhi: Council of Handicraft Development Corporations (COHANDS), 2007. Accessed 4 October 2017. http://www.cohands.in/handmadepages/book284.asp?t1=284&lang=English.
Sriramulu, Sindhe (2006 National Award–winning master leather craftsman) in discussion with the author, Paramparik Karigar Exhibition and Sale 2017.
'Bhaskar, Neela. *Tollu Bommalata*. Short film. YouTube video '"Tollu Bommalata"', 8:35. Posted by 'neela bhaskar', 12 October 2012. https://www.youtube.com/watch?v=waVqcW74QDs.

Arunachal Pradesh

Arunachal Times. 'When Did Dao Become a Weapon?' 4 February 2016. http://www.arunachaltimes.in/when-did-dao-become-a-weapon/ (site discontinued).
India Mapped. 'Arunachal Pradesh Ponung Adi Tribe.' Accessed 4 October 2017. http://www.indiamapped.com/folk-dance-in-india/arunachal-pradesh-ponung-adi-tribe/.
Indira Gandhi National Centre for the Arts. 'Bamboo and Cane Culture of Arunachal Pradesh.' Accessed 4 October 2017. http://ignca.nic.in/craft151.htm.
'In the Forest Hangs a Bridge.' Film trailer. Film directed by Sanjay Kak 1999. YouTube video, 2:45. Posted by 'Magic Lantern Movies', 24 May 2010. https://www.youtube.com/watch?time_continue=1&v=PUml8sKDws8.
Nabam Tuki, Chief Minister of Arunachal Pradesh. 'Dances of Arunachal Pradesh.' Accessed 4 October 2017. http://nabamtuki.org/political/website/nabamtuki/index.php/media-archives/media-archives/503-dances-of-arunachal-pradesh.html.
Pioneer (Bhopal). 'The Lord's "Raas" Draws Curtain on "Poorvotsav".' 5 May 2014. http://www.dailypioneer.com/print.php?printFOR=storydetail&story_url_key=the-lords-raas-draws-curtain-on-poorvotsav&section_url_key=state-editions.
Rao, Narayan Singh. *Tribal Culture, Faith, History and Literature: Tangsas of Arunachal Pradesh*. New Delhi: Mittal Publications, 2006.
Virtual Learning Environment, Institute of Lifelong Learning, University of Delhi. 'Chapter: The Adi Tribe.' Cultural Diversity Course. Accessed 4 October 2017. http://vle.du.ac.in/mod/book/print.php?id=6022.

Zephyretta. 'Adi Tribe.' *Pasighat: The Land of Rising Sun* (blog). Accessed 4 October 2017. https://pasighat.wordpress.com/adi-tribe/.

Assam

Assam Info. 'Ojapali Dance.' Accessed 4 October 2017. http://www.assaminfo.com/culture/40/ojapali-dance.htm.

Barua, Birinchi Kumar and H. V. Sreenivasa Murthy. *Temples and Legends of Assam.* Bombay: Bharatiya Vidya Bhavan, 1965.

Darrang District. 'Folk Art and Culture.' Accessed 4 October 2017. http://darrang.gov.in/Culture.htm.

Devi, Jyotima. 'An Introduction to Ojapali of Darrang District of Assam: Suknani And Biyahar Ojapali.' In *IJCAES Special Issue on Basic, Applied & Social Sciences* (Volume II), edited by Mrinal Kanti Ghose. Foundation for Interdisciplinary Research in Engineering (FIRE), July 2012. Accessed 4 October 2017. http://www.caesjournals.org/spluploads/IJCAES-BASS-2012-106.pdf.

———. 'Ojapali Institution as a Classical Dance & Music and Its Antiquity.' In *IJCAES Special Issue on Basic, Applied & Social Sciences* (Volume II), edited by Mrinal Kanti Ghose. Foundation for Interdisciplinary Research in Engineering (FIRE), October 2012. Accessed 4 October 2017. http://www.caesjournals.org/spluploads/IJCAES-BASS-2012-188.pdf.

Hazarika, Prabin. *Haate Mudra, Mukhe Pada, Mayur Sadrisya Naach: Lyrics with Body and Soul.* Documentary film. Produced by Krisangi Creation 2012. YouTube videos 'Ojapali - Lalit Chandra Nath' Parts 1–4. Posted by 'dhrubajyoti001', 1 December 2012. https://www.youtube.com/watch?v=erbKsOv2KhU; https://www.youtube.com/watch?v=6quDCL3h7k4; https://www.youtube.com/watch?v=fZHg5FCFY3o; https://www.youtube.com/watch?v=3Ll0U-Sb8rM.

McLean, Malcolm. *Devoted to the Goddess: The Life and Work of Ramprasad.* Albany: State University of New York Press, 1998.

Radice, William. 'Manasa's Triumph.' In *Myths and Legends of India: Volume 2.* Gurgaon: Penguin Books India, 2016.

Sharma, Mahesh. 'Goddess Manasa.' In *Tales from the Puranas.* New Delhi: Diamond Pocket Books, 2005.

Tate, Karen. *Sacred Places of Goddess: 108 Destinations.* San Francisco: Consortium of Collective Consciousness, 2006.

Bihar

Dayal, Bharti. 'On Mithila Painting.' Sahapedia. https://www.sahapedia.org/mithila-painting.

Devi, Shanti (National Merit Award–winning Madhubani painting artist) and Vijay Kumar Jha (Madhubani painting artist) in discussion with the author, The Handmade Collective 2016 and 2017.

Gupta, Charu Smita. 'Folklore: Literature, Art Craft and Music.' New Delhi: National Museum. Issued in National Science Digital Library, 2007. Accessed 4 October 2017. http://nsdl.niscair.res.in/jspui/bitstream/123456789/338/1/PDF%20Folklore.pdf.

Karn, Moti (National Award–winning Madhubani painting artist) in discussion with the author, Paramparik Karigar Exhibition and Sale 2016.

Kashyap, Shiva (Madhubani painting artist and founder, Mithila Vastram) in discussion with the author, Paramparik Karigar Exhibition and Sale 2016.

Mishra, Kailash K. 'Mithila Paintings: Past, Present and Future.' Kalasampada: Indira Gandhi National Centre for the Arts (Digital Library: Resources of Indian Cultural Heritage). Accessed 4 October 2017. http://www.ignca.nic.in/kmsh0002.htm.

Mithila Cosmos: Circumambulating the Tree of Life. Edited by Sangeeta Thapa. Kathmandu: S.C. Suman with Siddhartha Art Gallery, 2013. Exhibition catalogue. Accessed 4 October 2017. http://www.siddharthaartgallery.com/downloads/MithilaCosmosCatalouge2013.pdf.

Sahapedia. 'The Congruence of Tradition and Art-making in Mithila.' Sunanda Sahay. Accessed 4 October 2017. https://www.sahapedia.org/the-congruence-of-tradition-and-art-making-mithila.

Sivkishen. *Kingdom of Shiva.* Amazing Vedic Epic Series. Gurgaon: Partridge India, 2014.

The Craft and Artisans. 'Mithila Folk Painting of Madhubani, Bihar.' Accessed 4 October 2017. http://www.craftandartisans.com/mithila-folk-painting-of-madhubani-bihar.html.

Chandigarh

Daarji. 'Legends of Lohri.' *I Am Daarji* (blog). Accessed 4 October 2017. http://iamdaarji.blogspot.in/2011/01/legends-of-lohri.html.

Daniyal, Shoaib. 'Lohri Legends: The Tale of Abdullah Khan "Dullah" Bhatti, the Punjabi Who Led a Revolt against Akbar.' *Scroll.in.* 13 January 2016. http://scroll.in/article/801803/lohri-legends-the-tale-of-abdullah-khan-dullah-bhatti-the-punjabi-who-led-a-revolt-against-akbar.

Dilagīra, Harajindara Singha. *The Sikh Reference Book.* Denmark: Sikh Educational Trust for Sikh University Centre, 1997.

Kapoor, Subodh, ed. *The Indian Encyclopaedia (Volume 14).* New Delhi: Cosmo Publications, 2002.

'Lohri - India's bonfire festival!' Filmed by Wilderness Films India. YouTube video, 2:51. Posted by 'WildFilmsIndia', 13 January 2014. https://www.youtube.com/watch?v=faSZka9uK0s.

Punjabi World. '*Dulla Bhatti da Kissa:* Epic Story of Dullah Bhatti.' Posted 19 April 2009. Accessed 4 October 2017. http://punjabiworld.com/index.php?news=1707.

Singh, Surinder and Ishwar Dayal Gaur, eds. 'Mughal Centralization and Local Resistance in North-Western India: An Exploration in the Ballad of Dulla Bhatti.' In *Popular Literature and Pre-modern Societies in South Asia.* New Delhi: Dorling Kindersley (India), 2008.

Tribune (Chandigarh). '*Dulla Bhatti* Traces Heroic Deeds of Folk Character.' 12 January 2010. http://www.tribuneindia.com/2010/20100113/aplus.htm#6.

Vasudeva, Shivangana. 'Lohri 2016: How Did the Festival Get Its Name?' NDTV Smartcooky. Last modified 10 March 2016. http://food.ndtv.com/food-drinks/lohri-2016-how-did-the-festival-get-its-name-1265224.

Chhattisgarh

Baghel, Bhupendra Jaidev (state and National Merit Award–winning master metal craftsman) in discussion with the author, Paramparik Karigar Exhibition and Sale 2016.

Chhattisgarh: Full of Surprises. Published by Sampan Media Pvt. Ltd for Chhattisgarh Tourism Board, 2014. Tourism booklet. Accessed 4 October 2017. http://cgtourism.choice.gov.in/upload/publication/Booklet.pdf.

'Lost wax process Dhokra art making video with details by sushil sakhuja Kondagaon bastar INDIA.' YouTube video, 9:29. Posted by 'Sushil Sakhuja', 1 July 2007. https://www.youtube.com/watch?v=ffg07yxr_Vs.

National Museum, New Delhi. 'Pre-History and Archaeology: Dancing Girl.' Accessed 4 October 2017. http://www.nationalmuseumindia.gov.in/prodCollections.asp?pid=44&id=1&lk=dp1.

Paramparik Karigar. 'Gadwakam.' Accessed 4 October 2017. http://www.paramparikkarigar.com/getDetails.php?type=metalcasting&subtype=Gadwakam.

Paramparik Karigar. 'Gadwakam: Bastar.' Accessed 4 October 2017. http://paramparikkarigar.com/flipbook/files/assets/common/downloads/page0024.pdf.

Tripathi, Shailaja. 'Sweat behind Sweet Results.' *The Hindu*. 2 August 2015. http://www.thehindu.com/features/metroplus/sweat-behind-sweet-results/article7492065.ece.

Dadra and Nagar Haveli

Bhoir, Sandeep (Warli artist) in discussion with the author, Warli art workshop at Mumbai Return 2017.

Dnhonline.in. 'Tribal Heritage of Dadra and Nagar Haveli.' Accessed 4 October 2017. http://www.dnhonline.in/About/Tourism/Tribal-Heritage-Dadra-and-Nagar-Haveli.html.

D'source. 'Documentation of Warli Art: Traditional Folk Art.' Design resource by Sagar Yende and Ravi Poovaiah. Accessed 4 October 2017. http://www.dsource.in/resource/documentation-warli-art.

Kahankar : Ahankar (Story Maker : Story Taker). Documentary film. Produced by School of Media and Cultural Studies, Tata Institute of Social Sciences, Mumbai 1996. YouTube video by the same name, 38:06. Posted by 'SMCSchannel', 26 August 2014. https://www.youtube.com/watch?v=SyOyJ0tKWp8.

Know India. 'Folk and Tribal Art: Warli Folk Painting.' Accessed 4 October 2017. http://knowindia.gov.in/culture-and-heritage/folk-and-tribal-art/warli-folk-painting.php.

Save, K. J. *The Warlis*. Bombay: Padma Publications, 1945.

Seth, Radhika. 'Warli Folk Paintings: An Insistent Expression.' MPhil diss., Dayalbagh Educational Institute, 2013. http://shodhganga.inflibnet.ac.in/handle/10603/21896.

Tribes India Exhibition and Sale. Tribes India, TRIFED, Ministry of Tribal Affairs, Government of India. Chhatrapati Shivaji Maharaj Vastu Sangrahalaya, Mumbai, 2 January 2017.

Tribhuwan, Robin D. and Maike Finkenauer. *Threads Together: A Comparative Study of Tribal and Pre-Historic Rock Paintings*. New Delhi: Discovery Publishing House, 2003.

Warli Painting. Accessed 4 October 2017. http://www.warli.in/.

Daman and Diu

Ali, Shanti Sadiq. 'The Nizam Shahi Dynasty.' In *The African Dispersal in the Deccan: From Medieval to Modern Times*. Hyderabad: Orient Longman Limited, 1996.

Chari, Mridula. 'Rare Images Document the Centuries-Long History of Africans in India.' *Scroll.in*. 8 October 2014. https://scroll.in/article/682635/rare-images-document-the-centuries-long-history-of-africans-in-india.

Davies, Carole Boyce, ed. 'India and the African Diaspora.' In *Encyclopedia of the African Diaspora: Origins, Experiences, and Culture*. California: ABC-CLIO, 2008.

Deccan Herald. 'Siddi Dhamal: A Unique Dance Form.' Last modified 11 June 2011. http://www.deccanherald.com/content/168104/siddi-dhamal-unique-dance-form.html.

Eaton, Richard M. 'The Rise and Fall of Military Slavery in the Deccan, 1450–1650.' In *Slavery and South Asian History*, edited by Indrani Chatterjee and Richard M. Eaton. Indiana: Indiana University Press, 2006.

Herold, Christopher. 'Historical Background of Siddhis.' In 'Social Formation of the Siddhis in the Dharwad and Karwar Districts of Karnataka State.' DPhil thesis, Mahatma Gandhi University, 2010. http://shodhganga.inflibnet.ac.in/bitstream/10603/15838/9/09_chapter%202.pdf.

KAPA Productions. 'Sidi Goma: The Black Sufis of Gujarat.' Accessed 4 October 2017. http://www.kapa-productions.com/sididotcom/.

Rangarajan, A. 'Malik Ambar: Military Guru of the Marathas.' *The Hindu*. 12 October 2008. http://www.thehindu.com/todays-paper/tp-features/tp-sundaymagazine/Malik-Ambar-Military-guru-of-the-Marathas/article15402097.ece.

Shastri, Parth. 'Sidi Women Keep African Culture Alive in India, US Professor Says.' *Times of India* (Ahmedabad). 16 June 2013. http://timesofindia.indiatimes.com/city/ahmedabad/Sidi-women-keep-African-culture-alive-in-India-US-professor-says/articleshow/20611689.cms.

Shekhawat, Rahul Singh. 'Black Sufis: Preserving the Siddis and its Age Old Culture in India.' Paper presented at the 4th Indian Hospitality Congress, Haridwar, n.d. http://www.academia.edu/4206146/BLACK_SUFI_PAPER.

Shroff, Beheroze. 'Sidis of Gujarat, A Building Community: Their Role in Indian History into Contemporary Times.' In *Frontiers of Embedded Muslim Communities in India*, edited by Vinod K. Jairath. New Delhi: Routledge, 2011.

Tribal Research and Training Institute, Tribal Development Department, Government of Gujarat. 'Siddi.' Accessed 4 October 2017. https://trti.gujarat.gov.in/siddi.

WorldMusicCentral.org. 'Interview with Sidi Goma, African Indian Sidis from Gujarat.' Uploaded 7 July 2012. http://worldmusiccentral.org/2012/07/07/interview-with-sidi-goma-african-indian-sidis-from-gujarat/.

Delhi

Ali, Baqir. 'A Story in Urdū.' Delhi: 1920. Transcript and audio digitized by the Linguistic Survey of India, Digital South Asia Library. Accessed 4 October 2017. http://dsal.uchicago.edu/lsi/6826AK.

Ankit Chadha. 'Dastangoi: The Art of Storytelling.' Accessed 4 October 2017. http://www.ankitchadha.in/dastangoi.

Chadha, Ankit. 'Dastangoi Is the Most Minimalistic Way to Tell a Great Story: Ankit Chadha.' By Karan Kapoor. *The Alternative.in*. 15 January 2013. http://www.thealternative.in/lifestyle/the-art-of-dastangoi-forgotten-urdu-storytelling/.

Farooqui, Mahmood. 'Dastangoi: Revival of the Mughal Art of Storytelling.' In *Context: Built, Living and Natural* (Volume VIII, Issue 2). Gurgaon: Journal of the Development and Research Organisation for Nature, Arts and Heritage (DRONAH), Autumn/Winter 2011. http://www.academia.edu/1572349/Contextpdf.

Krishnan, Nandini. 'Dastan-e-Dastangoi.' *Fountain Ink*. 4 May 2012. http://fountainink.in/?p=1947&all=1.

Lakhnavi, Ghalib and Abdullah Bilgrami. *The Adventures of Amir Hamza: Lord of the Auspicious Planetary Conjunction.* Translated by Musharraf Ali Farooqi. USA: Modern Library, 2012.

Old Delhi Heritage. 'Culture and Traditions: Dastangoi.' Accessed 4 October 2017. https://olddelhiheritage.in/dastangoi/.

Sayeed, Vikhar Ahmed. 'Return of Dastangoi.' *Frontline.* (Volume 28, Issue 01). January 2011. http://www.frontline.in/static/html/fl2801/stories/20110114280109800.htm.

Victoria and Albert Museum. 'Hamzanama.' Accessed 4 October 2017. http://www.vam.ac.uk/content/articles/h/hamzanama/.

Goa

'Ghode Modni - Dances of Goa.' YouTube video, 5:04. Posted by 'Cidade de Goa', 20 August 2013. https://www.youtube.com/watch?v=jHtmCd2q1EU.

GoaHolidayHomes.com. 'The Ranes in Goa.' Accessed 4 October 2017. http://www.goaholidayhomes.com/information/the-ranes-in-goa.html.

Goa India Tourism. 'History of Goa.' Accessed 2016. http://goaindiatourism.com/goa/history-of-goa8.html (site discontinued).

Government of Goa: Department of Tourism. 'Ghodemodni.' Accessed 4 October 2017. http://www.goatourism.gov.in/culture/folk-dances/114-ghodemodni.

Kerkar, Rajendra P. 'Shigmo's Battle Stance: Horses, Swords & the Twirl of Ghodemodni.' *Times of India* (Goa). 2 April 2013. http://timesofindia.indiatimes.com/city/goa/Shigmos-battle-stance-Horses-swords-the-twirl-of-ghodemodni/articleshow/19335823.cms.

Lotus Film & TV Production. 'Ghodemodni.' Accessed 4 October 2017. http://www.lotusfilmgoa.com/Ghodemodni.html.

Gujarat

Centre for Cultural Resources and Training. 'Miniature Painting.' Accessed 4 October 2017. http://ccrtindia.gov.in/miniaturepainting.php.

Da'ji, Bha'u. 'The Inroads of the Scythians into India, and the Story of Kalakacharya.' In *Journal of the Asiatic Society of Bombay* (Volume 9, 1867–1870). Bombay: The Royal Asiatic Society, 1872.

Exhibits in N. C. Mehta Gallery and Lalbhai Dalpatbhai Museum. Gujarat Museum Society. Ahmedabad, n.d.

Guy, John. 'From Palm-Leaf to Paper: Manuscript Painting, 1100–1500.' In *Wonder of the Age: Master Painters of India, 1100–1900,* co-authored with Jorrit Britschgi. New York: The Metropolitan Museum of Art, 2011.

Jainpedia. 'Paryusan.' By M. Whitney Kelting. Accessed 4 October 2017. http://www.jainpedia.org/themes/practices/festivals/paryusan.html.

———. 'What Is a Jain Manuscript?' Accessed 4 October 2017. http://www.jainpedia.org/resources/what-is-a-jain-manuscript.html.

Losty, Jeremiah P. 'Some Illustrated Jain Manuscripts.' In *The British Library Journal* (Vol. 1, No. 2). 1975. http://www.bl.uk/eblj/1975articles/pdf/article15.pdf.

Nahakpam, Indubala Joykumar. 'The Historical and Cultural Development of Jain Manuscripts Painting.' In 'A Cultural Study on the Jain (Western Indian) Illustrated Manuscripts That Are Preserved in the L.D. Institute of Indology,

Ahmedabad.' Thesis, Gujarat University, 2011. http://shodhganga.inflibnet.ac.in /bitstream/10603/4680/7/07_chapter%201.pdf.

National Museum, New Delhi. 'Manuscripts: Jain Kalpasutra.' Accessed 4 October 2017. http:// www.nationalmuseumindia.gov.in/prodCollections.asp?pid=92&id=10&lk=dp10.

Parameswaran, O. P. 'Decorative Designs of Illustrated Kalpasutra Manuscript.' PowerPoint presentation. Department of Fine Arts, Post-Graduate Government College for Girls, Chandigarh. http://cms.gcg11.ac.in/attachments/article/75/Decorative%20 Designs%20of%20illustrated%20Kalpasutra%20Manuscript.ppt.

Victoria and Albert Museum. 'Jainism: Illuminated Manuscripts and Jain Art.' Accessed 4 October 2017. http://www.vam.ac.uk/content/articles/j/jainism_illuminated _manuscripts-and-jain-paintings/.

Wiley, Kristi L. 'Chronology.' In *The A to Z of Jainism*. The A to Z Guide Series (No. 38). Scarecrow Press, Inc., United Kingdom: 2009.

Haryana

Dainik Jagran. '*Saang mein Prastut Kiya Jaani Chor ka Qissa*.' [Transliterated from Hindi.] 18 July 2012. http://www.jagran.com/haryana/kurukshetra-9482000.html.

Directorate of Information, Public Relations & Languages, Haryana. '*Haryana Soochana Jansampark evam Sanskritik Karya Vibhag Dvara Tri-city ke Logon ko Haryanvi Sanskriti va Lokvidha Saang Se Ru-ba-ru Karwane ke Liye Sector-18, Chandigarh ke Tagore Sabhagaar Mein Ek Saath Divaseeya Saang Utsav*.' [Transliterated from Hindi.] Press Release, 12 July 2015. Accessed 4 October 2017. http://prharyana.gov .in/hindirelease.aspx?relid=4687.

Folk Dances of India. 'Folk Dances of Haryana.' Accessed 4 October 2017. http://folk-dances .tripod.com/id14.html.

Hansen, Kathryn. *Grounds for Play: The Nautanki Theatre of North India*. California: University of California Press, 1992.

Haryana Tourism. 'About Haryana.' Accessed 4 October 2017. http://haryanatourism.gov .in/showpage.aspx?contentid=5049.

Indian Travel Portal. 'Swang (Theatre).' Accessed 4 October 2017. http://www .indiantravelportal.com/haryana/arts-crafts/theatre.html.

Lather, Anoop. '*Hamari Sanskruti ka Aaina Hai "Saang"*.' [Transliterated from Hindi.] *Dainik Bhaskar*. n.d. Accessed 4 October 2017. http://3.bp.blogspot.com /-tkjRMTXy9sA/UBn53iqRk2I/AAAAAAAAB9Q/G7nKtq223Xc/s1600/302135_26 1972600489031_100000288782570_1067764_6388651_n.jpg.

———. '"*Saang" mein Jhalakti Hai Samudayik Bhavna*.' [Transliterated from Hindi.] *Dainik Bhaskar*. n.d. Accessed 4 October 2017. http://1.bp.blogspot.com/-cz5zSc-4158 /UBn51L__cSI/AAAAAAAAB9I/MuG4P7Pwyfw/s1600/298738_264897676863190 _100000288782570_1080901_2090259_n.jpg.

———. '*"Saang" ne Saheji Hai Guru–Shishya Parampara*.' [Transliterated from Hindi.] *Dainik Bhaskar*. n.d. Accessed 4 October 2017. http://1.bp.blogspot.com/-mzHIiv-S8O8 /UCDxcfWXl4I/AAAAAAAACGU/Xa247EV_1as/s1600/Scan09062011_021014 .BMP.

———. '"*Saang" se hi Janme Hain Kayi Loknatya*.' [Transliterated from Hindi.] *Dainik Bhaskar*. n.d. Accessed 4 October 2017. http://3.bp.blogspot.com/-yuIwpavrkaQ /UBn6L-t3S6I/AAAAAAAAB9s/EJjSMxUtQoc/s1600/bhaskar+sang-4.jpg.

Mehrotra, Deepti Priya. *Gulab Bai: The Queen of Nautanki Theatre*. New Delhi: Penguin Books India, 2006.

'*Rahasyamayi baoli mein dafn hai beshkeemti khazana.*' [Transliterated from Hindi.] YouTube video, 5:15. Posted by 'Shrimad Home Remedies', 16 September 2016. https://www.youtube.com/watch?v=_v0ilM5ZaC8.

Tribune (Chandigarh). 'Preserving Rich Tradition of Story-Telling in Haryanvi.' 5 October 2006. http://www.tribuneindia.com/2006/20061006/haryana.htm#27.

Himachal Pradesh

Chamba. 'History.' Accessed 4 October 2017. http://hpchamba.nic.in/history.htm.

'Chamba Rumal: Life to a Dying Art.' Dr Bhau Daji Lad Mumbai City Museum, in collaboration with Delhi Crafts Council. Mumbai, December 2015–February 2016.

Himachal Tourism. 'History.' Accessed 4 October 2017. http://himachaltourism.gov.in/history.php.

Himalayan Quest. 'Minjar Mela: Popular Fair in Chamba.' Accessed 4 October 2017. http://www.himalayan-quest.com/minjar.html.

Naik, Shailaja D. 'Chamba Rumal of Himachal.' In *Traditional Embroideries of India*. New Delhi: A. P. H. Publishing Corporation, 1996 .

NIFTCD (Textile Design department, NIFT Kangra). 'Chamba Rumal.' *Chamba Rumal: The Poetry in Threads* (blog). Accessed 4 October 2017. https://niftcd.wordpress.com/chamba-rumal/.

Jammu and Kashmir

Core of Culture. 'Cham.' Accessed 4 October 2017. http://www.coreofculture.org/cham.html.

HubPages. 'Chham: The Devil Dance of Lahaul.' By Sanjay Sharma. Last modified 20 July 2017. Accessed 4 October 2017. https://hubpages.com/entertainment/Chham-The-Devil-Dance-of-Lahaul.

India.com. 'Ladakh Festivals: Monks, Dance and Celebration of Life.' By Parul Gupta. Last modified 14 July 2016. Accessed 4 October 2017. http://www.india.com/travel/articles/ladakh-festivals-monks-dance-and-celebration-of-life/.

Kumar, Ajay. 'Ladakh's Cultural Heritage: Its Unique Festivals and Dances.' In *International Journal of Social Science & Interdisciplinary Research* (Volume 1, Issue 12). December 2012. Accessed 4 October 2017. http://www.indianresearchjournals.com/pdf/ijssir/2012/december/5.pdf.

Pearlman, Ellen. *Tibetan Sacred Dance: A Journey into the Religious and Folk Traditions*. Vermont: Inner Traditions, 2002.

Tibetan Cham Dancing. 'Cham Dancing Masks and Costumes: A Short Introduction.' Accessed 4 October 2017. http://www.chamdancing.com/masks--costumes.html.

Jharkhand

Banerjee, Sudeshna. 'Dancing Dolls in a Box.' *Telegraph*. 5 April 2015. https://www.telegraphindia.com/1150405/jsp/calcutta/story_12736.jsp#.WJojYvl97Dc.

Basu, Manas. *Dhusar Tudung: Forlorn Tudung*. Documentary film. YouTube video 'Documentary Short Film - Forlorn(DHUSAR) Tudung | Pocket Films', 27:55. Posted by 'Pocket Films - Indian Short Films', 2 February 2015. https://www.youtube.com/watch?v=EpEwQzzDQks.

Bompas, Cecil Henry, trans. 'The Backwards and Forwards Dance.' In *Folklore of the Santal Parganas*. Reprint of the 1909 edition, Project Gutenberg, 2004. http://livros01.livrosgratis.com.br/gu011938.pdf.

'Cadence and Counterpoint: Documenting Santal Musical Traditions.' New Delhi: National Museum, New Delhi, 2015. Exhibition compilation on Google Arts & Culture by Ruchira Ghose and Rajalakshmi Karakulam. Accessed 4 October 2017. https://www.google.com/culturalinstitute/beta/exhibit/DwISi2xsSQFgKA.

Daricha. 'Chadar Badni.' Accessed 4 October 2017. http://www.daricha.org/sub_genre.aspx?ID=121&Name=Chadar%20Badar.

Das, Palash. *Saga of a Puppet Show* (2015). Documentary film. N.d. (YouTube link discontinued).

Sphoorthitheatre Steparc. 'Fading Folk theatre of Santhal Tribes of West Bengal, India – "Chadar Badar Puppetry".' *Sphoorthi Theatre* (blog). Accessed 4 October 2017. https://sphoorthi-theatre.blogspot.in/2012/04/chadar-badar-puppetry-of-santhal-tribes.html.

Times of India (Kolkata). 'Vanishing Art: The Last Master of Puppets.' 9 April 2016. http://epaperbeta.timesofindia.com/Article.aspx?eid=31812&articlexml=VANISHING-ART-The-last-master-of-puppets-09042016007005.

Tribal Cultural Heritage in India Foundation. 'A Tale of Tribal Puppetry: Adivasi Putulkatha, a documentary film – Bengal & Jharkhand.' Accessed 4 October 2017. http://www.indiantribalheritage.org/?p=13578.

Wali Hawes. 'Chadar Badar Puppets and Its Revival by Ravi Dwivedi.' *Claygun* (blog). Accessed 4 October 2017. http://claygun.blogspot.in/2011/02/chadar-badar-puppets-and-its-revival-by.html.

Karnataka

Bai, K. Kusuma. 'Dance Forms at the Time of Nayaka Kings.' In *Music–Dance and Musical Instruments: During the Period of Nayakas (1673–1732)*. The Chaukhamba Sanskrit Bhawan Series. Varanasi: Chaukhamba Sanskrit Bhawan, 2000.

Binder, Katrin. 'Re-Use in the Yakshagana Theatre of Coastal Karnataka.' In *Re-Use: The Art and Politics of Integration and Anxiety*, edited by Julia A. B. Hegewald and Subrata K. Mitra. New Delhi: SAGE Publications India Pvt. Ltd, 2012.

Encyclopaedia Britannica. 'Yakshagana: Indian Dance-Drama.' Accessed 4 October 2017. http://www.britannica.com/topic/yakshagana.

Gajrani, S., ed. 'Karnataka.' In *History, Religion and Culture of India* (Volume 2). New Delhi: Isha Books, 2004.

Kanuga, G. B. 'Cry of the Heart.' In *Immortal Love of Rama*. New Delhi: Lancer Publishers Pvt. Ltd, 1993.

Karnataka.com. 'Yakshagana: Dance, Drama and Music.' By Jolad Rotti. Accessed 4 October 2017. https://www.karnataka.com/profile/yakshagana/.

Karnataka Temple Information System: Hindu Religious Institutions & Charitable Endowments Department. 'Karnataka: Culture.' Accessed 4 October 2017. http://karnatakatemplesyatra.kar.nic.in/homepage/html/Karnataka/culture2.htm.

Kasargod. 'Yakshagana.' Accessed 4 October 2017. http://kasargod.nic.in/profile/yakshagana.htm.

Miettinen, Jukka O. 'Yakshagana: Gorgeous Dance Opera from Karnataka.' In *Asian Traditional Theatre and Dance*. Digitized by Theatre Academy Helsinki with TEKES TULI-programme, 2010. Accessed 4 October 2017. http://www.xip.fi/atd/india/yakshagana-gorgeous-dance-opera-from-karnataka.html.

Singh, Chandra Sekhar. *The Purans (Volume 02)*. n.p.: Lulu, 2016.
Sri Yabaluri Raghavaiah Memorial Trust. 'Yakshagana: Origin and Growth.' By S. Ramakrishna Sastry. Accessed 4 October 2017. http://www.yabaluri.org/CD%20&%20WEB/yakshaganaoriginandgrowthjan58.htm.
Varadpande, M. L. *History of Indian Theatre: Loka Ranga, Panorama of Indian Folk Theatre*. New Delhi: Abhinav Publications, 1992.
Venkatraman, Leela. 'Focus on Rural Art.' *The Hindu*. 23 December 2005. http://www.thehindu.com/ms/2005/12/23/stories/2005122300250500.htm.
YakshaRanga. 'Welcome to Yaksharanga.' Accessed 4 October 2017. http://www.yaksharanga.org/.

Kerala

Deepa and Sujith (Kerala mural artists with Bhavm Murals) in discussion with the author, The Handmade Collective 2016.
D'source. 'Kerala Murals: The Art of Painting on Walls.' Design resource by Bibhudutta Baral and Antony William. Accessed 4 October 2017. http://www.dsource.in/resource/kerala-murals.
Kerala: God's Own Country. 'Krishnapuram Palace, Kayamkulam.' Accessed 4 October 2017. https://www.keralatourism.org/destination/krishnapuram-palace-kayamkulam/69.
K. I., Treesa. 'Mural Painting in Kerala.' In 'Mural Painting in Kerala with Special Reference to Vishnudharmottarapurana.' DPhil thesis, Sri Sankaracharya University of Sanskrit, 1999. http://shodhganga.inflibnet.ac.in/bitstream/10603/135967/11/11_chapter%20v.pdf.
Kumari, D. Latha. 'Introduction.' In 'EMS Namboothiripad Ministry in Kerala, 1957–1959.' DPhil thesis, Manonmaniam Sundaranar University, 2012. http://shodhganga.inflibnet.ac.in/bitstream/10603/133869/6/06_introduction.pdf.
Mural Paintings of Kerala. 'Padmanabhapuram Murals.' Accessed 4 October 2017. http://www.keralamurals.in/padmanabhapuram-murals/.
Panchavarna. Accessed 4 October 2017. http://panchavarna.com/.
P. V., Mini. 'Preparation Techniques of Pigments for Traditional Mural Paintings of Kerala.' In *Indian Journal of Traditional Knowledge* {Volume 9 (4)}. October 2010. Accessed 4 October 2017. http://nopr.niscair.res.in/bitstream/123456789/10308/1/IJTK%209(4)%20635-639.pdf.
Sadanandan.com. 'Kerala Murals.' Accessed 4 October 2017. http://www.sadanandan.com/keralamurals.html.
SA Krishnan. 'Gajendra, the Elephant.' *Stories from Hindu Mythology* (blog). Accessed 4 October 2017. http://hindumythologyforgennext.blogspot.in/2012/04/gajendra-elephant.html.
Vettakkorumakan. 'History.' By Balakrishnan Kartha. Accessed 4 October 2017. http://vettakkorumakan.com/history.html.

Lakshadweep

Union Territory of Lakshadweep. 'Bitra: History.' Accessed 4 October 2017. http://lakshadweep.nic.in/ISLAND_web/BITRA/history.html.
———. 'Lakshadweep Sahithya Kala Academy.' http://lakshadweep.nic.in/depts/lsk.htm.

———. 'Lakshadweep & Its People.' Accessed 4 October 2017. http://lakshadweep.nic.in/location.htm.

Bhatt, S. C. and Gopal K. Bhargava, eds. *Land and People of Indian States and Union Territories: Lakshadweep* (Volume 35 of 36). Delhi: Kalpaz Publications, 2006.

Jha, Makhan. 'Island Ecology and Cultural Perception: A Case Study of Lakshadweep.' In Lifestyle and Ecology, edited by Baidyanath Saraswati. New Delhi: Indira Gandhi National Centre for the Arts, 1998. Accessed 4 October 2017. http://ignca.nic.in/eBooks/Culture_n_Development_05.pdf.

———. *The Muslim Tribes of Lakshadweep Islands: An Anthropological Appraisal of Island Ecology and Cultural Perceptions*. New Delhi: M D Publications Pvt. Ltd, 1997.

Media Analysis and Research Center. 'Arabikadalile Kadha Ganangal Grabs Lakshadweep Kala Academy Award: Grabbing Minds by Traditional Songs.' *Mediamarx* (blog). Accessed 4 October 2017. http://mediamarx.blogspot.in/2011/01/lakshshadweep-kala-academy-award.html.

Mukerji, Sarit Kumar. 'Lakshadweep.' In *Islands of India*. Delhi: Publications Division, Ministry of Information and Broadcasting, Government of India, 1992.

S., Anitha. 'Where Tradition is a Way of Life: Traditional Knowledge in the U.T Of Lakshadweep, India.' Chennai: International Collective in Support of Fishworkers, 2012. Digitized by Aquatic Commons. Accessed 4 October 2017. http://aquaticcommons.org/17145/1/016%20Where%20Tradition%20Is%20A%20Way%20Of%20Life%20Traditional%20Knowledge%20In%20The%20Ut%20Of%20Lakshadweep%20%20India%20By%20Anitha%20S.pdf.

Madhya Pradesh

Adhikari, Subhrashis. 'Rise of Middle East (1200 to 1500 CE).' *The Journey of Survivors: 70,000-Year History of Indian Sub-Continent*. Gurgaon: Partridge India, 2016.

District Mahoba (U.P.) India. 'History.' Accessed 4 October 2017. http://mahoba.nic.in/history2.htm.

Government of Madhya Pradesh. 'Folk Songs.' Accessed 4 October 2017. http://www.mp.gov.in/web/guest/folksongs.

Talking Myths Project. 'Legend: Alha, Udal and the Devi of Maihar.' Accessed 4 October 2017. http://talkingmyths.com/alha-udal-and-the-devi-of-maihar/.

Varadpande. *History of Indian Theatre*.

Maharashtra

Srishti's Carnatica. 'Harikatha: An Article on Keertan Sastras.' By B. R. Ghaisas. Accessed 4 October 2017. http://www.carnatica.net/keertansastras.htm.

———. 'Harikatha: Tradition of Story Telling in South India.' Accessed 4 October 2017. http://www.carnatica.net/harikatha1.htm.

The Divine Life Society. 'Kirtan in Maharashtra.' By Swami Sivananda. Accessed 4 October 2017. http://sivanandaonline.org/public_html/?cmd=displaysection&section_id=1118.

Varadpande. *History of Indian Theatre*.

Venkatesh, Karthik. 'A Brief History of the Bhakti Movement.' *Livemint*. 12 November 2016. http://www.livemint.com/Sundayapp/0irwa2rMY1lUJKtPEtX4sO/A-brief-history-of-the-Bhakti-movement.html.

Manipur

Centre for Cultural Resources and Training. 'Manipuri Dance.' Accessed 4 October 2017. http://ccrtindia.gov.in/manipuri.php.
Cultural India. 'Manipuri.' Accessed 4 October 2017. http://www.culturalindia.net/indian-dance/classical/manipuri.html.
Eastern Zonal Cultural Centre. 'Manipur.' Accessed 4 October 2017. http://ezccindia.org/manipur.html.
E-Pao. 'Ras Lila: Manipuri Classical Dance.' By P. Kunjo Singh. Accessed 4 October 2017. http://e-pao.net/epSubPageExtractor.asp?src=manipur.Arts_and_Culture.Ras_Lila_Manipuri_Classical_Dance.
IndiaNetzone. 'Raslila, Indian Folk Dance.' Accessed 4 October 2017. http://www.indianetzone.com/38/raslila.htm.
Indira Gandhi National Centre for the Arts. 'Miscellaneous Arts and Crafts in Manipur.' Accessed 4 October 2017. http://ignca.nic.in/craft203.htm.
Jhaveri, Darshana (Manipuri dancer, of the Jhaveri sisters fame, Padma Shri awardee and director, Manipuri Nartanalaya). Performance at the 5th Margazhi: A Festival of Indian Classical Dance organized by Takshashila Dance Academy, Navi Mumbai, 7 January 2017.
———. 'Seeking Dance: A 100-year-old Story.' Lecture-cum-demonstration organized by Junoon Theatre, Mumbai, 9 July 2017.
Kothari, Sunil (dance historian, scholar, author and critic). 'My Journey through Dance.' Presented at Mumbai Local Arts Adda organized by Junoon Theatre, Mumbai, 16 December 2016.
Nongmaithem, Halley and co. *A Vaishnavaite's Odyssey*. Documentary film. YouTube video 'Manipur's Govindaji temple-a documentary', 14:36. Posted by 'halley nongmaithem', 6 August 2016. https://www.youtube.com/watch?v=jk0-GhyFB8s.
Pioneer (Bhopal). 'The Lord's "Raas" Draws Curtain on "Poorvotsav".'
Swami, Jayadvaita. 'Manipur: A Land of Krsna Conscious Culture.' *Back to Godhead* (Volume 29, Number 6). 1 November 1995. http://www.backtogodhead.in/manipur-a-land-of-krsna-conscious-culture-by-jayadvaita-swami/.
Utsavpedia. 'Manipuri Dance.' Accessed 4 October 2017. http://www.utsavpedia.com/cultural-connections/manipuri-dance-a-manifold-of-creativity/.

Meghalaya

C.P.R. Environmental Education Centre, Chennai. 'Sacred Groves in Meghalaya.' Accessed 4 October 2017. http://www.cpreecenvis.nic.in/Database/Meghalaya_899.aspx.
Jyrwa, P. Nicholas (lecturer, computer science and applications, Shillong College) in discussion with the author, n.d.
Kharmawphlang, Desmond. 'A Walk through the Sacred Forests of Meghalaya.' In *Glimpses from the North-East*. New Delhi: National Knowledge Commission, 2009.
———. 'In Search of Tigermen: The Were-Tiger Tradition of the Khasis.' In *The Human Landscape*, edited by Geeti Sen and Ashis Banerjee. Hyderabad: Orient Longman Limited, 2001.
Mohrmen, HH. 'The Legend of the Tiger Man.' *Shillong Times*. 31 October 2011. http://www.theshillongtimes.com/2011/10/31/the-legend-of-the-tiger-man/.

———. 'The Last of the Tiger Man.' *Shillong Times*. 12 December 2011. http://www.theshillongtimes.com/2011/12/12/the-last-of-the-tiger-man/.
Nongbri, Ailynti (associate professor, department of Khasi, Shillong College) in discussion with the author, n.d.

Mizoram

Gajrani, S., ed. 'Mizoram.' In *History, Religion and Culture of India* (Volume 6). New Delhi: Isha Books, 2004.
Greener Pastures. 'Folklore from North-east India - Rih Dil Lake, Mizoram.' *In Search of Green Pastures* (blog). Accessed 4 October 2017. https://thenortheasttravelblog.com/2012/09/24/folklore-from-north-east-india-rih-dil-lake-mizoram/.
Indira Gandhi National Centre for the Arts. 'Miscellaneous Arts and Crafts in Mizoram.' Accessed 4 October 2017. http://ignca.nic.in/craft205.htm.
Lalrindiki Ruala. 'Cheraw Dance, Popularly Called as Bamboo Dance.' *Mizoram Tourism* (blog). Accessed 4 October 2017. https://mizoramtourism.wordpress.com/2009/04/13/cheraw-dance-popularly-called-as-bamboo-dance/.
Mizoram. 'About Mizoram: Dances.' Accessed 4 October 2017. http://mizoram.nic.in/about/dances.htm.
———. 'About Mizoram: History.' Accessed 4 October 2017. http://mizoram.nic.in/about/history.htm.
Mizoram.gov.in. 'Rih Dil (Rih Lake).' Accessed 4 October 2017. https://mizoram.gov.in/page/rih-dil-rih-lake.
Mizoram Tourism. 'Rih Dil, Champhai District.' Accessed 4 October 2017. https://tourism.mizoram.gov.in/loc/22.
National Geographic News. 'Photos: Rat Attack in India Set Off by Bamboo Flowering.' N.d. Accessed 4 October 2017. http://news.nationalgeographic.com/news/2009/03/photogalleries/bamboo-rat-plague-missions/.
Tochhawng, Rosiamliana, Khiangte Lalrinmawia and Lal Hum Rawsea, eds. *Ground Works for Tribal Theology in the Mizo Context*. Readings in Mizo Christianity Series. Indian Society for Promoting Christian Knowledge, 2007.

Nagaland

Government of Nagaland. 'About Nagaland.' Accessed 4 October 2017. https://www.nagaland.gov.in/portal/portal/StatePortal/AboutNagaland/NagalandInfo.
Indira Gandhi National Centre for the Arts. 'Textiles of Nagaland.' Accessed 4 October 2017. http://ignca.nic.in/craft256.htm.
Joshi, Vibha. 'Dynamics of Warp and Weft: Contemporary Trends in Naga Textiles and the Naga Collection at the Pitt Rivers Museum, Oxford' (New Mexico, 2000). In *Approaching Textiles, Varying Viewpoints: Proceedings of the Seventh Biennial Symposium of the Textile Society of America. USA: Textile Society of America, Inc., 2001.* http://digitalcommons.unl.edu/cgi/viewcontent.cgi?article=1786&context=tsaconf.
Karolia, Anjali and Richa Prakash. 'Design and Development of Fashion Accessories Inspired from the Hand Woven Shawls of Nagaland.' In *Indian Journal of Traditional Knowledge* {Volume 13 (2)}. April 2014. Accessed 4 October 2017. http://nopr.niscair.res.in/bitstream/123456789/27951/1/IJTK%2013(2)%20416-426.pdf.
Longchar, Resenmenla. 'Origin And Dispersal of Nagas: A Folkloric Perspective.' In 'Oral Narratives of Ao Nagas: Constructing Identity.' PhD thesis, University of

Hyderabad, 2011. http://shodhganga.inflibnet.ac.in/bitstream/10603/105679/13/13_chapter%203.pdf.
Ministry of Development of North Eastern Region. 'Nagaland.' Accessed 4 October 2017. http://www.mdoner.gov.in/content/nagaland-2.
Patnaik, Soumendra Mohan. 'Consuming Culture: The Refiguration of Aesthetics in Nagaland Cultural Tourism in India's North East.' In *Arts and Aesthetics in a Globalizing World*, edited by Raminder Kaur and Parul Dave-Mukherji. Bloomsbury Publishing, 2015.
Ranjan and Ranjan, eds. 'Nagaland: Loin Loom Weaving.' In *Handmade in India*. Accessed 4 October 2017. http://www.cohands.in/handmadepages/book515.asp?t1=515&lang=English.
Sentinaro, I. and N. D. R. Chandra. 'A Discourse on Ao Naga Folktales.' In *Journal of Literature, Culture and Media Studies* (Volume II, No. 3). January–June (Summer) 2010. Accessed 4 October 2017. https://www.inflibnet.ac.in/ojs/index.php/JLCMS/article/view/141/140.
Siyahi. 'Woven Tales from the North East: Programme Details.' Accessed 4 October 2017. http://mongrel.in/s/woven-tales-programme-details.html.
TripAdvisor India. *International Dolls Museum: An Example of the Information Boards*. Traveller photo submitted by MrLukeLau, April 2013. Accessed 4 October 2017. https://www.tripadvisor.in/Attraction_Review-g297596-d3201157-Reviews-International_Dolls_Museum-Chandigarh.html#photos;geo=297596&detail=3201157&ff=62050295&albumViewMode=hero&aggregationId=101&albumid=101&baseMediaId=62050295&thumbnailMinWidth=50&cnt=30&offset=-1&filter=7&autoplay.

Odisha

Bariki, Akshay Kumar (2011 National Merit Award– and 2014 UNESCO Award–winning Pattachitra and Tala Pattachitra artist, member of Maa Dakhinakali Art and Crafts Culture) in discussion with the author, The Handmade Collective 2016 and 2017.
Das, Narayan (palm-leaf etching artist) in discussion with the author, Paramparik Karigar Exhibition and Sale 2016.
Ethnic Paintings. 'Palm Leaf Painting.' Accessed 4 October 2017. http://www.ethnicpaintings.com/painting-media/palm-leaf-painting.html.
Gaatha. 'Etched in Time.' Accessed 4 October 2017. http://gaatha.com/palm-leaf-pattachitra/.
Panda, Namita. 'Time for Trinity Worship on Tussar.' *Telegraph*. 17 June 2011. https://www.telegraphindia.com/1110617/jsp/orissa/story_14122518.jsp.
'Patachitra Art.' *Saritha Rao Rayachoti* (blog). Accessed 4 October 2017. http://saritharao.blogspot.in/2010/09/patachitra-art.html.
Shree Jagannath Temple. 'Legendary Origin of Lord Jagannath.' Accessed 4 October 2017. http://jagannath.nic.in/?q=node/83.
Visitors Guide India: Odisha. RBS Visitors Guide India Series. Rajasthan: Data and Expo India Pvt. Ltd, 2014.

Puducherry

D'source. 'Rangoli: Floor Art.' Design resource by Madhuri Menon. Accessed 4 October 2017. http://www.dsource.in/resource/rangoli/types-rangolis/kolam.

'How a stained glass window is made from start to finish.' YouTube video, 2:20. Posted by 'Derek Schmid', 8 February 2012. https://www.youtube.com/watch?v=xl2QOcFb6KE.

Indian Heritage. 'Arts and Crafts, Traditional Customs and Practices: Kolam.' Accessed 4 October 2017. http://www.indian-heritage.org/alangaram/kolams/kolams.htm.

Indian Mirror. 'Pondicherry: Culture.' Accessed 4 October 2017. http://www.indianmirror.com/culture/states-culture/pondicherry.html.

Khan Academy. 'How Stained Glass Is Made.' Accessed 4 October 2017. https://www.khanacademy.org/humanities/medieval-world/latin-western-europe/gothic1/a/how-stained-glass-is-made.

Mills, Margaret A., Peter J. Claus and Sarah Diamond, eds. 'Kolam.' In *South Asian Folklore, An Encyclopedia: Afghanistan, Bangladesh, India, Nepal, Pakistan, Sri Lanka*. New York: Routledge, 2003.

Nagarajan, Vijaya Rettakudi. 'Hosting the Divine: The Kolam in Tamilnadu.' In *Mud, Mirror and Thread: Folk Traditions of Rural India*, edited by Nora Fisher. Ahmedabad: Mapin, 1993.

———. 'Soil as the Goddess Bhudevi in a Tamil Hindu Women's Ritual: The Kolam in India.' In *Women as Sacred Custodians of the Earth? Women, Spirituality and the Environment*, edited by Alaine Low and Soraya Tremayne. USA: Berghahn Books, 2001.

Peaceful Puducherry: Puducherry Tourism. 'The Basilica of the Sacred Heart of Jesus.' Accessed 4 October 2017. http://www.pondytourism.in/iconics-innerpage.php?id=18&district=Puducherry&category=194.

Pepin, David. *Cathedrals of Britain*. Great Britain: Bloomsbury Publishing, 2016.

Rangoli. 'About Rangoli: Origin, History, Rangoli in the Lanes.' Accessed 4 October 2017. http://www.rangoliworld.org/rangoli_origin.html.

'Short Encyclopedia of Kolam.' *Jennie Kakkad* (blog). Accessed 4 October 2017. https://jenniekakkad.wordpress.com/tag/kolam-origin/.

Sridhar, R. 'The Hows and Whys for Women.' *Mumbai Mirror*. Last modified 17 March 2011. https://mumbaimirror.indiatimes.com/opinion/columnists/r-sridhar//articleshow/16110801.cms.

Yanagisawa, Kiwamu and Shojiro Nagata. 'Fundamental Study on Design System of Kolam Pattern.' In *Forma: The Beauty, Dynamics and Design of String Patterns in Folk Arts* (Volume 22, No. 1). SCIPRESS, 2007. Accessed 4 October 2017. http://www.scipress.org/journals/forma/pdf/2201/22010031.pdf.

Punjab

Ahmed, Mukhtar. *Harappan Civilization: The Material Culture*. Ancient Pakistan: An Archaeological History Series. North Carolina: Foursome Group, 2014.

Bagga, Neeraj. 'Khiloniyan Wala and Mishri Bazaars Abuzz Ahead of Diwali.' *Tribune* (Amritsar). 11 November 2015. http://www.tribuneindia.com/news/jalandhar/khiloniyan-wala-and-mishri-bazaars-abuzz-ahead-of-diwali/157131.html.

———. 'Traditional Bazars Come Alive on Festival of Lights.' *Tribune* (Amritsar). 3 November 2013. http://www.tribuneindia.com/2013/20131103/asrtrib.htm#2.

Ludhiana Tourism. 'Folk Toys of Punjab.' Accessed 4 October 2017. http://www.ludhianatourism.nandafurnishings.com/folk_toys.php.

Rajput, Chandana and Harinder. 'Resurgence: The Boundless Kalakriti of Punjab.' In *International Journal of Development Research* (Volume 6, Issue 2). February 2016. http://journalijdr.org/resurgence-boundless-kalakriti-punjab (PDF link discontinued).

Singh, Jagraj. 'Theology of Sikhism.' In *A Complete Guide to Sikhism*. Chandigargh: Unistar Books, 2009.
Swynnerton, Charles. 'Of the Gardener's Wife, the Potter's Wife, and the Camel.' In *Romantic Tales from the Panjab with Indian Nights' Entertainment*. New Delhi: Asian Educational Services, 2004.
The Hindu. 'Out of Play.' 7 November 2016. http://www.thehindu.com/features/metroplus/Out-of-play/article16439140.ece.
UNP: United Punjab. 'All about Our Punjab.' Accessed 4 October 2017. https://www.unp.me/f16/all-about-our-%60punjab-178892/.

Rajasthan

Bombay.indology.info. 'The Epic of Pabuji.' Accessed 4 October 2017. http://bombay.indology.info/pabuji/statement.html.
Chalto Phirto Devro: The Wandering Shrine. Documentary film. Produced by Illumine Films 2010. Vimeo video, 13:52. Posted by 'Saffronart Management Corp.', 10 April 2014. https://vimeo.com/91589496.
Hiltebeitel, Alf. 'The Epic of Pabuji.' In *Rethinking India's Oral and Classical Epics: Draupadi among Rajputs, Muslims, and Dalits*. London: The University of Chicago Press, 1999.
Joshi, Kalyan (National Award–winning Phad artist and member of Chitrashala: Phad Painting Training & Research Institute) in discussion with the author, Paramparik Karigar Workshop 2016 and Paramparik Karigar Exhibition and Sale 2017.
Joshi, Prakash (National Award–winning Phad artist and UNESCO's WCC Award of Excellence for Handicrafts awardee, member of Chitrashala: Joshi Kala Mandir) in discussion with the author, Paramparik Karigar Exhibition and Sale 2016 and 2017.
Joshi, Vijay (National Merit Award–winning Phad artist and member of Virasat: Nonpareil Shahpura's Phad Painting Training and Research Institute) in discussion with the author, The Handmade Collective 2016.
Kothiyal, Tanuja. *Nomadic Narratives: A History of Mobility and Identity in the Great Indian Desert*. New Delhi: Cambridge University Press, 2016.
Ranjan and Ranjan, eds. 'Rajasthan: Phad Painting.' In *Handmade in India*. Accessed 4 October 2017. http://www.cohands.in/handmadepages/book93.asp?t1=93&lang=English.
R., Shilpa Sebastian. 'Drawn into Family Tradition.' *The Hindu* (Bangalore). 1 June 2012. http://www.thehindu.com/arts/crafts/drawn-into-family-tradition/article3480283.ece.
Smith, John D. *The Epic of Pabuji*. New Delhi: Katha, 2005.

Sikkim

A View on Buddhism. 'Tibetan Buddhist Symbols.' Accessed 4 October 2017. http://viewonbuddhism.org/symbols_tibet_buddhism.htm.
Beer, Robert. 'Animals and Mythical Creatures.' In *The Handbook of Tibetan Buddhist Symbols*. Boston: Shambhala Publications, 2003.
Bhatt, S. C. and Gopal K. Bhargava, eds. 'Arts and Crafts.' In *Land and People of Indian States and Union Territories: Sikkim* (Volume 24 of 36). Delhi: Kalpaz Publications, 2005.
Eastern Zonal Cultural Centre. 'Sikkim.' Accessed 4 October 2017. http://ezccindia.org/sikkim.html.

Official Website of Sikkim Tourism, Tourism and Civil Aviation Department. 'Buddhist Circuit.' Accessed 4 October 2017. http://www.sikkimtourism.gov.in/Webforms/General/SikkimAtAGlance/Buddhism_Sikkim.aspx.

'Sikkim snow lions perform "Singhi Chham" dance.' Filmed by Wilderness Films India. YouTube video, 6:16. Posted by 'WildFilmsIndia', 27 November 2013. https://www.youtube.com/watch?v=Zj73aB5Az2M.

Subba, J. R. 'Folk Culture.' In *History, Culture and Customs of Sikkim*. New Delhi: Gyan Publishing House, 2011.

Tamil Nadu

Abram, David and Nick Edwards. *The Rough Guide to South India*. Rough Guides, 2003.

Department of Archaeology, Government of Tamil Nadu. 'Memorial Stones.' Accessed 4 October 2017. http://www.tnarch.gov.in/epi/ins11.htm.

Ilamurugan. 'Hero Stones (Nadukal), Devikapuram.' *Tamilnadu Tourism* (blog). Accessed 4 October 2017. http://tamilnadu-favtourism.blogspot.in/2016/04/hero-stones-nadukal-devikapuram.html.

Madhu. 'The Clay Horses Of Ayyanar.' *The Urge to Wander* (blog). Accessed 4 October 2017. https://theurgetowander.com/2015/11/24/horse-shrines-of-tamilnadu/.

Madurai Meenakshi Amman Temple. 'The Temple Towers.' Accessed 4 October 2017. https://www.maduraimeenakshi.org/the-temple-towers.html.

Murthi, V. Narayana. 'Pallava Era "Hero Stones" Found in Tamil Nadu.' *Archaeology News Network* via *Indian Express*. 30 September 2014. https://archaeologynewsnetwork.blogspot.in/2014/09/pallava-era-hero-stones-found-in-tamil.html#XgCSj9YyXKM6XIi6.97.

Pal, Pratapaditya. 'Southern India.' In *Indian Sculpture: (Volume 2)*. Los Angeles: Los Angeles County Museum of Art and University of California Press, 1988.

PBase.com. 'Ayyanar, a Powerful Village God in Tamil Nadu, India.' Accessed 4 October 2017. http://www.pbase.com/neuenhofer/ayyanar_a_powerful_village_god.

P.R. Ramachander. 'Village Gods of the Tamil Country.' *Village Gods of Tamil Nadu* (blog). Accessed 4 October 2017. http://villagegods.blogspot.in/2014_03_01_archive.html.

SFO Museum. 'Deities in Stone: Hindu Sculpture from the Collections of the Asian Art Museum.' Accessed 4 October 2017. http://www.flysfo.com/museum/exhibitions/deities-stone-hindu-sculpture-collections-asian-art-museum.

Tamilnation.org. 'Dolmens, Hero Stones and the Dravidian People.' By R. Nagaswamy. Accessed 4 October 2017. http://tamilnation.co/heritage/dolmens.htm.

Templenet. 'Temples of Tamilnadu.' Accessed 4 October 2017. http://www.templenet.com/Tamilnadu/tamilnatu_hist.html.

Telangana

B., Lavanya. 'Miniature Paintings of Golconda and Hyderabad School'. In 'Representation of Women in the Miniature Paintings in the Deccan School.' DPhil thesis, University of Hyderabad, 2004. http://shodhganga.inflibnet.ac.in/bitstream/10603/25652/11/11_chapter%204.pdf.

Deccan Herald. 'Timeless Appeal of Miniatures.' 26 February 2017. http://www.deccanherald.com/content/598289/timeless-appeal-miniatures.html.

Encyclopedia.com. 'Deccani Painting.' Accessed 4 October 2017. http://www.encyclopedia.com/international/encyclopedias-almanacs-transcripts-and-maps/deccani-painting.

'Indian Miniature Paintings: The Deccani and Paithan Schools.' New Delhi: Academy of Fine Arts and Literature, n.d. Compilation on Google Arts & Culture. Accessed 4 October 2017. https://www.google.com/culturalinstitute/beta/exhibit/eAIiY7nLvdXCIA.

India Picks. 'Deccan Miniature Paintings.' Accessed 4 October 2017. http://indiapicks.com/Indianart/Main/MP_Deccan.htm.

Moi'nee, Hina Fatima. 'The Deccan and Raiasthan Schools of Ragamala Paintings.' In 'A Comparative Study of Colour and Form in Deccan and Rajasthan Raagmala Painting.' DPhil thesis, Aligarh Muslim University, 2009. http://shodhganga.inflibnet.ac.in/bitstream/10603/60811/9/09_chapter%203.pdf.

Prajapati, Mohan Kumar (state award–winning artist and member, Balaji Miniature Arts) in discussion with the author, The Handmade Collective 2016.

Topsfield, Andrew, ed. 'In the Realm of Gods: Nature.' In *In the Realm of Gods and Kings: Arts of India*. London: Philip Wilson Publishers, 2013.

Unknown. *Chand Bibi Playing Polo*. Hyderabad, 1700 CE–1750 CE. Painting, 230 x 365 cm. National Museum, Janpath, New Delhi. Accessed 4 October 2017. https://www.google.com/culturalinstitute/beta/asset/chand-bibi-playing-polo/7AEWM_q-PKpBmg.

Tripura

Ayyar, K. R. Venkatarama, ed. *A Manual of the Pudukkottai State* (Volume II, Part II). Director of Museums, Government of Tamil Nadu, 2004.

Carman, John B. *Majesty and Meekness: A Comparative Study of Contrast and Harmony in the Concept of God*. Michigan: William B. Eerdmans Publishing Company, 1994.

Chakraborty, Shruti. 'A Magic Number: Into the Lost Hill of Unakoti, Tripura.' *Indian Express*. Last modified 27 March 2016. http://indianexpress.com/article/lifestyle/destination-of-the-week/a-magic-number/.

Ekaant. 'Unakoti, Tripura: Abandoned Sculptures' (Season 1, Episode 5). EPIC channel, 2014.

Press Information Bureau, Government of India. 'Unakoti Sculptures: A Bewitching Tourists' Attraction.' By Pannalal Roy. Accessed 4 October 2017. http://pib.nic.in/feature/feyr2001/fjul2001/f180720012.html.

Priti Mishra. 'Tripurantaka [Lord Shiva].' Speaking Tree blog. Accessed 4 October 2017. http://www.speakingtree.in/blog/tripurantaka-lord-shiva.

Storl, Wolf-Dieter. 'Shankar: The Yogi on the Mountain.' In *Shiva: The Wild God of Power and Ecstasy*. Vermont: Inner Traditions, 2004.

Taylor, William Munro. *A Hand-Book of Hindu Mythology and Philosophy: With Some Biographical Notices*. Madras: Higginbotham and Co., 1870.

Tripura, Land of Ten Million Statues. Accessed 4 October 2017. http://www.tripura.org.in/.

Tripura Tourism. 'Tripura: Origin and History.' Accessed 4 October 2017. http://tripuratourism.gov.in/Origin.

Uttar Pradesh

ANTIMAKHANNA. 'Sanjhi Art.' *Antima Khanna* (blog). Accessed 4 October 2017. https://antimakhanna.com/2013/12/28/sanjhi-art/.

AsiaInCH Encyclopedia: The Encyclopedia of Intangible Cultural Heritage/InCH. 'Sanjhi/Hand Cutting of Paper for Rangoli.' By Ritika Prasad. Accessed 4 October 2017. http://www.craftrevival.org/CraftArtDetails.asp?CountryCode=india&CraftCode=001174.

Goswami, Saurabh. 'Sanjhi: Folk Art from Vraja.' In *Music and Fine Arts in the Devotional Traditions of India: Worship through Beauty*, co-authored with Selina Thielemann. New Delhi: A.P.H. Publishing Corporation, 2005.

———. 'Sanjhi: Spirituality Expressed through Art.' In *Music and Fine Arts in the Devotional Traditions of India*.

Indira Gandhi National Centre for the Arts. 'Sanjhi: Ancestral Spaces, Maiden Desires.' Accessed 4 October 2017. http://ignca.nic.in/sanjhi/introduction.htm.

Rao, Shanta Rameshwar. *Krishna*. Hyderabad: Orient Longman Limited, 2005.

Soni, Vijay (state award–winning artist and member, Mathura Sanjhi Art) in discussion with the author, The Handmade Collective 2016 and 2017.

The Braj Foundation. 'Revival of Sanjhi Art Mela.' Accessed 4 October 2017. http://www.brajfoundation.org/braj_sanjhi.php.

Uttarakhand

Bajeli. Diwan Singh. 'Unmasking the Mask Theatre.' *The Hindu*. 4 November 2010. http://www.thehindu.com/features/friday-review/theatre/Unmasking-the-mask-theatre/article15675584.ece.

Balasubramanian, D. 'In Search of the Sanjeevani Plant of Ramayana.' *The Hindu*. 10 September 2009. http://www.thehindu.com/sci-tech/science/In-search-of-the-Sanjeevani-plant-of-Ramayana/article16880681.ece.

Indira Gandhi National Centre for the Arts. 'IGNCA Inventory on the Intangible Cultural Heritage: Ramman, Religious Festival and Ritual Theatre of the Garhwal Himalayas.' Description. Maintained by Molly Kaushal, Janapada Sampada Division. Accessed 4 October 2017. http://ignca.nic.in/ICH/ich_detail/ich00022.pdf.

Katyal, Surabhi. '10 Traditions of India That Find a Place in the UNESCO Intangible Cultural Heritage List.' *Better India*. 2 June 2015. http://www.thebetterindia.com/24394/traditions-of-india-included-in-unesco-intangible-cultural-heritage-list/.

Pande, Mrinal. 'The Sanjivani Quest: An Uttarakhand Village Hasn't Forgiven Hanuman for Defacing Their Holy Mountain.' *Scroll.in*. 31 July 2016. https://scroll.in/article/812802/the-sanjivani-quest-an-uttarakhand-village-hasnt-forgiven-hanuman-for-defacing-their-holy-mountain.

Press Information Bureau, Government of India. '17 States and 6 Central Ministries to Showcase Their Tableaux in Republic Day Parade, 2016.' By Ministry of Defence, 22 January 2016. Accessed 4 October 2017. http://pib.nic.in/newsite/PrintRelease.aspx?relid=135726.

Purohit, D.R. 'Ramayana in Performance, Garhwal Himalaya.' Paper presented at Festival of Ramkatha, New Delhi, 12–15 March 2008. Abstract digitized by Indira Gandhi National Centre for the Arts. Accessed 4 October 2017. http://ignca.nic.in/ramkatha_fest_abst_drpurohit.htm.

——— and Rakesh Bhatt. 'Satire and Civil Society in the Mask Theatre of Garhwal.' In *Folklore, Public Sphere and Civil Society*, edited by M.D. Muthukumaraswamy and Molly Kaushal. New Delhi, Chennai: Indira Gandhi National Centre for the Arts and National Folklore Support Centre, 2004.

'Ramman from Garhwal'. Performed by Saloor Dungra Gram Sabha at Festival of Ramkatha, New Delhi, 15 March 2008. Programme digitized by Indira Gandhi National Centre for the Arts. Accessed 4 October 2017. http://ignca.nic.in/ramkatha_fefst_garhwal.htm.

Sharma, Neena. 'Ramman Fest Gets a New Lease of Life: UNESCO Includes It in the List of Intangible Cultural Heritage of Humanity.' *Dehradun Plus*. 29 October 2009. http://www.tribuneindia.com/2009/20091029/dplus.htm#1.

UNESCO, Intangible Cultural Heritage. 'Ramman, Religious Festival and Ritual Theatre of the Garhwal Himalayas, India.' Accessed 4 October 2017. https://ich.unesco.org/en/RL/ramman-religious-festival-and-ritual-theatre-of-the-garhwal-himalayas-india-00281.

Zehra, Rosheena. 'Uttarakhand to Invest 25 Cr to Find "Ramayana"'s Sanjeevani Booti.' *Quint*. 28 July 2016. https://www.thequint.com/india/2016/07/28/uttarakhand-to-invest-25-cr-to-find-ramayanas-sanjeevani-booti.

West Bengal

Bajpai, Lopamudra Maitra. 'Intangible Heritage Transformations: *Patachitra* of Bengal Exploring Modern New Media.' In *International Journal of History and Cultural Studies (IJHCS)* (Volume 1, Issue 1). 2015. Accessed 4 October 2017. https://www.arcjournals.org/pdfs/ijhcs/v1-i1/1.pdf.

Chitrakar, Prabir (Pattachitra artist) in discussion with the author, The Handmade Collective 2016 and 2017.

Daricha. 'Patachitra.' Accessed 4 October 2017. http://www.daricha.org/sub_genre.aspx?ID=39&District=Birbhum&Name=Patachitra.

dokka srinivasu. 'Midnapore Patachitra Paintings.' *Heritage of India* (blog). Accessed 4 October 2017. http://indian-heritage-and-culture.blogspot.in/2014/01/midnapore-patachitra-paintings.html.

'*Macher biye* (Bengali scroll painting and song).' Folk song by Swarna Chitrakar. Filmed 2013 in Noyagram, Medinipur, West Bengal. YouTube video, 2:09. Posted by 'Chelsea McGill', 24 March 2013. https://www.youtube.com/watch?v=b81gC3cYqu0.

Manas. 'Pats: Bengali Scroll Paintings.' Accessed 4 October 2017. https://www.sscnet.ucla.edu/southasia/Culture/Art/Pats.html.

Midnapore.in. 'Pot Maya 2016: Patachitra Festival, Naya, Pingla, West Medinipur.' Accessed 4 October 2017. http://www.midnapore.in/festival/potmaya/pot-maya-naya-pingla.html.

Pal, Sanchari. '#TravelTales: Exploring Naya, Bengal's Village of Singing Painters.' *Better India*. 2 November 2016. http://www.thebetterindia.com/73787/naya-village-patua-patachitra-west-bengal/.

SenGupta, Amitabh. 'Potua's Village: Bangla Patua.' In *Scroll Paintings of Bengal: Art in the Village*. Indiana: AuthorHouse, 2012.